CW00701523

Out of The Dust

By the same author:

THE SHOP ON COPPINS BRIDGE
THE FAMILY ON COPPINS BRIDGE

OUT OF THE DUST

Elizabeth Daish

C

CENTURY
LONDON MELBOURNE AUCKLAND JOHANNESBURG

First published in Great Britain in 1987 by
Century Hutchinson Ltd
Brookmount House, 62–65 Chandos Place
London WC2N 4NW

Century Hutchinson South Africa (Pty) Ltd
PO Box 337, Bergvlei, 2012 South Africa

Century Hutchinson Australia Pty Ltd
PO Box 496, 16–22 Church Street, Hawthorn
Victoria 3122, Australia

Century Hutchinson New Zealand Ltd
PO Box 40–086, Glenfield, Auckland 10
New Zealand

British Library Cataloguing in Publication Data

Daish, Elizabeth
 Out of the dust.
 I. Title
 823′.914[F]   PR6054.A3/

 ISBN 0–7126–1719–1

Printed in Great Britain by
Anchor Brendon, Tiptree, Essex

To DEREK, SIMON and SALLY
who encouraged me and left me to get on with it.

Chapter I

Marian Verney put down her embroidery and walked to the open window. The delicate china bowl was half-full of water in which floated the petals of late May blossom. She rinsed her fingers in the water and dried them on the damask napkin hanging on the polished wooden rail by the small table.

'I've never known such heat in May,' she said.

Kate looked up and smiled. 'You feel the heat more than I do, Mother,' she said. 'Look, my hands are quite dry and cool and I've been sewing for far longer than you.'

Marian Verney watched her eldest daughter with a trace of anxiety. At nineteen, she should be doing more than sitting with her mother over a tapestry frame. It was high time she was married with babies of her own and a man to care for. Marian sighed. The Navy had so much of sadness to offer to young women. Kate might have been happy with Robert now if he had come back from the last naval sortie with the Dutch, a senseless matching of strength between young hotheads that smacked of piracy as war was not yet declared.

It was barely three months since Captain Holmes had attacked the Dutch in West Africa, seizing forts and property and sending the Dutch packing back to Holland. Such masculine stupidity, thought Marian. Any excuse to get at the Dutch, and it only needed the rumour that De Ruyter, the Dutch commander, had been guilty of atrocities against innocent English men, women and children to send men into a flurry of patriotic revenge that led to less than honourable engagement.

Kate forgot that her mother was watching her and stared out of the window. It was easier to appear contented than to bear the gentle sympathy that could be hers at the first sign of a tear. But I shall never know what happened. I shall never know if he thought of me when his ship sank under the cruel waves. Had he thought of the wedding that was to have been in June? She smiled, grimly, with a malice that was unlike her usual warmth. At least the scoundrel who had started the rumours of atrocities had been caught, a Dutchman posing as a Swede, who was sent to the Dutch Ambassador and had his ears nipped.

It didn't bring back her Robert and it did nothing to make the hot days of early summer easy to bear. What use was the investigation by the Royal African Company accusing Holmes of exceeding his instructions when nothing helped the loss of so many husbands, sons and sweethearts?

'I think I'll walk in the garden, Mother,' said Kate.

'Find Lottie and send her to me and ask Anna to bring Alice here to read her lesson,' requested Marian, and began to pack away her needles and silks.

Kate went to the kitchen but Lottie, the personal maid of Lady Marian, was not there and Kate had no wish to linger talking to Mary Creed the cook, who eyed her now with simpering servility and curiosity in the hard eyes. Next, Kate tried the bedrooms, empty and open-windowed and fresh with lavender, but Lottie didn't answer when she called.

The garden was even hotter than the house and Kate moved slowly, pausing only to call to Anna Maria Ruyter and Alice Verney who were reading under the shade of a

2

cedar tree. 'Mother wants you,' she said and went on through to the garden, calling for Lottie. There was silence and Kate sat on the bench that Anna had left, and wondered if Lottie was shopping.

From the loft above the stables, Lottie heard the distant calling and pushed Sam away. 'I told you they'd look for me, Sam,' she whispered, then smiled up into his eyes as he brushed aside her fair hair and bent his head to kiss her again.

'So soft,' he murmured. 'Was there any girl as soft, even in the bed of the King Himself?' His hands caressed her half-naked body and she stiffened. 'Stay a minute more,' he begged but she moved in an effort to lessen the weight of his body on hers, conscious of her taut muscles over the fullness in her pelvis and the instinctive need to protect it.

'I must go, Sam,' she whispered. 'If only I could live here and it be as it was.'

'Hush,' he said and tried to drive away the lurking dread that now spoiled their love. 'It may be nothing. It may be that you ate too much of Mary Creed's good food and it sickened you.'

'You know it's true, Sam. I was sick by the midden twice and when I saw my mother. She told you last week that I had a pinched look that meant one thing and I've missed a flux.'

'She told me all right,' he said grimly. 'Never a good word she's had for me ever since she knew we went together.'

Lottie looked at the good, strong face, now unsmiling and hard as he recalled the insults he had to bear from her parents. 'I know we can't marry,' she said. 'The master will turn me out and I shall have to go back to Cripplegate to have the baby and then be a wet-nurse or try to find a place with another family and leave the child with my mother.' She began to cry, and Sam reached out for her, holding her now with tenderness and no passion.

3

'Lady Marian won't let you go, sweetheart. The young ladies are fond of you and they would speak for you.' He fondled the white breasts, now slightly veined, with darkening nipples, and he knew that he had robbed Lottie of any future with the family she served and loved so well. 'I'll go too,' he said at last. 'There are others who need a good groom and it's been hinted that I could be coachman if I went into the country. We'll marry, Lottie, and live down in Surrey,' he said, impulsively.

'And you would hate it. You would blame me for making you leave and I would be unhappy in the country with all that mud and dark trees and nothing to do.' She touched his broad chest with her lips. 'What must be can never be changed,' she said. 'Now, I must go back. Miss Kate was calling and I can't stay any longer pretending to bring back the rosewater and herbs that Miss Anna wanted.'

She stood in the sunlight and stepped into her loose cotton dress that hung like a shift and hid any sign of the pregnancy. 'It doesn't show,' said Sam, hopefully. 'Maybe you'll stay small and they'll not know.'

She gave him a slow sweet smile that told him how silly men are when they want to believe something impossible.

'I'll see that there is nobody about,' he said, buttoning up his breeches, and went down the back steps from the loft to the lane beside the house.

Sam whistled softly and Lottie ran quietly along the lane before she reached the gate. She shifted the basket on to the other arm and walked slowly as if the heat was trying her and she had time to spare. Heavy footsteps hurried after her and she turned to see Joseph Creed, the coachman to the Verney family, coming up behind her. His thick livery was making him sweat and his face was red with exertion.

'Let me carry that for you, Lottie,' he said, and his eyes raked her face and body with ill-concealed lust.

'No thank you, Joseph. I have to get back. I'm late now

as I had to wait for the tincture that Miss Anna ordered,' she lied. His breath was stale and his eyes showed that he had drunk his fill while waiting for his master in the City.

Lottie quickened her steps. If Joseph was home, then Mr Verney would be here too, and she'd better make haste to be at Lady Marian's beck and call.

'I've some nice things I bought in St Paul's,' he said in a wheedling tone. 'A pair of slippers just made for your pretty feet and some beads that match those blue eyes.'

'I've told you before that I don't go with married men, Joseph. What would Mary say if she knew you chased me?'

'I don't care about her,' he said truculently, and Lottie breathed a sigh of relief as she spied Miss Anna walking towards them, and Joseph saw his wife Mary at the window.

'You have my herbs?' asked Anna. She glanced at Joseph with distaste. Such a coarse man and yet an excellent coachman who gave Mr Verney good service. He turned away and Lottie saw Mary Creed still watching from the window. What had she seen? There was nothing for her to see, but Joseph had walked beside Lottie from the gate and that would be enough to enrage the bitter-tongued harpy whom he had married years ago.

'It's so hot, Miss Anna. I hope I'm not late back,' said Lottie, innocently.

'Kate was looking for you to go to Lady Marian, but it's only to put away the tapestries,' said Anna, smiling. 'Go in now and leave me the basket. Lady Marian will want to know that they are back from the City.'

'Yes, Miss Anna.' Lottie smiled and relaxed. Maybe everything would be all right and she could marry Sam and stay with the Verneys. It was all so dear and familiar and she was treated well by all the family and every one of the other servants, except for Mary Creed who resented her youth and pretty face and almost accused Lottie of making

5

up to Joseph and perhaps more than just bantering and giggling behind Mary's back.

She'll never catch me with him, thought Lottie. After Sam, how could any girl think of someone like Joseph? Try as he may, I'll never go to him, she vowed and went up to the drawing room and tapped on the door.

Lady Marian looked up and gave a tired smile. 'I'm sorry I was late back, Ma'am, but I had to wait,' said Lottie, and was relieved to see that her mistress was not cross or concerned.

Marian looked at the girl in the doorway and envied the cool soft looseness of the shift she wore. Silk was far too warm and yet she couldn't change into muslin so early in the year. None of the ladies of her acquaintance would dare to flaunt such a breach of fashion. Only courtesans at the Palace of Westminster could afford to appear in the flimsy garments and not attract censure.

When Oliver Cromwell was ruling the country, between kings, rich clothes were not *de rigueur*, and the realm was grey . . . but it was like another dimension of living when the austere rules had been dashed away and England glowed again with colour and music and laughter and the dictates of high fashion once more, under the wanton eye of King Charles II.

But now, thought Marian, the King had been enthroned for long enough for the novelty of his return to have faded. In these early months of 1665, the country was prosperous but glancing sideways at a monarch whose appetite for good living, women and masques was only equalled by his need for more and more money to fill the depleted Royal Purse.

'You wanted me, my lady?' enquired Lottie.

'Is everything prepared for the master?'

Lottie nodded. 'Yes, my lady. His fresh linen is in the dressing room and the new *Intelligencer* is come. Sam fetched it when he took the bay to the farrier.' Lottie blushed, and turned half-away to tidy the pile of sewing

6

that Kate had left as if she might come back to it later. She dreaded the enquiring look that her employer gave her each day when she came to see to the clothes in the vast press in Marian's boudoir, and she bent slightly so that the loose shift would not cling to her figure.

'Very well, Lottie.' The girl moved towards the door but Marian called her back. 'What has been happening, Lottie?'

The girl burst into tears. 'Oh, my lady, don't send me away.' She placed a hand over the gently swelling mound in her belly. 'I'm strong and can work and when it comes I can send it to my mother until it grows older.'

'It is Samuel's child?' Marian paced the floor and tried to keep the anxiety from her voice. The heat was trying enough but this matter was something that made her head ache and her hands become moist once more.

'Yes, my lady,' whispered Lottie and failed to see the look of intense relief that made Marian look suddenly happy.

'Then he must own it,' said Marian. 'And you must wed.'

Lottie stared at her. 'But, what of the master? He will never let us live here together. Sam told me that he had refused any of the outside workers to sleep within the walls of this house, and so many had gone with their wives to other employ.'

'Yes, that is so,' said Marian. It was sad to think of losing the best personal maid that she had ever had and Edward would be furious if he had to lose Sam, the young groom who did more for their horses than any in the greater houses. It was a sobering idea that Sam could have work with many of their influential friends even if Edward refused him a good reference. Many had hinted that they would take him at a better wage than any that Edward would offer the man.

'My lady,' ventured Lottie timidly, 'if I went away when

7

I am confined, and came back without the child, I could stay with you, and Sam would have to live out over the stables as he does now.'

'You would do that? You would give away your child to remain here?' It was common knowledge that the lesser orders were hard and unintelligent, but surely Lottie had proved otherwise in the past? Marian saw the light blue eyes that were now dull with fear. Lottie's fair hair hung in untidy tresses and her dress was not as clean as it might have been, but the heat might have made this more apparent. 'Come now, child,' said Marian kindly. 'Do you not want an infant? I could never have given away any of mine.'

'Oh, yes!' The tears now began to fall and with them fell all pretence. 'I have not slept since I knew and I have been sorely ashamed, but I love it now, even in the womb, and when it is born, I think I shall die if I cannot be a mother.'

So Samuel *was* the father. Marian felt again the wave of relief that had restored her pride. If it had been her own son or, and this was an impossible thought, if it had been Edward, her husband, who had taken his fill of the pretty young servant, her heart would have broken.

This is not the Court at St James' and Westminster, she told herself angrily. It was common practice there for the young bloods to pleasure themselves with any good-looking serving wench they found in their own households and in those of their friends, but this was an honest household, with prayers each morning and no dalliance with the lights of love of the city. Even the servants were sober and Godly and went about their work with good hearts. True, Samuel was broad and strong and many a maid turned to look at him when he was in full livery.

But the child was his. Marian sighed. If Edward was tired, he could rage and turn them both away with no argument, losing two good workers and a lot of loyalty, but if he allowed them to marry, they would still have to

8

go, as he would never let the lads reeking of the stables come over the doorstep of even the back scullery, unless they carried vegetables from the gardener.

'My head aches, Lottie. Make me a tisane and bring it to the drawing room.' She watched the maid leave and felt a deep tenderness for the girl who was more than a servant and who made the house brighter with her smiling service and almost family pride. Now, she had ruined this situation. She would have to go and so would Sam and even if Edward sulked for a week, there was no other way unless he changed his rules.

'Mother!' Alice, trying to appear more grown-up than her bare fifteen years, burst into the drawing room and kissed her mother. 'I have learned another poem. Anna Maria taught it me in French and I can say if off without prompting now, or almost,' she added, with an anxious glance at the dark-haired girl who followed more slowly.

'You have learned it like a little parrot, Alice,' said Anna, laughing. 'If I asked for the last three lines, you could never say them without mouthing all the first ones, and then only if you peeped at the book.'

'You are horrid, Anna,' said Alice, without rancour. 'But I did work hard, Mother, so may I come with you to the theatre?'

'It's too hot,' began Marian, then remembered that Edward would expect her to appear with him in the box of the man who owned far too much of the City of London to be refused anything on the simple grounds of inconvenience or heat.

'It's tomorrow, Mother, and I can wear my red silk with the stomacher that Anna made for me.' Alice looked up into the serene face of her governess and friend. 'You *did* promise, when Lord Chalwood asked Father at Christmas.'

'And now we shall be expected,' said Marian. 'You will join us, Anna?' The girl inclined her head, and Marian was made aware that Anna Maria Ruyter was not just a

9

governess and companion but had a very satisfactory dowry of her own, invested by Edward in safe stocks, and enough means to buy her own good clothes. Now, she wore a gown of plain brown velvet that showed pale blue silk at the neck and edgings, and her bearing was of someone of rank.

'And will Christopher come with us?' asked Alice.

'Your brother has no time for such frivolity,' said Lady Marian Verney. 'He will stay with Kate, and Lottie will serve them supper.' She loosened the lace at her wrist, and decided that a cooler gown would be acceptable at the theatre, if this unseasonable warmth persisted. If Lottie was dismissed, who could she trust to look after her children when Edward asked her to go with him on visits to his family in the north and to her relatives in Surrey?

Alice was far too young to be trusted with the other servants and would be up to every kind of mischief even if she was nearly a woman and, as such, marriageable. My baby, thought Marian with a pang of sadness. They grew so fast and Kate could have been married and a mother by next Easter. Christopher, at eighteen, was already a man with a man's ideas of what he wanted from life but, as yet, no sweetheart who could be accepted into the family. Young girls who flirted with him, very prettily, but who were ignored if a new horse came to the stables and Sam was there to school it with his help, came and went without making an impact on the young man's natural yearnings. The only woman he seemed to respect apart from his mother was Anna Maria; an orphan and a distant cousin of Edward's, she was the daughter of an English mother and a Dutch father, both dead long since of smallpox, leaving the girl of nine to be brought up within the large and elegant house outside the City of London.

The estates in Holland had been sold after the last brush with the Dutch, Edward wisely foreseeing that they would lose value or be forfeit if another Dutch war was started. So Anna had a small fortune, enough to satisfy the most avaricious of in-laws, and a name that should have been changed long ago, to avoid embarrassment, by being similar to the notorious Dutch captain, De Ruyter. Even just 'Anna Maria Ruyter' was enough to make tongues wag whenever there was trouble with the Dutch, and with her grave dark looks, Anna appeared foreign to many who saw her against the lighter-complexioned Verney children. Kate might escape undue attention but Alice promised to be a beauty with her curling fair hair and dancing walk, the pink and white skin and delicate wrists and a figure that showed the promise of perfection. With Anna, the contrast was pronounced and men of rank eyed them both with interest.

It was too hot to think of matchmaking, but at seventeen, Anna should have suitors and must be given the advantages of soirées and visits to the Court. This, however, was difficult. Edward never admitted it but the name with which Anna was encumbered was a barrier to a good marriage while the Dutch war progressed, and national hatred against everything foreign and smacking of Free-Thinking or Papist practices brought rumblings of violence wherever they were encountered. Marian watched her ward and wondered if the old Huguenot background still had an influence on the girl. A legacy of fine sewing and lace-making was good, but anything bordering on Free-Thinking in a country sensitive to the religions imposed on it, might further impede her opportunities for marriage.

Alice turned back from the window. 'It isn't fair, Mother. Kate is wearing summer clothes while I am far too hot in this dress.'

Marian looked out. 'That flowered silk is warmer than you think, Alice,' she said. 'If you change into summer things too soon, you will take chill and have the ague.' It was an argument she used every year, but this year, with the lack of rain and the warm sunshine, it was hotter than many Julys.

11

'But I may wear the red silk tomorrow?' begged Alice.

'Yes,' said Marian, but longed to keep her baby for as long as possible. Surely the blossoming could wait a while?

Kate came to the doorway. 'Father is coming,' she said. Marian glanced at the ornate French ormolu clock and hurried to the front door, leaving Anna to follow, and Alice to linger in the cool room and so avoid any conflict with her father. To come home at this early hour meant that Edward Verney was out of sorts, out of temper with his clerks in the City office or had suffered a loss at the Stock Market.

The horses drooped under the shade of a tree, waiting to be taken to the stables, and Joseph Creed strode from the stable yard with Sam, to whom he flung the reins contemptuously and said nothing. The carriage that Mr Verney used each day to go to the City was dusty now. The distance from the borders of Holborn and Gray's Inn Fields to the City was not great, but the roads between, used by a huge volume of traffic in the over-crowded City, were mires of mud in bad weather and a dust-bowl in this dry spell, and so equally impossible for a gentleman to use unless he had a closed carriage.

The triple-collared cloak of the dark green livery that Joseph wore was more suited to a journey through wintry lanes and the way had been hard and filled with carts as traders went into the alleys and stews off Smithfield and St Paul's. He was hot and angry and gladly left the horses to Sam while he went to the back of the house where he shared rooms with Mary, for they were the only servants allowed to stay as a married couple that Edward Verney employed, with Joseph acting as coachman and sometimes butler and Mary as cook.

'The horses are sweating, Sam,' said Edward. Sam nodded and unharnessed the two black horses, then threw rough blankets over their withers before taking them to the stables. The carriage could wait. Horses were more

12

important than the tidiness of the front lawns and the empty beauty of the well-ordered flowerbeds and lawns. Marian closed her mouth without remarking on the carriage. Edward was right and so was Sam, and she must put up with the view for as long as it took Sam to bring men to manhandle the carriage into its shed.

'You are very early, my dear,' she ventured. Edward strode past her and into the wide hall.

'Where is the *Intelligencer?*' he demanded.

Kate handed the newspaper to him without a word. She knew that her father objected to anyone reading it before he came home and saw it first, so she had carefully put the pages together again after looking at it earlier. She watched his face, and wondered what interested him so much. He had news of Stock Market dealings fresh from the City, and the latest legal advice from his lawyers in Lincoln's Inn, so he had no need of the stale news of these bits of business. Even the war news was widespread now, in various pamphlets and by word of mouth, and the doings of the Court had never interested him.

Later, Alice would devour every bit of gossip about the King, his brother the Duke of York and the various wives and mistresses on whom they lavished extravagant pleasures and elaborate entertainments, sighing that one day she might be allowed to see such wonders and even to take part if her father would only let his daughters mingle with the right people.

Edward sank into a deep cushion on a wide wooden seat by the window. His shirt was sticking to him and his hose were hot but he felt none of this as he searched the page for the Bills of Mortality that had to be published each month for the general public to see. He read and threw down the paper with a mixture of disbelief and amazement.

'Lies,' he muttered. 'They are too intent on pleasing the Court and so print less than the truth.'

'Surely if it is in the *Intelligencer*, it is the truth, Edward.'

Marian was shocked. 'The King himself gave the concession to Roger L'Estrange, so it must all be true.'

'And there are many at Court who do not wish to know the truth,' said Edward, his face reddening even more. He tapped the paper with a finger that threatened to pierce the page. 'The Bills of Mortality have to state the cause of all deaths within the City and within the out-parishes.'

'They do that in detail. Poor souls,' said Marian. 'Many pass away with the most horrifying conditions, such as I have never seen. Some say they die from the influence of the planets. A man died from that in the last list of deaths and some die of the gripes, and French pox, and a rising of the lights. Surely these diseases are not found in houses such as ours?'

Edward gave a laugh of derision. 'What can the planets do to bring death? I fear that these names are but a disguise for something far more serious. There have been plague victims in the City that have not been noted in this journal.' He read aloud. 'Swelling and tympany! What is that, Madam? Head-ache and mouldshot? Pshaw! Water in the head I believe, if it means that the men who find these figures are mad, but I do not believe that this is true.'

Kate appeared in the doorway and set down a tray of cool water and lemons. 'Is the sickness spreading, Father?' she asked calmly.

'There's no need for you to worry,' said Edward, taking a gulp of the cold drink and sighing his thanks. 'It's not bad and will pass over soon but figures are sacred and should never be tampered with. I know of three cases that have not been noted in this report. My brother had to close up a house in St Giles-in-the-Fields and he told me of others, and yet the *Intelligencer* says that only sixteen deaths from the plague have occurred since the big frost.'

'That is few,' said Marian. 'If that is all, then it will soon pass and we shall have the blessing of fine weather to keep us in good health.' She smiled. 'Go and change into fresh linen, Edward, and Mary will bring cool water to wash your hands and face.'

'This will do,' he said and went to the bowl of water by the window. He bent over it and the florets were limp and browning in the now warm water. They had lost their first light fragrance and smelled stale. Edward seemed to recoil and then picked up the bowl and threw the water out of the open window. 'I'll wash in my room,' he said. 'Don't have those flowers in this house again. They are bad luck and they smell of death.'

Mary Creed who was hovering in the doorway waiting for her orders slipped away, smiling in a thin-lipped way. 'I told them it was bad luck to bring May blossom into the house,' she told Lottie in the kitchen. 'It's very late in blooming this year, after the hard winter,' she added, as if this made the bad luck worse.

'I don't believe it,' said Lottie. 'All flowers are sent from heaven and they can never harm anyone. You and your portents, Mary, are enough to frighten a body out of her wits.'

'Or a baby out of a womb,' said Mary, with a sly look at the girl in the loose shift.

'There's no call for you to say that, Mary Creed!' Lottie turned on her angrily. 'At least I can bear a child, and I shall give it a father.'

'Oh, you know the father, do you? And will this man wish to marry you now that he's had his pleasure?'

'I've told my lady,' said Lottie in a low voice. 'She knows it all and it's none of your business.'

'I don't work with sluts. Who knows what distemper you bring here with your whoring?'

'Oh, you horrible witch!' shouted Lottie and went to tear at the other woman's hair.

'What's this?' Christopher ran forward and seized Lottie by the waist, dragging her clear of the now-cringing woman. 'Whoa there!' he said, as if to a restive mare. 'What

15

is happening?' He grinned. 'Now get on with supper. I'm hungry and my father is in no mood for burned chops. Debbie!' he called, and the scullery-maid came into the kitchen. 'Stay here and help, and if they fight, come and fetch me.' He smoothed Lottie's hair as if gentling a dog and smiled at Mary. It was none of his business what made women fight. There were more important matters on hand. He came back to the kitchen with a linen cloth and linseed and ignored Mary's annoyed clucking while he took up one table to make a poultice for the older of the horses.

'Good enough to eat,' he said, as the fragrant oil became hot. 'She strained a leg against one of the massy posts in a narrow lane in Fleet Street.' But neither of the women listened. The congestion of the City was no concern of theirs, and many horses were bruised on the posts put to protect houses from the high wooden wheels of the carriages of the rich. They had enough to fill their minds; Lottie with worried thoughts of the future and Mary wondering if the young master had filled the wench's belly, or if Joseph her own husband could have had anything to do with it. She greeted him sourly and told him to wipe his boots when he came to find Christopher and to help with the plaster. He grunted at her and she saw how his eyes seemed to follow Lottie wherever she went. It could be his, she thought bitterly. Time was, when the Protector was ruling the land, that sluts like Lottie would have had to face the pillory or the ducking stool.

Mary smoothed the twin white points of her collar over the flat grey bodice. Oliver Cromwell lived on with people like her. Would the prophecies come true? She glanced at the well-worn book she studied so often. Joseph laughed at it and none of the ladies would read it, but it was all there. The Reverend Thomas Reeve who had lived at The Grapes in Chancery Lane had forecast evil for the depraved City. *God's Plea for Nineveh* told of a great plague to come . . .

16

'*That will cleare men out of their dwellings as if a fierce enemy was among them and shut up shop doors as if execution after judgement was served upon the merchants. There will be no music heard but the doleful knells and no wares to be borne up but corpses.*'

She thought of corruption and death and made light pastry for supper.

Chapter 2

'There's tragedy enough in the world without having to watch painted players enacting it on a stage,' said Edward Verney.

'But it's the King's players and you know you admire the acting of Mr Betterton, Edward. We have only to drive a step or two to Lincoln's Inn Fields and Mr Blackwell was exceeding kind to invite us to share Lord Chalwood's box.'

Marian hovered anxiously at the door to Edward's dressing room. Alice and Anna Maria had been dressed and ready for at least an hour, and Marian, cool after washing in lavender-scented water and now wearing a dress of cambric with tiny silk bows and an elegant shawl, was looking forward to the evening with her family looking handsome and prosperous and the excitement that Alice radiated becoming infectious.

Edward tugged at his silk coat and wished that natural hair was the fashion. His own hair was too sparse to be of any use and the periwig he wore now was the lightest he could manage but still over-warm.

'You look very impressive,' said Marian, smiling. 'You know that this evening is important to you so please try to enjoy the play. I am looking forward to seeing the outlandish costumes. Some say that the ladies of the Court have ordered dresses like the ones worn on stage, so that they can have tableaux and dances wearing them.'

'I'll have none of mine aping common actors,' said Edward, but his reflection pleased him and he took the long silver-headed cane and his lace handkerchief and joined the girls in the hallway. He stopped short of the door and frowned. Anna looked far too foreign to escape notice, with her lace shawl draped over her head to shield her from flying grit as the carriage went over the pitted and dusty road. She looks like a Catholic woman going to pray, he thought with a feeling of unease. Good teeth and smiling dark eyes did nothing to make her seem more English and he was glad when the shawl slipped on the smooth silk of her dress and refused to stay put.

Joseph Creed sat on the box of the carriage with the long whip in the leather stand by his hand. His tunic was dark green and immaculate and Mary, peeped out to watch the party climb into the carriage. She eyed her husband with displeasure. He was a well set-up man, and without the all-enveloping surcoat showed a figure that although slightly thickened, was still smart and might even be attractive to many women. With the fine weather, he would stay close to the theatre with the carriage, and it would not be necessary to bring the horses back to the warmth of the stables. A boy, given a coin to watch over the carriage, would free Joseph and other coachmen like him to drink in one of the many alehouses close by the King's Theatre until they collected their charges.

'If that's all he does,' murmured Mary. There were women who haunted the places of entertainment, and brothels full of tainted whores who would welcome men like Joseph. Mary's one consolation was that he dared not indulge in carnal activities when on duty in case he appeared crumpled and carrying the musk of the whore with him when he came back. She saw Lottie by the stable door and wondered if Joseph *had* tumbled her in the

19

hay . . . Once again, with a furious glance at the man she married so many years ago, she wished that she could be certain that he was not the father of the child that Lottie was expecting.

'It's a play by the Earl of Orrery,' Alice explained to Marian and Anna. 'I think it clever to write such things about a country so far away.' She sighed. 'I think I'd like to be an actress like Mrs Gwyn or Anne Marshall. I should adore the part of Roxalana. Don't you wish you were called Roxalana, Anna?'

Edward elected not to notice her prattling. Roxalana, indeed! Anna was dark enough to be a Turk as it was. He had a feeling that the *Tragedy of Mustapha, the Son of Solyman the Magnificent* would give him no pleasure and it would be impossible to talk business with Mr Blackwell, the banker and goldsmith, when everyone was chattering.

'Christopher has taken a liking to the theatre,' said Marian.

'The plays or the pretty rogues who play the leads?' said Edward. He laughed. 'It's time that he knew a skirt from a horse-blanket.'

'My dear!' said Marian. 'He's a boy, Edward!'

'I was married when I was nineteen, and you were younger than Anna,' said Edward. He wondered if the good dowry awaiting a suitable match would be enough to encourage any man to take on a woman like Anna in the times in which they lived. In many ways he would miss the gentle humour and good sense of the girl, but it was time she was off his hands.

Marian thought back over the past month. Christopher had started to dress with far more care than he had ever shown before and looked very handsome when he rode off on the young bay mare to the theatre. He usually attended the one in Drury Lane where many of the Royal Court followed the careers of Nell Gwyn and the Marshall sisters. There was no sign that he was infatuated with any of the actresses as yet, but it was bound to happen as this was a phase through which most young men passed, sometimes with disastrous consequences.

Marian fanned her face with the Venetian fan that Edward was given by one of the captains of the fleet of boats carrying his merchandise from the faraway places that Alice longed to see. The air was still oppressive but there was no sign of rain. Apparently water was becoming a subject of conversation in the alehouses as the water-carriers found it increasingly difficult to scoop up enough in their long leather buckets from the open ends of the culverts. Fights among the men were common-place as more and more houses found their wells running dry and needed to buy from the carriers.

The carriage stopped by the theatre and Joseph jumped down to assist the ladies from the high step. Men and women thronged the space before the wide doors, waiting to see who came, and who was with what party. They remarked on the dresses and the figures of the ladies, the bearing and clothes of the men, and assessed the wealth of the families by the patina of prosperity on coachman, carriage and horses. Sometimes a coat of arms on the doors would show who was the host and it gave entertainment to the idle crowds to know which insignia belonged to which great house.

Joseph Creed whipped up the horses and drove the carriage clear of the theatre as a cry went up that the King's coach was coming. The crowd pressed forward to see the beautiful ladies of the Court and Charles walked into his box with Lady Castlemaine at his side. Alice tried to get a better view of the royal party and leaned over the edge of the stairway, her face flushed and her eyes sparkling.

'Stand back, girl!' said Edward. 'It is bad manners to appear as if you have never seen the King.'

'But the other people are staring and jostling for a better look, Father,' she said resentfully.

21

'They are common people, idle chatterers and most likely cutpurses, the half of them,' said Edward. He looked back at the seething mass of people who would never see the inside of a gentleman's house unless they worked there as servants. He frowned. So much dirt and poverty in the shacks round Lincoln's Inn and Westminster, so much crime and depravity in the thriving alehouses that dotted the City of London and the out-parishes, and yet the colour and luxury of the Royal party, and to a lesser extent that of the King's followers, was enough to turn the head of a pretty girl like Alice.

Edward saw the way that men looked at his young daughter and was aware that she was about to become an even greater headache than Anna. 'Daughters!' he said, and glared at a young man with his natural hair worn loosely tied back in a thick swathe, and his body taut with youth and vigour. Alice saw the exchanged glances and sensed the aggression in her father's manner. She looked again and saw that the man had finely-woven clothes but was not dressed as elaborately as the Court. A clerk, like Father's men in the City, and so quite unworthy of a smile. She turned to watch one of the ladies whose wig was almost white, showing off the delicate colour in her cheeks.

Edward saw Alice turn away, and sighed with relief. Let the child be dazzled by the coloured baubles and so be unaware of the threat of such men as young Lord Carnegie's crowd. He glanced again at the young man and saw that, although he was with the Earl's son, and the wife he had married knowing her to be hardly better than a whore, yet he seemed not of the usual party, but as if he had been asked to join in an entertainment that held no pleasure for him.

During the performance, Edward sat with his host at the back of the box, intent on talking business and having little time for the antics on the stage. It was clear that as the play progressed and the audience became used to the colourful spectacle before them and were restless, as the play itself was poor, many were talking and ignoring their surroundings. Pretty wenches selling oranges and sweetmeats went between the standing crowds in the stalls, and the King's party drank wine and flirted and quizzed every likely face that was not entirely plain.

Edward was well satisfied. It was as private a place as he could wish for apart from his rooms in the City. Here, he could talk and there would be no spies to wonder what new dealings Edward Verney, the merchant and property owner, had with Mr Blackwell, the banker and goldsmith.

'So, you wish to transfer more into gold?' Mr Blackwell smoothed his badly-shaven chin and frowned. 'Ships may be less safe now that we are at war with the Dutch, but what they do bring home through the pirates reaps a good return . . . There's more if the war continues.'

'If they survive,' said Edward. He lowered his voice. 'I saw more red crosses today, and some close to my rooms. They say that the infection is spreading and it will be worse than the last one.'

'You aren't thinking of retiring to the country?' Mr Blackwell looked mildly amused. 'Is it the plague you fear – or the virtue of your pretty daughters?' He chuckled. 'I have sons and thus no need for such thoughts, and I bless the saints that I am not encumbered with two pretty wenches like yours.' He coughed and reddened. In the religious climate of May, 1665, a prayer to the saints was hardly tactful in a crowded place.

'That too, I admit,' said Edward, 'but I have noticed that with the heat, disease comes faster and destroys more.' He looked towards the actress on stage but saw nothing. 'The ships returning from the continent tell of huge numbers afflicted, the distemper spreading now almost to the Channel ports. It has run through Italy and Spain and France and I think that one of the reasons we had to declare war on the Dutch, apart from their unlawful use of the sea, was that they are weak from the plague and have fewer to man their ships and to work the land to grow them food.'

'We take nothing from them apart from the trickle of goods smuggled over by the fishermen and lightermen of Yarmouth.' Blackwell looked grim. 'The wretches sail out into mid-Channel and exchange goods and money, and the customs men catch only half of them. There have been cases of the plague in that town and many houses are sealed.'

'That's what makes me afraid,' Edward admitted. 'More than the thought of sickness for myself, it is the thought of those who are *not* afflicted, having to be shut up with the sick for forty days or until the whole house is clear or dead. It makes me shudder. Imagine my Alice having to shut out the sun and stay in a sick house and probably taking the distemper herself.' He put a hand to his hot brow. 'This heat and the smell of the people makes it all seem closer. I shall take my family down to my wife's relatives if it gets worse. I shall stay here until I think it wise to go, and leave a clerk to oversee my work in the City, and please God *he* doesn't catch anything.'

'I think you worry too much, Edward, and that the sun will kill the plague, just as it stopped during the hard frost. The heavens rule these things and with each new moon, there are changes, so let's hope the new comet bears no ill omens.'

'Another comet in such a short time,' mused Edward, recalling very unwillingly the pamphlets that his wretched cook Mary Creed left around for everyone to see. Almost by accident he had read one that told of all the past appearances of comets, and each one foretelling some terrible disaster. Two kings and one who had been beheaded, were crowned when such heavenly signs occurred. Pestilence had come to the country after another and now there had been two, one for the coronation of King Charles II and one for the plague creeping presently over the sea, by what means no one seemed to know, making this outbreak likely to be more severe than any of the others.

The party with the King were lit up by wine and laughter and the gentlemen fondled the women quite openly. Some of the young men begged to be excused and mingled with the crowds, ready to pick up a pretty whore or to leave the theatre on their own business. Edward tried not to think of the dissolute faces around him. Oliver Cromwell had been feared and hated, and in his time life and clothes had been grey, but now all of London talked of the extravagances and lechery of the people surrounding the King.

Alice gazed at the actresses and wondered how it must feel to have so many people watching and admiring. How would it be to wear such clothes and to have cheeks reddened with forbidden powders? But when the bold-eyed gentlemen from the Court eyed her, she looked down modestly, still half-child in her unawakened mind and heart.

Anna was blushing. She sank back on the gilded chair and fanned her warm face, using the fan to great effect and hiding her eyes with it from the stare of Sir Richard Routh who seemed unable to concentrate on the play. She saw him touch the sleeve of the lady next to him and they now bent heads together as if discussing the lovely dark face in the goldsmith's box, and then, with greater attention, the girl with fair hair. The play ended with applause and catcalls, and Marian wondered if the Palace had been pleased. Christopher had stayed with Kate this evening as she was still in mourning for her fiancé. He took it on himself to keep her company on the days when the rest of the family went out for pleasure. Anna Maria was watching the stage and trying to ignore the glances from the man in the figured silk coat and yellow cotton stockings. He was a gentleman of some rank, and his demeanour told her that he was used to being obeyed.

Marian saw him too and smiled. Anna bore herself with

dignity and had none of the superficial coquettishness that made many girls an easy target for such men. The graceful fan, like the one that Marian herself held, was a refuge but also a very potent means of allure in a subtle way. Marian leaned across and asked Mrs Blackwell if she knew the young man. 'I thought he knew you, Madam, as he stares so at this box,' said Marian with an air of innocence.

'He's a distant kinsman,' said Mrs Blackwell carelessly. 'One of the King's captains and only lately back from the war.'

'Not wounded, I hope?' said Marian and glanced at Anna who was using her fan rapidly and hoping that she didn't appear to be listening to every word.

'A fever brought him back but it was not serious. He fought in the Dutch lands in Africa and they feared that he suffered from the shaking fever of malaria but it passed and he is enjoying the King's benevolence before returning to his post.'

'And has he a wife?' asked Marian.

'No, and not likely to have one on the pay of an officer who neither takes bribes nor exacts money for fines.' The lady looked at Alice. 'Your girl is too young and I doubt if she would suit him as he prefers women who have too many brains for fashion.' Marian ignored the assumption that Alice must be empty-headed because she had spirit.

'So he seeks a woman with a fortune,' said Marian. 'Has he chosen such a lady? Or has there been no time to look far?'

'He had a likely partner found for him by his mother but when he came to meet her, he balked and refused to consider her, even though she could have solved all his problems. Such arrogance deserves no reward and as far as his mother cares now, he can stay as he is, in penury.'

'And what of his father? Has he no inheritance from that source?'

'He is a third son and so has no estate apart from a

small income that barely pays for his coats.' Mrs Blackwell sighed. 'I like the boy and apart from his pride, I think he could go far once he had a place of his own and a family.' She laughed. 'Do you want me to ask him to call on your daughter?'

'I have more than one daughter,' said Marian.

'I had forgotten. Your Kate was disappointed in love, I believe?' Mrs Blackwell looked thoughtful. 'It is too soon to press suit after such a bereavement, but in a way, this might be the time to make her feel the need of a man's strong arm.' She smiled. 'There would be no harm in sending Captain Daniel Bennet to pay his respects and to deliver messages from me to you, Madam.'

'I shall make him welcome, Madam,' said Marian. Mrs Blackwell eyed the handsome girl with Alice. It was a pity that she was so foreign-looking and had no position. What was she – the governess-companion to the Verney girls? She dressed well, but then, the family would want her to do them credit if she went with them very often to the theatre and soirées, as the duenna for the girls. Age made no difference in the reckoning of Mrs Blackwell. A girl of seventeen was as likely to be classed as a governess or duenna as much as a matron of thirty, if she had no portion or expected none, and so could never be thought of in the same way as the daughters of the house.

The royal party left, and the crowd followed their carriages through the narrow streets to the fields by the Strand and along to Whitehall. Other carriages followed to take guests to sup with the King and his Court or to watch the Royal Household at their tables. More carriages came to collect their own and Edward was in no hurry to leave his business friend.

'Is everything going well, my dear?' said Marian.

'Very well,' said Edward. He felt more lighthearted than he had done for a week. 'We'll stroll in Tothill Gardens and take the air,' he announced. 'Joseph, put down the seats for the young ladies and we can take our friends for supper.'

'What of our carriage?' said Mrs Blackwell.

'It can follow,' said her husband. 'Or the young ladies might like to ride in it and leave us to talk.'

Alice laughed. 'I like to ride in other coaches,' she said and stepped back from her father's carriage. Anna followed and they were shown to the black carriage with the men in dark red livery. Alice giggled. 'I feel as if I am being abducted to be taken to a handsome lover,' she said.

'Instead, we have to travel in less comfort,' said Anna, looking at the closed windows and the dark curtains that were less inviting than the ones she knew.

The coachman opened the door for her and Anna gasped. 'I beg your pardon, Sir,' she said. 'We were told to travel in this coach after my uncle and his friends.'

The man who sat on the velvet seat stepped out of the carriage and gave a stiff bow. 'I apologise if I alarmed you, Madam. My cousin sent a message for me to call on her as soon as I could and suggested that I sup with her and her husband this evening.' He looked at the fast-disappearing back of the swaying carriage, then smiled. 'It seems that we are thrown on each other's mercy, Madam. If you refuse to take me, then I have a long walk to Tothill Fields and if I take the carriage, then you must drive, unescorted, by hackney carriage.'

'Then of course we go together,' said Alice. 'My father would not let me drive in a hackney and we could not make you walk, Sir,' she added demurely.

'Captain Daniel Bennet,' he said, and kissed the hands of the two girls.

'Miss Alice Verney – and this is my companion Miss Anna Maria Ruyter,' said Alice.

'Miss Ruyter?' The smile faded and when they seated themselves in the carriage, the Captain sat on the small seat where not even his shoe touched either of the girls. Alice

28

looked complacent. From his first glance, he had preferred
Anna, but now her name had done what it did so many
times, shocked and embarrassed men and made them look
away, especially if they had fought for the King. She bit
her lip after a minute of utter silence. Even if she had put
him off Anna, he was not looking at Alice. I am not a
child, she wanted to say, but with him she felt like one,
and a child who was not even suitable as a playmate.

The coach stopped and the footman put down the step
for Anna to alight. He helped her down and the Captain
followed, taking Alice's hand and giving her the courtesy
due to the daughter of an important man. They joined the
others and walked by the fields and down by Palace Yard
to Westminster Stairs where Joseph had gone before and
arranged for a room and supper for the entire party. The
manservant grinned. Even Mary couldn't tell him to be
home now. Mr Verney would not want him for at least two
hours more and he knew an alehouse along by Petty France
where the girls were clean and pretty.

The window overlooking the river Thames showed the
lights on the barges and the distant flares in the streets
south of the river. Dust settled as carriages went away to
the mews and the evening was clear and light enough to
see by moonlight. Anna sipped her wine and picked at the
well-cooked fowl before her, and kept her eyes downcast.
Alice laughed as she drank unaccustomed strong sweet
wine, pressed on her by Mr Blackwell who was amused at
her prattling, and the young Captain drank deeply and
grew more and more silent.

'I think that Anna made a conquest,' said Alice, loudly
enough for Captain Bennet to hear. 'Did you see him
staring at her in the theatre?'

'Who was that?' asked Mrs Blackwell. 'She is pretty
enough to attract many men,' she said kindly. She
wondered if she had made a mistake about the girl. Lady
Marian had hinted that she had a good dowry and was with

29

them only because she was orphaned. Many commoners married into titled families. Lady Marian Verney had a title in her own right even if her husband was a merchant, with good connections but with no title of his own.

'The gentleman in the box opposite,' said Alice innocently. 'There was a handsome man who stared and asked about her and was talking to his hostess.' She wanted to show this silent man that Anna was sought after, as she now felt ashamed of trying to make Anna seem just a foreign governess.

'He was looking at you, Alice,' said Anna. 'At first he saw me and then he was quite bowled over by your pretty face.'

'Do you mean Sir Richard Routh?' They were the first words that the Captain had spoken for fifteen minutes. He seemed to be annoyed and Alice was delighted to have goaded him to say something other than "Yes, Ma'am".

'He was with the royal party and went with them to Whitehall Palace,' said Marian. She frowned. Sir Richard Routh had a reputation for midnight brawls and drinking and even if he had not as yet been challenged to fight an enraged husband or father, it must be because some guardian angel stood over him and protected him. Edward looked anxious. There was no way to ensure that his daughters were safe from such men unless he took them all away from London, and if they were to find rich husbands, they would find none in the farmhouses and bothys of the country. The last of the meat stuck to the platter in its own fat and the wine was giving him the gripes.

'It's time we took you home, Alice,' he said. 'Enough faldedals for one evening, Madam.'

Chapter 3

'It's a sad day when I have to sell land for that purpose,' said Edward Verney. His head clerk handed him the documents and Edward looked them over again. 'I was saving that piece for two good houses built of fine brick and stone, but the Privy Council can bring pressure on me if I refuse them.'

'It's a good price,' said Roger Carter, the solemn man who ran most of the Verney businesses when Edward was away or working at Westminster. He pushed the papers close to the penstand and silently urged the signing. 'It is needed, Sir. There have been more dying in St Giles-in-the-Fields, and if there are no new pest-houses then many who are unaffected will be shut up with the sick and catch the contagion.'

'You are right, Roger.' Edward signed the papers necessary for the release of his land and the building of hastily-erected dwellings for plague victims. Many had already been constructed and it was becoming clear to anyone with half an ounce of intelligence that the Bills of Mortality were inaccurate. They gave no clear idea of the numbers dying from the plague, but simply accepted the word of ignorant Searchers that the sudden increase in deaths was the result of anything from French pox to pneumonia.

Roger hurried from the room and gave the documents to a messenger to deliver to the authorities, while his master picked up a walking cane and announced his intention of taking the air and seeing for himself what changes would be made and whether the new buildings would lower the value of the adjoining land which he also owned. He looked up at the cloudless sky and narrowed his eyes against the sun. Not a sign of rain, and the well that supplied his rooms in Lincoln's Inn was low. The great new conduit bringing water from the northern end of the out-parishes did much to lessen the burden of the people, but Edward had more faith in his own clean well than in the water travelling so far, often exposed to the air, to dust and dead animals.

The narrow streets were thronged with people carrying goods to market on two-wheeled carts or on longer four-wheelers drawn by donkeys or nags. Ordure from the tall houses on either side of the roads filled the central drain that ran stinking down to the Thames, after filling the Fleet River. Rakers with long hooks released the stream from the masses of rotting rubbish, carting it off to laystalls outside the city limits, where it lay heaped and exposed to rats, dogs, cats and carrion crows.

Edward stepped away from the houses as the road widened into a way that could take two carriages. It was safer to walk in the middle of the road to avoid the hazard of water and night-pails being emptied from upper windows regardless of who passed beneath. He began to wish he had come on horseback as the dust thrown up by cartwheels was stifling, and his highly polished shoes were now dull and a disgrace to Sam's early morning efforts.

From the chimneys of a house by Southampton Market smoke belched in choking clouds, the smell of cheap coal mingled with the scent of bitter herbs and brimstone. On the front door was the red cross, two feet high, and the message, 'May The Lord Have Mercy On Us'. Edward

32

went to the other side of the road and wondered what made a sealed-up house have a fire in hot weather. The air was bad enough outside, so what the poor wretches must be suffering in the house was beyond his comprehension. The guard by the door leaned on his halberd and yawned and watched the passers-by as if there was no sadness, no impending death and no plague in the house he kept sealed.

Edward turned. What did it matter to which purpose his land was put if it stopped the pestilence from spreading? There would be time enough to think of any loss he might bear when this bigger threat was over. He hurried to the house where his brother William lived with his wife and son, and hoped that his brother was out and that he would not feel obliged to stay in the house of a doctor who tended the sick.

Jane Verney opened the door and undid the catch on the door leading to the private sitting room. She knew that Edward shared none of her husband's disregard for safety where infection was concerned, and tactfully took him to the one room that had none of the paraphernalia of a busy doctor in it. 'William is over at Cripplegate,' she said, 'and Thomas is with him.'

'He takes his son into houses where there is risk?' asked Edward.

Jane shrugged. 'You know your own brother, Edward. He thinks nothing of such danger if there is someone to tend. He also believes that only those who fear the plague and tremble when they see the red crosses are affected by it. He follows the teaching of Dr William Boghurst who has worked with many plague victims and gives relief in the pest-houses.'

'Is the man immortal or a fool?' asked Edward. He tried to forget the heavy feeling in the pit of his own stomach when he saw the first of the red crosses on the doors in Drury Lane.

'He's a good man,' said Jane simply. 'They need

33

everyone who has any knowledge of medicine. Even the pharmacists are working as doctors and trying to do good in the face of much false teaching.'

'Do you mean selling of nostrums against the plague?' enquired Edward. 'There are many advertisements in the *Intelligencer* and other pamphlets, and who can believe half of them?'

'It isn't only that. Some may help as they contain valuable herbs of proven worth, but others have a bad effect, and kill those in an enfeebled state if they are bled or blistered as well. No, I was thinking of the way that some seal up all windows and doors in the belief that the air is the bearer of the contagion, and they burn noxious substances in the infected houses to kill off whatever is in the air.'

'There is a house in Southampton Market leaking smoke from every fissure in the bricks as if the place is on fire. Surely, those the plague doesn't kill will be dead from suffocation.'

'William believes, like Dr Boghurst, that fresh air is good. He tells his students to eat well before visiting the sick, to sleep well and to walk slowly and never to arrive breathless at the bedside. All this builds up a guard against any infection. William does what he says and makes us do the same. We have clean linen and wash the grime of the City from our hands when we come home. If that does not protect us then God will, for men like William were sent to help the needy.'

'Does he chew tobacco?' asked Edward.

Jane shook her head. 'I believe that even the King uses tobacco in a pipe, and others swear by its prophylactic powers, but William does not care for the idea as he has seen the experiments at the Royal Society where they gave a cat, a hen and a dog some of the decoction of tobacco that the King had sent over from Florence, which is said to produce paralysis. William says that if it did nothing

34

more than stupefy the animals, it was still noxious and to be avoided when every man needs his wits.'

'It did not kill the beasts?'

'No, and some swear that chewing the raw plug is the best remedy.'

Edward remembered that Joseph chewed tobacco and that he had rebuked him for the habit, but now it might be as well to encourage it among all his servants. Some had friends and relatives in the more densely-populated and stricken areas of London like the wattle-and-daub houses across the filled-in drains by Westminster and Covent Garden and if, as some said, the plague could pass from one person to another by way of breath, then it was as well to have something bitter in the mouth to repel it.

'I have work to do,' said Edward, after refusing a glass of Sack.

'It would be good for you, Edward,' said Jane. 'Dr Boghurst drinks half a pint of Sack before visits and again at night, so William insists that I drink a glass before I go to market or to visit friends.'

'Perhaps a glass, then,' Edward relented. He held the thin crystal to the light and watched the sun play on the golden liquid. 'If all nostrums were like this, I would gladly use them,' he said. The warm, fortified wine sat sweetly on his stomach and he felt more relaxed as he left the house. Perhaps he was making too heavy weather of the news and of the sight of houses cursed with the red cross. He went back to his office and worked without pause for two hours and then decided to ride home on the hack that Joseph had left in the stable by the side entrance.

The smell of the livery stable was less sweet than the stables at home and the remains of wet bedding straw lay in untidy heaps waiting to be raked away. A black rat fled across the yard and disappeared under the broken fencing. Edward shouted to the ostler and told him to get a good ratter or lose his custom, then mounted and turned to the road towards Wich Street and Chancery Lane. At the end of Fleet Street he paused and dismounted, leaving his horse with a small boy who held out his hand for alms, then went into the tailor where he had ordered a suit of thin silk for the hot weather.

The street smelled sourly of dried dung and refuse and even the cries of the street vendors sounded stale and listless in the heat. The oyster shop had a fresh supply and Edward ordered two barrels to be sent at once to his kitchens. In the busy shops and stalls, life was unchanged and people laughed and argued and made deals, but small items of news filtered into the talk, and couldn't be ignored.

'Have you heard that the King has proclaimed that he will receive any with the King's Evil until the end of May and then will see and touch no more until November?'

'It is rumoured that the Court will leave London if the plague gets worse and then where will our trade be if the courtiers buy from Salisbury or Oxford instead of our shops?' demanded a mercer.

Edward took his horse and rode back home, slowly. There was food aplenty for those who could afford it, water, as yet, and enough remedies against the plague to cure the whole of Europe, and yet he was more apprehensive than he had been at any time since the other King had lost his head.

Even the sight of Cromwell's rascals strung up with their heads on pikes on Tyburn had not filled him with as much horror as the sight of the crosses on the doors now in view in many a street. He breathed the pure air of the fields and listened to a lark singing and thanked God that his house was well away from the stews of London.

Sam was whistling in the yard and the four dogs lay in the sun, the bitch suckling her pups and the half-wild outdoor cats eyeing the young with curiosity and malevolence. Sam looked up, his face expressionless, but Edward flung the reins in his direction and strode into the house

36

after nodding at his groom in a manner that showed he had not heard of Lottie's condition.

'Warm water!' shouted Edward and Lottie came running from the kitchen. 'Everyone in the house must wash in warm water each time they come back from the City,' he said. Lottie looked at him as if he were mad. 'My brother says that it keeps away the plague,' he continued. The strong Sack was still making life more easy. 'And tell Mary to order more Sack.' He laughed. 'Tell her it is better than all those remedies in her books and we shall take it and so shall she, even if she does not approve of strong drink.'

Lottie smiled. It would be a pleasure to tell this to the woman who had been taunting her all morning with snide remarks about babies born out of wedlock having the stamp of the Devil on them.

'You look well, Lottie,' said Edward. 'I think the air of Gray's Inn suits you. The City was hot and smelled like a midden and it is good to breathe again.'

'Yes, Sir.' Lottie bobbed and hurried back to the kitchen, sharing Sam's relief that the Master obviously did not know of her condition. Men are blind to such things, she thought. Perhaps my lady will not tell him for another month when it will be apparent to even the most blind of men. She put fresh water in the ewer in the dressing room and found her mistress in the small boudoir, sorting ribbons.

'The Master is home, my lady,' said Lottie.

'He didn't use the carriage? I heard no wheels on the gravel.'

'He came by hack, Ma'am.'

'I have not told him, Lottie. I cannot bear to think of you and Sam being turned away.' Marian looked worried. 'If you left us, you would have to live in Cripplegate with your mother and I hear that pestilence is there.'

'Sam can find work, my lady,' said Lottie with pride.

37

'He has been asked many times to leave you and go into the country where there are large stables for racing.'

'I do not doubt it,' said Marian. 'Sam is very good at his work and has a way with horses, but would you want to leave London, Lottie? You were born and bred here and I fear would find the country far too quiet.'

Lottie began to cry. 'I know, my lady. Sam and me have talked about it and neither of us wants to live away from London. Where would I buy any of the things hawked on the streets here? Where would we walk in the evenings to watch the fine clothes of the gentry as they arrive at soirées, and go walking in Vauxhall? Sam would miss his friends in the alehouses and I would have no one to gossip with.' She sighed and dried her tears on her apron. 'And my mother is not well and needs to see me whenever I am free.'

Kate looked up from the box of buttons that seemed to contain every colour and shape that she did not need. 'They could stay, Mother,' she said.

'Your father will never hear of it, Kate,' said Marian sadly.

'Sam lives above the stables,' said Kate. 'I went over to see what could be done and found a disused hayloft there: the stable under it is now a grain-store and so the hay can no longer be dropped down into the stalls. If the loft was cleared and lime-washed and added to the room that Sam has now, with the landing included as a place for a fire-grate and sink, they could both live there.'

Marian marvelled at the girl's calm efficiency, and Lottie caught her breath. She knew the hayloft only too well. It was the one place where Sam and she could be alone and undisturbed, and it had seemed so natural to make love among the swathes of sweet-smelling hay.

'A hayloft?' asked Marian doubtfully.

'Oh, my lady, if we could,' said Lottie, her eyes shining. It would be better then the small cramped room under the eaves that was all she had now, and she would have Sam for always, and their child.

'Don't tell Father until it is done,' said Kate. 'He will be angry at first but if there is no tax on his time or energy, he will accept the idea, and secretly be glad to keep Sam here.' She smiled. 'Lord Chalwood came at Christmas more to entice Sam away than to pay us a visit, Mother. He made Mr Blackwell organise the evenings in His Lordship's private box at the theatre and at the new Whitehall Theatre to place Father under an obligation to him and so let him have Sam.'

'Kate, you mustn't even think such things,' cried Marian, deeply shocked. 'Lord Chalwood acted as a friend and business associate.'

'He left Sam a Christmas box and told him that there were some employers who would value a good man and give him more!'

Lottie giggled at Kate's rejoinder. 'Sam told me,' she said. 'But he doesn't like the country any more than I do.'

Marian pushed the ribbons back in the same untidy heap in the drawer where she had found them. 'Tell Sam to clean the place and he can take the old stove that is in the barn. There is a pump below the windows of the loft and a drain for swilling down the waste, or the dung heap by the stables.' She looked at Lottie severely. 'But if you bring one whiff of the stables into the house, the Master will not tolerate it, Miss.'

'I need not use that way, Ma'am. There is a back ladder to the lane.'

'So that is how you met Sam,' said Kate, laughing. 'No one saw you cross the stable yard.'

Lottie blushed and hung her head. 'I'm sorry, my lady,' she said.

'What's done is done,' said Marian briskly. 'Tell Sam to get this accomplished as soon as maybe and then we'll arrange for the parson.'

It was such a relief to have Kate at home. In her quiet way she was wise and full of good ideas. If only she could look happier, then life would be wonderful. And now Marian had no need to lose Lottie.

Lottie sang as she washed the linen in the deep slate sink in the scullery. This was work for the scullerymaids and the girls who came in as extra help from the overcrowded dwellings in Cripplegate, but Edward was particular over the cleanliness of his shirts and Lottie decided that anything that could keep him sweet was worth the sacrifice of her status as personal maid to Her Ladyship.

'I don't see that you have anything to sing about,' said Mary Creed. She saw the girl's sparkling eyes and the bloom of health and pregnancy and hated what she saw. 'You'll not escape the wrath of God by singing lewd songs from the playhouses. You should fall on your knees and ask Divine forgiveness and sing hymns, my girl.'

Joseph had come back from the theatre evening wearing a very knowing grin and with his underwear soiled, but was mildly aggressive after the ale he had drunk and Mary had not dared to reproach him, and she bore the humiliation of having to clean his livery with deep resentment.

'It's a fine day, Mary,' said Lottie. She sighed. 'It's far too good a day to quarrel. I'm happy and I want everyone in the world to be happy, too.'

'And what if they turn you out? Have you thought of that, my girl?' Mary eyed her with hopeful malevolence. 'Just you wait until the Master finds out! Not all your hairdressing for Her Ladyship and your touch with lace will save you then.' She pursed her lips. 'The Master has no time for sinful servants. He allows me and Joseph to live in because we are God-fearing and he knows that we would never bring shame on this house.' Mary glanced at the girl, hoping for some reaction. Was Joseph the father? The artful minx could smile now but there would be ructions when Edward Verney was told. Mary was torn between the desire to tell him and the dread that if she did, Joseph might be named and disgraced.

'I'm to stay,' said Lottie. Her face clouded. 'At least, my lady knows and wants me to stay and is making plans so that I can live close to the house.'

'You'll not live in our rooms.' Mary blazed and her hands trembled with rage. 'There may be rooms there but the Master would never let anyone else use them as he gave them for our use! And what would I do with a squalling infant about the place?'

'There'll be no infant near you, Mary Creed. You wouldn't know what to do with one if you had one, any more than you know how to treat a man. I wouldn't let you touch any of my flesh and blood!'

Lottie pounded the clothes against the stone and tried not to cry. If only she could be rid of the woman. All the servants detested her, but she was sweetness itself when Edward Verney spoke to her and she was a very good cook.

'That's all you are fit for,' said Mary. 'You make a good scullery-maid,' and she tossed one of the pieces of dirty linen over towards Lottie. 'Go on, scrub. Sluts' work for sluts.'

'You sound waspish,' said Joseph from the doorway. He eyed Lottie with approval. 'Give me a bit of meat and bread or something, Mary. The Master wants the horses in a quarter of an hour and he's not in the best of tempers.'

Mary disappeared into the huge larder and brought out a piece of cold rabbit pie and pickles. 'There,' she said. 'There's not enough for them and we can finish it down here.'

Lottie recognised the remains of the special pie that had been served for mid-day dinner the day before in the upstairs dining room. She said nothing but hoped that she could take a piece over for Sam later when Mary was away from the kitchen. Not that the servants ate badly as Marian often asked Lottie what she had eaten and rebuked Mary if she provided badly for the people in the kitchen.

'You'd better eat some too, Miss,' said Mary acidly. 'Or they will say I'm starving you. Go on, eat for two. Isn't that what Her Ladyship will say?'

Lottie looked startled, but she pretended not to hear and twisted the clean linen to rid it of excess water. She shook out a shirt and placed it in the basket ready for hanging in the yard, and reached for another. The thin gown clung moistly to her front and Joseph saw the outline of her pregnancy. He grinned, knowingly. So that was why Mary was so ill tempered. It was bad enough that Lottie was full-blown and pretty, with breasts that promised all the delights of the flesh, and a sunny nature into the bargain, but to know that Lottie was with child must make his wife feel murderous. How many years had they been married? Joseph had lost count and had almost given up even pretending to want his wife for any purpose other than her cooking and cleaning and the very good housewifely attributes she possessed. They had long given up any ideas they once had of raising a family, and now this girl couldn't avoid goading Mary unto jealousy and hate just by looking as she did.

'Eating for two?' he asked, laughing. 'You're a sly one, Lottie.' He speared a piece of pie on his knife and ate it with relish. Mary slapped a tankard of ale down beside him and cut some pie for herself and some for Lottie.

'Thank you, Mary,' said Lottie, and wondered if the woman was at last showing a vestige of interest and sympathy.

'I do as I'm bid,' said Mary. 'They say that pickles go sour on you when you're carrying. If you eat them and get sick, just remember I warned you and don't run with tales to Her Ladyship.'

'I would never do that, Mary,' said Lottie.

42

'When is it?' asked Joseph. He stuffed his mouth full again and struggled into his tunic.

'The end of September or near enough,' said Lottie. Now that these two knew about it, there was no point in hiding dates or anything from the rest of the household. Besides, she was tired of pretending that all was normal, and the lump was showing now. She could almost see the way that Joseph's brain was calculating, and she reddened.

'Must have been the cold weather brought that on,' he said with a wink. 'Last winter was one for cuddling up in the hay or in a nice warm feather bed.' Mary looked angry. What did he mean? Was that wink a kind of message shared between them? She dared not ask him and she dared not, as yet, hint to Lottie that she knew that Joseph had rolled her in the hay, but it took all her self-control to stop her tongue from accusing them. Jealousy stole any logic she possessed and when Joseph left the kitchen, she worked in the larder until Lottie went up to her mistress with the tisane and biscuits after dinner.

Kate took a thin almond biscuit and handed the dish round for Marian and Anna to take some. 'I went over to the loft again, Lottie,' she said. 'You'll need a quilt and some other bedding. Sam hasn't anything that you could share.' Lottie poured the lime-blossom tea and hung her head, hating to be of any trouble. 'I've put a bundle of things ready for you to take as soon as the lime-wash has dried, and Mother has talked to the parson.'

'Oh, my lady,' said Lottie. 'I don't know how to thank you.'

'Not yet, Lottie. Tomorrow you must get it all done before I tell my husband, and for that I must pick the right moment.' Marian was uneasy. Edward could be stubborn and if he once refused to consider the couple remaining in his employ, there was nothing she could do about it for as the head of the family his word was law.

'I hope we are doing right,' said Marian when the girl

43

had left the room. 'I dislike deceiving your father in any way but it will be easier to tell him if we have arranged everything beforehand.'

'Is it fit for a newborn child?' asked Anna.

'It is clean and dry and warm and better than they might have in Cripplegate,' said Kate.

'When I marry and have babies, I want a crib lined with blue silk and a canopy of white lace,' said Alice.

'What would a servant like Lottie do with lace and silk?' said Anna sensibly. 'I shall make some good flannel binders for her and some cotton pads. That's the kind of thing she will need, so if you want to help her, you can sew the calico baby garments.'

Alice turned up her nose. 'I can't sew calico, Anna. It makes my fingers ache and reddens the skin.'

'Then cut down my old woollen shawl and make that up for the baby,' said Anna. 'That at least will be soft.' She frowned. 'Surely a baby born to a servant girl has soft skin and can be chafed by rough material just as a son or daughter of the gentry?' She shrugged and went back to her embroidery, wondering if Captain Daniel Bennet was always as stiff and cold as he had been at the supper by Westminster Stairs, and whether the gentlemen at the Court of St James were all as bad as Kate hinted.

Chapter 4

'Your father will not like it, Miss Kate,' said Sam.

'That is why I want you to drive me in the small carriage, Sam,' said Kate patiently. 'We need several things from St Paul's and Covent Garden and if I am in a closed carriage and not a hackney, how can I come to any harm? I refuse to stay here and do nothing, as if the plague will catch me if I so much as breathe.'

Sam looked anxious but he knew that Mr Verney was busy in his office in the City and that Lady Marian was receiving ladies in her drawing room with Anna and Alice and would not want to be disturbed. He went back to the stables to get the light carriage ready and had it waiting by the side of the house as soon as Kate was dressed for shopping and had her list and basket.

'There's a bundle of old clothes and a basket of food to be put in the carriage,' Kate ordered. 'First, drive to Dr Verney's house and then on to Covent Garden.'

Sam collected the bundles and climbed onto his seat without further comment, but took Kate such a long way round to the house where Mr Verney's brother lived that she called to him to take a short cut. Sam pretended not to hear as he knew he was avoiding two streets where every house had the red cross of the plague on the door and the middle of the roads were rank with filth as no raker was

45

willing to clear the ordure. He whipped up the horse and eventually they stopped and Kate stepped down and went up to the house, followed by Sam carrying the old clothes.

'Shall I bring the food, too, Miss Kate?' asked Sam.

'No, that is for the parson's family,' said Kate.

'I don't think you should go there, Miss Kate,' said the groom unhappily. 'They live by one of the infected areas and it is said that they mingle with the sick to give comfort.'

'And eat so little themselves that they grow weak and may catch the pestilence if good friends do not make sure they have enough food,' said Kate firmly. 'Dr Verney maintains that good food and Sack are the best shield against any sickness and I believe him.'

Only the housekeeper was at home and Kate left a message that all was well with the family and that the clothes were for the poor. She was secretly relieved not to see the doctor, as however he risked his own life, he might rebuke her for running into danger when she was unprepared and of no real use to the sick. Kate too had heard ugly rumours that one of the parson's family was ill, and every illness now, unless proved otherwise, was believed to be the plague. Yet it could simply be a cold in the head or a distemper of the bowels from eating bad food in the heat, she told herself now. Sam followed slowly with the carriage while Kate bought the things she needed and gave orders for meat and fish to be delivered to the house high above the City where the air was pure and the Verneys lived in comfort.

'I don't think you should go down there, Miss Kate,' said Sam as they came to the end of the road where the parsonage was situated.

'Bring the basket, Sam,' said Kate, tilting her head in a way that showed she would not be denied. She walked carefully as the rutted street was full of loose cobbles and dust and the smell of stale cabbage stalks and excrement hung heavy on the still air.

From the closely-packed houses came the wailing of hot babies and the shouts of anger exploding in rooms too stifling and dank for comfort. Kate tightened her mouth to shut out the smells and to stop the cry of distress that threatened to surface as she heard also the moans of the doomed in a house where the red cross still gleamed wetly and the guard was fixing the last of the chains across the door. She took the bunch of herbs that Lottie had thrust into her hand as she left the house and pressed the bitter-sweetness to her face, inhaling the good scent and praying that this was not the house she sought.

'Kate!' she looked up, startled, and Sam hastily supported her as Kate saw a face at an upstairs window that she knew only too well.

'Agnes?' she breathed. 'Oh, Sam, it *is* the parsonage.' She gazed upwards and other faces appeared, with the parson's wife trying to keep her family away from the window.

'It's Kate Verney,' called Kate, and the woman looked down at her and shook her head, hopelessly. 'You are not sick!' said Kate. 'Who is it?'

'My husband. The Lord has seen fit to burden us as He has so many of our flock and now we are sealed until he recovers and there is no more sickness in the house.'

The woman sounded calm, but already two of the children were crying bitterly. Kate turned to the guard who sat on an upturned barrel by the front door, paring his fingernails with a small knife. The halberd by his side and the chains and locks on the doors and lower windows showed that any attempt at entry or escape was impossible.

'They are not sick,' said Kate firmly. 'Take the parson to the pest-house and leave the others free, or they will all die.'

'The Searcher says he has the ague and a fever and I have my orders, Ma'am,' said the guard.

'Ague?' said Kate. 'That means nothing. You can let the

47

others go,' she pleaded. 'The parson may not have more than a heavy cold and should have air.'

'The doctor saw him, Ma'am, and he has buboes on his chest. They'll stay for forty days and nights or go on the cart with the rest,' he added, without emotion.

'They must have food! Thank God I brought the basket, Sam. Have they ropes to lower or can you pass it through one of the lower windows?' she asked the guard.

'They have ropes and baskets,' he said, and called up to the window for one to be lowered. Kate was pale and her hands trembled as she unpacked the food and Sam placed it in the empty container.

'*I wish it was more*,' she wrote on the back of her shopping list with a blunted piece of charcoal she had in her purse. '*I will send food each day until you are well and will ask the guard to get you ale and mead, and plague water.*'

'Do you think he is honest?' she whispered to Sam.

He snorted with derision. 'Not he, Miss Kate! Do you see the scars on his neck? They are healed sores, so he feels safe from catching the plague again. Once they are close to death, he will rob the sick and be off with whatever he can carry.'

'Will he do as we ask? Buy things for them if I give him the money?'

'Wrap some money in your kerchief, Miss Kate, and put it with the food. When they need anything, they can throw down enough to buy it and even if he cheats them, they will have something.'

'Oh, Sam, I can't believe this is happening. They are my dear friends who comforted me when I was unhappy. I must help them to escape. How can anyone be locked up when they are not sick?'

Sam tugged on the rope and the basket was taken up to the bedroom window. 'Leave well alone, Miss Kate,' he said. 'Come away now, and tomorrow I'll bring more food for them if Mr Verney allows it.'

48

'He will want to help, too!' Kate stared at him, wide-eyed. 'He *will* help, Sam. All of us must do something. They are our friends!'

He turned away sadly. What could she know of the suffering of the tainted? How could anyone help when the law was so harsh and so many were condemned without mercy to stay in stinking rooms with the dead or dying? 'They say that the disease is lessening, Miss Kate,' he said, hoping to comfort her.

'But not for them!' She dashed the tears away. 'Come home, Sam. My father must see the magistrate and get them freed.'

'It's no use, Miss Kate. Once the red cross is on the door and the Searcher has said there is plague there, nobody on this earth can do anything.'

'Who are these wicked people, Sam? Who are the Searchers?'

'Women mostly, who don't fear death or have had the sickness. Some are nurses but most are ignorant and dishonest and thieving.'

'And lives depend on their word?' Kate climbed into the carriage. 'Can they be bribed, Sam?' she asked as he bent to fold the step back and close the door.

'Many can, but it's too late for the parson. Once the watch is set at the door, it would be known and bribes would be useless.' He swung up on to the box and whipped the horse with unaccustomed fury, while Kate tried to think of ways and means to help her friends. She averted her eyes as they passed a newly-dug pit outside the walls of an overcrowded graveyard. The huge vat of lime waited to be added to the thin veil of earth on the next layer of bodies, and in the distance she heard the sound that matched the tolling of the bell.

'*Bring out your dead, and the Lord have mercy on their souls!*'

Kate put up a hand to cross herself, then lowered it

49

again. She was not of the old religion and yet she suspected there might be more comfort in it than in the whining teaching of Retribution that Mary Creed preached. She dried her eyes and when Sam swung the carriage to the front door of the house, she ran in to find her mother.

She stopped short in the doorway of the drawing room, unprepared to see her father home so early. He turned and smiled. 'Kate! Your mother was asking where you were, and as I am home early, we can eat and drive in the fields.' He didn't notice her pallor or the traces of tears on her cheeks, and Kate busied herself fetching the soft linen jacket to replace the coat he wore outside.

He shrugged into the jacket and sipped the cold drink ready on the tray. 'The news is better,' he said, smacking his lips with satisfaction.

'What news?' asked Kate bleakly.

'Even if we believe only half of what is printed in the *Intelligencer*, there has been no contagion in the City of London now for almost three weeks.'

'Mrs Mead, Uncle William's housekeeper, says that there are many cases in St Giles-in-the-Fields that have not been notified,' said Kate. She was shocked that her father could look so relaxed and complacent while the Reverend Ewing was lying ill and his family imprisoned, but she hesitated to tell him as she hated to upset him.

'And when did you see her, Miss?' asked Edward testily. 'I forbid you to go anywhere near the City, and as for that house of his, it must carry some sort of infection as he has no thought for his own safety and mingles more and more with the poor wretches in the pest-houses and in closed houses.'

'I took some old clothes for the poor, Father,' said Kate. I must keep him sweet, she thought, or in this mood he will desert his friends and they will starve. He grunted. 'They are well and after I went there, I collected your linen bands from Covent Garden and your new hose.' She smiled,

50

but her eyes showed her desperation. 'I was careful, Father. I went with Sam in the closed carriage and didn't call on anyone in the City, only the shops.'

Edward grunted again. 'If the pestilence is waning, I suppose you can visit the shops, but I forbid you to enter any streets with red crosses on the doors.'

Kate bit her lip. 'The Reverend Mr Ewing is sick, Father. They say he has a fever and the ague,' she added, to make it sound innocent, and decided not to mention the buboes. 'His wife and family are with him and they need food and lack comforts and herbs, but I can take them supplies.'

Marian eyed her daughter with alarm. She was pale and her face was tear-stained, her eyes swollen with weeping.

'No, I forbid it!' Edward sat down heavily and mopped his face with a silk handkerchief. It had been stifling in his office and he had left it gladly and come home anticipating being tended with love and attention by his family, not to be pilloried by Kate who looked defiant now and was obviously hiding something from him.

'I know you are fond of the family, especially the young children, and Mr Ewing does good work among the poor of Cripplegate, but young women should have better things to do than run into trouble and risk life and health.' She was staring at him and making him feel very uneasy. He struggled for words, and hated the expression of disbelief and anger that reproached him as Kate listened.

'They will think they are outcasts,' she said. 'If they are sick, they need our help and love. We go to church, Father! We pray, and yet may we not help as good Christians should?'

'Even so, until I hear more, you must not pass their threshold, Miss!' He turned to Anna, who was composedly sewing. 'I hope you are listening, Anna. No lady from this house goes into any dwelling of the poor, nor to visit the sick without my permission!'

51

'If the sickness is abating, there will be no need,' said Anna, biting a thread with her strong white teeth.

'Exactly,' said Edward, more calmly. 'The disease is fading and we worry too much. Don't go into the house until you know that the parson is better, and be careful – but the worst is over,' he finished, heartily.

'They are sealed up with the red cross on the door, Father,' said Kate quietly.

Marian gasped and put out a hand to her daughter, but Kate ignored it. '*Sealed?*' Edward spoke as if he doubted his own ears. 'All sealed? Even the children? Even your friend Agnes?'

'I saw her at the window, Father, and they had to let down a basket for the food I took them.'

'You touched nothing? You give me your word, Kate?'

'How could I touch them? They were in the upper windows and the door was chained.' Her hands hung at her sides as if she suddenly lacked will-power. 'How could I touch my dear Agnes when she is a prisoner, and Sam wouldn't even let me touch the basket they sent down. He filled it and sent it back, but I gave a note with the promise of more food and more money, Father. I must keep faith with them.'

'Make up a basket tomorrow,' said Edward. He grunted. 'But send one of the servants. Tell Debbie to go with it and leave it at the door. Take an old basket that need not be returned and tell her not to linger to gossip,'

'I must know how they fare,' said Kate. Her face was set in a firmness that he had not seen since she had defied him and was beaten for it when a child. My gentle Kate, he thought. My dear child who has had her own grief so early in life. How can I protect you except by taking you away where you can never see or touch contagion?

'They will be given anything I can send with safety, Kate, but I insist that you stay away. It is sad that our friends are sick, but the news generally is good and we may

52

walk safely in many places now.' He smiled in an effort to lighten the atmosphere, and walked over to Anna who was gathering cuttings from the garment she had unpicked to re-shape into small baby clothes. The soft thick cotton of her old dress was warm to the touch and far more comforting to a baby's skin than the coarse calico used by the lower orders for their layettes.

'What nonsense are you making now, Anna?' asked Edward, somewhat ashamed of his fears. He attempted a hearty interest and picked up one of the tiny garments. 'Dressing dolls again?' he said indulgently. 'Such fine work for so mean a return. Alice is too old for dolls, so I suppose these go to some poor child so ignorant that she cannot care for such work in the way it should be treated.' He put the material down and saw that his wife sat tense and pale behind her tapestry.

Edward picked up the cut-out gown again and examined it more closely. He looked across at Kate who was hurriedly wrapping flannel binders in a piece of uncut cloth and then saw the girl standing in the doorway as if turned to stone. Lottie looked as if she would collapse at any moment and she clutched the tray she carried as if she was afraid of dropping it.

Kate went to her and took it from her cold hands. 'Go now,' she ordered in a fierce whisper. 'Go where he can't find you for an hour and I will say you have gone on an errand.'

Lottie fled from the room and Edward wondered if his entire household had gone mad. His wife was pale and obviously frightened, a servant girl looked as if she hoped the earth would swallow her and two girls were poised to defy him! Even Sam, the equable and good-tempered man who was his right hand in everything in the stables had been sullen of late, even shifty, if his sideways looks were to be interpreted as furtive. Mary Creed had a wicked gleam in her eyes these days as if she had witnessed the

53

hanging of a Royalist in the days of Oliver Cromwell and relived the enjoyment as she worked, and each time he returned from the City there was a flurry of activity as if everyone was on edge at his coming.

'Dolls?' he asked. 'Dolls *or babies?*' He looked at his wife. Not Marian. Her vapours and change had finished these two years and she could never make another child. He eyed the two older girls with apprehension that he dared not show. Kate had been engaged to be married, but surely had never indulged in sexual activity with her fiancé? No, that was not possible. Robert had been gone long enough for the result of any such activity to have shown well before this. Anna, then? He often wondered if a deep and sultry passion lay dormant under those dark eyes but where did she have the opportunity to meet a buck of the Court in private? Anna half-smiled as if reading his thoughts but she was calm and had none of the dismay that he read in the eyes of his daughter and his wife.

He swung round to Alice. She was a child still. He stared. Was she looking pale? Her fair hair was swept up in a coil to keep her cool and she now appeared to him to be a very grown-up child indeed. Many daughters of his friends in the City were married or at least betrothed at fifteen. His mouth tightened and his eyes showed an agony that he couldn't hide from his wife.

Marian went to him and put a hand on his arm. 'It's one of the servants, Edward.' He let out his breath in a long sigh. 'Please don't be upset, my dear. It's only natural and it will never have to bother you or upset the running of this establishment if you will leave it in my hands.'

Kate poured cool lemon water into his glass and smiled. Anna brought light slippers and took off his shoes and Alice came to sit on the arm of his chair as he liked to see her. Edward relaxed. He knew many of the servants but Marian saw them each day and he seldom spoke to any not connected with the dining room, the kitchen or the stables.

It would be one of those, easily replaced when she had to leave, and why shouldn't his womenfolk show this charity by making things for the infant?

Edward sipped the cold drink and flexed his feet in the unrestricting slippers. Alice bent to touch his hair and told him about the poem she had learned, and Marian hovered like a mother hen about to be taken by a fox.

'Who is it?' he asked. Alice took away her soothing hand and Kate returned the jug of lemon to the pewter tray in case it was knocked over. Anna closed the purse string top to the reticule in which she kept her sewing scissors and threads, and pushed the sewing into a small chest by the window seat.

'It's Lottie,' said Kate. Marian put a hand to her mouth to stifle the muted groan that refused to stay quiet and wondered why she felt so deeply for a girl who was of no real consequence.

'Lottie?' Edward jumped up from his seat, sending the glass flying. 'Lottie with child?' His face reddened and he glared at his wife. 'Why did no one tell me? Do I have to be the last to know what goes on in my own household?'

'We found out only a few days ago,' said Anna gently. 'Lottie was afraid to tell anyone in case you were angry.'

'Angry? Why should I be angry? Tell me that, Madam! Why should it matter to me if one of your women is a whore?' He paced the room, leaving wet marks where his slippers went through the spilled liquid and nearly slipping on the polished wood. 'She'll have to go,' he said.

'Oh, no please, not that, Edward!' pleaded Marian.

'You know my rules,' he said stubbornly. 'If you have spoiled the wench beyond anything that is your affair, Madam, but she goes before the child is born and there's an end to it!'

'If she goes, Father, then you will have to lose Sam, too,' said Kate calmly.

'Sam? What has Sam to do with this?' Alice sniggered and turned to look out of the window.

'Sam is the father and they are to be married next week.' Marian spoke quietly. 'He owns the child, and Lottie and he will marry.'

'Sam? But he is the best groom and stable manager that I have ever had!' shouted Edward.

'If Lottie goes, he will go too,' said Kate again.

'That doesn't follow. He can find another girl who will not land him with this kind of trouble, so long as he keeps her away from this house,' said Edward. 'They know the rule that I will have no farm or stable lads within these walls except for Joseph, who does not rake the stalls or bring in dung.'

'If you let them stay, nothing need change, Father. Sam and Lottie can live over the stables and never bring a breath of horses into the house.'

'She goes, but he can stay,' said Edward. 'I will speak to him.'

'When they are married, they will expect to live together,' said Kate reasonably.

'Do you want members of your household to live in sin, Edward?' asked Marian, gathering courage now that her daughters were rallying round and Edward had lost his first fury. 'How can you face the parson knowing that you set your face against the Church's teaching?'

'Will you all leave me alone! I need to think,' he said. Women could twist a man's thoughts before he even had them in focus.

'My lady! Master!' Lottie burst into the room with Edward's best silk jacket over her arm and his light periwig in her hand. She showed none of the fear of the previous hour but bustled in, intent on the important matters needing her attention.

'The coach of M'Lord Chalwood is at the door, Sir!' As if thrusting a child into a too-tight coat, Lottie held the jacket for Edward as he slipped off the house-coat and turned to her with arms ready for the silk and the wig. Anna forced his feet back into his leather shoes and Marian wiped his brow with cool water. Kate bustled round the room, making everything neat, and tidied away all signs of the sewing except for the elegant tapestry on the frame. Alice undid the thick swathes of fair hair and shook them over her shoulders and Anna buttoned the tight cuffs of her dress.

'Thank you, Lottie,' said Edward, forgetting that a minute ago he had condemned her to the narrow lane where her parents lived in Cripplegate, in the huge old house that had once belonged to a member of the aristocracy but was now bursting at the seams with too many families, above the dark alleys of the wattle-and-daub huddles of the slums.

'Just in time,' breathed Anna. 'Thanks to Lottie,' she added in a pointed whisper as Mary Creed appeared in the doorway and announced that His Lordship was calling and was the family at home?

Edward nodded, and gave no hint of the inner turmoil that had ruffled the surface of the family tempers. He walked slowly to meet his visitor as if he had been waiting for just the moment. Anna curtseyed and showed the nobleman to the best chair and Kate whispered to Lottie to bring Malmsey and Sack and some of Mary's special light biscuits. Marian sat at her tapestry and listened but said little after the first greetings. The men talked of the weather and the price of timber for building, the state of the fleet against the Dutch and the fact that the plague had paused over the past weeks.

'And yet, I feel that I need country air,' said Lord Chalwood. He sipped the wine with appreciation and wondered where Verney had his supplier. 'My horses call to me and I am not happy about two of my new colts.' He eyed Edward warily. Seen in his own home, Verney was impressive and his household was obviously very well-

57

ordered and prosperous. There was no hint here of any need for patronage and indeed, there was much to be gained by the friendship of this shrewd businessman who had interests in most of the countries of the known world. The loan of a theatre box and a few invitations to the Court seemed little exchange now for what he wanted most

Edward watched his illustrious guest with caution, and outward courtesy. He talked of the state of the roads and of the order from the Lord Mayor for every household to swill down the fronts of their houses with water each morning and to put refuse in the middle of each road ready for the rakers to collect and take to the laystalls outside the city limits. 'That will take away the pestilence,' he added. 'It is a measure used long ago and never proved to be useless, but until the Crier had been out twice with an extra threat of fines or imprisonment, the first order was largely ignored.'

'Cats and dogs!' said Lord Chalwood. 'Too many scavenging cats and dogs. Get rid of the strays that roam the streets and dunghills and you kill the plague, too.'

'We need dogs to kill the rats,' said Alice, thinking of her pet, and the docile and well-fed dogs in the stables.

His Lordship smiled indulgently. 'We wouldn't take your pets, child, not the ones that earn their keep in the stables and farms, but the rest should be killed.'

'But are there not rats to be killed in the culverts and in the City?' asked Alice.

'There are but they pose no great danger to health and do not turn on men as dogs do.' He turned back to Edward. 'You have a boy at Eton, have you not?'

'Peter, my youngest son,' said Edward, with pride. 'He writes a good hand and sends letters on the orders of his tutors, in Latin.' He didn't think it necessary to add that only Anna could understand what was written and that she had a very low opinion of the standard of the Latin used. 'Would you like Anna to read one to you, Sir?'

'No, I can well imagine their excellence,' said Lord Chalwood hastily. 'My own son sent similar missives to us and quite honestly, I could not make head nor tail of them.' He laughed. 'When he wanted money or food, he wrote an appendix in good English.'

'So does Peter,' said Edward. It was a relief to know that he wasn't the only bad scholar in business. 'He asked for oysters and some of Mary Creed's best cakes in his last letter, as his Name Day is next month, so I suppose I have to indulge the rogue.'

'You will visit him or send them by coach?' Lord Chalwood examined the ends of his fingers. 'You could send your groom and he could rest his horses in my stables for a night. My estates lie close to Eton and make a good stopping place on the way.'

'How kind of you to think of it, Sir,' said Marian. 'It is hard for the boy to be away for his anniversary and even if he will be here for the summer, I like him to have some treats.' Her eyes softened. Peter was dear to her and she saw so little of him now.

'Then it is settled. You send your man with the hamper and he can use my stables to rest the horses each way. Perhaps on the way back, he could stay for a few days to look at my colts?'

Edward glanced at his wife with less than approval but resigned himself to losing Sam's services for a week. 'I am obliged to you,' he said. 'By all means let Sam see to your colts and be of use to you before he comes back for his wedding.' Anna hid a smile, and dared not look at Kate, and Alice slid out of the room to hide her laughter.

'A wedding?' Lord Chalwood looked annoyed. It was one thing to steal a good groom but it was more difficult if the man had encumbrances. 'Need it be so soon? I had thought it possible if my horses needed attention that you might lend Sam to me over a period of time. Lord Carnegie is bringing some nags down to pit against mine in a race or two and you would be welcome to join in the sport, Verney, if you had a mind to it and if Sam was there with my horses.'

'How very civil of you, Sir, but I hesitate to leave Lady Marian for long and we have a duty to our servants. Sam has been with me man and boy and his pretty young wench is my wife's personal maid. By all means make use of Sam on the way back from Eton, and I hope he sees what your colts are lacking, but what did you say the date of the wedding will be, my dear? Next Saturday two weeks?'

'If it suits you, my dear,' said Marian demurely. 'We must make it a joyous occasion for such faithful servants who assure me that they never want to leave us.'

'Just so,' said Edward shortly. 'Now, shall we visit the stables, Sir, and tell Sam what we have in mind?'

'God bless the noble Lord!' said Anna as soon as the two men left the room. Kate seized her hands and danced her round the room, and Marian sank back on the cushions as if exhausted.

Alice peeped in and saw the girls laughing. 'What happened?' she asked, with envy.

'You should have controlled yourself and stayed,' said Anna.

'Tell me,' pleaded Alice. 'Are we to visit Peter at Eton?'

'No, but Sam and Lottie will stay and be married in just over two weeks,' said Marian. 'I believe that your father suddenly realised just how much they mean to us all and he doesn't want to lose Sam to that man, Alice.' Marian regarded her younger daughter with gentle reproof. 'Just because a man has a title does not mean that he is completely honest, my love. Please remember that when the young men come visiting.'

'Nobody comes to see me,' said Alice resentfully, tossing back the golden hair.

'They will,' said Anna quietly. 'Lady Marian is right, Alice.'

'What do you know about it? I have seen no carriages at the door with messages for you, Anna Ruyter!'

Marian looked annoyed. 'Hold your tongue, Miss. Anna will make a good marriage and a better one for not flaunting herself whenever a handsome man appears. I was ashamed at the way you sat making sheep's eyes at Captain Bennet during supper the other evening.'

'I don't want to marry a soldier,' said Alice. 'I was being polite.' She smiled. 'At the play there were men far more handsome than the sober soldier. Lord Carnegie was looking at our box and so was another man who was in the royal party.'

'Lord Carnegie looks at any pretty woman,' said Kate. 'It isn't safe for a young girl to accept that man's flattery.'

'You weren't there,' said Alice.

'I saw him often enough when I went to the theatre,' answered her older sister. She looked sad but smiled as if she cast off a cloud. 'We saw him often and heard that he had married a woman who had been passed from hand to hand and had the clap. She gave it to one of the royal Dukes just to spite him for her husband.'

'So Lord Carnegie might be infected?' Alice looked revolted. 'How does a woman know?' she demanded.

'You remain pure until you are wed and you marry a man with sense and goodness and no vices,' said Marian. She smiled. With her to look after them, her daughters need have no sleepless nights over such matters if they remained prudent.

'It sounds dull,' said Alice. 'Surely none of the men we saw could be bad?'

'You are very innocent,' said Anna. She blushed. 'I have worried about this, Lady Marian,' she said. Marian took the folded paper that Anna gave her and raised her eyebrows, first in laughter and then in annoyance.

'No name but a vow of love from an unknown? Who sent this, Anna?'

'I do not know. A boy brought it and gave it to one of the servants, the day after we were at the theatre.'

'I know that crest,' said Marian. 'The sword and the castle are as the ones on my family shield, but we have no bar sinister,' she said with pride.' She laughed. 'So, a distant relative asks you for an assignation at Vauxhall, Anna.'

'How romantic,' said Alice. 'Shall you go masked, Anna?'

'Anna will not go there, but I think that my husband will know what to do.' Marian refused to say more but a sense of foreboding made her restless. London was a wicked city and her girls were no longer children. Alice was far too trusting and impulsive and in the sunlight, her hair was a mass of golden lightness.

'The horses are being put to the shafts, Mother,' said Kate.

'We must take leave of Lord Chalwood and wish him God speed.' Marian led them to the door and knew from his expression that the nobleman had not had all his own way with Edward. Sam hovered in the background in his leather apron and other servants peeped down from upper windows to see the magnificent carriage depart.

'Not a word to your father about Lottie until I have spoken to him,' warned Marian. 'It costs him much to go back on his word but now he has done so, the weddding will be held and he will given them a good present.' She waved Alice off to her books. 'No laughing and no hints about what was said before Lord Chalwood came. I shall send word to the parson at once to make sure he is free to wed them. Now, Kate, it is not fitting that I should attend but you may do so if you wish, with two of the maidservants to go with you as chaperone.'

'May I go, too, Lady Marian?' asked Anna. Marian hesitated. The church where the wedding would take place was in an area of good houses surrounded by the tightly-packed dwellings of continental workers who had fled one kind of oppression or another, religious, political or racial, and the rougher elements might be a threat to the foreign-looking girl with the dark hair.

'If you go, and there is a crowd, you must promise me that you will retire to the house of the woman who makes my gloves.' Anna nodded, knowing what Marian was thinking.

'We can use the small closed carriage, Mother,' said Kate, 'and come back as soon as the vows have been exchanged.' She laughed. 'I doubt if Anna or I would relish the kind of celebrations provided by Lottie's family in Cripplegate, and we shall give them wine when they return in the evening to their home.'

'Hush, I hear your father coming in,' said Marian, and when Edward returned, Kate was waiting with cool jacket and slippers, and Anna was absorbed in her sewing.

'Sam is going to Eton with a parcel of fripperies for your son, Ma'am,' said Edward. 'Please have it ready by tomorrow noon and tell Mary to make her best cake and a pie.' His manner was stiff with embarrassment and Marian ignored the brusque manner and suggested a list of things that might divert young Master Peter.

'You will let Peter come home for the summer, Edward?' she asked.

'He shall come for a visit, but if he loses himself in Whitehall as he did the last time he was in London, he will go back that very day. I feel safer with him out of harm's way at school and many of the pupils at Eton now stay during the recesses to avoid the pestilence. In his last letter, Peter asked for tobacco of a mild variety, as he is made to smoke it or be beaten.' Edward pulled off the hot periwig and Kate arranged it on a stand to air.

'William did say that tobacco was widely approved as a nostrum against the plague, but it seems hard to flog any boy who refuses to smoke when the tobacco makes him sick.'

'They are learned men, my dear, and know best. Flogging never hurt me when I was a boy and it will make a man of Peter.'

Anna gave a slight cough and rose from her stool. She folded her sewing and looked quickly at Marian before she left the room. Kate followed her and Edward eyed his wife with a sheepish air.

'Thank you for being so generous, Edward,' said Marian and kissed his cheek.

'I couldn't let that mountebank steal Sam,' said Edward with heat. 'You'll see to it? Servants' weddings are none of my business and you must tell me what you need for them, within reason,' he added gruffly.

'I'll do it all and you'll find that Sam will give even better service and loyalty if he has your approval for this.'

Edward poured more Sack and sipped it. It had been a mistake to tell Lord Chalwood that Sack was the perfect prophylactic against the plague. He held up the crystal decanter and wondered if the noble Lord could stagger from his coach. 'Did Mary order more Sack?' he asked.

'Before I ring for her, I think you should see this, Edward. Anna gave it to me of her own free will and wants nothing to do with it.'

He took the note and his face darkened. 'S'death!' he swore. 'Who dares to send this to a member of my family?' He read it again. 'It smacks of looseness, Madam, and an assumption that we have no standards here. He thinks of our Anna as a common strumpet to be seduced in some closed carriage in the fields of Vauxhall or in a house of assignation.'

Bless you for saying 'our Anna', thought Marian. He tapped the edge of the table and stared out into the cloud of gently floating branches of the silver birches by the red-brick stable walls. 'What shall we do?' asked his wife.

64

'If I was ten years younger, I'd confront him and have satisfaction,' said Edward. 'Christopher is too young and has none of the sword skills that all these jackanapes seem to have, and yet I cannot let this pass.' He, too, had seen the crest of the FitzMedwins and knew that the two sons had reputations for every sin they could commit within the law and some that came close to treason.

'No violence, please, my dear,' pleaded Marian, safe in the knowledge that her husband had never unsheathed his sword in anger beyond the first threat and avoided strife of any physical form.

Edward nodded gravely as if he was restrained only by her plea. He chuckled. 'He shall have his assignation – but not with Anna. Now, who shall we send who will come to no harm? Joseph will drive the coach and can deal with any violence if the young buck brings a bully with him, and who better to protect but his own dear wife, Mary?'

Marian fanned her hot face and wondered if she could risk sponging her body in cool water for the second time in a week. Edward seemed very amused, and perhaps he wasn't as blind as he seemed to be at times. Mary Creed must have shown the waspish side of her nature in his hearing once or twice and she needed putting in her place.

Chapter 5

'She may feel insulted, but no more than that,' said Edward Verney. 'No man would want Mary Creed when he expected someone as pretty as Anna.'

'But it is wicked to send poor Mary into any danger,' pressed Marian.

'No danger in taking a note of polite refusal from her mistress, is there? With Joseph present, no violence can occur and she is tough and wiry.' He looked solemn. 'If insult is all she gets, then she is lucky. The town is full of wickedness and sickness and strife and I wish we were well out of it. I worry, Marian. I worry about our girls.'

His wife glanced at his flushed face and knew he was far more upset about the family of the Reverend Ewing than he cared to admit. He had also been drinking more than usual, first with Lord Chalwood and then alone, brooding as he gazed unseeing out across the bright flowers and well-trimmed trees.

Marian sighed. Life under the Protectorate had been harsh in many ways but there was law and order of a kind not met with under the first Charles and now the new king. Death had come mostly from old age, diseases long accepted as the will of God and from wounds in battle not the dreadful curse that now swept the land.

'Does Mary know what to do?' Marian went on. She was

very uneasy and thought that Edward was acting without consideration.

He spoke with the deliberation of one who has drunk deeply and has to think out his words. 'She knows that this evening she will be taken in the coach when Joseph drives us to Westminster Stairs where we take the boat to Vauxhall for supper. He and Mary then go on to Vauxhall for the assignation. Joseph will see that she delivers the note and then will send her home by hackney while he waits to bring us back late.' He smiled, obviously amused by the idea.

'What if Sir Rollo is angry and makes a scene? Has Joseph the right to do anything likely to provoke him?'

Edward glowered at her. 'If the rascal has any sense, once he reads my note he will know that he is escaping my anger lightly. He'll make sure he leaves Anna alone in future.'

'Do we all go to Vauxhall, Edward?'

'Just Anna and Alice, and I think Christopher, to make it safe. Enough to fill the carriage with Mary and us.'

'I'm not happy about it, Edward.'

'Trust me,' he said expansively. 'Be patient, Marian. The plague is abating and we can take the air safely. In time, we may once more walk in Tothill Fields with the Ewing family.' Marian looked sad. 'It's getting better each day,' he continued firmly. 'They've closed many of the alehouses in the worst areas and killed off most of the dogs and cats so it may be that the authorities know what causes the sickness and have stopped the spread by these measures.'

'It isn't the plague that worries me, Edward.' Marian sat with him by the window. 'When we were betrothed, we were lighthearted and full of plans for the future, but can our children have any future in a world that has grown sick and evil? The men who come as suitors are sometimes no better than animals, in spite of rank. And Mary may be hurt.'

'Your heart is too tender, Ma'am. Mary will take no harm.' Edward looked at the timepiece on the table. 'I must go back to my office and make sure that Roger has all he needs for the new agreement over ropemaking. The Admiralty need more and more as our fleet are hardpressed and the ships have little time for repairs. Mr Pepys has ordered tar and coir and it is rumoured that a battle off Lowestoft has cost the Dutch their fleet, but that means we for our part have lost grappling nets, ropes and sheets.'

'Take care, Edward, and avoid the alleyways. Sam told Lottie that there is much sickness in Long Ditch and Thieving Lane by Westminster.'

'I have no need to go there today,' he said, 'and the pestilence will be over by next month.'

Anna finished sewing the last of the baby gowns and added them to the parcel that Kate had made of flannel binders, into which the baby would be sewn for a few days after birth, and the shawl cut down to fit a newborn child.

'We have worked hard and much too soon,' said Kate. 'I wanted to get them done in case Lottie was sent away, but now she can store them in the chest that Sam found in the stables and have everything ready.' She sighed. 'It might be cooler on the water this evening, and it's far too hot to sew.' She closed the lid of the workbox. It was hard to work on baby clothes for another woman's infant when she should have been the one married by now.

'There's a horseman coming by the birch trees,' called out Alice. 'I can't see his face but he shows a shapely leg.' She giggled. 'Another caller for you, Anna?'

Anna blushed and joined her at the window. 'A messenger for Uncle, more like,' she said, and turned away just as the man emerged from the shade of the trees and looked up at the windows.

68

'Oh!' said Alice in a disappointed voice. 'It's that solemn man we met at Westminster.'

'Mr Blackwell?' asked Anna. 'Perhaps he brings more invitations to the theatre from Lord Chalwood.' She patted her hair and smoothed down the front of her pale violet dress and turned to the door, smiling.

'Excuse me, Miss Anna, but Captain Bennet is below and are you ladies receiving visitors?'

Anna stepped back, disconcerted, but Kate politely told Lottie to ask the Captain to join them. 'And make a cool drink of wine and water, Lottie,' she added.

Alice made a face and when Captain Bennet came to greet her, she smiled briefly and then turned to assemble glasses on the tray, as if he had nothing to do with her.

Kate smiled and held out her hand to be touched, then sat with her tatting again and her small-talk faded as the pattern became intricate, leaving Anna to entertain their unexpected guest.

He held her hand in a firm grip for longer than courtesy demanded and Anna felt her colour rising. What can I say to him? she thought. He doesn't like me and if he's come to see Kate, she is being very discouraging. Politeness and good breeding made her make an effort and she was aware that he followed her when she went to the wide settle and waited to be asked to sit with her.

Her slim hand fluttered and he bent his head in acceptance and sat by her side, so close that she had to draw aside her delicate skirt to avoid crushing it. She blushed, not for his nearness but because the gesture seemed like a withdrawal, a rejection.

'You ride a handsome beast, Sir,' she said, then bit her lip as it showed that he had been observed approaching the house and he would think that Anna had peered at him through the shutters like any servant girl, spying from a window.

'He is a gelding of fifteen hands, Ma'am. A good mount

69

and jumper with a splendid temper,' said Captain Bennet politely. 'Your groom has taken him into the shade and is seeing to him while I visit.'

There was silence and Anna creased her gown far more by puckering it with her fingers than Captain Bennet would have done while sitting on its folds. 'Your relative, Sir, I trust is well?' She couldn't recall if he was related to the lady or her husband.

'My aunt sends her regards, Ma'am and is in the best of health.' So it was his aunt and not his uncle; not that it concerned her. Anna searched for inspiration.

'And you have been to the King's theatre to see Mrs Gwyn, Sir?'

'My aunt kindly gave me a place in her box but I have little time for painted orange wenches.' He looked stern and Anna wondered if he regretted the passing of the Protector and the emergence of more liberal days. If only he would smile! His mouth was full and firm and his natural hair hung glossily smooth and healthy, and as he moved, the scent of good pomade came to her notice, strangely masculine and almost sensuous in a house where men were in the minority.

She glanced down to avoid his gaze. His calves were well-shaped and hinted at a virility and strength that many men would envy.

Captain Bennet coughed and Anna looked up at him, startled. Had he seen her staring? 'My aunt commanded me to offer my services this evening,' he said. 'To *all* the ladies if you venture abroad,' he added, as if the invitation might include Anna but she was not to suppose that she was important.

Anna rose to fetch him a glass of wine and water and set it on the small table by his side rather than risk touching his hand, and he left the glass where she put it.

Even old Sir Roger, Edward's cousin, would have made some gallant remark, such as it tasting better for being

70

poured by her fair hands, and this was a young man free to make far more gallant advances.

'You are going to the theatre, Sir?' Anna smiled faintly. 'We have other arrangements made, but your offer is most kind.'

'Not the theatre. Have you not heard?' Anna shook her head, and even Kate looked up from her work, dreading every new mention of another outbreak of pestilence. 'The Dutch are routed at Lowestoft and their Admiral Opdam has lost twenty ships and ten thousand men.' A sudden smile illuminated the dark eyes. 'Victory over the Dutch, Ma'am. Victory over De Ruyter and nothing to fear from him for a very long time. Tonight, all good Englishmen will make merry and rejoice.' His smile was set and his eyes held a kind of sad challenge.

'What has that to do with me . . . with us?' asked Anna. Her cheeks were burning as she sensed his curiosity to know if she would rejoice at the defeat of a man bearing her own family name.

'Tonight, it will not be safe for ladies to walk alone or abroad without escort.'

Kate put down her work. 'You are most kind, Captain Bennet, but tonight Anna and Alice and Christopher go with my parents to Vauxhall, driven in our own coach.'

'First we go on the river,' said Alice. 'It may be cooler on the water and we shall have supper at the Gardens.'

Anna regarded him with calm eyes. Her name would always make her unworthy of his attention. 'I think we have no cause for concern and no need of your kind offices,' she said, and wished that it wasn't so.

'I'm sorry to have bothered you, Ma'am,' he said stiffly. He rose and gave each of the girls a small inclination of his head that was less than polite and then he begged to be excused.

Anna watched him go and willed him to look back but he paused only to pick up a book that he had brought with

71

him and not shown to anyone. The back of his head was stiff and his neck showed a kind of anger in its rigidity. Anna wondered if he ever relaxed enough to be passionate, then blushed.

'Lottie told me that Captain Bennet is here, Kate.' Marian stood in the doorway and her smile of welcome faded. 'I heard a horse leaving, but surely that wasn't the Captain?' She looked cross. 'Mrs Blackwell said that she would ask him to call and now I have missed him through bothering to change my gown. It's too bad. You should have kept him here longer.'

'He didn't come to visit us,' said Alice. 'He came on the command of his aunt, Mrs Blackwell, and was so stiff and formal that I nearly fell asleep.'

'Captain Daniel Bennet is a distant cousin of the Blackwells and very well born,' said Marian reprovingly. She watched the faces of each of the girls as they talked of the man who had left. There was no hint that Alice or Kate was impressed by his good looks and Anna wore the closed expression that invited no questions. Alice dismissed him as boring and solemn, the worst attributes that she could give to any man. Kate thought him ill-at-ease in feminine company and when asked, Anna just said, 'He rides well.'

She looked out at the trembling birch leaves, newly green. 'He offered to escort us this evening if we walked abroad to see the fires. There will be fireworks and music in Tothill and Vauxhall and his aunt, or cousin, whichever you prefer, offered us the use of his strong arm.' She smiled slightly. 'He did nothing to persuade us,' she added.

'That was a generous enough offer,' said Marian, dismayed by the manners of her girls. 'I should have been here to show better hospitality.' She glanced at the jug of wine and water, hardly touched. 'No man drinks such thin stuff. Why didn't you ask Lottie for some good Madeira and some of Mary's thin biscuits?'

She grumbled on and the girls began to feel guilty. Anna

72

made the excuse that Alice needed her help with letters and departed to the writing room. Marian tried to guess if the Captain was interested in any of her family. They would never find out if they treated such a good-looking and eligible man in such a shabby way, she decided. Had he come to see Kate? Her daughter looked well this morning and had lost much of her pallor as she thought more of others and less of her own bereavement. She was young and would marry in time.

'Do you think that the Captain came to see Alice?' Marian asked, once she was alone with Kate.

'Alice?' Kate laughed as if the idea was ridiculous. 'He came because he was asked to do so and not for any other reason, Mother. He was as stiff as a yard broom and hardly looked at Anna although she was the one who tried to talk to him and to serve him wine.' Kate shook her head, knowing how her mother's mind worked. 'Not Anna. She was being the perfect hostess as usual when you are not here. I was busy and saw no reason for setting aside my work. He could have come to talk to me if he wanted to do so, but he stayed rooted to the settle and looked awkward. Alice was too bored to be polite, but I should have shown him more attention.' Kate looked contrite. 'I'm sorry, Mother, but I have lost the habit of small talk and it doesn't come easily.' Her mouth trembled. She seemed about to say more, but turned away.

'I didn't ask him to court you, Kate,' said Marian. 'I know it is too soon and I doubt if he could capture your heart or even your attention.'

'Thank you,' whispered Kate. 'I need time to recover but I know I must marry some day.'

'You are a good daughter and a joy to us all. There is no need to leave us for a household not to your liking.' Marian smiled. 'You will not die an old maid, but there is time yet.'

'Captain Bennet told us of the big victory over the Dutch.

73

He has a special interest in it as he fought in Dutch Africa and was ill of a fever there. He hates De Ruyter as if he is a personal enemy and I think that he believes Anna to be related to the Dutch Admiral and that's why he never smiles at her.'

'I wish that Anna had any other name,' said Marian. 'Your father wouldn't have it changed when she first came to us as he knew her family in the old days and is distantly related. Anna's family may have been connected with De Ruyter long ago, but not for many generations and not in direct line. Her forebears were powerful merchants and had the entrée to the noble houses of Europe. In times of peace, she could be presented at any of the Royal Houses, including France.'

'Many think Anna is no more than our governess,' said Kate. 'Alice is wicked at times. If she is cross with Anna, she introduces her as her companion and makes no explanation of her place with us or the fact that she is half-English.'

'I see. I must speak to her about it. Alice must mend her ways, Kate. That would account for the distant manner of many of our guests when they meet Anna.' She wondered if it accounted for the distant manner of the Captain, too. 'Are you sure you will stay here tonight, Kate?' asked her mother.

'Quite sure. I'm glad of the victory over the Dutch but I have no heart for celebration. It isn't only my own loss, but I think of Agnes and her family, sealed up with a sick and dying man and having nothing to celebrate.'

'Hush, dear.' Marian kissed her. 'Prepare another basket of food and put in any fresh under-shifts we can spare. They will have water for washing but will need spare clothes.' She shook her head. 'We can do so little, but we can at least give them food for as long as we are here or for as long as they need it.'

74

'As long as we are here?' Kate was startled. 'I thought that Father wouldn't hear of us all leaving the house.'

'We have talked and he thinks that you and Alice and Anna should go to the country.'

'Not without you, Mother,' said Kate quickly. 'I would like to live in Surrey, but not if we aren't there together.'

'I told your father that you would feel like that and for the moment, with the news getting better, he has forgotten it, but if you go, Peter could join you from Eton and have a few weeks on the farm. Think about it, Kate. The farm would be good for you all, and Edward might forget that he intends keeping Peter at school for the summer.'

The air grew more sultry as the first of the bonfires were lit in early evening. The City of London was oppressive and filled with smuts and heat. The highly-polished carriage swung to the doorway and Anna, Marian and Alice climbed in, with Christopher, Mary and Edward sitting opposite them.

Marian couldn't decide if the carriage was more comfortable with the windows open and the curtains drawn back or when they sat in semi-darkness screened from the smuts and smells and sounds of London waking up to revelry.

There was a sense of relief that perhaps with this wonderful victory, all the other problems would be resolved, as fires had long been thought to destroy disease and so it followed that the smoke would have the same effect. The authorities seized the opportunity to press for every street where there were no wattle-and-daub walls to have fires at each street corner. The spirits of London rose when the word went round that all the Royal Family walked freely again in the Gardens or were taken by Royal Barge on the Thames. If the Court had no fears left of the plague and the fires dispersed the evil by means of noxious fumes, then tomorrow new hope and health would be born.

The carriage stopped by Westminster Stairs and the river glinted sullenly as if aware of the contagion it carried, as the bodies of those dead of the plague and tossed overboard from boats floated on the tide. By the light of flares, however, the scene was pretty enough and the bonfires made the night glow and sent exciting tongues of light along the river bank.

'Take care, Joseph, and be sure you hand the note into his own hands, Mary,' said Edward. 'No harm will come to you and you shall have a piece of silver for your trouble.'

'Thank you, Sir,' said Mary meekly, but her eyes gleamed with excitement, and Joseph turned the horses towards Vauxhall Gardens.

Mary clutched her shawl close and peered out between the drawn curtains. Loud laughter came from two coaches, each trying to pass through a narrow lane with neither of the coachmen willing to give way until the rank of one crest gave precedence and they unlocked wheels like stags disengaging at the rut, and one followed the other down to Tothill.

'Sodom and Gomorrah,' whispered Mary, as painted whores hung on to carriage doors and were admitted to spend an hour or so down by the river. Her pulse raced with pleasure and a thin spittle formed at the sides of her mouth when she thought of all she would say to the profligate man who wanted to seduce Miss Anna. Her eyes widened. It was seldom that she had the opportunity to see the crowds and hear the laughter and the cursing of the wicked.

Joseph drove slowly now to circle the drive in Vauxhall and to show Lady Marian's crest under the flickering torches. A cry went up and the crowds parted to wave to the King. He sat in an open carriage, resplendent in silk and lace, gracefully accepting the acclamations of the crowds. Lady Castlemaine, replete with food and wine and, some murmured, a new royal bastard in her belly, lay back half-asleep with her mouth slightly open.

The curtains were hiding some of the view, but Mary had been told to keep them drawn so that Sir Rollo FitzMedwin would not see who was there until Joseph had spoken to him, to explain. 'But I am the one to give him the note,' she exulted to herself. 'I shall curse him to his face and tell him of the prophecies.'

A bright yellow carriage, light and with room inside for two in great comfort and privacy, driven by a man in the livery of a noble family came slowly by the line of carriages waiting to enter the gardens. Joseph nudged his horses forward and to the side as if ready to give way until the press eased, and the yellow carriage came along by the off-side.

Joseph grinned. He knew what would happen. The young buck inside would come out, all lace and flourishes, expecting that a simple governess might just have managed to arrange a ride with the family coachman this evening, or had pleaded a headache and been left in the coach while the family went about their amusement, and if she wasn't in the coach, then a bribe would loosen the tongue of the man on the box who would tell him where in Vauxhall he could find her.

Joseph toyed with the idea of taking the bribe and telling where the family supped. It was tempting and no harm would be done as Christopher and Mr Verney would make sure that the ladies were well protected, even if they were discovered. He sighed. Mary had the note ready and so would do as she had been told. If one of the other maids had been given the task, perhaps the young man would have settled for less sophisticated company as Joseph turned a blind eye to seduction.

The man on the yellow box touched his hat with his whip in salute and the two carriages stopped. Mary peeped out but could see nothing. A door opened and Joseph was talking in a voice heavy with subservience. His shadow appeared at the window. 'Her Ladyship discovered the billydoo, Sir, and sends a message.'

The flickering lights on the carriages faded and the

77

torches were borne further away as the crush eased, and there was no light now inside the carriage where Mary huddled, half in fear and half in ecstasy of wonder that she might see a dissolute seducer face to face. Link-men went with the royal party and left twilight in the gardens where no flares were lit.

'I don't believe you, you rogue!' said a voice harsh with anger and ale. The door of the carriage was wrenched open and Mary felt a strong hand grip her wrist. The shawl hid most of her face and in vain she held the note up to be taken. The grip lessened and a face, handsome and young but showing all the excesses of a mis-spent youth, peered in at her.

'I have something for you, Sir,' said Mary. She forgot the sermon that had filled her mind as they drove to Vaux-hall. The heady feeling of carrying Godly counsel to the wicked vanished as she smelled the ale-sharp breath and the reek of sweat and French perfume.

'You have indeeed, my love. Let's take a kiss now and then drive down to the water.'

'No, Sir. I have a note.'

'Your man told me. I thought I had been discreet but if Lady Marian discovered my note, then of course you have been instructed to refuse me.' He took the note and tore it across. 'The fact that you came shows you to be willing, and tonight I conquer more than the Dutch.' The carriage was still scented with lavender from the ladies and the good smell of herbs on the floor. Mary tried to draw back into the corner of the seat but the man came into the vehicle and almost fell on her.

'No, Sir!' squeaked Mary. 'Joseph!'

'Come, my rose,' said Sir Rollo FitzMedwin, and pulled at the shawl. He fumbled for her breast and his mouth clamped down on hers like a warm, wet sponge, and when Joseph pulled the man away from his wife, after hesitating far longer than was gallant, Mary was half-fainting.

'That isn't Miss Anna!' Rollo sat up and looked down at the thin body that had given him no satisfaction. His own coachman, on Joseph's urgent instruction, had retrieved the torn note, and now the men lit lamps on the boxes and Rollo saw his light of love for the first time.

'No breasts, begad!' he said in wonder. 'Nothing for a man to take.' He was saved the need for apology as Mary moaned and refused to open her eyes to be defiled further by the sight of her assailant.

'The note, Sir,' said Joseph, shaken more than he would ever admit by the sight of his wife in the arms of this nobleman.

Rollo shook his head free of ale fumes and read the note. Quickly,he sobered and stood pulling at his coat and shirt to get them to rights. Edward had made it clear that Anna was of good family and not a servant. He hinted that she came from a very influential background and that Edward Verney was aware of the name of her would-be seducer. He reminded him that men of rank had been sent to the Tower for abducting girls with far less influence than Anna Ruyter and the Verney family.

The note ended with a warning that Rollo FitzMedwin and his brother did much to stain the name that was distantly linked to Lady Marian Verney.

'Has the lady a fortune?' asked Rollo, recovering his aplomb. Joseph frowned and said nothing. 'Here, man, tell me about her,' said Rollo, slipping a gold piece into the willing hand.

Joseph drew a picture of vast estates in Holland and wealth invested in shipping. He repeated all the gossip he had heard in the servants' quarters about her background and made up what he didn't know. The gold piece was generous enough to demand a good tale.

Rollo leaned against the door, and both men ignored the faint moanings from a now-pettish Mary. She vowed revenge on her husband for his tardiness in rescuing her, even if no real harm had been done, and she saw the money change hands. That would be hers tomorrow, to add to the growing store she had hidden under her bed.

'Perhaps I should pay court at the front door,' said Fitz-Medwin. 'She's the loveliest creature I've seen since I left France, and with such a fortune might be a catch worth having.'

'She has many suitors,' lied Joseph.

'Then I must make haste and come with my abject apologies to your master,' said Rollo with a grin. 'There are other ladies? I seem to recall a child with golden hair who bemused Routh at the play.' He laughed. 'It may be time we all took wives and retired to the country. This Court leaves a man destitute, and living under the royal gaze is no place for retrenchment.'

He leaned over the now wide-eyed woman in the back of the coach. 'My apologies, Madam.' He placed another gold piece in her lap and turned away, convinced that he had bought her silence and future help. 'If I come calling, I may expect your help?' he said, and waited for no answer.

'I must see if my master needs me and then make sure my wife gets home safely,' said Joseph.

'Your wife?' Rollo FitzMedwin laughed. He had seen the Puritan dress and the sallow skin and felt for himself the lack of anything that made a body inviting. 'I heard that you carouse with my men at the Rose, and no wonder. Tell your master that I beg his pardon and will come to present my apologies tomorrow.'

He turned away to his own carriage. 'Come back for me in three hours,' he ordered. 'I go on foot to find supper and solace by the Gate.'

'The alehouses there are closed,Sir.'

'The devil they are! Where then, my man?'

'Whitehall or here in Vauxhall. There are many places where my master does not go, down among the smaller chophouses. He will be higher up for supper,' said Joseph.

Rollo nodded. 'Did you hear? I'll be by the river in the tavern close by the landing.' He looked at his coachman more closely. 'Are you asleep, man? Come down and let me look at you.'

The man passed a hand over his face as if to dispel a fog. He climbed down unsteadily as though drunk and stood reeling before his master. Mary saw his flushed face in the glare of the torch that Joseph had lit for Sir Rollo to take on foot. The thick tunic was tight and hot and the air was hardly less warm than at noon-day.

She forgot her humiliation in her sense of having everything to rights. It was one of her worries that hot uniform and ale would one day give Joseph apoplexy, and she clambered out of the coach. 'Undo your buttons,' she ordered. 'He is overcome by the heat,' she said. The man sank to the ground with a groan and Mary rapidly freed his neck and chest from the tight uniform. The shirt underneath was sodden with sweat and he gasped for breath.

Mary bent forward and then sank back on to her heels. She put up a hand that had sudden authority and stopped the two men from coming closer. On the swollen glands of the neck was a round soft swelling ringed with red. With a twig she took from the ground, Mary pushed aside the shirt and found, protruding from the armpit, another, as big and more tense. For the first time in her life, she saw and recognised the Tokens of the Plague.

'May God Have Mercy On Him,' she prayed. Then she tugged at Joseph's sleeve. 'This is none of our business,' she said, her eyes glinting with triumph. What better sign from the Good Lord above than this? He had struck down the servant of the wicked and shown his displeasure. Her soul was filled with joy as she pushed her husband away and told him briskly to drive her to the nearest hackney carriage, so that she could go home and tell the rest of the servants what was the tribulation for wickedness.

81

Chapter 6

Lottie backed away. 'It's all right, I tell you,' said Joseph. He stepped towards her and she put a hand over her smooth abdomen as if to protect what was inside.

'Go away or I'll scream,' said Lottie. 'Don't you touch me or I'll kill you!'

'Come on, now. Sam away and you all alone and wanting a cuddle?'

The window of the loft was high in the roof and the door through which the grain had originally been shunted was sealed now that the room was to be a dwelling. The floor gleamed wet from recent scrubbing and the smell of fresh lime-wash made everything wholesome. A mattress of straw lay in one corner covered by the old feather bed that Marian Verney had spared for the couple. The other bedding lay on a low shelf of wood and various pots and pans showed that the preparations for living here were well in hand.

'What's the harm, Lottie?' Joseph was pleading now.

'If Sam was here, you'd never dare touch me,' she spat at him. 'Get back to that stick of rhubarb you call your wife, if she isn't carrying the plague.'

'She didn't touch him,' lied Joseph. 'He fell on the ground and his shirt flew open to show the buboes.' He took another step. 'I'm clean, Lottie. Never went with a dirty tail in my life, and nobody ever missed a slice off a cut cake, did they?'

'I'm not like that.'

'You went with Sam, so what's the difference? It's done now and no man can add to that.'

Lottie made for the wooden steps leading from the loft down to the room where Sam had lived before now. With Joseph making her nervous, she would rather risk crossing the stable yard than feel unsafe on the ladder. 'If I go out this way, I shall tell Lady Marian that you were after me,' she warned. Joseph hesitated. He had watched for this opportunity ever since Sam left three days ago and he knew that nobody would hear her even if she screamed, but Mary might see the girl emerge through the yard and that was more frightening than if Lottie told her mistress.

'Horses!' said Lottie and laughed. 'What's it to be, Joseph? Do I walk out with you from here or do you leave me alone and I'll not tell on you?'

He gave her a furious glance and ran from the stable. With Sam away, the stable lads were slack and he had to be there whenever a visitor arrived, to see to the horses. Lottie poked out her tongue as he went and brushed back her hair. She'd ask Debbie or one of the other girls to come with her the next time she cleaned and settled the loft. Slowly, she climbed back and over to the ladder. It was still very hot and her ankles were tight, but nothing could dim the joy she felt for her future.

Joseph saw the yellow carriage and hurried up to the entrance. Sir Rollo FitzMedwin stepped from the coach and Joseph could smell a whiff of rue and rosemary. Bunches of bitter herbs were tied inside the doors and more decorated the box on which a young man sat, in dark buckskins and jacket that had none of the swagger of full livery.

FitzMedwin saw him and nodded. 'I came to call on the master of the house, but if he is not at home perhaps Lady Marian would be gracious enough to see me.' He spat out a plug of tobacco and grimaced. 'It's bad enough to kill the devil,' he said, then lowered his voice. 'What was said here the other night?'

'Nothing, Sir. Mary told Her Ladyship that we saw the buboes but we didn't touch him.' He grinned. 'We said that you didn't even see them and called for men with boards to take him to the pest-house.'

'Good. Very good – and I'll not forget it. They took him away and didn't get as far as the pest-house. He died on the way.' He spat again, trying to rid himself of the taste. 'So, I lost a good man and a new set of livery.'

'That too?' said Joseph, who had always thought the livery one of the smartest and most expensive in London.

'Would you want it now?' The cynical eyes glinted. 'We are clean and may we remain so.'

Joseph looked at the new man and wondered if he was aware how the position had become vacant, then unhitched the horses and led them into the shade while one of the maids ran to tell Lady Marian of the visitor.

'Must we see him, Mother?' asked Alice. 'What if he did touch the man whom Mary saw? Is it possible to bring the plague on his clothes?'

'Hush, Alice. Your uncle says that unless the discharge from a token or some blood touches a sore place on the skin, then nothing is passed from one to another.' Marian spoke with far more conviction than she felt and braced herself to meet this man, whom she didn't know, and felt as if she was close to a plague pit. The bunches of herbs hawked by women in the streets were everywhere, and more herbs from her own garden added to the subtle bitter scent.

'Your servant, Madam,' said Sir Rollo. Today, he looked clean and his eyes were no longer bloodshot. At twenty-two, he was young enough to be able to shake off the worst of his excesses and to appear none the worse for wear after only two days of frugal living. The occurrence in the

Gardens had frightened him badly and he had never before felt so helpless as he had done when Joseph was tugged away by the woman and he was left with a dying man and a carriage and pair.

'My husband is busy in the City, Sir, but Alice, my daughter, will bring you refreshment.' Alice inclined her head slightly and went to fetch Malmsey and Sack. Marian decided that she would break her rule of having nothing strong to drink before Edward came home, and took a glass of Sack, explaining that it was her husband's order against infection.

Rollo eyed Alice without enthusiasm. Routh was the one for her. What was the attraction of girls with unformed bodies? Routh took them virgin at ten if he could get them but FitzMedwin glanced towards the door time and again, hoping for a glimpse of Anna Ruyter.

'I came to apologise most humbly, my lady.' His blue eyes were innocent. 'I lay myself at your mercy.' He sipped his wine and wished that Alice would stop smiling as if she knew of his discomfiture. 'I sent a note in jest, not thinking it would be taken amiss and knowing that this is a noble house where such innocent jests would be ignored or put down to the rude behaviour of youth. I expected a wench to come with a rebuke, and that the girl might not find me amiss.' He saw Marian's icy glance and knew that she didn't believe him.

'I now come to pay suit to Miss Anna Ruyter,' he said. 'My father will write to Mr Verney to state my case and my credentials and I wish to say that I was overcome by her beauty when I saw her at the theatre.'

'You are kind, Sir Rollo,' said Marian, 'but my ward is slightly indisposed and cannot see you today.'

Alice giggled and Rollo went red. How had he come to make such a blunder? The house was everything a gentleman could wish and more, and now that he knew of

Anna's fortune, greatly added to by Joseph's enthusiasm, he wanted her more and more.

Lottie hovered in the doorway. 'My lady,' she said, softly. 'There is a visitor.'

Marian walked over to the girl and spoke quietly. 'I know I asked you to come in so that Sir Rollo would leave but this is too soon for politeness.'

'There is another gentleman, Ma'am. He came the other day with messages from Mrs Blackwell.'

'Show him into the library and explain that I am with a guest who will leave soon.'

Lottie clattered down the stairs to the hall and asked Captain Bennet if he would wait. She opened the door to the library and left him there, closing the door behind him.

A book fell from a high shelf and Captain Bennet looked up at Anna perched on a pair of high library steps. Her skirt was caught up and showed a leg in a fine silk stocking and a petticoat of pale blue cambric edged with écru lace. He stared and then looked away sharply. Dust from the books that Anna was moving on the top shelf hung suspended in a golden haze where the sun streamed in through the open window, and she seemed to be sitting on the edge of a sunbeam.

'Your pardon, Madam,' said the Captain and his alarm was not for the possibility that a heavy book might fall on his head. He stepped back to the door but the oak was fast and it would be humiliating to fumble for the latch before making an ignominious retreat.

Anna pointed to the fallen book. 'Would you be so kind?' she said softly. 'I am tired of running up and down these steps.'

With eyes averted, he bent to pick up the heavy volume. The wasted terms of a Classical education had at least shown him a little Greek and Latin, enough to recognise Homer and the great philosophers. He weighed the book in his hand. 'Heavy indeed, Madam.'

Anna laughed. 'As you say, Sir, but that is not my choice. I teach Alice a smattering of the Classics but for my part, I read tales of adventure and daring, and the papers of the Royal Society on new discoveries.'

She felt more at ease now that Captain Bennet was literally at her feet and seemed far more startled than she did at the sudden meeting, but she couldn't think why she ventured to tell him her taste in books.

'I applaud your taste, Ma'am. My father was a member of the Royal Society and I have all his papers. Have you heard of the paper on Microscopy?' Anna nodded. 'And the description of the slide rule that His Majesty had a hand in inventing?' Anna looked amazed and shook her head. 'You know nothing of that form of measurement? Then, with your permission, I will send it to you.'

He put a hand on the ladder and looked up. The skirt had blessedly fallen into soft folds hiding the delicate ankles and he could go closer. 'You say the King invented it?' Anna smiled, disbelieving anything but the King's profligate ways.

'He is a great man, Miss Anna. He attends many of the meetings of the best physicians and surgeons that this country has ever known. He watches experiments and listens to learned papers and has a care for the health of the poor.'

'He has stopped touching for the King's Evil,' said Anna, 'and it is rumoured that he will leave London if the plague grows, and if *he* goes, then others will feel that they may leave also. My father is afraid that trade will slacken and many more wretches will have to beg a living or starve or steal, and no house will be safe.'

'The King must not be endangered,' said Captain Bennet firmly. 'If there is disease, then he must, on the persuasion of his councillors, be taken to a place of safety. Believe me, Ma'am, he is no coward. He knows hardship and has been an unhappy exile for long enough to know what suffering means.'

Anna looked down into the fervent eyes and knew that if this man gave his loyalty . . . or love, it would be for ever. For a moment, hastily quelled, she felt envy for the King.

Sounds from the hall indicated the departure of the other guest. 'I have taken up enough of your time,' said Captain Bennet. 'I came to pay my respects and to ask Lady Marian to meet Mrs Blackwell for dinner.' He placed a note on the table. 'If Lady Marian is engaged, then I will take my leave, and she can send an answer by messenger.'

'Please wait, Sir, and I will see if her other guest is gone.' Anna climbed down the steps and smoothed her gown. She saw the heavy volume in the Captain's hand. 'Oh, I didn't put it back,' she said.

'Allow me,' he said and ran up the steps with the book. Anna opened the door and walked out into the path of Sir Rollo FitzMedwin and Marian. Alice was watching from the main stair to the drawing room and two of the servants peeped from the passage to the kitchens.

For a moment, Anna could not see who it was silhouetted against the bright light from the open front door. The silk coat gleamed peacock blue and silver and the shape of the man was elegant. She smiled, and then knew her mistake.

Rollo advanced to take her hand. He bent over it, kissing it and holding it firmly as she tried to draw away. 'It gives me joy to see that you have recovered from your indisposition, Madam,' he said. He turned to Marian. 'May I offer my carriage to take the air? For you and your daughters, too, Ma'am,' he added, as he sensed Marian's disapproval.

'You are most kind,' said Anna, 'but we are bespoken for dinner with Mrs Blackwell and Lady Marian travels only in our own carriage now that the plague is about.'

Rollo flushed angrily. Was this to be the pattern in other

88

houses? Just because the wretch died after falling from his coach, did it mean that no one would drive with him in the distinctive yellow giant that might be tainted? Marian nodded, well pleased. 'Then I'll bid you good day, Lady Marian, but I hope to visit your young ladies again in a day or so.' He kissed Anna's hand again, savouring the flower-scented skin and glancing up at the softly swelling bosom. A prize if he could get her, and not only for her money.

As the yellow carriage scattered the gravel, Captain Bennet emerged from the library, with the note from Mrs Blackwell. 'It seems that Anna has accepted,' said Marian.

'Then I will ride with your carriage and see you safely there,' said the Captain, as if this was his duty. He led his horse from the shade and followed the carriage, having spent the waiting time in the garden alone.

Mary saw the yellow carriage leave and hurried to the herb garden which was as close to the stables as she dared to go. Joseph tried to ignore her imperious wave but had to bring fruit to the kitchen and knew that there was no escape.

'Did he give you any more?' Mary asked.

'What more do you expect, woman? You had a gold piece and so did I.' He scowled. 'Not that it did me any good. It disappeared from my pocket in the night.'

Mary smiled. 'It's safe enough and we'll need every penny when we leave here.' Joseph's heart sank. He wanted no part in Mary's plan to buy a chophouse where she would cook and attract any who liked good food and Joseph would be pot-boy, host and anything he had to turn a hand to. It would be a comedown for him and he would miss the life he led in the alehouses, but he admitted there might be money to be made, and Mary had an obsession with money these days.

He eyed his wife with anxiety. She had touched the man dying of the plague, and last night she had been willing for the first time in months to lie with him. He looked away, remembering her skinny body and her thin lips, and knew that he had managed to climax only when he thought of Lottie.

'What did he want?' asked Mary. She had seen the young buck swagger from his carriage and in spite of her rigid convictions she had felt a tremor of something like lust when she recalled that this handsome man, with his silks and breeding, had tried to seduce her. She had seen wickedness and felt it close at hand and had resisted, she told herself, piously.

'Well, he didn't come for a second helping of you, that's for sure,' said Joseph. 'He's after Miss Anna and he knows she's a good catch. Stayed with them up there for over half an hour and says he's coming back, so he must think he's got an even chance.' He glanced at his wife. 'I'll be out when Lady Marian is at dinner with her friends. I'll not be back here for mine. I said I'd tip Sir Rollo the wink when Miss Anna will be going shopping in Covent Garden.'

'She said she wants more books,' said Mary. She sniffed. 'What does a woman of her class want with books? Foreign ways,' she muttered. 'Some of them are wicked and deal with the dark side, I've no doubt.'

'She'll go with one maid?' asked Joseph.

'She takes one of the bedchamber girls and a hackney carriage as it is in daytime.'

Joseph nodded. 'Will Miss Alice go too?'

'Only if she shops for gloves or silks for her mother. She has no time for books, and no need with that pretty face.' She wondered what was in her husband's mind. 'Sir Rollo wouldn't court Miss Alice?'

'No,' said Joseph. He kept to himself the implied hint that Sir Richard Routh was interested in the young girl and might be with FitzMedwin when next they met Anna, quite by accident.

Mary seemed to forget about the family and looked at

the masses of fresh raspberries and strawberries in the baskets. 'These will have to be made into preserve or show mould by nightfall,' she said. 'There was enough labour making cakes and pies for Master Peter without all this.' She called to Debbie to carry the heavy baskets, and within an hour the gardens were filled with the fragrance of jam-making and raspberry vinegar. Lottie came to pick fresh herbs and sat on the back step making up bunches for the ladies to carry when they walked in crowded places.

She took large oranges and stuck them with cloves before dousing them in orris root and bitter herbs and hanging them to dry in the shade, smiling as she pictured Lady Marian's face when she saw them tied up in blue ribbons. She would be pleased, as the royal Family carried pomanders and bitter herbs when they walked in Vauxhall, and many of the noble families believed that this was the best protection against distemper, but they were fussy to make and needed a deft hand to get the cloves into pretty patterns.

She made an extra one for herself, thinking to hang it over the bed in the loft for a good luck token. Sam would be home soon and he would look after her. The wedding was close and she felt strong and healthy, with the child beginning to move in her belly. God is good, she thought. Away from the dust and noise of the City, she had the best of all worlds. Birds sang and the grass smelled fresh and she had good food and a place to live. Beyond the gate was life and entertainment and the stalls and shops that she loved.

Lottie stuck another orange too deeply and the juice ran out. She frowned. There was less entertainment since the decree went out by Crier, closing many of the alehouses in areas where there were red crosses. The theatre had closed too, after near-panic had ensued when someone screamed that a man who fainted in the heat had plague, but that was last week and the place might well be open again. She tried to forget that her parents lived in Cripplegate and that a pit had been dug by the graveyard there in which bodies from the pest-house were now buried. There was not time enough to dig proper graves, and fewer men were willing to bury those who had died of the contagion.

She heard the family returning and went to meet them, carrying bunches of herbs and a basket of pomanders. Alice fell on them with eager fingers. 'How pretty they are, Lottie!' She waved the heavy orange on the ribbon.

'They have to dry out,' said Lottie, 'but they are like the ones carried by the royal party.'

Marian looked pale. She held a bunch of herbs and picked at them, sending dried leaves into the air. 'The vicar is still sealed up with his family, Lottie, and they say they all have the plague now.'

'Not the children, too, my lady?'

'Yes. Dr William Verney is angry as he says that if the sick are removed to pest-houses at once, the healthy could be kept apart for a week and then allowed out instead of being exposed to the sick in a closed house until they all catch it, but that law has never been repealed and many of the magistrates have left the City.'

'And the clergy? Is my marriage safe, my lady?'

'Your church is allowing services in the courtyard or in the vestry, Lottie. The church has been used for burial services and so is no longer safe.' Marian forced a smile. 'You will be married, never fear, Lottie, but we must all be careful now that the latest Bills show a sharp increase this month.'

Anna said nothing. If she carried herbs and drank Sack before going into the city and kept a kerchief to her mouth if she saw someone sneeze, then she could go to buy books from the stalls in St Paul's Churchyard. People of rank went there all the time, and she had seen the Secretary of the Navy, Mr Pepys, and many more of her uncle's business friends there. Books didn't interest the masses and nor did the rich and expensive clothes sold there, so the risk must be less. Lady Marian needed more stationery, too, she remembered, and the last of the lace cuffs for Mr Verney might be ready, so when she went in the small open carriage with her maid, Anna felt safe from all evils.

'No one must use a hackney,' Edward had said at supper the previous evening. 'Some have been used to take infected cases to hospital or the pest-house and if they are not aired, might well be dangerous.' He grunted. 'Sam has the small coach and there is only the little curricle, so the ladies must wear shawls against the dust.'

The stable lad trained by Sam and known to be honest, drove the light two-wheeled vehicle, but Anna winced as they jolted over every stone and cobble on the way along Fleet Street to St Paul's. She looked up at the noble edifice and sighed. The English did nothing to care for such a place. Cromwell had objected to the papish-looking facade and torn down much of the new structure before using the nave to stable his horses. Since then, itinerant traders and stall-holders had set up shop within the church and its environs, making it a defiled house where money changed hands and God was forgotten.

Anna strolled along the book stalls and tried to find an account of the instrument that Captain Bennet had mentioned. Her interest was acute and she grew quite excited and animated as she found an allusion to the maker of such things. From time to time, she held the bunch of herbs to her nose and made the girl with her do the same. Grace was bored and couldn't think why her mistress liked to waste time in such a place, so Anna sent her into the shop where Edward bought his linen and told her to be no more than ten minutes.

'By what happy chance are you here, Madam?' said Fitz-Medwin, who had followed Anna for the past quarter of an hour. He was dressed soberly and his dark green coat made no impact on the milling crowds of the City. He had

93

his own hair dressed simply and appeared young and rather ingenuous. Anna glanced beyond him but her maid was fast disappearing into the shop. Rollo smiled and made no attempt to touch her hand. 'You are on serious business, Miss Anna?'

'Yes,' she said, annoyed at the intrusion on her precious free time. She put down the book she held and found another, bound in fine leather with gold lettering on the spine. 'I may not be able to come here again for a time if the plague increases,' said Anna, 'so I must choose carefully.'

'Alchemy?' said Rollo, eyeing the book with benevolent disbelief. 'What interest can you have in such a subject, Madam?'

'I enjoy reading about scientific matters,' said Anna. She moved away to another stall and lifted one book after another, but it was difficult to concentrate when she was followed closely and every book she touched provoked some reaction.

'You must allow me to show you the library at Mersley Manor, where my parents have a fine collection of books.'

Anna nodded briefly and wondered if he knew one book from another. 'You must excuse me, Sir. My maid is taking too long over the linen and I must see that she doesn't get muddled.'

'But your books, Miss Anna! You have chosen only one.'

'I shall come back when I am alone,' she said stiffly.

'You have no need of alchemy,' he said. 'Your touch would transmute the basest of metal into gold.' He smiled engagingly. 'Even such rough metal as Rollo FitzMedwin. I feel better just to be with you, and if you will drive with me, I might even become completely reformed.'

In spite of her annoyance, Anna smiled. She knew of his reputation and she had seen him at the play, flushed with wine and over-dressed even for a courtier, but today he was completely different and she began to feel safe. She saw her maid come out of the shop and breathed a sigh of relief. Ladies didn't talk to men in a public place unless they were chaperoned. 'Does the King have no use for you, Sir? Has the Court become sober and religious?'

'The King left for the Nore to see his mother off to France and then to Portsmouth to review his triumphal fleet after Lowestoft.'

'And you are not needed?'

'I have served my stint in his entourage and now can stay, unless I am commanded to go to Salisbury or Hampton Court.' He kicked a stone from his path and Anna saw again the spoiled coxcomb she had thought him to be. 'Salisbury is the saddest bore a man could endure. If the Court goes there, we shall have cramped quarters and the local landowners are rough and supply little amusement and hospitality. I hope we go to Hampton.'

'You are certain that the Court will leave London, Sir?' Anna was appalled. In spite of what Captain Bennet said, that the King must be protected as the Head of State, it seemed to her that he was deserting his people.

'Parliament has been prorogued until July and the Admiralty will move to Winchester soon, leaving the Navy Office at Greenwich until the Dutch war is over completely, and much has been said of a move to Nonesuch House near Epsom for the Royal Exchequer.' He shrugged. 'Soon there will be nothing for a gentleman to do in the City and we might as well all leave before the plague catches everyone.' He frowned.

'Surely the sickness attacks only those living and working in dirty houses, and they say that it came from the ships.' Anna looked about her. There were far fewer people in the stalls than she remembered in the past. On the roads, the way had been rough and tiresome in the heat, but there were fewer vehicles to hold up her progress.

Rollo matched his step to hers as she walked distractedly along the cloistered side of the church. A side entrance to the crypt was roped off and from the depths of the stone vaults she heard cries of pain and delirium. 'What is down there?' she cried. Her maid backed away and tried not to make the sign of the cross as a hurdle carried by two men came through the bushes.

'Come away,' said Rollo. He took Anna's hand and tried to pull her back, his own fear making him rough.

'What is it?' said Anna. She watched with horror as the man on the litter groaned and attempted to get off the hurdle, throwing aside the linen covering and showing his naked body. She saw the hard black swellings and the weeping sores and heard the rattle in his throat. The man at the head pushed him back and they hurried inside the crypt with him and were lost to sight.

'There are so many, Miss,' said Grace. 'They've made the crypt into a pest-house, but none come out of there alive.'

Anna put her posy of herbs to her face, finding comfort in the clean astringent smell and hardly noticing that Rollo FitzMedwin held her firmly round the waist. 'Come back to the books, Ma'am,' he said, and released her. It was too early to do more than he had already achieved and the more he saw of Anna, the more determined he was to possess her.

Anna smiled, grateful to be allowed to regain her composure without comment. 'Yes, I shall order stationery enough for a month or so, and all the books I can find of interest.'

'You should leave London,' said FitzMedwin. Anna shook her head. 'You must have relatives in the country where you could stay out of danger?' He looked concerned only for her safety, but was filled with triumph when she said that there were relatives in Surrey who would welcome the whole family if the need arose. A day's ride from his uncle's estates and the stables of Lord Chalwood where a man could have good sport.

'But I hope we stay,' said Anna. 'I am not a country wench and I would miss all this.'

With a restraint foreign to his nature, Rollo kissed her hand and left her to her shopping, but begged to be allowed to visit the following day. 'Please tell Lady Marian that I am at her service if you leave London,' he said. 'Unless the King commands me to Hampton, I shall visit my uncle who has estates on the Surrey hills.'

An hour later, Anna had the books and stationery loaded on to the curricle with the new linen and some silk for a gown, wondering when she would go there again. People seemed to keep to themselves, moving away if anyone came close enough to touch or to breathe over them. She had never noticed this before she saw the man with the plague but now she was increasingly aware of the mark that the disease was making on the City.

Chapter 7

Edward Verney stepped off the boat on to the landing-stage and peered up the stairs hoping to see the outline of the carriage that Joseph should have ready to take him home. The river trip from Westminster had been bad enough, with the choppy water making the boat wallow but the darkness of the shore was worse.

He tried to forget the words of his clerk Roger Carter, who seemed to take a morbid delight in bad news.

'More dead of the plague, Mr Verney. The Bills of Mortality give figures of over three thousand and the roads at night are not safe for any man without two link-men and a guard.'

'The *Intelligencer* says less,' said Edward.

'Even the news-sheet admits now that the King has gone to Salisbury with the Court after staying at Hampton until one of the retinue died of the plague.' Roger gave a grim smile. 'That made them jump and think again and the next we hear is that the whole entourage is in Salisbury.'

'We all thought the City walls would contain the disease and that it was dying out at the time of Lowestoft,' said Edward. He sighed. Walls no longer shut off the squalor and misery of the poor. Plague was no respecter of rank or wealth or goodness. The Reverend Ewing dead with all his family and the house robbed of everything of value made a mockery of virtue being rewarded, and the numbers of beggars grew daily. The threads of death reached out into the homes of every kind of citizen, and men no longer offered a hand in greeting to old friends.

'Nobody is allowed to leave the City for the country without a bill of health from the authorities,' Roger said. 'There is plague in some of the out-parishes brought by people fleeing from the City, and some left whole in houses now free of the disease have sold bedding and bed-curtains instead of burning them.' It was common knowledge that Searchers and Bearers of the Dead plundered houses and sold the contents or stored them until such time when buyers would think them clear. It was hard to know what measures should be taken. William Verney still worked hard among the sick and enough were cured to make the work of such dedicated men and women worthwhile, but what cured one was useless to another and only one brave man had attempted a post-mortem examination of a death from the plague. He found such inner destruction that it showed how difficult it was to treat all the different signs and symptoms.

Edward braced himself to leave the well-lit platform and walk up the dark steps to the road. One man shouted and his link-man appeared at the parapet and for a minute the stairs were visible, but the young man ran up quickly, leaving Edward to follow more slowly.

In the corner where the stairs turned, a heap of clothes stirred and moaned. Edward held his breath and edged along the far wall, then drew his sword as the man under the rags stood and leaned against the corner. A thick arc of vomit followed by curses made Edward move faster than he had done for years. Drunk or dying? he thought as he gasped his way to the top of the stairs, and when he saw the coach waiting, he hung on to the door for a minute to gain breath and strength enough to climb inside.

'Are you sick, Sir?' asked Joseph.

'No, just out of breath. There was a man down there who looked like a cutpurse. I drew my sword and he didn't attack me,' he added as he regained his confidence.

'And ran up the stairs! Very wise, Sir. The place is full of such people and the sooner we get home the safer I'll feel. It isn't just the thieves about now. The afflicted are out for air and the night isn't safe for God-fearing men, Sir. It's after nine and all who are whole should be locked inside their own safe houses.'

'What are we coming to, Joseph? Time was when we would be starting out for an evening of entertainment now, not scurrying home as if the Devil was after us!' He knew that his hands were shaking. Robbers were bad enough, but the sorry procession of the sick allowed out under guard at night was far more blood-chilling. The cold sweat of fear made him ashamed of his own feelings but the sight of the man reeling about on the stairs haunted him.

The door of the coach, tightly shut, gave a sense of security and Edward was glad that he had never to depend on men walking with him carrying flaming torches to light his way. Houses blighted by red crosses were everywhere in the congested streets and only a few showed the white cross indicating that all was now well and the house was free.

The coach stopped and Edward gazed fearfully out into the hazy light of bonfires at a crossroads. Joseph moved the coach into a side alley to let the death cart go by. The horses stamped restlessly as they smelled death and Edward saw for the first time at close quarters the dead piled haphazardly, some wrapped in linen sheets and some naked, as wood was almost unobtainable for coffins and only the rich could afford to be buried decently. Everything was against a good man's sense of what was fitting, and Edward was sickened. To die without the blessing of the Church and without care from family and friends was sacri-

100

lege, and even to think of masses of bodies, tossed carelessly into the same lime-pit like cattle, revolted him.

'Whoa! Hoof over!' shouted Joseph, more to make sure that Sam heard his return than to control the horses who knew they were near warm stables and food. Edward climbed down and walked slowly into the house. He called for Debbie and sat in his office for half an hour drinking Sack before he went up to the drawing room.

All was quiet and from the remote kitchen he heard laughter, soft and poignantly carefree. Half-smiling, he walked upstairs. Lottie sounded happy and the house was as he had left it, clean and wholesome and well-ordered. From the doorway to the drawing room he watched his family as if he might never see them again exactly like this, with Marian at her silks, his daughters playing sweet tunes and his son reading with great concentration. It was another world that must never be touched by the horror in the two cities of London and Westminster.

I have to save them from that, he thought and when Marian looked up and saw him, he was seized with a pang of such love and protectiveness that he wanted to hold them all close and make sure they were flesh and blood.

'Kate? Call Debbie and bring supper. Edward, we were beginning to worry that Joseph had missed you.' She smiled and put aside her silks.

'You waited for me?' he asked.

'I did, but the young ones were hungry and ate an hour ago,' she said apologetically, as she knew how much Edward liked to eat with his family.

'Good,' he said briskly. 'We'll eat in my office. I want to talk to you, Ma'am, and this is as good a time as any.'

Alice eyed him curiously. Her father looked stern but she couldn't recall doing anything lately to give him cause for anger, so she was sure that he wasn't about to discuss her. Maybe Anna had been too cold and had driven away Captain Bennet, or Peter had written again complaining

101

about Eton. She selected a piece of soft fudge from the pile on the dish and turned to talk to Anna.

'What is it?' asked Marian anxiously as soon as they were in the study with a tray of food on the table and a decanter of wine open before Edward. 'You look pale, my dear. Are you sick?' She touched his hand and found it cold. 'Edward? What is wrong?'

He drew her close and embraced her with such fervour that she was startled. Edward had been a good husband, had fathered four children in the lust of early marriage but had never been a man of hot passions. She glanced towards the door. Surely he hadn't brought her into the quiet study to ravish her? She blushed, trying to deny to herself that she felt any response. He released her as if ashamed of his action and poured wine into two goblets.

'I am nearly out of my mind with worry,' he said bluntly.

'You *are* sick!'

'No, I am hale as many men half my age,' he said impatiently. 'We all are, thank God, but *for how long*, Marian?'

Marian sipped her wine and tasted the rabbit stew and onions that Mary Creed made so well. 'You have heard bad news?' she said quietly and urged him to eat.

'Tonight I saw such sights that must come from Hell. I have heard tell of it all, but until I witnessed the cry of the Bearer of the Dead and saw the cart not five yards from our coach, it meant nothing more than any distant news.' He began to eat, more to hide his emotion than from hunger.

'The Bills are worse again and I have told the servants that if they go anywhere infected they shall leave our service,' said Marian. 'Lottie and Debbie and Mary Creed will obey, but some of the sewing girls and those in the dairy live out and I worry about them. Are you sure of Joseph? He goes out at night, or so I hear from Debbie,

102

and even if most of the alehouses are closed, he could bring infection back here.'

'Mary would kill him!' said Edward, and smiled for the first time since coming home. He finished his food and took more wine while Debbie cleared the tray and brought a lime-blossom tisane for Marian.

As soon as they were alone again, Edward cleared his throat and sat straight in his chair. 'I think we should send the girls into the country,' he said.

'Bless you, Edward, that's what I want but they say they will not leave without us. When I suggested it, Kate refused to go and Alice was in tears.' Marian frowned. 'If you order them to go, they will obey but I see much unhappiness if you separate us, and who would make sure that Alice behaves as a young lady should?'

'She can run wild in the country with only the cows to judge her,' said Edward easily. 'That is nothing. Life and health and the future is all that matters.'

'I would miss them, Edward, but I know you are right.'

'You would be there, Marian, with Lottie to take care of you.'

'You forget, Edward – Lottie will be here with Sam after they are married in two days' time. You can't send her to the country without him and Lottie would not go. She *hates* the country.'

'Stubborn women,' muttered Edward. 'Sam is back from Lord Chalwood's stables and I shall need him tomorrow to do some work for me for a change.' He stood and stretched in an attempt to appear at ease. 'What if we all go?'

'All of us? You would consider leaving London?' Marian was amazed. 'Leave your office and businesses and this house?'

'I have given it much thought and until this pestilence has eased, I see no disgrace in leaving to preserve my own family. The King has gone and any who can afford it are going to friends and relatives in the country.'

'We could go to Uncle John and Aunt Mattie,' said Marian. Her eyes lost their earlier sadness. 'They have said we would be welcome to use the cottage or to live with them at the Manor.'

'I have been in touch with them,' Edward confessed. 'I said nothing as I hoped the sickness was abating, but now the whole of London seems like a midden and who knows if it will stay down there? My business is steady and Roger Carter is a good clerk and honest. He will look after my office and give a good account to me by mail each month. My ships are not expected for another month or so and I have most of my documents and a good sum in gold here that I have brought in over the past week so that I was not observed.'

'You have been planning to go!'

'I planned for an emergency and I think we are at the gates of one now. Tonight made me fear for us all, Marian, and I see no other way.'

'How can we leave? The authorities forbid any who try to leave the City.'

'We are not in the City and my carriage can pass to the offices in Lincoln's Inn and back at any time as I am recognised. I have brought cases of documents and money in the carriage and if no trunks are seen outside, it is thought that I am on my daily business.'

'I must pack everything,' said Marian. 'The sooner we go the better.'

'Tomorrow, you take the girls down the river to Greenwich. Joseph will drive you to Wapping Stairs and do some errands for me which will keep him busy until he collects you again at Wapping. Mary Creed asked for time to see a friend and will be away, and because of the sickness, I have told the other servants to visit any relatives who are not sick in case they can see them no more until the plague is over.'

104

'I wondered why you allowed Mary to go,' said Marian. 'And you gave her money for the river, too!'

'The house will be clear but for Sam, Christopher and me and we have work to do so that even if death or thieves catch up with some of us, there will be money and stocks hidden safely under the stables. Roger Carter will have papers in my office and more documents but we must make sure of something here.'

'I shall say nothing to the girls, but tell them to sort out any clothes they can spare for the sick, and make sure they have nothing left that we can't take with us.' Marian began to enjoy the challenge that was lacking in her well-ordered life. 'Alice and Anna will hate the country,' she said with a laugh. 'No men of distinction or handsome boys to satisfy Alice, and Aunt Mattie will see that Anna learns country arts.'

'It will be good for them,' said Edward. 'Good for all of us,' he added, without much conviction. 'Now, not a word to the girls or to any of the servants, not even Lottie. If we go, we go quietly and leave this house closed unless we can find a caretaker whom we can trust.'

Alice had gone to her room to fit on a new dress and Anna was reading when Marian went back to the drawing room. She wondered how they would react to the tearing down of everything that made life safe and homelike, and whether she dared risk a new venture after such stability and luxury.

Edward went to bed early and soon the house was dark and still, with only the barn owls and the cats sharing the dark.

If only the rain would come and wash away the ordure and the sickness, Marian thought as she went to sleep, but in the morning she heard a cock crow and bright sunlight slotted through the shutters and another hot day began.

Edward was up early, dressed in sturdy fustian trousers with heavy shoes and a plain shirt. Joseph eyed him with curiosity and wondered what was in the Master's mind. No day at the office, well-dressed and carrying his silver-topped cane? No orders above simple errands that would take Joseph a long way on trivial matters, and a silver coin for Mary to keep her away for the day?

Joseph shrugged. Maybe even the Master needed a day to himself at times without a bevy of women to hector him. He whipped up the horses and Alice waved to Christopher from the window as they all set out for Wapping and Greenwich, deep in the lush country by the river.

Edward Verney waited for the carriage to leave and turned back to the house. Everything was strangely silent and Sam waited for him on the back step of the kitchen. 'Good,' said Edward. 'You know what to do, Sam. Everyone has gone and we have about four hours to accomplish what we discussed.'

He smiled to himself. It wasn't easy to rid the house of all the family and servants at the same time, but they were gone now and he could put his mind to the future. He walked by the baskets of fruit picked early that morning and checked to see that the fowls and meat that had been delivered at dawn from farms outside the parishes had been put in the cool. Food was plentiful and an early harvest brought on by the hot sun made vegetables and fruit plentiful even in places where the farmers were afraid to touch anyone but left food on flagstones and took the money from jars of vinegar from another place.

If the house was quiet, the streets near the house were quiet too, for no street vendors plied their trades or cried their wares as London mourned.

'Sam?' Edward walked across the stable yard and opened the door to the middle stall. Sam was stripped to the waist, his skin shining with sweat and his face red with exertion as he dug up the hard earth under the flagstones.

'Take some ale, lad,' said Edward, walking round the now-deep hole and nodding his approval. Sam rested on a bale of straw and drank deeply from the earthenware jug. He wiped his mouth with the back of his hand and looked to his Master for instructions. 'Nice and dry even in wet weather, Sam, and just right, I reckon.' He listened but could hear nothing but birdsong and now the morning was under way, he could hear cart wheels as more and more wooden carts laden with worldly goods left the City for a new resting place in the country.

'Is Master Christopher coming soon, Sir?' asked Sam.

'He should be here by now. I can't think what keeps him.'

'The roads are full of carriages and carts, Sir. Many people are walking with bundles on handcarts if they have no nag or donkey. I found it clogged up out by the Strand and had to come by another road that would take a horse but not a cart,' said Sam. He put down the jug and picked up the spade again. 'Best get it done deep, Sir.' His back bent and arched and bent again with a rhythm that Edward envied.

'Don't wear yourself out before your wedding tomorrow, Sam.' Edward walked out into the sunlight and wondered if it would ever rain again. Whitewashed walls sent the heat back like a blow from a hot torch and the cobbles stood proud as earth was blown from the crevices. Tired hens made a plaintive sound in their shady boxes and the two horses in the other stalls hung their heads listlessly.

Edward looked up and listened again. The sound of wheels on the gravel driveway came louder. 'It's Christopher,' he said with relief. He went to meet him.

Sam took the reins as Christopher jumped down from the box and together they unhitched the horse and let her into the grass enclosure where there was shade and water and hay. 'I was held up by the crowds, Father.' Christopher was hot and dusty and took the jar of ale and drank from it. 'The City is in a panic,' he said. 'Carts are trying to

107

leave by all the gates and only a few people have bills of health.'

'You had no difficulty?' asked Edward anxiously. He eyed the small carriage with its drawn curtains and empty rack.

'No, they know our carriages and that you go to the City on business. The carriage looks the same as usual and anyone trying to leave the City with bundles on the roof, on the racks and jutting from the windows shows at once that they are trying to escape.' Christopher laughed grimly. 'One rascal offered to buy the coach and hung on to the reins trying to force me off. I had to whip him away. They are using anything on wheels and every nag they can lay hands on.'

Edward and Sam smiled. Christopher was peace-loving and even-tempered, but it would take a very brave or determined man to try to take from him anything he valued. They opened the doors and the men unstacked the mass of small boxes and packets inside. Edward wrapped the documents in oiled silk and tar paper to keep out the damp and the metal and wooden boxes were smeared with oil before they were placed in the bottom of the finished pit.

The pile of packets that Edward had prepared earlier went in too and the pit was covered with earth, tamped down, and one by one the heavy flag-stones were replaced as they had been before the pit was dug. The two young men filled buckets with the soil left and carried it to the back of the midden so that no trace was left of the digging.

'You saw Roger?' asked Edward.

'He's made an inventory of everything here and all that he has in the office that he'll need for business while you are away and I can be in touch with him if he needs anything.'

Edward looked at his son sharply. 'We all go to Surrey,' he said. 'You, too.'

Christopher looked stubborn. 'I can come later, Father. There is no need for me to travel with you. Sam can drive the big coach and leave me this one. Kate is capable of driving the curricle and Anna can take a turn. They are good with horses. If Roger is to live over the offices, he will need me here to look after the property.'

'It's no use you looking like thunder, my boy. I have everything planned. You come with us as Sam is staying here.' Christopher looked back but Sam had gone to fetch rushes and straw to cover the floor of the stable. 'Does he know he is staying?' Christopher was disturbed. 'You wouldn't cast him out, Father? Sam is more than a mere servant. He is a trusted friend.'

'I know that,' said Edward drily. 'Would I trust him here today if I didn't believe that? No, Sam and Lottie will stay here and look to my house and interests. It is their choice, not mine. I tried to persuade them to come but they refused. I take no toll for what might happen to them, but having decided, it will be a relief to know they are here. I am glad to leave everything in their care.'

'Have you money enough to take with you, Father?'

'I have sent my Will and some more documents to a lawyer in Oxford and I have money enough for the journey and to tide us over when we live on the farm, but not enough to cause us distress if we are robbed on the way. We must have means of support if we live with your mother's relatives. They will make us welcome, but Sir John doesn't harbour idlers or beggars. Anna's inheritance is safe in Oxford and Roger will deal with shares if there is any market left.'

Sam led the horse into her stall and filled the wicker rack with hay, spilling some on the floor and making everything look normal. An hour later, when the straw was soiled and wet, the stall looked used and no one could suspect that anything had been hidden under the flags.

'That's all done then, Sir,' said Sam.

'I was telling him that you and Lottie mean to stay, Sam.' Edward laughed. 'If it's that painted actress you're mooning over, Christopher, forget her. They moved to Salisbury with the Court and the theatres are closed until the King returns to London. The Whitehall Theatre is shut and the theatre in Drury Lane is surrounded by red crosses.'

'Closed the theatres?' Christopher was crestfallen.

'If you stay, Master Christopher, you will be safe here but it's best to avoid the City. Most of the alehouses are shut and there is no entertainment.'

'You seem to know all about it, Sam.' Christopher was resentful.

'Lottie's parents are in Cripplegate and we went to see about the wedding,' said Sam.

'After the wedding, you must stay away from that place, Sam. You must promise me! I know that Lottie worries about her mother, but with the child coming, you can afford no risk to either of you.'

'Is Joseph to go with you, Sir?' Lottie had told Sam about what Joseph had tried to do to her and he was still angry. 'I don't know.' Edward smoothed his chin with one hand. 'He's an able rogue but I never trust him completely. Not a word about this day's work to him or anyone in the house.'

Sam went to the pump to swill away the sweat and dust and Christopher followed his father into the house. He washed his hands and face and found Edward cutting into the thick pasty that had been left for their dinner.

'You wouldn't turn away the servants without some support, Father?' Christopher helped himself to food and filled two glasses with ale.

'Many do,' said Edward defensively. 'I saw two men who had worked for the Ryans and they were asking for work. It is a pity, but who can feed so many with no return?'

'You would have Debbie steal or sell her body?' stated Christopher bluntly.

'Not Debbie,' came Edward's hasty denial. 'When it comes to personal maids and men, they must have something.' He wished that he could leave such matters to Roger or some neutral party, as there were women he didn't know who worked in the scullery and in the dairy picking fowl and preparing fish. He couldn't pretend to care what happened to them. There were casual workers, too, who came in for seasonal jobs like painting and cutting wood. What of Marian's maids?

'Who, then?' said Christopher with relentless intensity. 'If I stay, I can see to their welfare and make sure they don't starve.'

'And go into the City stews to find your actress friends and catch I know not what apart from the plague?' said Edward brusquely.

'Sam and Lottie can look after me.'

'That is enough, Son. If we go, we all go and I shall need your strong arm if all I hear is true about villains on the road.' His expression softened. 'There'll be sport in the country and if the plague diminishes, you shall come back to open up the house for us. As soon as it abates, and I can spare you, you shall come back.' He smiled. 'It can get no worse and with the streets empty, there can be no spread after this month. We'll be home by autumn.

'It will be good to see horses running free,' said Christopher. He relaxed. If the theatre was closed, then he would find better things to do than moon about the playhouse in the hope of seeing Anne. He wondered if Sir John still had the foal he had seen born when they had visited four years ago. He recalled the haymaking and the harvest and the long evenings spent under the stars with cider and fresh bread and cheese.

'I wish that Sam was coming, too. We could race horses and even take on neighbouring farmers. Did you know,

111

Father, that Lord Carnegie has estates there? Richard Routh races his horses with them and many of the Court who are not needed by the King take their leisure with them.'

'You'd be safer in the City than with that crowd,' muttered Edward as Christopher went to change from his dusty clothes into something that didn't make him seem a stable lad. Edward sighed. It was miles away and yet the world in which he and his class moved was smaller and getting smaller all the time. People talked of visits to Scotland, changing horses and making good speed on the stage coaches, or had done until the coaches were stopped by decree.

The Kingdom of Cornwall, in England but still not a real part of it, was available if the dangers of highwaymen and bogged-down wheels were overcome, and Surrey was only two or three days away without changing horses.

'Sam said that Peter was miserable,' remarked Christopher when he came back to the drawing room and sipped the red wine and water that Marian had left for them.

'Why miserable, the ungrateful jackanapes?'

'He is still made to smoke and likes it no better, but the floggings are severe if the boys refuse. He was sick last week and even Mary's good cakes did little to cheer him.'

'It was only the tobacco?' asked Edward anxiously. Eton was not far from Hampton and Windsor, and both places had enough of the plague to cause concern. Christopher told him that it was only the strong tobacco, and Edward breathed again. 'The mild stuff I sent is partly herbs,' said Edward. 'I have been at odds with your mother about him. She wants the boy with us this summer but I feel that he is safer where he is.'

'When we are settled in, he can come to the farm, Father. I'll see to him,' said Christopher, and Edward knew that his elder son had reconciled himself to leaving London. 'But you have not said what happens to Lottie and Sam,'

112

his son pressed, and Edward was reminded of a dog with a bone that everyone tried to hide but was dragged out into view smelling of decay when an important visitor was there.

'I shall leave them a small pension,' said Edward. 'They shall not starve.'

'And Mary Creed and Joseph?'

'They may come with us, but I cannot see a place for them in Sir John's household.'

'Mary would upset all the maids in half an hour, Father, and Joseph would try to tumble all the village girls.'

Edward raised an eyebrow. Christopher looked grim. It was amazing that everyone but the Master of the house found out about his own servants. 'Has he that reputation?' asked Edward mildly.

'He tried to rape Lottie when Sam was away.'

'How do you know?'

'Sam told me. He had to tell me as I stopped him from marking Joseph for life or worse. Joseph denies it but I believe Lottie and Sam. They have never lied to me, Father, and they are very loyal to you.'

'I know it, Christopher.' Since giving his consent to the marriage, and arranging for them to look after the house, their gratitude and devotion were almost embarrassing and Edward wished that they would come to the farm with the family, but Lottie was adamant in her intention that her son would be born in the place she loved.

'Father,' called Alice. 'You should have come with us.' Her eyes sparkled and she looked very young. 'Why don't we use the river more? It is so much better than the dusty streets and we could see for miles.'

'You had your eyes on some things nearer,' said Anna. She laughed. 'At Greenwich, there were several boats coming back from the King's barge and Alice caused one poor sailor to lose his mooring.'

Alice blushed. 'They were looking at you, Anna.'

'Not that boat, Alice.' Anna looked pensive. Alice had

113

been far too busy making sheep's eyes at the young sailors to notice the other boat that followed them back to Wapping and tied up behind them. Coincidence – or did he have prior warning that the Verneys would be on the river at that time? Whatever it was, Sir Rollo FitzMedwin was there at the landing ready to assist the ladies ashore. The carriage that awaited him was more modest than the yellow giant he flaunted in public places and his manner had been restrained.

'What brings you to Wapping, Sir Rollo?' asked Marian, who had been too busy keeping an anxious eye on her young daughter to notice anything a yard from her nose.

'Business, Ma'am,' he said airily. 'My father has concerns in the City and asked me to manage them as he fears the plague and cannot come to the Exchange.'

'The Exchange is closed, Sir,' said Anna demurely. 'Have you not heard that it is closed for cleaning and will not be opened again until the autumn?' Rollo laughed. 'I hope that you have no other fruitless business?' she concluded.

'I hope not, Madam,' said Rollo and his eyes were bold enough to make her lower her own glance.

'So much has changed,' sighed Marian. 'I have not been in the City for a week or so and there seem to be no townspeople left. The only ones I saw looked poor and Oh! What a preponderance of beggars and ruffians.'

'Then I insist on escorting you home, Madam.' Rollo gestured to his coachman to go on alone and meet him at the house, and then stood back to allow the ladies to enter their own coach. He followed and sank into the velvet cushions by Anna's side, and she felt his leg pressed against hers. She moved away slightly and he didn't move closer, but talked to Marian with wit and charm all the way back to the house.

Anna looked out of the window. The refuse in the streets was worse than ever as few would take the work of raking when they could get more for bringing out the dead and driving the plague carts. An old woman in a long white gown walked slowly behind a man tolling a bell. She carried a long white stick and people ran away as soon as they saw her.

'They have Searchers out by day and night now, Lady Marian,' said Rollo when she commented on it. He looked contemptuous. 'They are ignorant and most have had the plague and recovered, but they still give false returns.' He shrugged. 'What can they do when they have no other employ? Their masters leave them on the streets and they have to do this or starve.'

'Where can they live if they touch the plague day after day?' asked Alice.

'There are alehouses where they admit them at a price. None other goes there and often the landlord dies of the plague from taking goods stolen from infected houses.' He looked serious. 'The man in my employ who died went to such a place not knowing it was frequented by Searchers and drivers. It is closed now, sealed up and the contagion contained.'

Rollo dismissed it from his mind and when they came to the door of the house, Marian felt obliged to ask him in for refreshment. He wore good clothes and his whole manner was without reproach and she wondered how she had come to think him a worthless idler. Anna, she noticed, seemed a little distrait and disappeared with a murmur of asking Mary for refreshments, forgetting that she and the other women were absent visiting their families and friends.

The wine and water was warm and the biscuits left out had lost their first crispness, so Marian served Sack and Rollo sat by the window watching Joseph and Sam manhandle the carriage. He glanced towards the door but Anna kept away and at last he had to make the choice of asking if his horses could be put in shade, or of taking his

115

leave. He moved restlessly. Alice chattered and his head ached. He looked at the Sack and wondered if he should leave it alone. He hoped it was the heat and the strong wine that made his head ache and he wished he was in bed.

He rose to take his leave and Alice went with him to the door as Marian explained that they were without servants today. Rollo sank into the oven-hot carriage and gasped. The sun was relentless and he had stayed on the deck of the boat with his head uncovered, wearing his own hair and no wig. He closed his eyes and wondered if he would ever touch Anna's soft hand again.

'Anna?' Marian sounded annoyed. 'Not at your books again? Our guest has gone and seemed put-out. I hope you were not rude to him?'

'Rude, Lady Marian?' Anna looked offended. 'I went to find Mary but she is still away, and so is Lottie. The kitchen was empty so I left ale on the step for Joseph and Sam. Uncle asked me to do so. He is in the stable yard, looking at the horses, and he will be here for a cool drink shortly.'

Marian looked at the tray that Anna carried, with water fresh from the well, cold and clear, and fresh oranges. 'I had no idea that Edward was here,' said Marian, now transferring her annoyance to him. 'He must have seen the carriage and Sir Rollo arrive.'

'I don't think he likes Sir Rollo,' said Anna. She smiled. 'I didn't think you approved of him, either.' Alice had told her that Lady Marian had said that Anna was indisposed when he called, but now Her Ladyship seemed under his spell.

'I think we misjudged him. He is a gentleman of breeding and wealth with excellent family prospects and he is looking for a wife.'

'He has a host of well-bred young ladies from whom he may choose,' said Anna. She poured out a drink for Edward who came in wearing shirt sleeves and dusty shoes.

'Your jacket, Edward,' said Marian, in mild reproof.

'I might be wearing less good clothes soon,' he said. He took a long drink and sighed. 'That's good. I've been with the horses,' he said. Marian turned up her nose. 'They're in good fettle,' he went on, ignoring the fact that he had broken his own rule and brought the smell of stables into the house.

'Sam is good with them and you have a coachman,' said Marian, wondering why he needed to come in looking as he did, and why he couldn't leave horses to the men paid to look after them.

'A man ought to know his own stables,' said Edward. 'I believe we have a wedding tomorrow.' It seemed a sharp change of subject and Marian was glad to talk of the details still to be observed.

'You promised them a present, Edward. Have you given Sam some money?'

'Yes, and I have decided to give them a pension.' He lowered his voice. 'God alone knows who will survive this pestilence, and they are good people.'

'But Edward, while they work here with us, they need no pension.' She looked at her husband anxiously. Had the news made him morbid? Depression could lead to catching the plague, or so she had heard.

'If we go away and leave them here, they will need a pension,' he said.

Marian smiled. 'I see. You wish to arrange it so that if we go, they will have it then. It's a good idea, but hardly a wedding present. Lottie needs money to buy things for the baby. The carpenter is making a crib and I have given them old linen but there will be other expenses, like a good midwife when the time comes and perhaps even a bill from a doctor.'

'If there are any left in London,' muttered Edward. 'William says that many doctors have followed the King to Salisbury and many more have fled to the country. Nurses

117

are not to be found, as most of them died, poor wretches, as they nursed the sick and those left are not worth a candle.'

'I shall send a clean woman from the country,' said Marian firmly.

'Who would come? Have you not seen the straggle of carts leaving the City? Heaven knows how we shall get through, even from here,' he said.

'We are not going to the wedding, Edward. Anna and Kate will go in the small carriage and come away as soon as the vows are exchanged.'

'Ah, yes, the wedding.' Edward rose wearily. 'I have to go into the City on horseback. Joseph says that it is easy using the backstreets where there are no carts and I can come back early.'

'You will take care, dear?' The brief glimpses that Marian had seen that afternoon had worried her beyond anything she had experienced. 'I hate the thought of you going to the City day after day.'

'Not for much longer,' he said in a low voice.

'May I tell the girls?'

'Not yet. Alice would blurt it out to Mary and then everyone would know, but I have only a little more work to do.'

'If only it would rain,' she said, looking out at the glassy sun and the one heavy cloud over the City. A distant rumble of thunder and a flash of lightning hardly stirred the heavy air and the cloud passed with no pity on the parched land. Everything was humid today and the fruit picked in the morning was bad by the next day. Fish lost its lustre in two hours, even in the slate-shelved pantries, and milk was sour and solid in the ewers.

'I shall be back for supper,' said Edward. Even chop-houses were places to avoid now and eating at home was fast becoming the fashion.

Sam brought the horse, saddled up and ready with

paniers of leather for anything that Edward might bring from the offices. 'Will I go with you, Sir?' asked Sam anxiously. 'I have the bay ready and can be here in five minutes.'

'No, it is not far and the side streets are empty, Sam. I can be home again soon and you have work to do.' He stepped onto the mounting block and swung into the saddle. 'Not a word, even to Lottie until after the wedding,' he warned. Sam nodded and handed up the reins. 'What's wrong with your hand?' asked Edward. The knuckles were bleeding.

'It's nothing, Sir.' Sam backed away.

'You've been fighting.'

'I had to, Sir. Joseph said just too much and I struck him.' He sounded defiant and yet pleased with himself.

'He isn't injured?' Edward tried to look concerned but he knew that he could see Joseph leave without a lot of sorrow. 'Is Lottie back yet?' he asked.

'Yes, she's in the kitchen helping Debbie. Mary is still away.'

'The devil she is! What of my supper?'

'Lottie is a very good cook, given the chance,' said Sam.

'Best warn her to keep away from Mary when she finds out about your fisticuffs, lad. There's no love lost between them, I know.'

He rode down the path to the main street and trotted the horse gently through the deserted cobbled lanes. Houses that nearly met above him cut out the sun and made cool patches that were welcome. The houses seemed quietly blind and dead as if they had no inhabitants.

He hastened, the silence and darkness in the alleys becoming oppressive. A cold menace that he had never before experienced made him sweat and as soon as he saw the road to his Chambers, he pressed the horse on and arrived out of breath.

Roger Carter, his head clerk, was waiting with a sheaf

of papers for signing. He was pale as always and composed, and seemed unconcerned that his Master was about to leave him in charge of everything for an indefinite period. 'You will bear with me, Sir, if I cannot get news through to the country easily. The post is bad as the stages are confined to few routes and there are many highwaymen on the road.'

'Do what you know I would want, Roger. I trust you and know that you have my interests at heart. Live here if you will and make use of funds as you need them. I shall leave a man and his wife at the house and if the plague gets worse, then you must decide if you can stay here or go there to live. Here are keys to both establishments.'

'I shall remain here. The College of Physicians was closed up for only a month and all the silver was stolen. It was in vaults but still the rascals got in and stripped the place.'

'Will you be safe?' Physically the man looked dried up and narrow-shouldered.

'I have this, and the locks are good,' said Roger calmly, producing a large pistol. 'Of swords I know nothing, but I have a pair of these and am a good shot. Have no fear, Mr Verney. I shall not have the plague. I drink plague water night and morning and carry a hare's foot and have a bag of herbs round my neck.'

'Then, goodbye until better times,' said Edward, with emotion. 'I must get back before the carts are out.'

He left the offices and gazed over the roof towards Covent Garden. There were other matters he wanted to follow up in businesses there but he turned away to go home, and saw a horseman riding towards him. Edward tried to place him. I've seen that face somewhere, he thought.

'Mr Verney?' The man drew rein beside him.

'You have the advantage, Sir.'

'Sir Vincent Clavell. I saw your family at the theatre a few weeks ago and Lord Carnegie told me of you.'

'I recall,' said Edward. He smiled, liking what he saw, wondering again how such a man came to be in the party of the notorious Lord Carnegie. Suddenly, he saw again the interested glance that this young man had given to Alice and her complete lack of response.

'I came to warn you that the Bearers of the Dead are that way and that two houses have the Searchers in them.'

'You saw the red staves of the Bearers?' Edward paled, knowing that the dead and afflicted would be dragged from the houses and put on the carts as soon as they were hooked down from their bedrooms, or from the hallways if the family had dared to touch them. 'I am obliged to you, Sir. I am not afraid for myself, you understand, but I have a family to consider.'

'And beautiful daughters, who must never be exposed to such a risk,' said Clavell gravely. They rode side by side in silence for a minute, taking a slightly longer route, through what Edward knew was an area frequented by men looking for cheap prostitutes. Two women looked down from high windows and laughed. There were red crosses on all but two of the doors and one of these was the house with the women in it. If they didn't get the plague, they must be riddled with pox, he decided, and kept his face towards the front.

'Need we go this way?' he asked, and made towards a side turning. Clavell followed reluctantly and put a hand on the hilt of his sword. The way before them was narrow and dark and Edward began to wish he had stayed with Clavell. A movement from the shadows made his horse rear and the cobbles rang as he regained control. Clavell slapped the rump of Edward's horse sharply. 'Ride, Sir! Out of this alley and turn right.'

Edward didn't look back but bent over the neck and spurred the beast until he found the sunlight again. He looked back. Clavell was riding out, his sword in hand and on it, Edward saw blood. They gained the main thoroughfare and halted. Edward calmed his mount and had time to look at his companion.

121

'Are you hurt?'

Clavell grinned and wiped the blade of his sword on the hedge of privet that grew shoulder-high to the horse. He sheathed it and brushed the dust from his jacket. 'A rogue flew out of a doorway as we passed and tried to catch your horse by the tail. He saw me too late, thank God, and he has a bloody ear to pay for his mistake. This is no place for you, Mr Verney. Allow me to ride with you to your house.' He looked back but they were not followed. 'The City is full of beggars and the sick and there will be no return to honest living until the King comes back and sets an example,' said Clavell.

'You think he should have stayed?'

'I think he had no choice with the pestilence reaching up to the gates of Westminster and now at Hampton Court, but the people will not understand his going and those left will resent it. Most of the rich have left and their servants starve.' He glanced at the man he had saved. 'But you, Sir, you will not keep your daughters here? Women are precious and should not be put at risk.'

He seems anxious about my family, thought Edward. 'Where do my daughters and my ward find good matches if we hide them in the country?' he said out loud.

'Soon, all the eligible men will be there, Sir, and not in town.' Clavell smiled. 'If you leave for Surrey, where I hear you have relatives, may I call on you?'

'You seem to know all about my family, Sir Vincent,' said Edward drily. 'I wonder at and am flattered by your concern.'

'Your servant, Sir.' Clavell refused refreshment and turned his horse at the gate. He rode away without looking up at the windows where Alice and Lottie watched him go.

'He might not be a clerk,' said Alice. She frowned. If he *was* more than that, he could have brightened up an idle hour, but he didn't even look back.

Chapter 8

'You look pale, Kate,' said Marian anxiously. She felt her hand and found it cold in the heat.

'I'm not ill, Mother.' Kate took away her hand and tried to smile. 'Just tired and miserable. I had no idea that seeing a wedding would bring back so many memories of what might have been for me.'

'It was a poor affair,' said Marian, unable to see any resemblance with a wedding in a fashionable church. 'You were kept outside and they allowed no strangers into the churchyard, or so Anna told me.'

'The churchyard was full of freshly dug graves, Mother, and we had to wait while the buriers passed by to fill a new pit. Cripplegate is badly affected and the church has only one curate now and he is considering leaving to go to the country.' Kate looked up. 'But nothing could take away the feeling that Lottie and Sam are now joined before God. They saw no corpses, no dirt, no misery. They saw only their union and the life they will make when the baby is born.' She took a deep breath. 'That child will be born of love and be given that priceless gift.'

'Your father and I loved you all,' said Marian.

'I know, but that is different. I didn't expect to see it in a servant.' Kate sipped her tisane and the colour returned to her cheeks. 'I'm all right, Mother,' she said. 'Lottie and

123

Sam will come back tonight and I want to make sure they have everything they need in their new home.' She produced a large key from her pocket. 'I'll go over now and see that all is well.'

'It is locked?' Marian was shocked. There were locks on all the doors in the house but they were seldom used in a home where servants and family were there and the house was never empty. 'We have no robbers, here Kate.'

'Christopher sent for a locksmith to make all secure,' said Kate. 'He doesn't trust Joseph or Mary.'

'Mary is a good cook and a quiet woman, and Joseph has given us good service,' Marian stated firmly. 'I have never had to reprimand Mary for her work at any time.'

'She shows one side to the family and another to the girls in the kitchen. Lottie has been in tears more than once because of her.' Kate picked up the key and walked through the stable yard to the steps leading to the room that Sam and Lottie were to use. The dogs greeted her with lofty tails and bright eyes and the two horses left in the stables munched quietly as she passed. It was peaceful and clean and there were no rats.

At the wedding, there had been rats. Not blatantly running before them but slipping away into the bushes and making holes in the wattle fencing. She had been conscious of them without seeing them, and as always she hated their stealth and their love of dirt. Her Uncle William had told her that there were more rats in the City than at any time he could recall, made bold by the lack of cats and dogs that had formerly kept them under control.

'They eat and soil good food and I cannot think that it is wise to kill the dogs,' he said. 'In the stews of Westminster, there is plague and rats aplenty, and yet the rats thrive. It is as if the two evils walk hand in hand and do each other no harm.' He considered the problem with a frown. 'In clean houses where there is no vermin, there is much less contagion and yet there seems to be no connection. People do not readily touch rats, to be infected by anything they carry, even if they leave their fleas to worry and irritate where they bite.'

Kate mounted the steps and heard a movement above her. Sam and Lottie would not be back for at least two hours and Joseph was driving Edward this afternoon. The stable lads were busy mending harness and cleaning the silver-chased bridles and yet someone was on the stairs.

Kate went up softly, and smiled. Debbie or one of the servants who couldn't be spared for the wedding must have thought to lay a gift at the door. She heard the door rattle as someone tried to get in, and then a more furious rattling as if whoever it was could not wait or was frustrated to the limit of his or her patience.

'Slut! Slut and whoremonger!' cried Mary Creed.

'What are you doing here, Mary?' asked Kate.

Mary Creed swung round, startled. 'Nothing, Miss Kate.' She gave a thin forced smile and tried to hide the pail she held behind the folds of her long skirt.

'What is in that pail?' questioned Kate. She could smell the midden from here or was it fresh dung from the stables that sent this stench up to the loft?

A mixture of fury and guilt made Mary Creed even uglier than usual. 'It's nothing, Miss Kate.' She tried to come down the stairs, hiding the pail, but Kate stopped her.

'Show me, Mary!'

Reluctantly, the woman brought the bucket into view and Kate's nostrils were assailed by the awful smell of rotting manure. Wordlessly she stared at the woman who now rushed past her into the stable yard, then Kate unlocked the door and went into the clean room smelling sweetly of herbs and scrubbing. She saw the shelf of kitchen utensils above the small stove and the orange pomander hanging by its blue ribbon from a nail above the bed in the corner.

She gulped back tears that were not wholly for what

125

Mary Creed might have done here. Lottie was a happy woman, fulfilled and healthy and had no need of pity or patronage. She couldn't believe that Mary Creed or anyone would want to sully this homecoming, and yet she had had the means to ruin everything in her hand. Christopher was wiser than any of them. Kate locked the door again after her and went slowly back to the house to tell her mother what she had found.

'I don't know what your father will say, Kate. Are you sure that Mary meant to foul the room with it?'

'I can think of no other reason, Mother. It isn't the thing to take into a clean house, is it? There was no cause for Mary to have that pail at all as she has nothing to do with the midden or the stables. She was cursing Lottie when I saw her and I have never seen such evil in a woman's eyes in my life.'

'She never had children,' said Marian thoughtfully. 'Some say that it leads to madness at the Change.'

'Madness – or jealousy?' said Kate.

'Who is madly jealous?' asked Alice as she came in, wearing a new gown with bright pink ribbons. 'May I ask Lottie to dress my hair, Mother?'

'Not on her wedding night,' said Kate. She looked at her mother. 'I think I will go to the kitchens and see the food prepared for them when they return.'

Marian looked startled. 'You don't think that she would . . . ?'

'She might already have done so,' said Kate. 'Alice, take off that gown and change into something old. We shall wait on the bride and groom tonight and give Mary the rest of the day off.' Alice opened her mouth to protest and then shrugged. It was a strange idea but rather pleasant. She had never played at being a maid. She ran to her room.

'Inspect everything,' said Marian, who was over her first shock and now became practical. 'If you have any doubts, then use whatever is there and make sure that it is tasty.'

126

'Our supper will be fine,' said Kate. 'Mary would never dare to tamper with that, and usually they make far more than we eat and I suspect that Mary and Joseph have it or give it to Joseph's brother who seems to hang about the back door far too much.'

She went down to the kitchens and found Debbie stirring a pot. 'Where is Mary Creed?' said Kate.

Debbie stopped stirring. 'She said she had to go to buy herbs that we didn't grow in the garden.' Debbie giggled. 'It's too late to give herbs for love. Lottie showed today in that thin gown.'

'Is this for Sam and Lottie?'

'Yes, it is a thick mutton broth and it is very good.'

'Did Mary taste it before she left?'

'She did, twice, and relished it, but she laughed and said it needed something more to give it zest.' Debbie dipped in her spoon and held it to her lips. 'It needs no more than a grain or two of salt.'

'Then that is how it shall be served,' said Kate. She lifted pot-lids and peered into the hot oven. The pies had been made the day before and would be all right. She backed away from the heat, and wondered how the kitchen girls managed to live in this temperature all day in summer. Was that why Mary was dried up and bitter?

Debbie was curious as Kate sat on a stool to wait for the cook's return. It must be the wedding that made Miss Kate so interested. I wonder if they will give me a good wedding present if I marry? the servant girl thought. The ostler in the Rose Inn was about to declare for her, and as things stood, now that half of London was dead, she might as well marry him. She hinted that she might marry soon, and waited with lowered eyelids for the response. Kate seemed distracted and spoke little, but just smiled and said she must think of a present. Debbie stirred the pots again and dreamed of a new room as neat and sweet as could be, with a good featherbed like Lottie now had and a husband to make love to her through the hot summer nights.

Kate heard the carriage return with Edward and Joseph. She bit her lip and wished that Christopher or Sam could be with her when Mary came back and if Joseph came into the kitchen, but she had no need to worry. Five minutes later, with Mary still away, Edward strode into the kitchen and one look at his face told Kate that Marian had spoken to him.

'Is all well?' he demanded. Kate nodded and Debbie looked puzzled. It only needed Miss Anna and Miss Alice to come and bring Lady Marian with them to make this the oddest day of her life.

'Mary has gone to buy herbs for the pot,' said Kate in a level voice.

'The devil she has!' Edward sniffed the air. 'It smells good, my girl,' he said to Debbie, who bobbed as if she took all the credit for the savoury dish.

'Send her to me directly,' he said, leaving the kitchen. 'I'll be in the library. Christopher!' His son poked his head round the library door. 'You had keys made for the loft, I believe.'

'Yes, Father.' Christopher hesitated, not knowing if his father approved.

'Good, I want you to check all the locks in the house and make sure there are keys to fit. Do it now and if any lack keys or fail to work, get the locksmith in today.'

'I'll ride down as soon as I know how many need work on them.'

Edward paced the room. The sooner they left the better. As yet few people knew of his intentions and if he could get rid of Mary and Joseph Creed before they made the last preparations, the safer his family would be. Small incidents in the past which he had ignored now came back in memory. Insignificant sums of money missing and pieces of tackle having to be replaced far too often for economy

128

and the amount of food that the servants were said to consume, all added up to modest but steady pilfering.

He looked up as Anna came in with a book. 'Lady Marian told me about Mary,' she said. 'I can hardly believe that anyone could be so wicked.' She eyed him with speculation. 'Lady Marian also asked me to go through my clothes and look out those that I have done with and put them on the landing.'

'Yes, child. I asked her to look out clothes for the poor. William needs as much as we can provide and there are many garments that you girls can afford to lose.'

'Are we going away, Uncle?' She lowered her voice. 'I know we may do soon, as a whisper was heard in the City, but *how* soon, Uncle? Have we time to say goodbye to friends?'

'Soon,' he said. 'Make a good pile to send away, Anna, and see that Alice keeps nothing that isn't useful.'

'I saw Christopher drag trunks out of the storeroom,' said Anna.

'You might as well know. I trust you to keep a still tongue, Anna. We have every right to leave. We are not inside the City wall and we have no red crosses here.' He pulled at his wig until it hung over one ear and gave him a plaintive look. 'There are many who would condemn me for this but I have you all to consider. If we stay, you will want to shop in St Paul's and Christopher will find some mischief, and as for Alice, why she is like a honeycomb and attracts all the young rakes in London. I've seen the way they look at her, and as yet, she notices their interest but does not respond.'

'Alice will do very well,' said Anna soothingly. 'She will never take a lover as she respects you too much and she will marry where money is, and love him.'

'You suggest that she will marry for money?'

'No, that is not the same,' said Anna gently.

'And you, Anna. I feel that I have failed you,' he said.

129

'Marian tells me that Sir Rollo FitzMedwin is after your hand. D'ye fancy him, my dear?' He looked puzzled. One day his wife told him that Rollo was a rake and probably had the clap and then she suddenly changed her mind and sang his praises.

'He is good company and has wit,' she said, but her face gave nothing away. 'If we leave, who will know where we are?' She flushed. 'If callers come, will they be told where we have gone?'

'Sam will know who to tell and who to keep guessing. I have no creditors to hound me and Roger will live at the chambers to oversee everything.' He went to the open window but there was no sign of Mary. 'Some of our friends have left for Winchester and for the Court at Salisbury. The King likes to have young men around him and that poor Captain Bennet has been summoned there.' Edward pushed at a pile of papers on the desk. 'I forgot. He brought this for you, Anna.' He laughed. 'Not the way to woo a maid but he would make a very good friend.' He shook his head over the heavy volume and its contents. '*Experiments On Animals In the Royal Society*? *The Chart of the Heavens and the Planets*? Such learned stuff and not for me, my dear. How did he think that this would amuse you?'

'It does interest me, Uncle,' she said, and took the book to her room. If Captain Bennet was in Salisbury, then she could think of him there, imagining it to be the King's will and not his own. Had he wanted to see her that day or did he leave the book out of courtesy?

Debbie knocked timidly on the library door. 'Mary Creed is coming in at the back,' she said.

'Send her to me,' said Edward. 'No, wait, girl. I'll see her in the kitchen.' He turned to Christopher who had come in with a list of the damaged locks and the order for keys. 'Come with me, and do that afterwards,' he requested.

They went to the kitchen and Mary Creed put a hand

over her heart. She glared at Debbie and then at Kate who went to stand by her father. The pocket of her dress bulged and she tried to slide behind the deal table where it couldn't be seen. 'It is all ready for the wedded couple,' she said. 'I have made a savoury dish for them and I hope they come soon or it will be spoiled.'

'You went to buy herbs?' said Edward, smiling. 'Tell me, Mary, what do we lack in our own gardens? They run rampant and grow like weeds.'

Mary licked her lips and forced a laugh. 'You are right, Sir. I found nothing new and only dusty stale herbs culled yesterday.'

Edward walked round the kitchen. 'Tell me, Mary, do you use the same herbs for cooking as we have in the posies against the plague?' He eyed her with interest. 'If so, then surely if we eat them, we are doubly protected – unless some are poison.'

'Poison? None of our herbs is poisonous,' said Mary. She looked even more pale than usual. 'Taste this, Sir, and tell me if it is poison!' She went to the big pot and dipped in a long spoon. 'It is the best mutton stew I have made,' she said, and sipped from the spoon. 'Would I eat this if it was harmful?'

'So it is complete and there is no need for more herbs?' said Edward.

'It is ready and I hope they give me credit for my trouble,' she said crossly.

'Let us greet them well,' rejoined Edward heartily. 'Debbie, put on your frilled apron and Mary, change yours for I see gravy on it. Kate and Alice will be maids tonight and my son will open some of my best wine.'

Reluctantly, Mary handed her soiled apron to Debbie who held out her hand for it to take with her own to the scullery.

'Wait!' Edward strode across the room and took the apron. From the pocket he shook out a handful of small

131

mushrooms. 'What is this?' he said, in a low voice heavy with menace. 'What is this, woman?'

Kate gasped. From early childhood she had known that these were not edible. Mushrooms grew in the open and were dark-gilled under pale tops. These, she knew, were the sinister but innocent-looking fungi that lurked under trees and could bring death in three days.

'I make an infusion of them for the rats,' said Mary. 'I hate vermin.'

'We have cats and dogs to keep down rats and mice and I have no wish for my dogs to be poisoned if they eat a rat filled with this,' said Edward.

Mary burst into tears of fury and frustration and Kate had the sickening feeling that she felt no remorse. 'I meant no harm, Sir. It was to rid this house of vermin,' the cook insisted.

'You are lying, Mary.' Edward turned to Debbie who was watching wide-eyed and seemed glued to the ground. 'Fetch Joseph,' he said.

Edward flung the death-caps in a heap on the table and waited. It was the first time he had become involved in domestic affairs like this, but this was no mere squabble among servants and he knew that it was his duty to deal with it.

Joseph came in, wearing his livery. He eyed his wife with disfavour and looked about him at the servants, and the people who seldom came down to this level, sensing that something was terribly wrong. He took in the drawn expression on his wife's face and then the small pile on the table. His mouth tightened.

'I see you know them,' said Edward. Marian now hovered anxiously behind her husband and gasped.

'They are mushrooms?' said Joseph, cautiously. Mary looked hopeful. 'There are plenty better than that in the fields but not until later in the year after heavy dew.'

132

'But you will eat them for supper if your wife gives them to you?'

'I never eat mushrooms, Sir,' said Joseph firmly. 'They give me the gripes.'

'These would give you gripes enough,' said Edward grimly. 'My brother has had dealings with these and few people live after eating them.'

Joseph moved away from his wife as if that absolved him from any conspiracy. 'It must have been a mistake, Sir.' he said.

'A great mistake. Now, Mary Creed, go and pack your bags and be out of this house within the hour.'

'Mr Verney, Sir!' Joseph went red in the face and took a step towards his master. 'It wasn't meant, Sir. Mary is the best cook you'll ever have and if she goes, then I go, too.'

'So be it,' said Edward calmly. 'I think that you have finished your time with us, Joseph. Christopher, see that these two wretches are gone before nightfall, but first do that errand I asked of you.' He eyed the couple grimly. 'I feel that it is even more necessary now,' he said.

'But where shall we go?' asked Joseph.

'There are inns and places where they will take you. Here.' Edward flung down two gold coins. 'You will not starve. There are many who want coachmen and cooks and I shall not send a bad character after you. We are leaving shortly for the country, so none will think that you left in disgrace.' Joseph turned to leave, ignoring his wife completely. 'One minute,' said Edward. 'You go without a bad character but if I hear of one word that you say against any member of this household, or one action that might endanger any one of them, you shall be dragged before the magistrates.'

Edward put an arm round his wife and led her from the room. 'You were hard, Edward,' she whispered.

'Would you have Lottie die? Or my Sam lie in agony?

That woman is a witch and a hag, my dear, and heaven help Joseph if he has to put up with her for life.'

'Lottie is here, my lady,' said Debbie, whose head was in a whirl with all the excitement.

'Not a word to her yet,' warned Marian. 'Let her come home with pleasure and have this night to remember.'

Christopher came back with the locksmith and then opened bottles of wine. From the library, Edward heard the sounds of laughter and smiled, imagining his daughters playing at servants and enjoying it. He watched from the window the departure of the couple who had betrayed his trust and was glad that he had let Christopher give them a cart and a nag to take their belongings. It meant that they had everything with them and there was no excuse for returning on any pretext.

Mary hadn't seemed as upset as the dismissal warranted, and he wondered what new evil she had in mind. 'The devil!' he said suddenly, and almost ran to the window. It was too late. The pair had gone and he had no way of knowing where they were. It was only now that he recalled that Joseph was wearing full livery, the new set bought only a month before and marking him as in the employ of Mr Edward Verney. So, Joseph could say he was still employed but wanted a change as the family might move away from London. Edward shrugged. They were gone and the Verneys had seen the last of them.

Lottie drank the remaining drops of her wine and felt light-headed. She gathered up the small presents from the servants and Sam took them in a large basket to their rooms.

'Come to the drawing room before you retire, Lottie,' said Kate. 'Lady Marian wants to see you.'

Rather unsteadily, Lottie followed her and Marian and Anna smiled as they saw her radiant face. 'My lady, I shall never forget your kindness,' said Lottie. 'I shall remember

this day for the rest of my life and tell my child about it.'
She rested a hand on her stomach and her eyes were misty.

'You must take care,' said Marian. 'You know now that
we leave for the country as soon as we can pack?' Lottie
nodded. 'You can come with us, if you wish. If you change
your mind, there will be the small coach that my husband
will leave here and a couple of horses.'

'It won't be for long, my lady, and we'll have everything
clean and ready for your return. I can't leave London now
that I am expecting. I need my friends close to me at my
time.'

'If you lack anything, get in touch with the clerk, and
eat well, Lottie. There is enough growing here to feed an
army and Sam must get good meat from the farmers at the
gate and fords.'

'We shall be very happy here.' Lottie hesitated. 'The
Master has forbidden us to go into the City now that the
Bills are high, but my mother has the dropsy and I worry
about her.'

'Keep away if you can, but take heed of what you hear,
and avoid the plague pit over by Aldgate. They say that it
is forty feet long now and almost as wide, and growing
each day as more and more are buried there.' Marian knew
that it was impossible to forbid Lottie as the girl would do
as her heart told her, so she sketched out ways of avoiding
the plague-ridden streets. 'And ride if you can, with Sam
as protection.' She told Lottie of the encounter that Edward
had had with the footpad and of the timely intervention of
Sir Vincent Clavell. 'There are desperate men about, my
girl, and some would have no conscience about a woman
with child.'

'I hate to think of you so far away, my lady.' Lottie's
eyes filled with tears. 'I have so much to thank you for,
you and the Master and Miss Kate.'

'Your enemies have gone, Lottie, and you may never see

them more. I could never have Joseph and Mary in this house again.'

'It is the best wedding present I could have, and now I will go to Sam, if it please you, my lady.'

She walked down to the kitchen and saw that Sam had left. Debbie was yawning and piling the dishes in the sink, leaving them to soak in soda water until the morning now that Mary was no longer there to make her work until midnight. The house was quiet and Lottie made her way across the stableyard, thinking that tonight she could go that way and not have to climb the ladder. Her limbs felt heavy with wine and love and Sam had the lantern lit by the door for her to see the way.

She smelled the new hay and the clean scent of horses and felt the warmth of the summer night as she stepped out of her dress and shift. Honeysuckle that climbed unpruned up the stable wall in an extravagance of pale yellow fragrance brushed the skylight window and made a bower. The deep featherbed needed no cover and Sam laid her down naked in the golden light that made shadows where her full breasts pointed over the living mound of new life. He kissed the moving limbs of his unborn child and took his wife with care and gentleness.

Lottie clung to him when he sank back. 'Sam, do you think we shall ever be as happy again as we are tonight?' she whispered. 'Today, we were married before the church and became man and wife. My lady and the Master gave us their blessing and we have this place all to ourselves for as long as we want it.'

'You love me, sweetheart?' he murmured into her hair.

'For ever, Sam, and nothing can ever harm us, can it?' She looked up to the rough-cast ceiling, more beautiful to her than the frescoes in a lofty church and saw the pomander ball swaying gently above them. With the herbs and good food and clean water and a little care, there was nothing that could reach them that was evil. They slept like children in a hayfield until the dawn cocks crowed away in the fields and the cartwheels rolled in Mary-le-bone, taking families from the City – and the plague – as soon as the gates were opened.

Chapter 9

'I know where to go,' said Joseph Creed. 'You'll have to stay with the nag and cart or he'll know we've been turned out.' He laughed. 'I had a good look round his stable and there is a stall never used that would take this. I can sweeten his man and say that we are on our way to join the Master, but we need to see people in the City first and can't take our belongings there because of getting out again.'

The City Gates were well-guarded and, as fewer people could find doctors who would give them bills of health to leave, many were trapped with loaded carts or had to fight a way through when the crowds were too big to control. The road to the Strand was empty and they passed the houses of many titled families. Lady Essex had left her huge mansion in the charge of servants and the smaller houses where men like Sir Rollo FitzMedwin had London residences looked almost as abandoned. Some new crosses had appeared on doors and on two were white crosses and signs of life again.

Joseph turned the horse into the lane leading to the stables and wondered why nobody came out to see who entered the yard. He called and then looked into the stalls. A horse stamped impatiently and Joseph noticed that his water trough was almost empty. The feeding racks had not been filled and wisps of hay lay everywhere in the ordure.

He led the horse and cart into the yard and fetched water and fodder from the store for the two horses and for his own which he put in the spare stall. He was filling the last bucket from the pump when Mary ran in to him.

'I've been up to the loft where the coachman lived,' she gasped. 'It's empty and everything has gone.'

'Are you mad, woman? The coachman died of the plague!'

Mary brushed aside his fear. 'That was long enough ago to make it wholesome again, and with not a stitch nor stone there to show that anyone lived there, there is no place for the pestilence.'

Joseph thought for a minute. 'Yes, you may be right. The man who drove after that could not have lived here, but perhaps stayed in the inn or even in the main house. Many of the rich families bring in staff and place them out in inns if they have no room for them.'

'Where is he?' Mary looked at the heap of muck that Joseph had raked from the stalls. 'Gentlemen do not like their horses to be neglected. He must have been away for two days.'

Joseph backed to the door. 'Do you think that the second man died too, or is in the pest-house?'

'Leave this until later, Joseph. Go to the nearest alehouse and find out what is happening.' She smiled slyly. 'I'll go to the front of the house and ask for Sir Rollo and if he's there, I'll say that Miss Anna sends him messages.' She laughed. 'It would be something to warm my heart and to revenge us for our dismissal if he took her away and ruined her.'

Joseph washed the dirt from his hands and brushed the dust from his livery. He strolled out and along the road to the one alehouse still open in the Strand. Lounging by a barrel, he asked about the house and family. 'I heard that the coachman was taken sick a while back. How are the rest?'

The innkeeper stared at the smart livery. 'You're with Lady Verney, aren't you?' He handed over a brimming pewter mug of ale and laughed. 'What brings you here asking after Sir Rollo's family? Not the kind that the Verneys would entertain are they?'

'They might,' said Joseph significantly. 'They've got three girls to marry off.'

'Oh, the wind's in that quarter is it? I don't think I'd want one of mine to be mixed up with Sir Rollo, but some will do anything for rank and money.' The man looked round the empty room. 'No trade now. Might as well shut up like the rest and be safe from the plague. I had to turn away a Searcher yesterday. She tried to sidle in but forgot that she still held her white staff.'

'Is there much round here?' Joseph took a long draught of ale. 'I called at the stables but there was no one there. I suppose the man who took over the horses lives here or in the house?'

'Not here since yesterday. He left in a hurry and I suppose he was needed to take Sir Rollo into the country or to join the Court at Salisbury. He took all his clothes and didn't say when he'd be returning.'

Joseph walked back slowly. The stables had been left in a hurry too. No water and little food for the beasts and the door unlatched. The huge carriage was still at the back of the yard and he didn't know enough about the place to tell whether that was the only vehicle usually there. Two horses left when the master of the house went away for a long time? It wasn't likely, as he now had no permanent and reliable coachman or stable hand.

Mary came to meet him, her pale face agitated and yet full of a kind of pleasure. He said, 'I found that the man who had care of the horses has gone with Sir Rollo and they left in a great hurry.' He saw his wife's face and faltered. 'At least that's what the inn-keeper believes. The man left yesterday.'

The evening sun slanted between the houses on to the dusty grass and showed the sails of boats on the river, bright and flower-like on the tide. 'Come and see for yourself what has happened,' Mary said.

Joseph looked up at the sky. 'It will be dark soon and we have no roof for the night. We must find something to eat and a bed.' The red glow before sunset made the stone walls soft and as Mary tugged at his arm and Joseph saw the front of the house for the first time, the red glow was echoed in the crimson cross on the door.

A man stood with a halberd at his side and he picked it up as Joseph approached, as if he might be attacked.

'Who is in there?' asked Joseph.

'Just one,' said the man. 'The rest fled before the Searcher came, after telling the Bearer of the Dead when he went to the house over there.' Two shapeless bundles lay on the ground a few yards away in a doorway over which the red cross scored the wood.

'Sir Rollo or his man?' asked Joseph.

'Oh a fine fellow he was, but raving when the Searcher looked at him, and hot, she said, and ripping off his clothes.'

'And now is he dead?' asked Mary.

'Not he!' The man laughed. 'Some die quietly and some rant and rave. This fine fellow curses and shouts and tries every way to get free, but I have locked all the doors with chains and padlocks and he will never be free.'

'How long do you stay here?' asked Mary.

'Until all is quiet inside and he has asked for no more food to be bought for him.' He rattled coins in his purse. 'I have made all doubly secure while I go to the market for him. He wants food and wine and swears that he isn't tainted. I have never know a plague victim with his appetite. Perhaps he will recover and then I will have this job for forty days.' He spat in the road. 'He's generous, I will say that for him, but he can't bribe me to let him go.' The

141

shifty eyes lightened. 'If he dies, there will be good pickings in a house like this.'

Mary eyed him with respect. 'You do well, do you?'

'The Searchers do better,' he admitted. 'They can get into houses sooner and if all are dead, then they take the best and put it away before the Bearers come to take the bodies.'

'Are you afraid of the sickness?' she asked.

'There are some who get it and some who don't, whatever they do with the sick. I believe that if you've had a bad disease like the pox or smallpox, then you don't get the plague.'

'I've known men who had all of that and more and still died of the distemper,' said Joseph scathingly, but Mary fingered the pockmarks on her face and smiled.

'Prostitutes get it and they are riddled with the clap,' said Joseph. He backed away from the door. 'We have to find a place to sleep,' he said.

Mary didn't move. 'We left our horse and cart at the back in the stables and we fed Sir Rollo's animals,' she said self-righteously. 'Poor creatures, they had no water and no fodder. He would want my husband to care for them.'

'I had not thought of horses,' said the guard.

'The loft is empty and we could sleep there. I saw fresh clean straw that we could lie on and the place is clean.' Seeing the man's hesitation, she added quickly, 'The Verney family where we work have dealings with Sir Rollo FitzMedwin and would want us to be of service while they are away in the country. Do you want the animals to starve and be of no value when this is over?' She gave him a knowing wink.

'Ah, I see that you have sense, Ma'am. There's no contagion apart from the house and you can come and go by the back lane as you wish.' Joseph looked unconvinced. 'The coachman who died didn't live there, and stayed at the alehouse while he found a few sticks of furniture. He was new and had only just been given livery.'

'But he touched Sir Rollo.' Joseph looked at his wife, remembering her fingers clawing aside the unbuttoned livery to give the dying man air. The guard shrugged and lit a torch which he thrust into a holder by the door. Night was falling and Joseph was torn between his desire to get out of the dark, plague-filled streets and the pressing need for food and sleep.

'Come,' said Mary impatiently. 'The loft will be safer than an inn, and quiet.' She asked the guard where they could buy food and ale and he gave them a torch to light the way. Half an hour later, Mary gave the guard ale and one of her own pies, a supply of which she had brought with her. It paid to keep him sweet, she thought, and her mind worked long after Joseph lay snoring beside her, lost in an oblivion of fatigue and strong ale.

Sir Rollo had called on the Verneys, and had travelled with them in their coach since the man died. He had kissed the hands of the ladies and sat close to Miss Anna. Mary smiled. There was still time for the plague to take its toll there and the idea of Anna, that foreign witch, lying in agony covered with the tokens of death, made her sigh and turn over to sleep peacefully.

'A judgement on the wicked City,' she murmured. The prophets were right and there would be more to come.

Joseph roused himself and couldn't think where he lay. He reached over to touch the woman by his side thinking that he had spent the night with a whore, but the thin flanks and bony ribs of his wife soon made him wide awake.

He got up and washed his face in the pump water in the yard and put a ewer to fill for the horses. The flow of water was small and it took time to fill the vessel and by the time he had finished, Mary had bread and cheese and ale ready for him.

'We stay here until you get work,' she said. 'Put on

working clothes and I'll brush your livery so that you look smart when you see someone wanting a coachman.' Already, the loft looked as if they had lived there for weeks, as they had brought all their worldly possessions in from the cart and Mary had distributed them over the big room.

Joseph was given confidence by the sight of familiar things and his fears faded. He walked round to the front of the house in time to meet the guard for the day and to give him his morning draught of ale, establishing the fact that he had a right to be there.

'I guard the houses in this street,' said the man. 'There are four and I think they will not need me soon as no sound came from two yesterday and nobody asked for food.'

Joseph saw that the two shrouded bodies in the far doorway had gone. 'Did the cart come in the night?' he asked.

'By night and by day now,' said the guard. 'There are so many that they can't leave them for darkness when the whole are safely in their beds, and many are naked, as shrouds are hard to come by.' He looked tired and Joseph shuddered. If only everything had been different and he had been asked to go to Surrey with the Verney family. Only now did he value the good quarters and food and conditions of work that he had formerly derided as insufficient. He went back to Mary, disgruntled and ready to blame her for everything.

'I'm going out,' she said.

'Selling your body?' said Joseph, openly sneering at the drab figure she made in her grey dress and black shawl and the severe collar and cap of white.

'You may be glad of the money I make,' she said, smiling in a way that made him uneasy. 'I'm not sitting about doing nothing when there is good money to be earned.' She came closer and the three deep pockmarks were clearly visible. 'I can never catch the plague. I have my prayers and these

144

scars to protect me. I carry a powerful remedy against disease, next to my skin, and I believe in the prophecies.'

'What do you mean, woman?'

'I mean that they need more Searchers, Joseph. I mean that there is money and goods to be taken at will and none to stop me once I carry a white wand.'

'You can't go into infected houses!' Joseph recoiled as if she had the taint on her breath. 'Stay here and I will get a position of good value.'

'I am going to look round and keep my ears and eyes open,' she said. 'You go looking for work and if you find some, then I will stay and keep house. If not, then you have no choice, Joseph.' She handed him some money, grudgingly. 'You'll have to buy ale to loosen a few tongues, but keep a clear head yourself.' She looked round the loft and smiled. It would hold a lot of valuable pickings and nobody would dare to try to steal from a house with the red cross on the door and a guard at his halberd.

She clutched her shawl closely although the morning was already warm and went out through the deserted streets. Faces appeared in windows and vanished again as Mary was too soberly dressed to attract attention and any who lurked in doorways waiting for someone to rob took her to be poor and not worth the trouble.

Joseph dressed neatly but also looked like a working man who would arouse no interest. His first thought was to find an alehouse that still served customers and to drink himself into a euphoria that would put away the dread he suffered each time he saw Mary's avid face. She might do what she said, he decided, and the idea made him stride quickly to the place where many coachmen and flunkeys met in the mornings for the first draught of the day.

He bought bread with his ale and sat waiting in the nearly empty taproom. An hour passed and there were three more men there, drinking alone and suspicious of anyone who came close to them. None of the men were coachmen that he had seen on the driving boxes of a noble house but were hackney coach drivers and men about their business of trade. Joseph went to another place and found it was the same there. Houses that he had not noticed from the high perch on the carriage looked dusty and forbidding and twice he stepped into another alley to avoid the plague cart, piled high with naked bodies. He watched, fascinated, as the driver reached over to tug a thin gold chain from a dead woman and as he did so, his hands roamed over her breasts as if he still found them alluring.

Sickened, Joseph went back to the loft. He sat on the stool that Mary had put by the open door and wondered where she was. Dinnertime came and went and he ventured out again for food. This time,he met a man who wanted to hire a cart to take his belongings to friends in the village of Hampstead, but Joseph knew that if he let the cart out of his care he could say goodbye to it. The man became belligerent and tried to strike at Joseph's face. Joseph wished that he had kept quiet about the cart. It was becoming clear that every cart and carriage that could carry goods had long been sold, stolen or begged for the exodus from the Cities of London and Westminster.

By late afternoon, Joseph was dispirited and tired. The loft was empty and for the first time in his married life, he wished that Mary was there. He went round to the front of the house and saw the night guard arrive and stood talking to him for a while. 'He's been quiet today, the other man said,' the guard told him. 'In the last stages no doubt and I'll be in there soon.'

Two more bodies awaited collection in the doorway of a house not far away and there was no light to be seen in the curtainless windows. Joseph went back to the loft and drank more and more as he waited for his wife. He would have been anxious about her if he had not been tipsy and even through his fuddled state he knew that she was out late and could be in danger.

146

At last he saw a flickering along the lane and heard his wife's voice. 'You can leave me here. My husband is there. You can see the candle.' Joseph heard a man's voice, but the words were indistinct. 'No,' said Mary in an angry voice. 'No further or you might have the sickness. Look on the front door of the house. There is plague there and in these stables a man died last week. We are staying here because we have no other bed and the Lord will protect us.'

The torchlight wavered and dipped its way back to the road. Joseph stumbled to the stairs and shouted. 'Mary! Where have you been? I thought the Devil had taken his own at last!'

Mary climbed the stairway and looked about her at the dishevelled room and her bleary-eyed husband, and her eyes were cold. 'I can see that you have been busy,' she said sarcastically. 'Were they falling over each other to have you drive their coaches? I have seen but one coach in the whole City today and that went by so fast that I couldn't see who was in it. Another was by the river waiting for a crossing, but the boatman would take only the smaller carriages and carts, so it looks as if there is no call for you, my dear.'

'It can't last. They'll all be back next week and we have plenty to see us through,' said Joseph.

'We haven't a lot,' said Mary, 'and what we have, we'll need for later.'

'Then why pay a linkman to see you home?' Joseph sat heavily on a stool and wanted only to sleep now that he knew Mary was back home again. It wasn't in her nature to waste money and she had never been afraid of the dark.

'I didn't want to be taken for someone with the sickness, walking abroad at night for air,' she said. 'I was told that many are killed and stripped if they are seen, as they are weak and have no protection.'

'Who would attack you?' he said. 'One look at your sour

147

face and they'd know that you had vinegar enough to kill all contagion.'

Mary ignored him and prepared for bed, and by the time she drew the quilt over her Joseph was asleep. Mary pinched out the candle and stared up into the darkness. The City was silent and the river boats sounded far more than she had ever heard them when she worked for Lady Essex in the big house on the Strand. She smiled in the darkness and wondered what Joseph would say when he knew what she had done.

The big houses were either deserted or had perhaps one or at best two servants living in to care for them. Mary had met one in the inn where she had dinner and another in a shop near the bridge. That was a good and easy position to have but it was very poorly paid as the owners gave only board wages and none of the perquisites that were usual from well-stocked kitchens.

She had gone next to the magistrates and asked what they paid Searchers for their dangerous work, and had been pleasantly surprised.

'You can start today, Ma'am,' said one official. 'We have need of more than we can elect and you can have rooms and food beside your pay.'

'I want no infected rooms,' said Mary. 'I've heard that Searchers are given rooms where many have died and so catch the disease themselves. My husband and I are living in a clean loft in the mews behind the house where Sir Rollo FitzMedwin is imprisoned. If I can have a paper giving me permission to stay there, then I will come tomorrow to pick up my white staff.'

'You will come back?' asked the official anxiously. 'We have so few women of character who will do the work honestly and with good sense.' He saw the sober garments and the meek expression that belied the sharp eyes and thought of the contrast between this woman and the

148

drunken or half-mad trollops who were all that the authorities could now find.

'If I am better than the others, then I must have extras,' said Mary firmly.

'If you come, you shall oversee at least five of them and make sure that all goods belonging to the sick are secure.'

'Then I will come tomorrow,' said Mary. Five other houses to inspect when the Searchers had given their opinion as to the cause of death? It would make her fortune. A lifetime of making young servant girls feel worthless would stand her well in this. She remembered the cart that Christopher Verney had given them to take away all their things and it was like an act of Providence. For a while she toyed with the idea of Joseph using it and becoming a driver and bearer, but she knew that his horror of disease would never be overcome by greed and that he could not touch a dead body, leave alone a body riddled with pestilence.

Briefly, she wondered if he would stay with her now that she had made up her mind, but as she fell asleep, she was confident that he must stay or starve and he'd have to earn his keep by carting anything she found in the houses of the dead.

'And if you die, my fine buck, it will revenge me for your making free with other women.' That whey-faced wench Lottie *must* have been one of his whores, or why would Sam have beaten him? Perhaps the child was his . . .

149

Chapter 10

'I can find nothing!' snapped Edward Verney.

'You must be patient, my dear. We are trying to pack as fast as we can and we cannot hope to be ready by tomorrow if you interfere and ask for things that were packed in the first of the boxes.' Marian was flushed and hot and was fast losing her temper. It was bad enough to have the whole of her well-ordered life turned upside-down in a few days, but added to this was fear for her family, her servants and even for herself.

'I wonder if I should go into the City again,' said Edward, pacing the room in an irritating way.

'You promised me that you would not, Edward, and it wouldn't be fair to the girls if you risked anything now.' Marian looked reproachful. 'You forbade Christopher to visit his friends, so please stay here or he will think that he has made a sacrifice in vain.'

'What sacrifice does he make, Madam? He will have the run of a great estate and farm and enough sport for any gentleman.'

'He is a man now and needs to have feminine company,' said Marian.

'Actresses!' snorted Edward as if he in his youth had never waited cow-eyed for the scented hussies of the stage to come and sup with him. 'He can make do with fresher, country stock.'

'May I take the kittens, Mother?' asked Alice, pulling one of the mewling litter from her apron pocket. 'They will be welcome on the farm and if we leave them here, they will be caught and killed.'

'Leave them with Lottie,' said Marian. 'We can't rescue every animal in the house. We need all our space for clothes and food and it will be a tight squeeze for even one of the dogs.'

'Your uncle will have dogs and cats enough to feed without adding to them,' said Edward. He wondered how well he would get on with his wife's family if they all had to be together for more than a few weeks, and he wanted nothing to make his family unwelcome in any way. He strode from the room and went to the stables. 'Joseph?' he called, and then remembered that he had sent his coachman packing.

'Sir?' said Sam. He went on brushing the older of the black horses.

'Are you sure, Sam?' Edward Verney asked for the tenth time. 'I need you and I know that my wife will grieve if Lottie is left here and runs into any danger.'

'We shall be all right, Sir,' Sam grinned. 'You will see, I shall barely have the time to get this place cleaned up ready for when you come back. I doubt if Lottie will be delivered of the baby before you all return, and the young ladies will look on it as a holiday and no more.' He went on brushing and the dust fell in clouds. 'The streets get worse and I've never seen such dryness. When I went for hay, the stocks were low and I had to go further as the crop was so poor, but I have a man willing to deliver hay for the next two months and then we can go back to the usual dealers.'

'I hope you are right, Sam, but the Bills of Mortality

151

grow longer each week and the sights in the City are straight from Hell.'

'It must end soon, Sir.' The sounds of the steady brushing and the deep stolid voice were soothing. 'Most of your friends are gone and Miss Alice would be lonely if you stayed now.'

'Yes, I shall be glad to take Alice away,' said Edward. 'I was hoping to have company or at least an escort. The highwaymen on Hampstead are bad again and the footpads in Kensington grow bolder every day, or so I'm told.' He frowned. 'Captain Bennet would have come with us for at least a part of the way, I know. It would be good to have a Captain in His Majesty's Army to guard us but that is not to be as he has been called to Salisbury.'

There were other men, all victims of the charms of Alice or Anna who might have gone with them, but they, too, seemed to have vanished over the past few days. Edward smiled grimly. That jackanapes Sir Rollo FitzMedwin hadn't been of much use. He must have gone with the raffish set to join the Court as he had not shown his face over the past few days. Lady Marian made excuses for him but he was a coward and a braggart, thought her husband. Better at kissing a lady's hand than riding to protect them from villains.

Sam looked up and put down the brush and curry comb. 'I think I hear a horseman, Sir.' He rubbed his hands on the leather apron and went to the front of the house. Edward followed, hoping that this was not an important visitor as he was wearing only a plain white shirt and dark trousers and his wig was perched on its stand in his dressing room. Sam came back with a man leading his horse.

'Sir Vincent Clavell!' greeted Edward. With many men of rank, he would have felt at a disadvantage wearing such plain garments, but young Sir Vincent never seemed to dress extravagantly and wore his hair naturally even at the theatre. Edward eyed him, noting the slim figure and clear

152

eyes and wished that this man was the heir and not the third son of one of the richest and most respected titles in the Home Counties.

'I came to enquire of your health, Sir,' said the young man. 'I'm afraid that you had a shock when that rascal attacked you.'

'It was you who suffered the shock, Sir Vincent. I was well protected by your sword.' Sam took the horse and led him away and Edward urged his visitor to take some refreshment with him. 'Not that you may have more than a mug of ale and some cheese. We are all at odds, trying to be ready to leave for Surrey tomorrow.'

'Then I'll not hinder you.'

'You shall, my dear boy. My wife will want to thank you for your intervention and it will do the ladies good to see a fresh face and to leave their work for an hour.'

Sir Vincent followed him with a show of reluctance, but when Marian came out of the drawing room, brushing down her dress in an effort to appear as if she had been doing no more than tend the flowers, he was the soul of courtesy and kissed her hand as if it was perfumed with roses and not with the mothballs that she had placed in the boxes with the clothes.

Alice ran in wearing a lace shawl over a high comb, like a mantilla. 'Look, Mother,' she said, and pirouetted round the room until she saw that they were not alone.

'Oh, I beg your pardon, Sir,' she gasped in confusion, and ran out again.

'Miss Alice is like my sister,' said Sir Vincent, and he smiled indulgently. 'About the same age – fourteen? A child one minute and a woman the next.'

'Just fifteen, Sir.'

'Is she?' The young man looked pensive. 'Does she like the idea of being buried in the country? The times are bad for young ladies about to blossom and make their mark on society.'

'She would like to stay here but that is impossible,' said Marian. 'Two servants will remain to look after our interests and my husband's clerk will see to the business in the City but there would be no suitable person to care for Alice. Besides, with the Bills giving a total of over five thousand deaths in the Cities of London and Westminster this week, we can no longer stay and expose her to danger.'

They sat at the long oak table and ate a dinner of bread and cheese and boiled fowl. Kate joined them and made pleasant conversation and Anna came in with Alice who now blushed and sat quietly, as if ashamed that this man should have seen her playing the fool. Sir Vincent talked of life at Court and gradually, Alice forgot her shyness and began to ask questions. 'Do all the ladies of the Court travel with the King and Queen wherever they go?'

'They take it in turns,' Sir Vincent informed her. 'If a lady is summoned to be a lady-in-waiting or a woman of the bedchamber, she may not refuse. It is a Royal Command and would bring shame and even some penalties if the honour was refused.'

Edward frowned. 'Is there no way round it?'

'Father!' cried Alice in disgust. 'Who would want to avoid being a member of the Court? Just think of the wonderful entertainments and the clothes that they enjoy. If only I was old enough and important enough to be chosen.' She pouted. 'Who will see me if I live on a farm? Who will ever know that I live?'

'My sister lives in the country,' said Sir Vincent. 'I think not far from where you will be staying. She is fourteen but nearly fifteen and would like your company, Miss Alice.' Alice smiled. 'She is a little like you,' he went on. 'She has fair hair and a delightful smile and a lot of spirit.' He looked at Marian. 'May I send word to my mother that you will be neighbours and would value a call?'

'That is very kind, Sir Vincent. It will be good to make new friends as well as to visit many who have moved away

154

from the City.' Marian was flattered. The Earl of Lamark had a very prominent place in society and any contact that Alice could have with his family must be advantageous to her future.

'And will you be there, Sir Vincent?' asked Anna.

'Not for a while.' He shrugged. 'It isn't only the ladies who are commanded to attend Court. I am back from sea and have to make my Obedience to the King at Salisbury.' He pushed away his platter and Edward sensed that he was not anxious to go to the Court.

'Then you may see Captain Bennet,' said Marian. 'He is another who has deserted us. I had hoped for his company on the road until we are clear of the out-parishes and danger, but it was not to be.'

Her guest nodded. 'I know him and hope to meet him when I am free from my duties.' He gave a wry smile. 'We shall console each other for the time spent away from our real work.'

'Do you love the sea?' asked Anna.

'It is a good life for a young man if he is above decks, but a poor one for the wretches we press into service,' said Sir Vincent.

'And were you in the Battle of Lowestoft?' said Alice. She giggled. 'Did your ship sink and so make you come ashore?'

'No, we didn't lose our ship but it did suffer some damage and is being refitted.'

'Were you hurt?' Her mood changed and her eyes widened with concern.

'A little, but it is over,' he said smiling, and Alice dropped her gaze before his quizzical eyes. If he would only dress like a courtier then he could look handsome, she thought, and he was not a mere clerk after all.

'May I give your regards to Captain Bennet?' he asked, and was looking at Anna as he spoke.

155

'I'm sure that we all wish him well.' she said demurely. 'As we wish you, Sir.'

Marian rose from her chair and Anna followed her. 'I hope we meet again soon,' said Marian.

'Very soon, Ma'am. I would like to put myself and my sword at your service tomorrow when you leave. I can ride by your carriage as far as the good road beyond Kensington. I believe that most of the danger lies close to the City and that once you are clear, the grassy lanes being dry, you can make good progress.'

'I'm grateful, my boy,' said Edward. 'It will give me a chance to get used to driving again. Christopher will take the coach and I shall drive the curricle and we leave the smaller carriage with Sam and Lottie to keep safe until our return.'

Sir Vincent nodded and bent over Lady Marian's hand. He turned to Kate. 'Do you like the idea of living away from London?' he asked and seemed to hold her hand a long time while she replied.

'It doesn't matter, Sir,' she said sadly. 'My family fill my life and I am happy to be with them.'

'We must make sure that you have some amusement,' he said, and Alice felt an emotion that was strange. He's only the same age as Kate, she thought resentfully. He's much too young for her. What does he offer *me* for amusement? His sister who is a child! Younger than me by four months!

'And you, Miss Alice,' he said as if she was a polite afterthought. 'On my father's estate you will find many ponies suited to your height and needs and many young animals that are amusing.'

'Thank you, Sir,' she said with dignity. 'I think I have outgrown puppies.'

Edward hid a smile. She was a sweet little minx and it was time to take her away from London. He went with his

156

visitor to the stables where Sam had the horse ready, cool and calm beside the carriage horses.

'If you need to change employ . . .' began Sir Vincent, with a laugh.

'Others have tried to rob me of Sam,' said Edward complacently. 'Lord Carnegie wanted him for his stud and tried to get him to stay when he was at Lord Chalwood's a while ago.'

'Carnegie?' Sir Vincent looked solemn. 'I advise you, Sir, to keep your young ladies away from his friends. Some of them are sober enough but Rollo FitzMedwin and Richard Routh are dangerous.' He flushed. 'I should not say this as they are friends of my family insofar as they are distantly related and our fathers know each other, but I am glad that my sister is safe in the country and cannot come within the lecherous intentions of those two.' He spoke with passion and turned away to the driveway. 'Take care of Alice,' he said. 'She is worth more than that.'

Why Alice? thought Edward as he watched the young man ride away. He shrugged. Sir Vincent had a sister like Alice, so naturally, he was protective.

'Sam,' he called, and they went on with the business of trying to get six boxes in where only four would fit comfortably. 'I've told my wife that she can't take everything in her press and as for the girls, I never knew that women had so many fripperies.' But at last, everything was strapped tightly to the coach and on the roof and the smaller packages were ready to put inside, containing items they would need for an overnight stay at an inn.

Lottie came with rugs. 'You may need them if the nights are cold and you can find no beds.' She bit her lip. 'I haven't told my lady this, but I heard that many trying to leave London are refused help in the villages lest they carry plague. I have packed a big basket of food and drink in case you have difficulty, Sir.' She dragged the heavy basket along to the coach and Sam took it from her.

'There's no call for you to lift things, Lottie,' he said. The mound in her abdomen was firm and getting higher each day and she still had the bloom of health in her cheeks and the softness of pregnancy. Sam eyed her with devotion and treated her with care. Now that the family were leaving life would be easy and she could rest more until the baby was born. He hated to see Mr and Lady Verney leave but if they must go, then this was the best time for Lottie, and as they stood at the door, waving, the next morning, he was thankful that life had treated them so well. Lottie was in tears and so was Alice. They clung together and promised to write as often as the stage could carry letters, even though they both knew that most of the hired coaches were off the road in fear of the plague.

Sir Vincent Clavell rode with them along the Oxford Road to Tyburn and beyond and gradually the dirt of the City was far behind them and fresh fields stretched before them.

Grass was parched and the way was rutted but out in the open there was little cover for footpads, and the notorious hiding place of highwaymen was safely passed. Edward stopped the coach and refused to let Sir Vincent go with them further. 'You have enough travelling to do to reach Salisbury. I insist that you go back and rest until you leave tomorrow.'

'Your servant, Sir. My lady.' The young man bared his head and turned away, spurring his horse and not looking back.

'He never looks back,' grumbled Alice. 'Doesn't he want to know if we will miss him?'

'And will you miss him?' asked Anna, smiling.

'No. He thinks I am a child,' said Alice and hugged the kitten that she had hidden in her pocket until they were far enough from the house to produce it in safety.

'And you, of course, are quite grown up,' said Anna, still smiling.

'I am older than his sister,' retorted Alice, determined that she wouldn't like any girl who was forced on her as a friend.

Edward urged his horses to go faster as the gap between the coach and the curricle was growing wider every minute. 'Christopher' he called. 'Not so fast. The coach is over-laden and the horses will sweat.' The wheels crunched the dry earth and dipped into the deep ruts that in wet weather would have made the going slow and treacherous.

He slackened speed. 'I want to go with Christopher,' whined Alice. It had been amusing at first, travelling in the coach and imagining that she was being carried off to Spain or France or one of the exciting places she had heard about from her father's business friends, but now she was cramped and hot and the kitten had scratched her hands in an effort to escape.

'You will stay where you are, Miss,' said Edward. 'Christopher is our guard and must have speed and the ability to turn without having screaming females tugging at his arm.'

'Do you think we might be attacked, Father?' Alice leaned forward and saw that her brother had a long musket and pistols beside him on the driver's seat. She looked at the innocent summer hedgerows and the breeze stirring the leaves of the beechwoods. Roses over cottage doorways shed pink and white blossom on the yellow grass and in distant meadows cattle moaned softly. She wriggled into a more comfortable position and dreamed that she was captured by a handsome highwayman. He would surely not harm her but be overcome by her beauty and leave her with her jewels and money, content just to kiss her hand.

She woke with a start to find the kitten licking her hand where it had been scratched. It was hot as the sun rose high and the girl was thirsty.

'Stop when you see shade and water!' shouted Edward, and a few minutes later Christopher drew up under a group of trees on common land. A small stream ran by and it was clear and pure compared to the water that the City had used during the drought. 'We'll eat our dinner here and then drive on for another few miles before we find shelter for the night. We can't press the horses too far in this heat and over such ground.'

Christopher led the horses to the brook and tipped a pile of hay for them in the shade, knowing that they would not stray even if he didn't hobble them. 'I respect the stage-coach drivers now,' he said. 'It's bad enough making way in these conditions but to drive a heavy and tall coach with much more baggage and many more passengers than we have must test a man's skill to the utmost.'

'You travel light, my son,' said Edward, stretching his tired arms. 'It's a long time since I sat up there and I must say I wouldn't like to do it often. How many stops do you think we need?'

'Sam made Eton in two days, resting his horse overnight, and of course when he came back he stayed at the Chalwood estate, so the horses rested well.' Christopher drank from a flagon of cider and reached over for a pie that Marian was setting on a cloth on the grass. 'But remember, Father, he was alone in the small coach which is fairly well-sprung and had no great mass of baggage.'

'You think we should take longer?' Edward was disappointed. The journey was becoming monotonous and he was very hot. Alice was getting restive and the other ladies looked pale with the heat.

'When do they expect us at Dunstan Manor?' asked Kate.

'I had word that we can go there any day this week and that they are ready for us,' said Marian. She sighed and dipped her kerchief into the cool water. As she bathed her temples, she smiled. 'This is the worst part, Alice. Soon, you will have a room again and the freedom of the farm. This heat will seem less fierce in the country,' she added, though without much conviction as she had seldom felt the

160

heat as much as she did now. The shade was wonderful and the horses seemed quite fresh after two hours' rest, so the men harnessed them again with the help of Kate and Anna, who were glad to do something other than sitting in a hot coach and trying to look cool.

Alice picked wild flowers and chased the kitten among the trees, until everything was ready and the remains of the food were safely packed away again. 'Come along,' called Edward. 'Alice, there is no more time for play.'

'I wasn't playing,' she said. 'The kitten needed exercise.'

'Well, pick it up and get into the carriage,' said Edward testily. He had pinched his thumb between two pieces of harness and knew that a black blood-blister would give him trouble for days.

Kate and Marian climbed into the coach and waited for Alice to join them. 'What now?' demanded Marian, as Alice disappeared into the trees.

'I can't find her,' said Alice. 'I've lost Kittie.'

'S'death!' Edward swore under his breath. 'Find it or leave it. We go in five minutes.'

'I can't leave it. A wild animal would kill her and eat her.'

'We left all the wild animals in London, my dear. Cats have nine lives and this one will manage very well on fieldmice and water.'

'Father, you have no heart,' said Alice, who was close to tears. 'The poor little thing would have no chance here. There are foxes and stoats and who knows what else in these woods at night. Owls and . . .'

'Oh, go and look for it, Christopher, or we'll be drowned in tears,' said Edward. 'We must get on.' He glanced up at the sun and hoped they could find a village soon where they could relax and eat well and have beds for the night.

Kate joined the search and Alice beat the bushes with a stick to drive the kitten out if she was hiding. Suddenly,

161

Christopher gave a shout and laughed. 'Wash your hands in the stream, Alice. She was asleep under the coach.'

'Now can we go, Miss?' Edward was annoyed. He had eaten well and the cool water had been a blessing, but now he was as hot as ever and knew that he couldn't drive far again that day.

'Shall I take the coach?' suggested Christopher, who saw that his father was flagging.

'No, I couldn't fire a shot in anger, Son. My eyes aren't as sharp as yours and I'd see no danger until it was too late. I can manage and Kate can take a turn later if we have to go further than I fancy.'

Christopher looked anxious. 'Then we must stop soon and find an inn.' He smiled. 'What does it matter if we are gypsies for another day, Father?' He squinted up at the sky. 'At least we have no chance of rain.'

'Why does no one wave to us in passing?' asked Alice as they saw another woman stare and run inside her cottage as the coach passed by.

'They see very few along here,' said Edward, but he knew that this wasn't true. This had been one of the fastest and busiest stage routes before they were stopped for the duration of the plague. He recalled the same people running out to sell fruit as the coaches paused on the rise of the hill. They would buy from the pedlars who sat on the roof and some even begged or offered beds for the night for travellers who were tired or queasy from the motion of the vehicle.

He whipped up the horses, feeling ill-at ease. To fear the many highwaymen and footpads was normal, but this dread of infection was something he couldn't fight with guns or offers of money. The inkeepers would have more business sense unless they wished to starve, and anyone could see that the coach belonged to a gentleman and his family. Indeed, with the coat-of-arms of Lady Marian's

162

family on the doors, who could suspect them of carrying contagion?

In the distance were the first gentle slopes of the Surrey hills, but they had never seemed so far away as the weary party viewed the scene and wanted only to find a village or a hamlet with a few houses with rooms to spare. Smoke from a chimney showed life in the valley and they made towards it. Dogs barked and Alice clutched at the trembling kitten which had heard them, too. A man with cows prodded them through a gap in a hedge and into a yard for milking.

'We can have fresh milk,' said Alice. 'For us and for Kittie.'

Christopher dropped the reins and jumped down, leaving Edward high on the lane in case there was no resting-place here. The heavy coach was difficult to turn and any deviation from the route was inadvisable unless they were certain of being accepted.

'The man is running to get a milk bucket,' said Alice, with satisfaction. 'I have not had milk fresh from a cow since we visited that farm last year, Mother. Do you think they make their own cheese, too?'

'The devil he is!' cried Edward, in alarm. Christopher was backing away and now ran to his curricle. A blast of stones and old nails was fired into the air from an ancient fire-arm and Christopher had to seize his horses' reins to stop them bolting with the carriage.

Christopher led the frightened animals up to the other coach and sat on the grass, panting.

'Are you hurt?' Marian climbed down and bent over him.

'No,' he said. 'Only shaken. There's no rest here,' he added grimly. 'They think we are plague carriers from London and wouldn't listen to anything I had to say.' He picked himself up and dusted off his clothes. 'I can understand them,' he admitted.

163

'I shall go to the Constable,' said Edward. 'They are no better than murderers.'

'I doubt if you would find anyone ready to act for you, Father,' said Christopher sensibly. 'Think. If a man came to your house and you suspected that he had the plague, what would *you* do?'

'I'd have the rascal . . .'

'Flogged or worse? These are only protecting their own, too.' Christopher climbed back to his seat. 'Make up your minds that we might have that reception again, so keep back whenever we meet people and leave the asking to me.'

'You'll be armed the next time,' said Edward.

'No, Father. If they saw a pistol, we might be in trouble. I saw another man at a window with a pistol at that farm and I think he would have shot me if I hadn't turned tail. These are dangerous times and we must be as we truly are, innocent travellers, or we could all be killed.'

'I want no fighting,' said Marian. 'Better we sleep in a field than to be harmed.'

'You might have to do that, Mother,' said Christopher.

'I hate spiders,' said Alice. 'Things creep about in the night and bite people.'

'If that is all you have to bear, Miss, then you are indeed fortunate,' said her father, but he saw that the whole party was unnerved. 'It will not come to that. Over the next hill there is a village with a fine inn. They will not act as those savages did. We shall laugh about this tomorrow.'

The sun glanced sideways at the ripening wheat and over the stream below the hill. A glow that was warm and rosy made the dusty coaches glint and Alice felt drowsy. If they had known where to sleep, this would have been a pleasant time, less hot, and with the countryside peacefully beautiful. Edward wondered if his arms were still in their sockets as he followed Christopher past one village which was tightly shut up, through another that had one child running back to a cottage where the door was slammed after him, and past a farm where only the animals showed any sign of life.

It was as if a messenger went before them, carrying the news of their arrival. Edward saw birds flying and wondered if pigeons were the messengers. Dovecots full of soft-breasted birds graced every cottage eaves and could well be used. His mouth watered. A brace of plump pigeons roasted on a spit with fresh bread and ale would serve them well. He was hungry and very tired, with a weariness that was not wholly physical. Would this time of trial never come to an end?

Christopher gave a cry. Ahead in the twilight was a light and the outline of a big house. As they came closer, they could see that this was the inn that Edward knew well, and had used before on the stage-coach journeys.

'Stay with the ladies. I will go this time. They know me well,' said Edward. He pulled at his shirt and wished that he looked more presentable. He made sure that he had a purse of money ready and walked firmly to the door.

It was fast shut when he tried the latch and he banged on the wood in an authoritative manner. Inside, a dog barked but no other sound came to him. He banged again and shouted, 'I am Mr Edward Verney. I am no robber! You know me well. I have used this inn many times and have found your welcome warm.'

Still no sound but the shuffling of feet. Edward stood back and looked up at the shuttered windows. A small gap appeared with a light behind it.

'Go away. We want no plague here.'

'We are clean and tired and will pay well for rooms for the night.'

'You came from London?'

'Not the City or from Westminster,' said Edward. 'We have no plague where we live.'

'Then why leave like rats from a ship?' the man said, and someone behind him laughed. 'If it's so grand in your mansion, there is no need to trouble poor country folk who want only to be left in peace.'

'You are an innkeeper and yet you refuse help to genuine travellers who have money to pay?' said Edward scathingly. 'The law says that you *must* serve us.'

'And does the law say we have to bring the plague into our beds? Does it say we have to see our children die?'

'My good fellow,' began Edward. 'If you will not let us in, then all we ask is food and drink. We can eat here', he added desperately. 'My good man, you *must* give us something.'

'We'll give you something, all right!'

The window opened more and Edward stepped back hastily as the contents of an evil-smelling pail swooshed down over his shirt. He spluttered and ran back to the coach and the window above slammed shut.

'My dear!' said Marian helplessly. Edward shook his head and the foul droplets scattered.

'Come Father, you must bathe in the stream,' said Kate firmly. 'Who knows what was in that pail?' She led him to the bottom of the hill and he stripped naked. Kate pushed the shirt and trousers into a bush and was glad that he had worn so little. Marian rummaged in a bag for fresh clothes and after the first shock of the cold water, Edward felt clean and refreshed. Christopher eyed him with envy and took off his clothes for a plunge into the pool hollowed out of the gravel, and when they were dry, the moon had risen and chased away the daylight.

'Well, we have no bed and only the food we brought,' said Kate. 'Over there, I noticed a barn that can't be seen from the inn or from that farm. We must find somewhere and that is the best we can do.'

Marian hugged her youngest daughter. 'You wanted adventure, my dearest, and now we are gypsies.' Anna took the kitten which was now exhausted and fast asleep and

166

shut her in a basket, covered by a cloth tied at the corners. At least that was one less bother, she thought.

The barn loomed dark and forbidding but Kate had candles and soon they found clean straw and some wood for a fire. From the gloom came a snowy owl which hooted disapproval at the sudden light and fled on silent wings to hunt.

Christopher came from the well outside with a bucket of water for the horses and then settled down with the others to eat what was left of the food they had brought.

'We must leave enough bread for the morning,' warned Kate. 'Eat the rest of the pies or they will go bad and leave things that will keep, like cheese and bread and ale and smoked fish. We have enough left for at least another day,' she stated cheerfully, and even Alice didn't grumble when she was securely wrapped in one of the rugs that Lottie had put ready in case they were needed.

'Dear Lottie,' said Marian. 'How I shall miss her.'

'Not for long, Lady Marian,' said Anna. 'We shall be back before her baby is born.' It was a comforting thought. There were all the books she had never read in the library at home and people with the same interests as she had. Captain Bennet came into her thoughts again and again. He doesn't like me and yet he studies as I do and takes time to send me books. She sighed. He was correct in everything he did and showed interest in her because it was the polite way of men of breeding. If he sends books, he will never send me flowers, she thought, and wondered why it made her sad. With my name, no captain of His Majesty's Army will ever look at me as Sir Rollo does, she decided.

Chapter 11

The sound of oars and the shouts of watermen came
through the shutters of the upstairs windows of the house
near Whitefriars Stairs; the silence of the other buildings
that belonged to the great names of London, Dorset House
which was close, and further away the huge mansions of
Lady Essex and other noble families who had left for
country estates while the plague raged, was even more
pronounced now that all street vendors were mute.

Sir Rollo FitzMedwin stirred on the wide four-poster
bed and pushed away the coverings. Was it day or night?
He had been asleep and yet he dimly recalled seeing figures.
First he had seen his servants, staring at him as if they saw
a ghost; his new driver, looking white and fearful and
shouting for the other servants to come to see to the Master.

Rollo shook his head to rid it of the ache and the lost
hours. Then he remembered the hiss of indrawn breath as
his housekeeper spoke softly. 'The pestilence,' she had
said, and there was a flurry of movement and nobody would
give him the water his body craved.

Then came silence, with distant hurrying as if some were
packing boxes and leaving. He had left the bed, almost
crawling to the ewer on the washstand and in his eagerness
to drink had spilled most of it over his shirt, soaking it.

It was cooling and yet sent him shivering back to bed in

the heat of the room. Hot and cold, sleep and nightmares came and went without really awakening him, until he became aware of a new sound. Footsteps on the wooden stairs and coarse laughter, and by now he was hot again even with his wet shirt. The old woman who entered his bedchamber might have been a part of the nightmare and the white staff she carried might have belonged to a witch for all he knew, but she was real enough when she bent over him and he smelled the drink on her breath.

'A pretty lad,' she said. 'A very pretty lad with many nice things that he'll leave behind.' She laughed and the cackling was of unholy crows that wait for the dying to be still.

'Then is it the plague?' said a man's voice. 'The driver called me when I was taking two corpses from the house over the way.'

'You'll be needed here before long, but until he dies, tell the magistrate that the watcher must look to this one, too.'

'I'll do that when I report back and I'll add this one to your tally, Mistress.'

'But I'll collect my own fee,' she said hastily. 'He's rich enough to pay a nurse.'

'There isn't one to be found from here to Cripplegate and not a coffin in the whole of London. I'll tell the guard to bring chains for the doors.'

Sir Rollo tried to sit up. 'I want water,' he said. 'My head aches and my eyes are dim.'

'If I give you water, you'll die, Sir. The cold makes you shocked and then the Almighty takes you.'

'Water, I say!' he cried.

'Poor young man,' the Searcher said. 'He is out of his mind, and see the sweat soaking his shirt, and he is hot.'

'There are no tokens as yet,' said the Bearer of the Dead.

'Some never have them and some die as they form, while others who have several recover. It is never certain,' the woman said.

'I haven't got the plague!' Rollo sat up and tried to get out of bed. His head swam and his eyes felt as if hot balls of iron were pushing out through the irises. 'I'm sick but not of the plague, woman! Bring me water and fresh clothes and send my servants to me.'

'They have fled, Sir. Now rest quietly and the guard will bring you all you need if you send down money in this basket.'

'All gone? I don't believe you. My housekeeper must be here.'

'The coachman took a small carriage piled up with things and there were four people in the carriage.'

'The devil there was,' said Rollo weakly. He sank back, feeling sick, and when he opened his eyes again, the two had gone. His head was aching less now and with difficulty he used the night-pail and drank some more water. He had no idea how he had come to be in bed nor how long he had been there. The coach had been devilish hot and the driver had brought him here at a pace that nearly threw him from the seat. And then? Somehow he had come to bed, with or without help, and had been hot and cold and aching ever since.

Later, when the sun had gone and only the lights from the torches of link-men showed between the cracks in the shutters, he moved with more assurance. His legs felt weak but his nausea had gone and he felt empty.

'Martha!' he shouted. The old crone had said she was gone, but he couldn't believe it. He dragged on a gown and lit a candle before groping his way to the door. In his own house, he had never ventured as far as the kitchen and it took several attempts to find it. He clung to the stair-rail and paused to listen on the way down and heard the sound that everyone dreaded. *'Bring out your dead'*.

In the hall, he was confronted by his own pale reflection. The staring eyes and dishevelled hair made him start. He put down the candle and lit two more. He regarded himself in the mirror and with increasing dread opened his shirt-front and examined his chest for signs of the plague. He felt under his armpits but there was nothing but sweat and hair and in his groin were no signs of swelling.

If I have the plague then it doesn't show and I feel better, he thought. He took the candle and found the kitchen and saw that a meal had been prepared and left uneaten. It was still fresh enough to be appetising even though the fire had gone out in the range and he had to eat the lamb-broth cold.

Strengthened, he found ale and brandy and took both back to bed with him, after inspecting the larder and seeing that there was cheese and bread and cold meat to last for a day or so.

At midnight, he looked down from the window and hailed the guard. The man looked up. 'Get back to bed, Sir,' he called. 'Go to sleep.'

'I am not ill,' shouted Rollo. 'I am not infected and I want to be let out!'

'The Searcher has set her seal on your door and you must stay there for forty days before you can be said to be whole.'

'I am not ill, I tell you. Let me out, you wretch!'

'Poor soul. You must rest, Sir. 'Tis part of it, Sir, this restless raving.'

'Let me out! Let me out! I command you to let me out!' said Rollo, with a growing sense of panic.

'Now if you are quiet and send down money, I can buy what you need and it might keep up your strength, but if you shout like that, there'll be some who would come in and finish you. I wouldn't do it, but there are many on the streets who would overcome me and get to you. You don't want your fine house stripped, do you?'

'If I die, the Devil can take it all,' said Rollo. 'Buy me fresh bread in the morning and cooked fowl, and take some for your first draught of the day.' He flung down a coin

171

which the man picked up with tongs and put in a jar of vinegar, and it was at that moment that Sir Rollo Fitz-Medwin, man of wealth and influence, knew that he was forsaken, untouchable and likely to die.

He went back to bed and slept fitfully until morning, when a knocking on the door made him go to the window.

'I put your food in the basket, Sir. Pull it up before I hand over to the day guard.'

Rollo hauled it up and found that it was all fresh and well-cooked and that he had not been swindled. He set about the food with a healthy appetite and became more and more convinced that he did not have the pestilence.

He looked down at the new man who stood with a halberd by his side. He looked a rogue, thought Rollo and decided not to trust him to buy anything. His mind worked well now and he recalled the day before he was ill. He had been on the river with his head uncovered and in his desire to see Anna Maria Ruyter, had stayed in the open as his boat followed the one on which the Verneys travelled. The ladies had wide hats and the gentlemen had periwigs and hats, both discarded by Rollo as hot and impeding, but a safe shield against the dazzling sun that beat down on the river and reflected back again to double its intensity.

'A touch of the sun!' he said, in disgust. A footman travelling on the back of his coach had once collapsed with it after a hard ride in the middle of July, and had been ill for two days, but it was recognised to be the sunstroke and nothing more serious. Rollo pictured his new coachman and hoped that he died of the plague! The fool, to panic and send for the Searcher before he found out what was wrong. And the housekeeper? What was she about? But all his mind-searching did little to solve the immediate problem. He could really be shut up for forty days and nights if he couldn't escape.

Escape? Rollo went down and tried all the doors and lower windows but they were locked and chained from the outside. He couldn't even go into the yard or to the stables, and they were at the back of the house away from any help he could get from a passerby. He shook the doors but knew that they were firm. He tried all the windows above stairs but when he looked down there was only one window where escape could have been possible, over the low porch at the front door below which the guard rested from the sun.

He changed his clothes and brushed his hair and felt as if he was back to normal health. He noticed that several valuables were missing from the dining room and smiled grimly as he pictured the revenge he would have on his servants once he brought them back from the magistrates.

It was time to plan and he must make his escape good. If he was seen to go by any who thought he had the plague, he would be seized and bound and taken to the pest-house or shot if he was violent. Rollo packed a small bag with clothes that he would need on a journey of two or three days and put a basket ready in which he would carry food. Once he got away, he could keep to the side roads and not ask for help in the villages. He could go to Carnegie or any of his friends in Surrey or beyond until he could sort out his future movements.

From time to time, he watched from the windows and saw that the day guard went from one front door to another of four houses, each with the red cross on the door, but he was never out of sight and it would have been impossible to slide down on to the sloping porch roof unobserved and get to the stables for a horse, *if* those villains had left any.

On the third night, he called to the guard. 'What of my horses?' he shouted. 'They will starve if they are not fed and watered.'

'They are being cared for, Sir. A couple came and offered to look after them if I let them sleep in your loft.'

So that meant there were two horses, and one of the carriages. Rollo watched again and the night guard sat in the porch with a torch above his head and one in a stand by the wall. It was too well-lit to move now so he went to bed heavy with misery and boredom. He thought of Anna and longed to touch her. He tried to imagine what she would be like in bed and could not see her there. She was the untouchable, not he, and yet she must become soft and yielding and his to possess if he was to have any happiness. All the trollops he had bedded faded from his fantasies and were nothing. He even examined his body for signs of the clap and was relieved to see that the slight infection he had once had was gone and he was clean.

'A miracle! I need a miracle,' he said aloud. Thirty-five days more in this prison would kill him quicker than the plague.

The day guard was there again and when the plague cart came, in daylight now as well as at night because there were bodies stacked with no pits dug to hold them and few Bearers left, the house along the street gave up two more corpses and when the Bearer went in, the guard followed and came out carrying a box of clothes. The door was sealed and Rollo knew that there were no more alive in that house. Two houses left to guard and less chance of him escaping as the man had less to oversee.

The next day, Rollo sat in his bedroom above the porch and made a rope of sheets and another of hempen twine he had found in the store. In this one he made a noose that slipped easily when he had dipped it in oil. The day guard sat in the open as if he was cold, and he didn't make any attempt to try the doors or shout up to the windows. At five in the afternoon, he collapsed in the street and when the cart came, he was hooked up on to it without comment from the Bearer.

With rising excitement, Rollo waited for the night watcher and made sure that all the doors and windows were locked from the inside. If he could escape, he would make sure that the house was sealed from within so that no looters

174

could enter. He stood by the window and noticed that the man was puzzled.

'The other man went away early. He was sick,' called Rollo.

'The plague?' The man seem unconcerned. 'It takes many in the street, and I think he went into infected houses. I'll report it in the morning.' He settled down with a flagon of ale and some cheese and Rollo waited for dark and silence. He ate a good meal and dressed well but soberly, showing that he was a gentleman but with nothing to attract attention. He listened and heard drunken laughter coming from the alley leading to his stables. It faded with the banging of a door and he smiled. If the rascals that took his loft were drunk, so much the better.

The man at the door yawned. This one lasted well and maybe didn't even have the plague, but he was generous and forty nights here would do him nicely, thank you. The brandy he had recommended was good and strong and enough to keep the Devil at bay, with the ale to chase it down.

'Hey there,' called Rollo, softly. The man stumbled to his feet and went out far enough to see the man in the window above him. The light from the torch shone down and made shadows. He peered upwards.

'Too late to buy anything. I'll go as soon as it is light,' he said.

'I want you to have this,' said Rollo. 'In case I feel worse tomorrow. Bring me more wine and more roasted pigeons.' He flung coins to the ground and the man bent to pick them up. As he rose, the noose slipped over his head and tightened. A muffled grunt and a brief struggle made everything easy and when he was dead, Rollo let down the rope and swung down, pulling the end to bring the whole rope down from round the bedpost. He set the bundles on the ground and wrapped the watchman in a sheet, then propped him in the doorway for collection.

In the distance, the death cart came, with the torchbearer at the head and the red staff of the Bearer after him. The bell tolled and the sad cry went up again and again as each alley was reached and each harvest of corpses was gleaned. Rollo went softly along the alley to the stables sword in hand, but there was no sound. He nearly tripped over a bucket of lime wash and smiled to himself.

A few minutes later, the red cross on the door was replaced by a white one and the care that Mary Creed had shown for her new home was appreciated as Rollo put the bucket back where he had found it.

A horse whinnied and he paused, but no candlelight appeared in the loft. Rollo led the horses to the great yellow coach that was in the back of the yard and hitched them up, thankful that he was as skilled as any groom in such matters. The animals seemed in good heart and he silently thanked whoever was caring for them. He put his bundles in the coach and made sure that his money belt was secure then led the horses slowly to the lane and held his breath. Surely someone would hear? He reached the end of the lane and jumped up to the box, taking the reins with eager hands, and as Mary Creed woke and tried to rouse her drunken husband, the horses gathered speed and the coach swayed out into the Strand and off to the West.

'Joseph! Wake up.' Mary Creed shook the man who lay beside her, snoring. He grunted and coughed and turned over, away from the urgent hand. 'Wake up, Husband. I heard something.'

'Owls,' muttered Joseph. 'Leave me be, woman. It's the middle of the night when there is nothing on the streets but the sick from the pest-houses and the death cart.'

'It wasn't on the street, or not at first. Someone has been in the stables. I heard wheels on the cobbles and the horses trampling.'

'If they've stolen anything, we can't see until it's light,'

176

said Joseph, grumbling and feeling to see if his head was still firmly fixed where it should be.

'I heard wheels, I tell you,' she insisted. 'They may have stolen our cart and then what will I do when I bring home bundles?'

'Nobody but the guard on the street knows that we are here and have a cart,' said Joseph, but he was slowly gathering his wits. 'There is a night-watcher as well as a day one and they are all rogues. He could have taken our cart and concealed it in an alley to take when he goes home.'

'Go now! I'll light the lantern and you get dressed, Joseph. If he has hidden it close to the house, you can find it.'

Grumbling and cursing Mary, the night prowler and Sir Rollo FitzMedwin for being ill and not able to help them, Joseph dragged on a coat over his nightgown and took the lantern. He also clutched a heavy stick and wished that he had drunk less the night before. The darkness in the lane, made heavier by the overhang of trees, was stabbed only lightly by the yellow beam of the lantern. The moon was hidden by a flurry of vaporous cloud and he walked cautiously to the stables. Inside, he lit another lantern and held it high. The nag that Christopher Verney had given them was still there, viewing the light without curiosity. Joseph went on to the next stall and found the door wide open and the soiled straw still warm.

The next door was open too and with slow steps he went to the back of the yard. The cart was there as he had left it but the huge yellow coach with the coat-of-arms on the doors had gone, leaving a patch of earth where weeds grew in the shade it had given. He bolted the stable doors and went back to Mary.

'Is the cart gone?' she asked and he wondered how he had ever married this woman with the greedy eyes and avaricious mouth. If he had been able to come back to bed and take comfort in soft warm arms, none of this would seem important.

'No, it's there and the nag we brought with us.'

'What then? I swear I heard the horses.'

'The carriage is gone and the two horses,' said Joseph. 'Make sure that whoever took it didn't stay here. No one could hide that in a back alley until light.'

'You must go to the guard and ask if he saw anything,' said Mary. 'Go now! He will be gone in the morning and another man will be there.'

'Devil take you, Mary!'

'If we don't try to get it back, then Sir Rollo or his relatives will say that we stole it,' said Mary. Her eyes glinted with anger. 'If we'd thought, we could have sold it for a good sum and said it was stolen. Even the magistrates have had to buy carts to use for the dead as there are none left to hire and any they tried to buy on the open market were sold to the highest bid. With so few wheelwrights left alive, even that was difficult.'

'How do you know?' asked Joseph scornfully.

'I spoke to a very important official,' said Mary complacently.

'When was this?' he asked, with growing suspicion.

'I told you, I keep my eyes and ears open, Joseph. Now get along to the guard and ask what he saw.' Joseph just surfacing after a drunken evening was unpredictable, Mary knew, and she decided that her news could wait until she had him in his usual submissive role. 'I'll trim the candle for you and then the light will be better. When you come back, I'll have something nice for you,' she wheedled. When you hear my news, my beauty, you'll not want your Mary close to you again, she thought, knowing his fear of the plague.

In many ways it would be a relief to sleep alone, but it would lessen her power over him if he no longer wanted even occasional pleasure with her.

Joseph peered at her through the dim light. She was up to something. It was only when she wanted something or needed to tell him news that he wouldn't welcome that she offered herself, but who was he to refuse when there was little opportunity now to find women clean enough and free of the sickness?

He picked up the lantern and went out into the lane. Over by the river were lights and the sound of boatmen shouting. There was a splash and Joseph didn't go further. It might be a body taken from a ship and slipped into the river at night to prevent the vessel from being sealed, and let her go away on the tide as if she was not carrying the plague. He shielded the light with his hand. It could be the pressmen come to take whoever walked at night if he had no tokens of the plague on him. The navy was short of good strong men for the fleet that had once more faced the Dutch and this time had lost many ships and men. He hurried to the front of the house.

The lantern showed little until he came close to each house. A torch burned over one doorway but no guard sat beneath it. Joseph went on, past the red crosses on the doors and over to the house where Sir Rollo was imprisoned. There were two bodies which he avoided, one under the torchlight and one in the doorway of this house. The hairs at the back of his neck crawled as Joseph saw the tightly-wrapped bundle in its winding-sheet. Could this be the young buck who swaggered over London so full of sex and aggression? Did life end here for all of them?

Joseph held up the lantern and saw that instead of the red cross on the door, this one had a bold white cross that still dripped lime wash. He grinned. It could mean one of two things. Either Sir Rollo had bribed the watchman to let him go and had taken the coach with him, or the guard must have stolen it and gone away. Joseph looked at the corpse and knew that Rollo was dead. There had been no other person in the house. The poor devil, thought Joseph, without real feeling. He tried the door but found it locked on the inside. So the guard had taken out the body and locked everything, taking the keys with him. The white cross would allow him to come back and enter; to take whatever he wanted from the house. That must be what had happened. Rollo was dead and the guard had stolen the coach.

'He saw nothing,' said Joseph, when he returned to the loft. It was too late to do anything now and Mary had promised. Let it rest until morning, when her agile brain would tease out the puzzle. He didn't mention the body by the door or the absence of the guard, but rolled over on to the woman and used her roughly until he had the satisfaction of hearing her cry out, and his lust was spent.

That's the last time, thought Mary, as Joseph turned away and fell asleep again almost at once. With the horses gone, there would be more room for her store. It would be wise to wash everything before it went into boxes and not to take the bedclothes from under the dying. Bedcurtains, she thought, in the dark; bedcurtains from rich houses would fetch a good price once the people began to return to London and the City of Westminster.

The one house she would not touch in case friends of Sir Rollo came back and blamed them, would be his. In fact, Joseph could guard it for them and they would pay him well. Her body forgot the indignities it had suffered at Joseph's hands and she slept until dawn, then heated water for a tisane against the plague. Herbs from the garden grew straggly but still pungent, and she made a bunch of them to carry. The prophylactic she had against her thin chest was safe in its linen bag and the hare's foot was stitched into her dress.

Joseph was still sleeping when she went to the door and out into the morning air. They said she must report at Covent Garden today and she was glad that she didn't work on her own doorstep.

From a nearby doorway came curses and shouting and a man rushed out past her, nearly knocking her to the ground. He vanished into one of the tangle of alleyways and Mary stood back as two sturdy men carrying truncheons and chains ran after him. She saw the tarbrushed pigtails of the press gang and hoped they caught him. If I was carrying my white staff, she thought, they would have treated me with more respect. She licked her lips. The plague took only the wicked and the sick in mind or body. She walked faster. The Good Lord would look after her and favour her work, and tonight she would read again the prophecies of the destruction of the evil cities of the world.

Chapter 12

Christopher bent down to take the rabbit from the snare. He hummed softly. Two in one morning before the rest of the family was about was more than he'd thought possible. The meadow stretched far across the rise in the land and the hedges were full of rabbit warrens. Beyond the rise was the inn where they had been so badly treated the night before and he had avoided showing himself, keeping to the edges of the field and watching for any sign of human movement.

The barn was full of dark and sunlight as the door hung free at an angle that showed it was broken at the hinges. Edward scratched himself and yawned. He took a minute or so to get his bearings and then sat up with a worried expression on his kind face. He imagined that he could smell the ordure thrown at him from the window of the inn and he relived the ordeal of their departure from London. If they had been more lightly loaded and not so obviously leaving the city to escape the plague, then they might have been treated with respect, but this sickness made animals of sane and kind citizens, each eager to protect his own against anyone who threatened.

He brushed the straw from his breeches and went out to the stream to wash, acutely aware that the straw was thickly laden with thistles. He stood by the clear water and watched his son leaning over the bank, with his hand in the water.

'You'll never catch a fish like that,' said Kate as she came behind him and sank to her knees. 'Robert taught me how to do it.' She lay on her front and put her hand down to the gravel bottom of the stream, making the fingers seem to follow the flow of the water. The grey shape that Christopher had tried to catch now lay on the current, head to the water force with its tail gently moving. Kate moved slightly and the fish vanished. She laughed.

'You're no better than me, Kate,' said her brother.

'Neither of you will get any if you set your shadow over the water,' said Edward. He regarded his elder daughter with affection. She was good at country things and would make someone a good wife and be a fine mother. He was pleased to see her looking happy, and with a sense of wonder he realised that he too was happy in spite of sleeping in a barn with who knew what crawling insects ready to bite him. He also noticed that she could call her dead fiancé by name without losing her smile.

Only Alice seemed out of sorts and grumbled that she had cramp from lying on a stone and that she was bitten all over.

'Come and wash and pick some fruit from the hedgerow,' said Anna. 'There's an apple tree that must have been seeded by a bird, growing wild and bearing sweet fruit.' She bit into one and made a face. 'Or they *will* be sweet when they are ripe, in about three weeks' time,' she chuckled and threw the apple over the hedge.

Christopher turned out his pockets. 'I found plums in a cottage garden down there. It is deserted and there is a good vegetable patch running wild. There is also a pump in the yard.'

'Could we stay there?' begged Alice. 'We might hear that the plague is over, and we would be close to London.'

'Not here,' said Lady Marian nervously. 'It is too close

to those terrible people and we must go on. Aunt Mattie will expect us.' She smoothed the damp hair away from Alice's face and smiled. 'When you get there, you will be glad we didn't waste time. You'll find so many amusements that you'll wish you had left London sooner.'

'I shan't,' said Alice firmly. 'I want to be able to go to the play and to see the great coaches rushing down by St James'. I want to see the fashionable ladies of the Court and to hear the gossip.'

'If you find the gossip about the plague amusing, then listen to this, Madam!' Edward took out the penny sheet he had bought before leaving the City. 'For the week ending August twenty-ninth, there were six thousand deaths, out of a total of seven thousand, that died of plague. *Six thousand*, Miss, and you want to stay in the city? The total is twice that of the week before and growing more all the time. Soon, there will be only rats and stray dogs and corpses left and who knows where we shall be this time next year if we don't stay away.'

'But I'll miss going to the shops and seeing friends,' said Alice, with less heat.

'They've all gone, shopkeepers, fish merchants and mercers. All of our friends have gone, too, Alice.'

'We might meet a lot of new faces,' said Anna. 'We might even have callers among those we have met in London.'

'The King takes all the interesting ones to amuse him at Court,' said Alice. 'Not that Sir Vincent Clavell was very amusing. He treated me like a child.' She gave Kate a look of resentment. She was in mourning and yet she smiled and he had shown her all his attention.

'Captain Bennet said he would come to see us as soon as his duties allow,' said Marian. She watched the faces of the girls as they ate bread and cheese and salt herring and drank wine and water. None of them noticed that she had mentioned his name and she sighed. He would do nicely for Anna, or even Kate if she came out of mourning, but the girls laughed as if on a picnic and seemed in high spirits. Even Alice went to make a garland of leaves and daisies and began to chatter.

Christopher hung the rabbits to drain and then put them on the rail under the coach. They would get dusty but stay cool there and be ready for cooking as soon as they had another fire, but now the most urgent business was to get away before curious farm workers found them and insulted them further.

The horses were refreshed and the coach cool from a night away from hot sun and a morning in the shade before the heat of the day became bad. Marian packed the remains of the food and folded the rugs that they had used for bedding and Alice found her kitten, in the basket where Anna had kept it.

'If that creature gets free, we do not stop,' said Edward severely. 'Look after it if you wish to keep it, Alice, and don't make Anna attend to it for you when you tire of it.'

'I'll put it back in that basket when it gets too lively,' said Anna. She smiled at Alice. 'I know you want to have something from home and we must look after Kittie, mustn't we?'

Alice kissed her cheek. 'You know better than anyone that I hate the country, Anna. What are we going to do?' She sighed. 'You are sad, too. Where are we to find husbands or men to pay court to us?'

Anna tried to smile. 'We can ride more and walk in the fields and do whatever we did when indoors. We could learn to make butter and cheese and to make bread.'

Alice looked glum. 'I hate getting my hands covered with flour,' she said.

'There will be visitors,' went on Anna, trying to sound cheerful, but she felt as if life was passing her by without having the chance to prove anything, either to herself or to others. Even the company of Rollo FitzMedwin or Captain

Bennet would break the monotony and give them entertainment.

'Do you remember the night we sat at the play and the gentlemen watched us more than they did the stage?' asked Alice, with a giggle.

'I remember,' said Anna. 'We went to supper afterwards and were introduced to Captain Bennet.'

'He was so dull,' said Alice. She dropped her voice. 'I know that everyone says that Sir Richard Routh is not a good man, Anna, but he does have good eyes and teeth and made me feel as if I was a great beauty when he looked at me.'

'He's best avoided,' said Anna. 'Come and sit in your place. Lady Marian is ready to go.'

'I can take the coach, Father,' said Christopher. 'I don't expect to meet highwaymen now we are clear of the main road. I can carry one gun beside me and take the lead while you follow in the curricle with the other gun. Kate can drive with me on the box to take the reins if we are attacked.'

Edward gave way thankfully. The stiffness in his arms since driving from London had not gone completely and he wasn't looking forward to the same experience today.

Smoke appeared in chimneys as they passed tiny hamlets that prepared for the day, and they avoided all villages by taking to higher ground and going over the Downs. The turf was soft and springy and gave a more comfortable ride than along the rutted roads. Larks sang and the sky lacked the metallic glare of the city, where smoke and dust rose to make a hot mist. Alice dozed and Marian envied her ability to relax completely, like a cat draped over a settle. The kitten was back in her basket and Anna ignored the plaintive mewing.

The early dew dried under the thirsty sky and Christopher eased up to let the horses breathe freely. They had made better time across the turf and now he was not as scared of attack or the aggression of ordinary villagers. He saw a spinney and thought he spied the glint of water and made towards it.

'Do you think we should go on?' said Edward. The lighter carriage was easy to drive and Anna had taken a turn to relieve him so he wasn't as exhausted as he had been when they started from London.

'The horses need rest,' answered his son. Marian sighed. A cup of lime-flower tea would be so refreshing, but she saw no hope of having it from a thin cup until they reached Aunt Mattie and Uncle John. Anna gave her warm ale and smiled, knowing how difficult it was for Lady Marian to adapt to these rural conditions.

'Kittie needs milk,' said Alice, turning up her nose at the stone jar of curdled cheesy milk.

'Kittie will have to have water like the rest of us,' said Edward, drinking deeply from his mug of ale. The bread was past its best and the salt herrings were smelling badly but the cheese was good and he found that he was hungry.

'I don't think we'll stay long enough to make a fire and cook the rabbits,' said Christopher. 'If we press on after dinner, we could be at the Manor by nightfall.'

'By moonlight if necessary,' said Marian. 'I'd rather walk the last five miles than sleep in another barn.'

'Even if the coach has to stay, there is no reason why Anna should not drive you and Father in the curricle and we could rest the other horses overnight,' said Christopher.

'I want to go with Mother, and Kittie needs real food and fresh milk,' said Alice.

'I can't have young ladies open to danger,' said Edward. 'I can't leave them here.'

'We would not suffer if Christopher was with us,' said Anna. 'Let Alice go with you, and Kate and I will stay with Christopher.'

'Yes, Mother,' said Kate. If Marian wasn't there, sighing over her dusty clothes and the fact that she suffered heartburn after eating too much stale bread and cheese, they could enjoy the rest of the journey.

Marian hesitated. She longed for the comfort of a good feather bed and well-cooked food. She looked at her husband. His face was red from the sun and from over-exertion, and she decided where her duty lay. 'I think your father needs a rest and he will have that only if we reach the Manor.' She smiled. 'I think we must go on and leave you, my dears.'

Kate hid a smile. 'I think you are right, Mother. Father does seem over-heated. If you travel light, you should be there in the late afternoon, in time for supper.'

Christopher harnessed the two vehicles and made sure that the horses dragging the curricle were fit and their feet had not suffered from the rough roads. They could go over turf for the next few miles and then be on a well-worn track leading to the Manor. He knew that the family had done the worst of the journey but this last part would give him time to come to terms with the change in his life from young man-about-town to country bumpkin. 'We'll drive on and find a place for the night,' he said when Edward and the curricle vanished over the hill.

'Is it far?' asked Kate. 'I thought that when we reached the village down there, we hadn't much further to go.'

'We can make the Manor by nightfall if we go slowly and don't wind the horses. Do you want to do that?' He felt guilty now. Girls were different and might begin to regret this extra adventure, but he wished that he could travel gypsy-like and arrive when and where he chose.

'Let's stay the night again,' said Kate. Her eyes sparkled. 'We can cook the rabbits and we have enough other food and drink to last until tomorrow,' Christopher cocked an eyebrow in Anna's direction.

'I'd like to stay,' she said. 'I want time to think before we meet Sir John and Lady Matilda.'

'That's how I feel,' said Christopher. They drove in

companionable silence until they came to a heath covered with bright yellow gorse and purple heather. Bees worked hungrily among the flowers and startled birds flew up from nests among the bracken.

Anna stretched. 'This is a pretty place, with grass over there for the horses and water in the dew pond.'

'But no barn,' said Christopher.

'The night will be warm and we have blankets,' said Kate. 'Now there are only the three of us, Anna and I can sleep in the coach or on the heather and you can lie under the coach.'

'I'll make a fire,' said Anna. 'I seldom have the chance to do anything like this.' She hitched her dress up to make sure she couldn't trip over her skirt and tucked the fold into her belt, then foraged for twigs and small pieces of wood to start the fire. Kate followed her and walked across to the clump of trees by the water. Ripples formed and widened as moorhens fled to the other bank of the deep pond. Kate tossed a stone into the water. The circle of waves eddied to the shore like idle thoughts. She gazed into the water as it became still. There was no trace of the stone or the ripples. She picked up sticks and made a pouch of her skirt in which to carry them, like any farm labourer's daughter.

Robert was dead and she was alone by a clear pool, gathering sticks. Nothing remained of their hopes and plans for the future, and to others her life was as calm and uncomplicated as the surface of this water, but the ache was there this morning, more than if she had been at home. She finished gathering sticks and walked back with them as Anna called for more and bigger pieces of wood. Would the simple life fill her heart and make her content with her lot? Anna was smiling and her cheeks were pink. 'You'll have freckles,' said Kate affectionately.

'I never freckle,' said Anna.

'Then you'll go darker and Father will pull at his wig

189

and think you a Papist,' joked Christopher. 'And Captain Bennet will march you off to the Tower as a Netherlander unless you change your name.' He paused, embarrassed when Anna blushed.

'We might be back in London soon and then I shall have to powder my face like an actress or a lady of the Court,' said Anna, a mite put out by his teasing.

'Don't do that, either of you,' said Christopher. He regarded them with affection. 'I can't think why women put paint on their faces when they have such lovely skins.'

'Actresses do, and the men swarm after them like a hive of bees,' said Kate.

'It's only for show,' said Christopher quickly. 'It doesn't mean that they are wicked underneath. It's a mark of their profession. They have to paint.'

He tried to remember the face of the woman for whom he had conceived a passion when he saw her on the stage of the Whitehall Playhouse, and at Drury Lane Theatre Royal, but all he could recall was the painted face and not the sparkling eyes and good humour of Anne Marshall. He glanced at his sister and at his foster sister and wished that Anne could look as they did, then turned to skinning the rabbits again. Anne must paint on stage and so did her sister and Mistress Gwyn, all the rage in London theatre life. It made them apart from other women, the attraction of the forbidden in the minds of many who had suffered under Oliver Cromwell and had been deprived of such beauty and allure. In the minds of the young men, they were a challenge to be conquered – but a challenge rarely met as so many men followed their tawdry trains and practised smiles.

Here, it would be embarrassing to see her, unless she washed away the paint and replaced with a simple gown the costumes of the stage. He laughed, softly. When I go back, I will take her a gift. I will show that I am faithful, even if the rest of the men forsake her. He dropped the rabbit skin into the fire and watched it curl up and burn away.

'I wonder what theatres there are in Salisbury?' asked Anna. It was as if she read his thoughts and Christopher looked up. 'All the famous names have gone with the Court. Mistress Gwyn, Rebecca Marshall and her sister Anne and even some of the men who take the leading parts, like Betterton, at the Theatre Royal in London.' She laughed. 'They have their livelihood to consider. If they are out of the King's sight for long, other, younger women will take their place.'

Christopher forced a sharpened stake through the rabbit with unnecessary force. He suddenly knew that he had been deluding himself. What had Anne given him but a few smiles and a touch of her lips on his cheek after supper at the Rose? There had been far too many people there to be alone with her, and when it was time to leave, he had not seen when she left or with whom. I do love her, he thought. He hammered two forked sticks into the soft ground on either side of the now hotly-glowing fire and rested the wooden stake across it with the two rabbits impaled.

Kate brought fat bacon, salted and so not decomposing in the heat as so much of the food had done. She wrapped pieces of bacon round the rabbits and left the juices to keep the meat from drying out over the fire. Fat hissed on the bed of crimson heat and sent flames up to lick the rabbits, and the smell made the watching cooks sit close and will the meat to be done quickly.

Both girls had their skirts above their calves but Christopher was unconcerned. They fitted in to the scene so well and he was relaxed and grateful for their sisterly company. Anna had been a member of the family for as long as he could recall, and to him she was a dear sister and could be none other, in spite of many hints from friends that if

191

Christopher married Anna, her fortune would be his, and why not keep it in the family?

They tore hot joints from the rabbits and ate with a hunger that none of them remembered. Kate had found wild thyme amongst the heather and had added the herbs to the rabbit. The sweet heather made fragrant smoke and they wondered if they could have better food in any of the great houses.

'I never knew how lucky gypsies are,' said Christopher at last as he surveyed the pathetic remains of the meal. 'They catch coneys all the time and poach birds and deer. Imagine a haunch of venison cooked like this and eaten under the stars.'

'It would take hours to cook that,' said Kate, 'and by that time, you would be so cross at waiting that it would take away any enjoyment.' She found her smile was forced. 'Perhaps the best things in life have to be taken quickly before they fly away like butterflies.' She watched a Painted Lady butterfly pause on a floret of heather and then surge up towards the sun.

'Painted Ladies,' said Anna. 'They are so beautiful, but if you touch their wings, they lose that bloom and can't fly. Much better to watch and enjoy them but not to try to catch or net them.'

'Dear Anna,' said Christopher softly. 'I think you are a witch who should be ducked or pilloried.' He grinned. 'I saved some of the plums and we can drink the rest of the wine that Father left us.' They sat by the dying fire and each one was happy to be there, thinking their own thoughts, and in a subtle way absorbing the country and shedding the noise and clutter of the city better than if they had Alice with the miseries and Marian sighing for comfort. Here, they could think of the past without too much bitterness and Robert was fast becoming a wraith that grew less substantial under the dark sky. Christopher thought of the horses he might ride and Anna wondered if

192

there would be anyone who knew anything about science in a small country village. Anyone as educated as Captain Bennet.

Deciding that there might be adders among the heather, Anna slept in the coach. Kate followed her in half an hour when the rustlings in the heather disturbed her and made her think as Anna had done, but Christopher lay under the body of the coach and breathed the night air, content to be where he was and now ready for the country. There might be pretty girls in the village. His blood quickened. Many of his friends boasted of rustic conquests, even of abducting girls for a day or so and then paying them well. He turned on his side. He could never do that. Father would flay me, he thought, and he had very little money of his own. He breathed deeply. They might be in time for the harvest and the supper that went with it. That would bring in all the young people of the neighbourhood and the nights were dark and warm and who would mind a kiss or two?

Anna thought of St Paul's Churchyard on the day that she had bought books there and had met Sir Rollo Fitz-Medwin. He had been at the landing stage when the family came back on the boat but he had left in a hurry after escorting them home and taking wine with them. He had looked hot and as if his head ached badly. Anna touched the back of her hand where he had kissed it and all sleep left her as she recalled what William Verney had told her of some of the plague signs. If Sir Rollo was well, he would have called again as he had promised, and had even offered to go with them to Surrey.

'Are you awake?' whispered Kate.

'Drowsing,' said Anna, but her eyes were wide and dark and full of apprehension. 'How long does it take to show signs of the plague, Kate?'

'Are you feeling ill?'

'No, not me,' said Anna hastily.

193

'Then please don't frighten me like that. We left the plague back there in London, with all the dust and noise and bad water, and now that we are here, I'm glad. You can forget London for a while, Anna, even if you do long for all your books and the markets. Uncle John had a good library, or so Father said, but he might have got rid of it since Father was last there.'

'What if the pestilence follows us, Kate? We are whole but there are many who have come into the country to die. Christopher told me of hundreds of people camping in the fields because villages wouldn't let them over their land, but many slip through at night.'

'As we did,' said Kate seriously.

'I was wondering,' began Anna.

'What? You sound worried, Anna.'

'Rollo FitzMedwin was unwell when he came to the house after our river journey. Do you recall? He had a headache and was very hot and we haven't seen him since, nor did he send messages of God-Speed as he promised!'

'You can't believe that he has the contagion?'

'Many of the nobility have died and remember, his coachman collapsed and died in Vauxhall, leaving Sir Rollo alone with the coach. I heard Joseph telling someone about it.'

'I'm glad he didn't come back in that case,' said Kate. 'I didn't like him very much but I wouldn't wish him ill. Still more, I wouldn't have him infecting this family.'

'He kissed your hand, Kate. He kissed all our hands and I met him by chance in St Paul's a little while ago and he . . . I slipped and he caught me round the waist.'

'Uncle William would tell you that there was no danger in that. If he had kissed your lips or there had been more time close in his company, then it might not be so safe.'

'Of course he has not kissed me,' said Anna affronted.

'He wanted to,' said Kate. 'If he isn't dead of the plague, I think you'll see him again. Father says that he has relatives a day's ride away from Uncle John, and in the estate further on Lord Carnegie often stays at Lord Chalwood's stables, where they wanted to keep Sam.'

'I hope I don't see him again,' said Anna. At the time, in St Paul's, she had been far too upset to notice what was happening but now she wondered if her fast pulse and agitation had been solely due to seeing the plague victim being taken to the pest-house in the crypt. She recalled the insidious hand at her waist and his breath on her cheek, and her own sense of excitement at his touch.

'Poor man. He may be dead, Anna. I wish I'd liked him better and not said rude things about him.'

'We'll hear later,' said Anna. News would come to the village, she hoped. A fast horseman could ride unencumbered from London in a day with a change of horses, if there were any posthouses which would furnish travellers with a change of horse. Officials must have such means and nobody would think of them as carriers of more sinister messages than letters and packages on business of His Majesty's Mail.

'Do you enjoy the country, Anna?' asked Kate. All thought of sleep seemed to have vanished.

'I shall make myself like it,' replied Anna. 'I can make myself happy wherever I am if I try hard enough, and my ancestors had to move about when they were persecuted for religion. I suppose I am like the gypsy who gathers up her belongings and makes a home wherever she sets down for a while, but I shall miss the city and the colour and the gaiety. Alice and I are alike in that. We are not country girls, but our stay will not be for ever, so we must find what amusement we can.'

'Your name still makes people stare, Anna,' said Kate. In the coach, under the night sky, it was easy to talk of matters that Kate would not have mentioned at any other time. 'Why don't you change it? Father could arrange it.'

'My family did nothing of which I'm ashamed,' said

Anna proudly. 'I am only partly Dutch and no relation to De Ruyter. You know, we thought he was beaten at Lowestoft but Lord Sandwich made a bad decision and so we suffered heavy losses at Bergen – where Sandwich thought he had the support of the Danes. He was driven away from his attack on the Dutch East-Indiamen, and with the wind off the land, it was impossible to stay and use fireships.'

'Were our ships lost?' asked Kate fearfully.

'No ships lost but a great deal of damage and six commanders killed including John Windham, a gentleman volunteer known to Lady Marian,' said Anna.

'Sir Vincent Clavell serves with the fleet,' mused Kate.

'I hope we see *him* again,' said Anna.

'Yes,' said Kate. 'He is kind and understanding.'

'I don't think Alice would agree. He annoys her as he treats her as he would his young sister and not as the lady that Alice thinks she has become. Sometimes I fear she will never grow up and yet when she dresses for company, she is a young lady.'

'Well, she can be a child again here. If she is to play with Sir Vincent's sister, she will not have adult company apart from us, and you see, they'll be collecting puppies and kittens and motherless chicks before the month is out.' Alice was so young and carefree, spoiled by everyone. And who will take me under his wing? thought Kate as the dawn chorus eased her into sleep.

Anna lay awake still. London seemed far away and this new world of soft sounds and scents was soothing, with a hint of danger out there in the dark. She longed for something that would shatter the stillness and make her heart beat faster. All the latent passion of her nature would be stifled if she became a rustic. Perhaps I am foreign in my mind as well as in my face, she thought. Perhaps these feelings must be suppressed if I am to live here. She longed for voices to stimulate her, people with whom she could

196

talk as an equal about the book that Captain Bennet had brought her. I don't even know if his hands are soft or firm, cold or dry, she thought to herself. He kissed the hands of the other ladies but not mine. She pictured the young hard mouth and the steady gaze that had once become shocked when he heard her name. He was the perfect officer and gentleman, but she needed more than politeness.

Chapter 13

'I have to go,' said Lottie stubbornly. 'I must know how they fare.'

Sam took her by the shoulders and shook her gently. 'You must stay, sweetheart. You can have no idea of the City now. Even in these last few weeks since the family left, the streets have become graveyards, with heaps of unburied dead lying in doorways, in drains and in the halls of those too weak to bring them out. Beggars are everywhere and some are rogues. Think of the baby and stay here where you are safe.'

'I have to go and see my mother,' repeated Lottie.

'Then I shall take you in the carriage like a lady,' said Sam, laughing. 'You are too big to ride even side-saddle now and my son might not like horses at this stage.'

'Can we go now?' Lottie smiled. 'I have baked bread and cakes that would make even Mary Creed envious and we can take some with us. I promise that not a drop of drink nor a crumb shall pass my lips while we are there and I'll take a big posy of herbs.' She fingered the silver cross around her neck that Lady Marian had given her. 'This will protect me, Sam; and my faith in our future.'

Sam watched her pack the basket and cover it with a clean linen cloth. His large hands hung at his sides and he wondered how a clumsy oaf like he could have had the good fortune to marry someone as sweet and pretty as Lottie. When she looked up and smiled, he bent to kiss her and fondled the miracle that moved within her belly. 'Before we go?' he asked and pressed her down onto the featherbed.

'You'd think there was no work to do now we are left here,' said Lottie, but her eyes were tender.

'If they come back, we shall have no time for this and when the baby comes, you'll have your work cut out to see to him and to do your own chores.' He wondered if even the mistresses of the King could look like this, with the blue marbling on her breasts and the softness of her thighs. If they had been forced to leave and live in Cripplegate, they might be dead by now. He lay with his wife until she woke from the light sleep that now overtook her when they finished making love, then went to harness the small carriage and horse, conscious again of the generosity of the Verneys.

'Put herbs on the box with you, Sam, and more inside the coach,' said Lottie. She felt faintly tipsy and wondered how Sam could drive after drinking the mug of Sack that Edward Verney had ordered them to take before mixing with crowds, but men had strong heads for wine and he drove carefully. Perhaps, she thought as they passed the end of the road leading to Lincoln's Inn Fields, Sam might be taken on as full coachman when the Verneys came back. She reclined on the cushions and imagined herself living at the back of the house where Mary Creed had once dwelt. The rooms were big and the fireplace could keep a young baby warm in the bitterest of weather.

From alleyways came the stench of decay and an aura of despair. No shops were open and they passed a fresh pit that was already half-full, and the Bearer of the Dead stood by with his red staff to make sure that no person came near. All the houses in one road had the red cross on the doors and Lottie hid her face in her bunch of herbs until they were through. She began to wish that she was back at the house away from the smells and heat. Fires burned at street corners to purify the air but did nothing more than fill the atmosphere with black smuts and a choking fog.

Sam drove as fast as he dared over the loose cobbles. No care had been given to the roads for weeks and the going was hard and treacherous. At last he stopped outside the house where Dora and Henry Moor lived in two rooms. He gave a sigh of relief, as he had half-expected the house to be sealed as there were so many families living there, and most of this type of house had rapidly become affected.

Lottie climbed down and looked at the dirty windows. She wrinkled her nose in distaste, seeing what she had never noticed before she went into service with the Verneys. The cleanliness of the family, which she now took for granted, was in sharp contrast to this place. The squalor of the district seemed much worse than she remembered and when she went inside, the fire was smoky and foul, and the floor dirty.

'Lottie!' Dora opened her arms to her daughter and her welcome was warm. 'Your father is out trying to get food but it is hard now that they closed all the stalls in the market and the baker died.'

'Of the sickness?' Lottie blessed the day when she had learned to make bread and had no need to buy from a dirty bakery. Even this was new. As a child, she would play in the dirt with the other children and eat scraps that fell on the floor of the kitchen but now, perhaps because of the baby, she was sensitive to everything that offended the senses.

'You are in good health?' asked her mother. She touched the mound that moved slightly.

'Yes, but your grandson is naughty. He gives me not an hour at a time without him kicking,' said Lottie, with pride. 'I sometimes think he must come soon, but Dr Verney said that I must wait for another month at least.'

'He is a good man,' said Dora. 'He comes here to visit the sick and goes into houses with no thought for himself. His son goes with him and they bring comfort to many who are dying – and they have cured more than anyone could ever hope.' She put water to boil, as even in Cripplegate among the more ignorant, water was now boiled if it came from a public supply.

'We can't stay, Mother,' said Lottie. The thought of eating anything here made her feel vaguely sick and she longed for the clear air of the garden and the healthy smell of clean horses.

'You'll stay to see your father, Lottie? To come this far and not say a word to him will upset him more than you can know. He hasn't seen you for so long.'

'How are you managing?' asked Sam. He knew that Henry had been in service but his people had recently left for France, saying they needed no one but an agent to look after their property and that they wouldn't return until the last of the plague had gone.

'We had a little put by, but it *is* hard,' said Dora. Her normal cheerfulness cracked and Sam saw the worried face behind the brave smile.

'You must eat, Mother. Dr Verney said that only people who didn't fail to take care of their own bodies could hope to escape the sickness.' Lottie dived a hand into the basket and brought out the bread and pies that she had made that morning. She exchanged glances with Sam as her mother tried not to hurry when she took a pie to eat.

'Take another,' urged Sam. 'Lottie makes a good pie.'

'When did you eat, Mother? When did you and Father have your last food?'

'Yesterday. It gets harder by the day,' said Dora.

'What is Father doing?' Lottie felt a chill of concern.

Her mother turned away and put the loaves of bread into a crock to hide the trembling of her hands.

'This is good bread, my dear. Your father will be so pleased.

'Where is he?' asked Sam. He looked anxiously towards the street from the high window.

'We used all our money,' whispered Dora. 'We didn't have much and it's all gone.'

'Begging?' Lottie stifled a cry that shook her body. 'Not that, Mother?'

Dora hung her head. 'You should have told us,' said Sam. He shifted from one foot to the other. 'We haven't money as we are on board wages but we do have food. The clerk in Lincoln's Inn gives us our money, enough for food for us and for the horses. He never asks what we want it for but gives me what I ask if we need anything for the house or the stable.'

'That is because you are honest and never ask for much,' said Lottie.

'We do better than most,' said Sam severely, 'and I'll not take advantage of Mr Verney.' Below the window he could see the coach and the small boy who was watching that it came to no harm. The small coin that Sam had tossed to him without even thinking, might be all that one family had for a day's food.

Lottie emptied the basket and choked back her tears. It wasn't fair! Her parents were honest people who had never done a bad or spiteful deed in their whole lives and because of this pestilence, they were reduced to penury. She had never noticed that her mother had grey hair now instead of the soft brown swathe that she liked to show under her caps. Her skin was dry and her whole face showed her privation like a sucked peach.

'There is no work for even an honest man, Lottie, and nobody wants to buy our poor sticks of furniture. We are all the same in Cripplegate and each day more die and more

202

crosses appear so that I feel like a rabbit in a trap. When will our turn come?' She picked at her apron nervously. 'You are lucky,' she added with a hint of reproach. 'You have good food and a bit of air but at night the streets are full of smoke when the fires are lit to kill the contagion.'

'We live where we do because we have a charge there for Mr Verney,' said Sam. He reddened. It wasn't his fault that he had a good roof over his head. He wished that they had come on horseback instead of using the smart carriage as if he was of some importance. 'I have to look after Lottie. Her time isn't all that far away and she wants a healthy child.'

'There's many who lose theirs,' said Dora. Her first pleasure at seeing them had vanished. 'You don't know anything about us, living where you do, safe above the City. Remember Mrs James?' Lottie nodded. 'She died of the plague last week and her unborn child with her. They cut her open but the baby was covered with the tokens, and was dead.'

'Don't say such things!' cried Sam. 'It's bad luck to talk of that in front of a woman with child. Who knows what harm you might do?'

'Well, if there's harm done, I shan't be here to see it.' Dora's mouth set in a hard line. 'We might as well all be dead. What hope have we for the future? I say it's wicked to bring infants into this evil world when everyone knows the City is doomed.'

'It will pass,' said Sam desperately. 'There have been plagues from ancient times, they say, and they burned themselves out in time. I heard from one of the sailors that it's almost gone in Italy where it was bad last year.'

'Passed it on to us, no doubt, Sam, and I'd be wary about who I talked to down by the river.'

'You haven't been down there?' Lottie gasped, with a look of horror. 'They say the river stinks of pestilence and

203

that many bodies are put in there that never get taken away on the tide.'

'I followed a funeral cart to one of the pits,' said Dora. Her eyes gleamed.

'But that is against the law now.' Sam stepped back as if she had brought the cart with her and all its grisly burden.

'There were many without even a shift to cover them and not enough earth to cover everything.'

'How can you enjoy that?'

'It will be something to tell my grandchild, one day,' said Dora. 'If I live to see it born.' She took a cinnamon cake and ate it slowly now that her first hunger was satisfied. 'Have you see Mr Vincent's paper?'

'Who is he?' asked Sam.

'Mr Thomas Vincent? Surely you have heard of him, even living so far away from us ordinary folk. He writes tracts about the plague and about the wickedness of the City. The last one was called *God's Terrible Voice in the City.*'

'There have been many as mad,' said Sam impatiently. 'He is only copying Reeves, the mad preacher whose books Mary Creed used to read.'

'There must be truth in it – or why would we be suffering like this?'

Sam looked round the grimy room and felt stifled. 'I think we should go,' he said. 'I've work to do.' He gave Dora a belligerent glance. 'I do have work to do. It isn't all honey. I'm single-handed in the stables and Lottie finds it hard to do all that needs attention in the house even with the family away.'

'Did they say you could take on other servants?' asked Dora eagerly.

'No, they forbade us to take in anyone in case they brought infection with them. We can manage quite well but we earn our keep.' The thought of his mother-in-law and Henry coming to help was more than he could stomach. Neither of them had Lottie's brightness and life with Dora would be a mixture of warm affection one minute and tales of doom-laden resentment the next.

'Well, you won't have us to worry you much longer,' said Dora. 'They put a new cross on the house next door this morning early and I can still hear the screams.'

Lottie was pale and tearful. She looked at Sam and knew that she dared not mention what was in her mind, at least not until they were alone, but how could any daughter leave her parents in such danger?

'Come away, girl,' said Sam gruffly. 'We can't wait to see Mr Moor now.' He held out two silver coins. 'Take this. It will keep him at home for a few days and then I'll bring more food.'

'And when will your father see you, Lottie?' Dora looked satisfied with Lottie's distress. 'You wouldn't want your child to be born before he had seen you like that, all fat and well and without a care in the world, and eating for two, I hope.'

'We'll come again,' promised Lottie with a cautious look at Sam's set face.

'If we can,' he said. 'I'll bring the food as Lottie shouldn't ride now and I can't bring the carriage again.' It was the only way he could let them know that Lottie would never set foot in this place until it was safe. 'Say goodbye, sweetheart and come down,' he said firmly.

Dora kissed Lottie as if she was going to the ends of the earth and Lottie felt the thin body that had once been fat and self-indulged. She looked at the pile of food she had brought. On the kitchen table it had seemed a generous amount, but now she wished that it was twice as big.

Hardly seeing the stairs, Lottie clung to the rail and went down to the carriage. Children sat on the cobbles, too enervated to play and too badly fed to care.

Sam jumped up and took the reins. The boy who had

looked after the horses called after them. 'If you come tomorrow, I'll be here, Sir.' Sam wondered if he would wait all day in the hope of another coin.

'All that fruit,' whispered Lottie. 'The garden is glutted with fruit and lying bad on the ground and yet they starve. Can't we let them in to pick it all?'

'And have the whole of the house taken over by beggars and the sick?' Sam whipped up the horses and made for the main road.

'And herbs in plenty, and eggs from the chickens.' Lottie droned on until Sam spoke to her sharply. Melancholy was one of the prime causes of the plague, they said.

'I wish that Master Christopher hadn't let Joseph have the small cart,' said Sam as he helped Lottie down and handed her the empty basket. 'I could have loaded that with fruit and eggs and taken them down to Cripplegate for your parents to sell, or at least to eat themselves.'

'You'd have been robbed on the way,' said Lottie. In her familiar surroundings, she breathed more freely and regained her normal good sense. 'You could take a box in the carriage.' She saw his face. 'I wouldn't come,' she added hastily. 'You have to see the clerk tomorrow down in Lincoln's Inn, and you could leave the food on your way there.'

'Not the carriage again, Lottie. I was uneasy all the time it was there, but I will take the big saddlebags and I can tie a bundle or two behind me where you would ride.' Sam's face cleared. He hated to think of Lottie being unhappy but he also hated the thought of having Dora's snide remarks in his ears all day. He hurried to the garden to see what could be saved. If Lottie had been forced to have her child over there in that house . . . he dared not think of it.

'I'm in here,' called Lottie, later that evening. She pushed her hair out of her eyes and opened the door of the bread oven. As she worked in the house, keeping everything clean and tidy against the return of the family, she found it convenient to use the main kitchen.

'We might as well move in,' said Sam. 'Before he left, Mr Verney suggested it but I said we were comfortable.'

'I can't get up the ladder as easily now and the steps from the stables are almost as bad,' said Lottie.

'I looked at the rooms that Joseph had and they would suit us very well,' said Sam. 'We can return to the loft as soon as we have word from Mr Verney that they are coming back.'

'He might let us stay here,' said Lottie. 'He'll need a coachman and Lady Marian said she wants to keep me.'

She opened the rooms and sniffed. They still held the smell of Mary Creed's nostrums against the plague. Lottie brushed aside the accumulated dust from the window-sill and picked up a piece of paper that was all that Mary had left. She read again with distaste and uneasiness about the wrath of God and the vengeance He would wreak on all who followed the way of the King and his Court.

It was as if the woman stood in the corner watching her, and Lottie went quickly to the other room which Mary had used only during the day. This is where we'll sleep, she thought and went out into the garden to pick herbs to make the other room fresh. She burned rosemary and thyme and sage in a small dish in the middle of the floor of the empty room and added brimstone.

'That's enough to chase off the Devil!' said Sam.

'I hope it has,' replied Lottie and felt that she had exorcised the ghost of the woman who hated her. 'I will never see her again, and this can be my home now,' she decided as the fumes faded to leave a fragrance that was not of Mary Creed. She removed the dish with the ashes of the herbs and the charred remains of the pamphlet of prophecy.

'That's better,' said Sam. 'I wonder where they've gone?'

He brought over the bed and stools and handed down from the loft the bags of clothes for Lottie to put in the big press that even Mary Creed was unable to claim as her property when she left. Sam put a bed of fresh straw in the loft and left enough utensils in case they had to move back in a hurry, but by nightfall they had two homes, and the new one was far more comfortable.

Lottie lay awake and smiled. Sam was a good man. He didn't really like his in-laws as they had been less than welcoming once they knew that he had made Lottie pregnant and they thought that she would be dismissed, but now she wondered if he shared her idea, that if circumstances grew worse, Dora and Henry might have to come and live in the loft. They would never come into the house, I'd make sure of that, she decided. They could see to the garden and the fowls and go on errands.

She snuggled down into the soft bed and leaned over to touch the man at her side just to know that he was there. I shall not be alone when the baby comes, she thought. That had been a dread she had each night when Sam was asleep. A woman needed her mother or some other female relative with her at such times. She bit her lip. The baby stirred and she knew that she had only a few more weeks before it was born. There might be no midwife, as all she knew had gone away or died, and the dirty old drunks that attended death and birth would never touch her baby.

In the moonlight she saw the outline of the wooden crib that the carpenter had made and the bundle of baby clothes that she left in it ready for the day when the crib would be filled. Anna had made such pretty gowns, soft and warm, cut from one of her good dresses and gentle to the touch. Kate had made sure there were enough pads and binders for two babies and even Alice had helped to hem a fine woollen shawl and to trim the small linen caps. They were far away and only the clerk had news of them, or might do tomorrow when Sam saw him in the offices. Messengers had the freedom of the roads once the footpads were avoided and even the villages who refused help to refugees were anxious for news of relatives, friends and business contacts in the cities.

'God keep them safe,' she prayed. 'Make me a fine son for Sam and keep my mother safe.' Safety? Who could expect any safety any more? She threw back the hot cover and pressed her body against Sam's back for comfort. Surely the sound of the cart was closer tonight? Sounds that were ignored each night now seemed louder and she wished that she was back in the loft at the rear of the house. Even these rooms, well back from the main family apartments, were more vulnerable to street sounds and as dawn brought a streak of light through the shutters, she dressed quietly and went out into the cool air.

'This is the best time of the day,' she murmured. Suddenly she felt energetic and needed to work vigorously. She took baskets to the apple trees and picked fruit to store. Blackberries hung in black wasp-sweet clumps and she remembered the cordial that her grandmother used to give her when she had sore throats. It might be good for the baby. When Sam found her, she had fingers stained with the black juice and the wasps were waking up.

'There's sugar aplenty in the larder, Sam, and I can't waste this,' she said when he objected to her working so hard. 'Besides, I feel as if I must work.'

'Come away to bed again.' He grinned. 'You need the rest.' He had never seen her looking better and even her ungainly shape made him want her as never before.

She smeared blackberry juice on to his cheek and he slapped her hand, gently. 'I'll have to wash this off,' she said, but she went with him and they lay in the sun, happy and smelling of harvest, the ripeness of the year bringing a softer light, a softer breeze and a promise of calm happiness.

'I must make more pies,' Lottie said at last. 'What would Mr Verney say if he saw us now?'

'He'd envy me,' said Sam. He lay naked with his arms

behind his head, watching Lottie pull on her shift, then he bent to pick up his breeches. 'And I must sweep the yard and the stables,' he said. 'Later, I'll go to the clerk and to your mother, Lottie.' He kissed her, feeling heavy with love and indulgence. 'Try not to think of Cripplegate. I will see that no harm comes to them.'

'Even if they have to come here?'

'Pray God it never comes to that,' he said fervently. 'If they have food, they will keep well,' but he took a bunch of herbs pinned to his coat when he ventured into the City and drank plague water and Sack to fortify himself.

The horse was laden with food and drink and fresh fruit when he led her from the stables. The sky was overcast but he had seen that so many times, with no rain coming during the long hot summer, that Sam ignored it and went on to Cripplegate.

Henry was sitting in the front room and saw his son-in-law arrive. Two boys hurried to the horse, ready to fight for the job of looking after her while Sam was in the building, but he gave them a coin each and told one to carry the bundles up the stairs for him.

Henry hastened to meet him and to take some of the load. 'Where is Mrs Moor?' asked Sam as he put the still-warm bread on the table.

'She went out to see what she could get,' said Henry.

'If she has food here, why risk contagion?' asked Sam, sharply.

Henry looked embarrassed. 'She said that Lottie was upset and that you would be here today with more food.' He saw Sam's mouth tighten. 'We had a lot of bread left so she took it to sell.'

'And what if we hadn't come back?' demanded Sam brusquely.

'She knew you would.' Henry looked at him and smiled ingratiatingly. 'Lottie is a good girl. She wouldn't see her poor mother starve.'

210

'The fruit you can sell if you can find buyers here. The rest is for you. Make it last this time as I am not due to see the clerk again until next week and I shall not come again for many days,' he added firmly. 'Who has money for bread here?' he asked curiously. The children in the street bore testimony to hunger and acute need.

Henry looked away. 'Don't tell Lottie, but Dora's gone over to Covent Garden where there are still houses with clerks and workers paid to look after offices, and a little meat in the market.'

'And pits on the way!' said Sam. He tossed down the herbs from his own coat. 'Better take these as well as the ones that Lottie sent. She'll need them if she goes into that place.' He left abruptly and snatched the reins from the boy before riding off to see the clerk. It was good to give, wholeheartedly as he and Lottie had done, but she had better things to do than to slave in a hot kitchen making pies to be sold.

Sam left the horse in the shade but the sky was almost black now over the lighted fires at each corner. The air was heavy and when he reached the offices he was glad to be in the cool.

Roger Carter greeted him at a distance. He held a bunch of herbs which he placed on the desk when he saw who his visitor was, and seemed to relax. 'You are in good health, Sam?' It was fast becoming a familiar greeting and was often more than a formal nicety.

'Yes, Mr Carter. We are both well,' said Sam. 'How is it here in Lincoln's Inn?'

'Many have left, but those of us who stayed do nicely, thank you, Sam. We have ample supplies brought up by water from the country at Greenwich and enough work to keep us busy.' He coughed and reddened. 'How is it outside? I seldom venture beyond the gates and have seen nothing for a week.'

'Bad, Mr Carter,' said Sam. 'The Bills give grave figures,

211

and I have seen such sights as no man should have to look on.'

'So, you came by back ways and spoke to nobody?' asked Roger Carter.

'I spoke to no beggar nor touched an infected house,' said Sam cautiously. There was no need to lie but he knew that Roger Carter wouldn't approve of his visit to the house in Cripplegate.

'And you keep the house and horses in good heart?' Roger opened a ledger. 'I had word from the country that the Verney family are safe there and settled. My good Mr Verney suggested that I might increase your money because, as he said, you will soon have another mouth to feed.' He smiled thinly. 'I see no need for this but I obey my orders. I have arranged to have it ready for you now. With the sickness everywhere, there is no need for you to come so often. Here is enough for the next month and a note from Lady Marian for your wife.' He looked out at the sky. 'We shall have a storm at last,' he said with satisfaction. 'It will clear the drains and wash away the distemper and we might see the family back again soon.'

'Is the Court still at Salisbury?' asked Sam. 'Lottie likes to know the news.'

'The Court were due to go on to Oxford at the end of October, and it is only early September now but there are rumours of the King leaving sooner as the plague followed them to Salisbury.' He smiled 'I wish the people of Oxford well. The Court cleaned out the whole of Salisbury like ants round honey and the city will be glad to see them gone.'

'Does the King know what is happening here?' Sam was disturbed. He admired the King and it was good to have better times, when there was no sickness, after the sober years of Oliver, but he was disappointed that the Court had left London to fend for itself while the young noblemen and their mistresses still enjoyed a life of pleasure and luxury.

'He knows, but what can he do? If he stayed and caught the plague, we would have to stomach his brother as King or go back to a Commonwealth. He's better safe where he is and he can face the reckoning later. There are good men who have stayed, like Monkton who brought the King back from exile and became the Lord Albermarle. They have done their best to bring back the old plague laws but there are few magistrates left or officers to enforce them. The fires you see on the streets are a part of it, but I can see no truth in the belief that the air is the source of inection.'

Roger seemed pleased to have someone to whom he could talk and Sam reflected that the clerk must be lonely in the empty apartment and silent offices. He had no wife or family and from his buttoned-up mouth didn't seem likely to seek the company of light women.

'And what have you heard of my master?' asked Sam. He noticed that Roger sat away from him and offered no refreshment.

'They are well but the ladies miss their friends. I believe that they suffered badly from the villagers on the way to the Manor but they are glad to be settled there now.'

'Master Christopher will enjoy the horses,' said Sam. He recalled with slight nostalgia the few days he had spent on Lord Chalwood's stud farm.

'They will be back soon,' said Roger with conviction. 'As more die and the rains come, we shall see London clean again.'

'It is hot and clammy today but the clouds just pass over,' said Sam.

'I would go home, Sam. I think that this time, you may be wrong.'

The horse seemed uneasy and distant thunder spiked with bright flashes caused Sam to lead her through narrow streets with overhanging upper windows. He cursed the

213

fact that he had brought her as she had a history of fear of thunder. Now, heavy drops of rain fell warm on his head and became a torrent. Water sucked into the long-dry drains and welled out of blocked culverts. Refuse floated over the roads and the smell of ordure, freshened by the water, was almost intolerable. The horse grew quieter as her flanks became soaked and Sam mounted and rode her slowly back to the house. He was wet through to the skin but the air was still warm and he revelled in the laying of dust and the clear air of the upper roads. Lottie was waiting with dry clothes and a hot posset. Rain streamed down the dusty windows and made rivulets along the gutters.

A slow and sullen band of smoke rose from the doused fires of the City and hung on the air until washed away. For a few hours, the air was fresh and clean and hope began to rise, but by morning the steaming streets gave off a deadly heat as the sun shone again.

Chapter 14

'Where have you been, woman?' asked Joseph.

'I've been working,' said Mary Creed and pushed past him into the stable.

'What's that you're hiding?'

'A few things I collected from a house in Shoe Lane,' she said, eyeing him with a certain amount of caution. The bag was heavy and she put it down on the swept floor of the stable she had cleaned ready to use as a store. 'We'll need locks and chains to keep this place safe against robbers.'

Joseph bent down and opened the sack. He stepped back and stared at his wife as if he had let loose an adder. 'What is this, Mary?'

'It means that we don't starve,' she said bluntly. 'You can't find a place and we would be out of money soon if we didn't find ways of making some.'

'You didn't steal this?' Joseph knew that his wife was ruthless and cunning, but she had never stooped to thieving. 'The Constable will find out and then where will we be?'

'It isn't stealing,' she said impatiently. 'What is stealing but depriving an owner of his rightful goods? If there is nobody left to own it, then first come is first served,' she added, with a sly smile.

Joseph wanted to believe she was lying, but he knew that glint in her eyes only too well. It meant that she was well pleased with something she had done and that she didn't care what he thought. He leaned against the wall. The gleam of silver and polished pewter made a patch of brilliance in the dull place. 'You weren't given that,' he said sarcastically.

'I took up the white wand,' Mary said and looked defiant. 'I shall never catch the plague, because I am too well protected and I serve the magistrates.'

'You are unclean?' Joseph backed away further, his face showing his revulsion.

'I change from my smock when I come home and I wash my hands, and chew tobacco when I walk the streets, and now I shall take more plague water.'

'But you go into houses where there are sick and dying and touch their belongings. You even bring them back here, full of contagion!'

'I never touch the dead,' said Mary. 'I can tell at a glance what the cause is and if I'm wrong, then the man or woman is still dead. Nothing brings them back to life, so what does it matter if the Bills report the flux of the lungs or the plague?'

'And you seal them up?' Joseph had always been horrified at the thought of being shut away from the air and light until the occupants of the house died, or recovered and were released after forty days.

'They plead and offer money,' said Mary, and laughed. 'How they plead, like men on the rack, and if there are children, they cry and try to reach me to cling to my skirt but I use the white wand to keep them off.'

'You are a wicked woman, Mary.' He saw that she was enjoying reliving her power. 'These carry the sickness and I want nothing of it.' He kicked at the sack and it shed its contents.

'I bring no clothes and one of the other Searchers warned

216

me that bedcurtains do carry infection so I leave them, although this morning it was hard to leave such pretty hangings.' She smiled. 'But it was just as well because the Broker of the Dead comes after us when the house is empty and takes the rest to sell if there are no known relatives to claim anything. So, I leave everything but the silver and pewter and good jewellery, and coins.'

She dragged forward a bucket of vinegar and dipped each piece of silver and the coins in it, then rinsed them all in a bucket of water. In spite of himself, Joseph was fascinated. 'Where did you get these? It must be a rich house.'

'I started the other day in Covent Garden but the pickings are poor there and most of the houses are sealed and have time to go. I now work round Ludgate Hill and Thames Street and it is not far to come home from there.' She picked up a fine sugar pot and Joseph saw the chasing and the pattern on the sides. 'I could do with help if I bring heavy things,' she said. 'The cart would hold a lot and sometimes I have to be quick to avoid the Broker.'

'I would never go into a house of sickness,' said Joseph.

'You have no authority to do so,' snapped his wife, waspishly. 'I am a Searcher and all you could be would be the Bearer or the driver of the death cart.' She watched his face and knew that he was useless. 'No, you wouldn't help your wife, Joseph. I always knew you to be a coward.'

She washed coins and spread them to dry on a piece of wood.

'I could drive the cart but you would have to put everything on it,' said Joseph. He had spent his last angel and hesitated to ask Mary for more money, but the wish to survive now had two heads. Either he had money to buy food to stop starvation, earned honestly or wheedled out of Mary who kept the pursestrings tight, or he must get money from another source that had the risk of a death much worse than starvation. Either way, he felt doomed.

'I'll cook something nice for supper,' said Mary. 'I'm not hungry myself but you need something, Joseph.'

'I don't want your cooking, you witch. Give me some money and I'll eat at an alehouse.'

'More have been closed, my dear, and the streets are teeming with floodwater, after the storms.' She saw him hesitate. 'They thought that the rain would destroy the sickness but it only delayed it and now even the place where such men as Lord Brounkner and Mr Pepys took their ale, the Angel Tavern at the lower end of Tower Hill, has been shut, and many in Fenchurch and along by the Stairs.' She smiled. 'You will find no plague in my good broth, my dear. If I wanted to get rid of you I have other means.' She thought of the deathcaps she had used to try to kill Sam and Lottie. They could be useful if ever she needed a death to happen sooner than it willed.

'I'll eat here,' said Joseph. During the past few days he had eaten sparingly in taverns, eyeing the serving men and women and shrinking away if someone so much as coughed. One of the symptoms of the plague was sneezing, making it dangerous for anyone with a head-cold to appear in public in case they were taken to the pest-house.

'You can cover that with clean straw over in the corner,' said Mary. 'Nobody will look there even if they thought we had such things. With us living here and the white cross of health on the front door of Sir Rollo's house, it looks as if the place is used again and no robber would dare try to break in.'

Joseph picked up each piece and put it carefully away and when he went into the room where Mary was cooking, he shrugged. The meat smelled good roasting over an open fire and if he was to die, then at least he wouldn't die hungry. 'How much do you think it's worth?' he asked later, his mouth full of bread and meat.

'We can't sell it like that with a crest on it,' said Mary. 'It will have to be melted down even if we get less for it.

The pewter we can sell as it is plain and can never be sworn as not ours. There's plenty more where that came from, Joseph, and we could have enough to buy that tavern or chophouse as soon as London is back to itself again. There'll be many such properties waiting for people like us to purchase them.'

Joseph ate and drank, and drank again and Mary left him asleep with his arms on the table. Tomorrow, she'd make him bring in straw for his own bed and she need never have him snoring beside her again. She watched him and wondered if he would get the plague as a punishment for his ways with loose women. If he did, she must make sure that he was taken away before they sealed the place where they lived. She washed and scoured the pots with white sand and left everything spotless. Tomorrow, there might be more treasures.

After an hour in bed, Mary heard a thump and knew that her husband had fallen to the floor in drunken sleep. That might be the answer, to let him have enough money to drink himself into a stupor each night so that he hardly noticed what she was doing, so before she left at dawn, she put a generous number of coins on the table for him to find when he woke, and she crept from the loft without waking him.

Joseph stirred soon after and when he came to his senses, he called to Mary. He looked in the other room and saw that everything was put away and tidy. His gaze fell on the money and he grabbed it in case she came back and had second thoughts. He needed a draught of ale to take the dry staleness from his throat, so he brushed the mud from his clothes and boots, in case he met someone in service who needed another hand or two even for a short while.

The roads were thick with mud after the storms of the past week and were now drying to a dirty morass through which it was impossible to walk without being splashed from head to foot if a horseman or carriage went by, so

219

Joseph took the nag and rode slowly down by the river and along the bank. Mary had mentioned Thames Street and he went there out of curiosity. The road led him on to the Old Swan by the bridge and he stopped there for his morning draught. Carts and horses still used the bridge but there was little traffic there this morning. The shops lining the bridge as far as the gap where a fire had destroyed all but the bare bridge and the water pumps newly-fitted to give London more and fresher water, were closed and trade had stopped completely.

Joseph looked for old friends from the days when he and his fellow coachmen had swaggered in full livery and aped their betters in drinking and womanising, but there were none left, only the beggars and the sick who showed their sores and asked for money. He left as soon as he had drunk his fill and went on to the Tower. Here it was the same story, except that in the gardens of big houses there was clear air and no fires lit at street corners. Many old fires were dead, washed away by the storms and now left unlit as more and more people thought that the fires had been doused by a Divine hand.

Joseph swore softly. If only Mary had held her peace and pretended to like Lottie they could have been safe and well-fed in the country with the Verney family. He thought of Lottie and wondered if she was alone or if Sam stayed with her every hour of the day. It was too risky to go back there to see her. He imagined her looking fresh and full of the new life that he had never managed to give Mary. Mary was barren, he told himself. There must be bastards born of his seed among the women he had taken, but he had never seen proof of his own manhood.

Tomorrow, I'll go there, he told himself. Sam can't be there all the time and she will be heavy and clumsy. He turned the horse to go back and was nearly thrown as the loose cobbles made the nag stumble. Joseph dismounted and led the animal to a grassy place. It was hobbling badly and he knew that it wasn't fit to be ridden.

The path was muddy, and with a lame horse his temper rose. Nothing was going as he wanted it to. Mary was a worrying source of infection if he didn't make sure they never touched, he had no place of work and had to depend on a miserable woman to dole him out money when she felt so inclined, and now he had to walk through streets thick with slime to get home.

At the end of Thames Street he saw Mary, dressed in a long gown and carrying the white staff of the Searcher. She was followed by a man carrying a bell and the cart was driven by a man who looked little better than the corpses on it. Mary didn't see her husband. She saw nothing but the road ahead as if in a trance. Her broad-brimmed black hat gave her the appearance of a member of the old Inquisition or of any of the sects that made men fear religion. The bell tolled and the small procession went away from the river to the new plague pit by Cheapside.

Joseph found another tavern that still served ale and asked for the ostler. The nag was taken to the stable and poulticed and Joseph said that he'd leave it for a day. He paid the man well from the money he still had left and walked on, instinctively following the path that Mary had taken.

One of the great houses seemed busy and he saw a carriage he recognised. It was heartening to see an old friend even if he had never really been on good terms with this particular coachman. He might have news of the King and the Court and of the return to the City of the people who had fled in panic. There might be work here, if only as a footman.

Joseph went inside the gates and raised his hand in greeting. The coachman left the horses to his footman and came to meet him. 'You still here in this pest-ridden place?' asked Daniel. He eyed Joseph with contempt. His clothes were muddy and he looked half-drunk, if his blood-shot eyes spoke true.

'My family have gone to Surrey,' said Joseph. 'We are left to look after things,' he lied.

'No livery?' the man was sneering.

'I have it at home but who wants to use it when the family are not here?' He looked down at the mud splashes. 'I came out on horseback but had to leave it at the inn back there with a pulled tendon.' He grinned. 'So I get muddy and have to walk back.'

'You have to pass through the City,' said Daniel. 'Wait and I'll take you and we can talk about what is happening here.'

'I'm only going as far as the FitzMedwin house first,' said Joseph hastily. 'We are looking in there for Sir Rollo.'

'You do well,' said the man with more respect. 'We do as well but there is always a risk.' He shrugged. 'If they take fright again and leave, we may not be needed. There was news of the King coming back but now they say it is rumour and that he will be in Oxford until November. The Navy Office is at Greenwich and the Exchange is still away and we had no idea that the streets were so bad.' He looked at Joseph again. 'Come and talk. I passed two alehouses closed this morning and I need to know what to do here.'

They walked down to St Paul's and Joseph took delight in seeing the horror on the man's face as they saw the wretches taken into the crypt. Shops and stalls were shut and barred to stop the growing numbers of robbers. The man loosened the collar of his tunic. 'God help them,' he said. 'If my master sees this, we'll be heading back to Oxford even if he did want to avoid the Court.'

'Is there news?' asked Joseph.

'We won a victory over the Dutch which made up for the losses at Bergen and this time we sank many of their vessels. It means we have more ships to man if we turn these against the Dutch, and that in turn means the pressmen may be out. Wear your livery if you go abroad at night or you might be taken. Only the protection of powerful men can save anyone if the gang get them on board.'

He eyed Joseph again, only half-believing that he was still employed. He almost expected to be asked for money and was pleasantly surprised when Joseph paid for their dinner of bread and cheese and ale.

'Is your Mary out selling her body?' he said, laughing. Every coachman in London knew of Mary and the need for Joseph to pleasure himself elsewhere.

'We are well provided for,' said Joseph. He began to relax. With money, he could still meet men like this and be on equal terms. That meant that he must go along with Mary and even help her if necessary. He saw the thin faces and diseased bodies of the beggars. If he caught the plague, at least he would enjoy life until the end and pray it came quickly.

'I must go back in case they need me,' said Daniel. 'We can meet later. Why don't you go back by hackney?'

'They are not safe,' said Joseph. 'They used many to take the diseased to pest-houses and so infected many more. I'll walk and meet you by Blackfriars tonight. If you aren't there, then tomorrow here when I fetch my nag.'

The way back to the house was a nightmare. Away from the few roads still raked and washed, the streets were a mass of filth and rats ran away at the approach of any man on foot. Piles of rotting household rubbish and ordure were covered with flies and a few mangy cats that had escaped the wholesale killing of cats and dogs earlier in the year now scavenged for food.

On horseback or in a carriage, these sights were dimmed, for progress was faster and the rider had a certain isolation from the ground. On foot, however, and after the storms, having to pick a way carefully to avoid slipping full-length in the mud, the whole picture was frightening. Joseph

223

avoided the house fronts and kept to the river bank as much as possible. A few beggars held out hopeless hands to him but didn't come near and from upper windows women shouted after him without the vigour and humour of the strumpets he had once visited.

Twice, he stood back to let people pass and they looked at him as he did them, with deep suspicion, and when he reached the stables, he was glad to strip off under the cold water from the pump. He hung his clothes to dry before brushing off the mud, and decided to wear livery when he went to meet Daniel, if only to endorse his story that he was still coachman to the Verneys.

The water freshened him and as he hungrily ate cold meat and bread he thought again of Lottie and her soft womanly body. If I wear livery and go there, she will think I am back with the family and I can make up some tale about them sending her news . . . This idea pleased him and gave him back a little of his usual self-confidence.

'Doing some work?' asked Mary when she came home. She raised her eyebrows in mockery, taking in the cleaning materials and the boot blacking that Joseph had spread over the floor as he had once done at the Verneys' stables.

'I may get a job of work,' he lied. 'I met Daniel, who is back with that family over by the Custom House and he might get me something. The family are with the Navy Yard and came back to clear up all the work that has gathered while we fight the Dutch.'

'There is sickness there,' said Mary. 'Not in that house but close by, but no deaths as yet and they say they might recover,' she added crossly.

Joseph noticed with relief that Mary had shed her gown and the white staff in an outhouse and now looked much as usual, neat in her grey dress and white collar and cap. Her shoes were muddy but she had worn pattens of wood and steel which had raised her from most of the slime and

224

given her extra height that added to her dignity when wearing the gown and carrying the wand.

'Did you bring anything?' he asked.

'I thought you wanted none of it,' she jeered. She went out and fished in the vinegar jar for the money she had dropped in it on her way into the loft. 'Money today, but no goods,' she said. 'The Broker was there before we got the room empty and there was another on the bed in the other room who might get better, so he wouldn't take anything until they are all gone.' She chuckled. 'But they didn't see the sock under the bureau. If I can have such treats as this, we needn't deal in goods.'

She spread out the money and Joseph gasped. It was more than he earned in two years and more than he had ever seen in one place at the same time.

'Well, what do you think of your Mary now?' she laughed and goaded him further. 'Aren't you going to give Me a kiss for bringing such nice things for you, my dear?'

Joseph recoiled. 'I haven't led such a virtuous life as you, Mary. You might have the contagion on you and the Lord might take me.'

'It's as well you remember that,' said Mary. 'Keep clean and we may yet have that pothouse together.' She put the coins into a box and hid it on a rafter. 'I didn't see the nag out there. Is he sick?'

'I had to leave him with a stable by the Tower,' Joseph said. 'He strained a tendon and I have to collect him tomorrow. That's when I met Daniel.'

Mary cooked them both a meal and Joseph told her all the gossip that he had heard and the evening was more friendly than any they had shared for months. Joseph drank little under Mary's eagle gaze and she showed her approval by giving him two angels for the next day. 'Eat somewhere safe as I shall be away all day,' she said. 'You must buy drink for Daniel as he is a good source of gossip and might tell you where some of the great houses are affected. There

225

are some who still have the power to bribe watchers and escape, leaving all their goods locked away until the sickness has gone from London.'

'I might have a look at the old house,' said Joseph casually. 'I've heard nothing of them and it might be empty.' He waved a key. 'We could get in and nobody would ask us why if I wore livery,' he suggested.

'Keep away. That harlot is still there. I saw Sam yesterday but he didn't see me.' She chuckled. 'Many look away sharply as if my eyes carry the plague, and the broad hat does much to make me a stranger.'

'I'll keep away,' said Joseph. 'You bring in more than enough without us breaking into houses where they might find out about the robbery.' So Lottie was there, he thought. With Mary away, he could go where he chose and do what pleased him most.

Mary watched him clean her pattens under the pump and suggested that he wear them, too.

'I can't if I am to fetch the horse,' he said. 'By morning the worst of the mud will have gone and walking will be safer. I saw the rakers freeing the Fleet and the culverts leading to the river, and this new rain will wash it through.'

When the shower stopped the breeze was cool and drying. The air smelled fresh and Joseph began to be optimistic. Mary was brave and cunning and a fit wife for a man like him, if he never had to touch her. Now that he slept in the other room on the mattress of straw, he had no fear of her. He need never touch her body nor take her breath, and in the morning she slipped away before he was awake and didn't disturb him.

Today, I shall be myself, he thought with satisfaction. I shall dress up and look smart and talk with my equals. I shall eat well and drink good Sack and wine instead of ale and later, I shall call at the Verneys' house to see if Lottie is alone. He washed his face and scraped the beard from his chin, wincing at the touch of cold water. The road

226

outside was cleaner and the mud was drying. Soon, the problem would be dust again and he hurried over to the hacking stable with linen leggings over his livery to protect the cloth.

The nag was better and Joseph led him along the bank without mounting. He couldn't afford to have him lame again in case Mary needed him to draw the cart, so he left him grazing on a grassy bank under the care of a boy while waiting for Daniel. Dinner-time came and went and Daniel didn't appear. Joseph ate a venison pasty and drank more ale and Sack and the world was good. Then, the afternoon sun broke through the clouds and warmed the now-freshening air and Joseph was angry. He had come out to see Dan and the wretch had better things to do.

He fetched the horse and mounted, turning its head towards Blackfriars Stairs. If Dan didn't come there, it would be too late to see Lottie. In his mind, Joseph now saw her clearly, smiling a welcome when she saw how smart he was and how much money he had to give her for the baby. That would be his approach and what woman could resist that? The strong drink made him believe what he needed to believe and as time went on, he grew restless and eager to see her.

Abruptly, he left the tavern and walked along towards the Custom House and the house where Daniel worked. If he was there, he'd tell him a thing or two, keeping him waiting all day. It didn't cross his mind that Daniel might have work to do and couldn't get away. It happened in service and everyone took it for granted that they were on call for twenty hours of every day. He skirted the river bank, finding the muddy road more to his liking than the stench from the river, and he passed one or two people hurrying home with buckets of fish bought at the landing stages from fishermen bold enough to come up the river.

A large coach appeared at the end of the road, swaying as it gained speed and pushing up mud in swirling, drenching waves. Two men with fish ran into a doorway even though the red cross was on the door and Joseph saw that the coach was being driven furiously by Daniel, who whipped up the horses and took no heed of anyone. His face was tense as if he had suffered some horrendous shock and the curtains of the coach were drawn over the windows.

Joseph leaned on one of the massy posts that protected the house fronts from such hazardous driving and the coach lurched over the cobbles. 'Stop!' shouted Joseph. He put out his arms as if he could stop the coach but Daniel ignored him as if he didn't exist. Joseph backed but the massy post was there, firmly at his spine. He tried to move round it but his fuddled brain was slow to react and as the coach swerved, the near horse reared in terror and brought his hooves down on to the man, crushing him against the post and trampling him into the mud.

Angry shouts inspired by envy and fear made the horses panic even more and one tore away from the traces. The coach stood with one wheel lodged in the gutter in the middle of the road and Daniel was thrown from the box.

One man, more bold than the rest, opened the door to the darkened coach and looked inside. He gasped and crossed himself, caring nothing for mutterings of Popery. 'The plague!' he shouted. 'He was trying to escape with her.'

He struck Daniel as he lay on the ground. 'Murderer! Villain!' he cried and the pent-up fury of people deprived for too long of food and hope erupted. In five minutes, not only was Joseph Creed dead in his own bloodstained livery, but Daniel lay dying by the coach in which he had been ordered to drive away the beautiful mistress of Anthony Mercer, rich merchant and friend of the Court, who couldn't buy her cure. The buboes were plain to see and when the Searcher came and the Bearer, the road was once more deserted but for the two men lying dead and the woman in the coach who died even as they looked in at her.

Mary Creed dragged the rings from the still-warm fingers and the pin from her dress, and the Bearer laughed. 'This is the prettiest one I've seen, and still warm,' he said. Mary eyed him coldly. He had been ill with the plague and recovered. How did God allow that in the sweep of justice? And now he could do what he liked.

'I'll take her first and remove her clothes myself.' His mouth was wet with anticipation as he lifted her on to the cart and took her out of sight down by the river.

Mary said nothing. He never interfered when she took silver from houses and she turned a blind but sickened eye to his practices.

The colour of the bedraggled livery caught her attention and as she bent to see the torn face, Mary felt a momentary frisson of regret that Joseph would never go with her now to the pothouse she would buy.

Her pockets were heavy and she didn't wait to see her husband pulled up on to the cart with Daniel. Two good suits of livery, she thought, but she knew her duty and went to the magistrates to report that there was plague in the house of Mr Mercer, and for her there would be riches indeed.

Chapter 15

'Christopher!' Marian laughed in mock despair. 'You look worse than any of the labouring men.'

Her son leaned on the huge axe and grinned. 'After this, Mother, I shall take on any who come to the fair and beat them.' He looked up at the sun. 'I hope you've come to tell me that dinner's ready.'

'If you don't hurry, they'll have started and there are two extra mouths today,' said Marian. Her simple cotton dress and bonnet made her look younger and she moved over the rough ground from the spinney with ease and suppleness. The few weeks of country air and the increased exercise made her feel as well as look better than she had done for years. 'I'm anxious for you to try Kate's cheese. We must all say we like it even if we don't! She has worked hard in the dairy and is very serious about the work there.'

'I've tasted it and it *is* good,' said Christopher. 'She gave me some last night to try before it was set in front of the family.'

'You went down to the dairy after supper?' asked Marian.

'Kate wanted me to,' said Christopher, quickly.

'Because she is afraid of the dark?' queried Marian slyly.

'No, she just asked me, that's all,' said Christopher.

230

'Well, you'd best be clean in five minutes, Sir. Our guests might object to eating with the forester's axeman.'

'Who are they?' asked Christopher, but his mother walked away and left him to sluice his hands and face under the pump. He changed his rough shirt for a thinner one and shrugged into a dark fustian jacket. He was smiling as he went into the cottage, wondering if the vicar was calling to see Kate again, then as he saw who was seated at the table, he reddened. Abigail Lawrence, the daughter of the neighbouring landowner, looked up and smiled, shyly.

'Abigail stayed with Aunt Mattie last night as it was late,' said Marian. 'Cheesemaking takes such a long time and Kate kept her until it was unsafe for a girl to ride home.' Her eyes twinkled. 'I'm afraid that Christopher will have to leave his woodchopping to escort you home, my dear.'

'We'll all ride over,' said Alice. 'This is my brother Christopher,' she said to the girl by her side. 'Christopher, have you met Sarah Clavell?'

'Sarah is to stay with Alice for a few days,' explained Edward who was pouring cider from a big earthenware jar. 'Sir Vincent called and asked if we could entertain her.' He beamed at the pretty little fair-haired girl who seemed to be quite at home after only a few hours with Alice.

'Vincent told me about you,' she said. 'I knew all your names before I met you, and you all look exactly as I imagined.'

'Did he say what I looked like?' enquired Alice.

'He said you were fair-haired and a suitable companion for me,' said Sarah. 'I know we shall be friends. Vincent is usually right.'

'Is that all he said?' asked Alice. She was disappointed. Sir Vincent wasn't as dashing as many of the young men who had sighed after her, but he was rich and quite good-looking and he had no right to ignore her or to look at her as if she was a child. When he drove the carriage over, with Sarah and her box in it early on, he had busied himself

231

with his sister and talked to Edward for ages in a low voice, taking not a scrap of notice of Alice's sprigged muslin fichu, which made her bosom seem larger than it really was.

'He said he hoped we'd get on well,' added Sarah, looking puzzled. What more could he say to a girl who was not a lot older than his young sister?

Alice looked across at Kate and frowned. Vincent Clavell had kissed her sister's hand and told her she looked well. I look well! thought Alice. I'm prettier than Kate and she will be an old maid.

Abigail picked at her food and avoided looking directly at Christopher while he too seemed preoccupied and ate what was put before him without seeming to know what it was. However, when they all sampled some of the cheese made by Kate in the dairy over by the main farm, he managed to show some enthusiasm and Kate was soon blushing at all the compliments that her work attracted.

'You must take some over to the church,' said Marian. 'Young George Silke doesn't eat as well as we do with that yard of pump water for a housekeeper.' She smiled. 'And of course, when we go to the Manor for supper tonight, we shall take some for Aunt Mattie.'

Kate relaxed. 'Yes, Aunt Mattie taught me all I know about cheesemaking and I promised her some from the first batch. I made some butter, too, Mother. The dairymaid over at the Manor strained her wrist and the churn is too heavy for Aunt Mattie now.'

'I can make butter, Kate, but I need more help with cheesemaking,' said Abigail.

'Kate will carry on teaching you,' said Christopher eagerly.

'Yes, you must come over each day. It would be a great help to have you here, Abigail. We could work together,' said Kate.

'Mattie can use or sell all that you make, my dears,' said Marian. 'They have been so kind that I want to repay them in some way as they will take no money for this cottage.' She looked up at the dark oak beams in the ceiling and at the wide room in which they lived and ate.

The cottage was large and airy and about a hundred years old, with its original thatched roof and lathe and plaster walls, now dulled to a gentle greyish fawn under the lime wash, showing the wooden structure faintly but with a pleasing pattern. The three doors of yew fitted snugly into the arched doorways in one wall of the room, one leading to the utility services and scullery and another to the spacious larder. The third led to the upper floor, until recently only a store, as the yeoman farmer's family in earlier days had slept in one room the whole length and breadth of the house; after the erection of inner walls, there were now three rooms for sleeping.

John Dunstan had made alterations to the vacant cottage as soon as he heard that his relatives might be coming to live with them. Now, a brick-built chimney and fireplace filled one end of the main room, and the stain of soot and grease on some of the rafters was but a relic of days when the only fire was in the middle of the room.

Outhouses and a small stableyard made the cottage a pleasant and self-contained dwelling to which the Verneys had come as if to a refuge.

'I've made up a box for Peter's things,' said Christopher.

'Are you sure that both of you can fit into that small room at the end of the kitchen?' asked Marian.

'We shall be comfortable, Mother, and when we get up early to work, we shall disturb nobody but Debbie in the kitchen.'

'I'm glad that we sent for Debbie,' said Marian. Her face clouded. 'I wish that Lottie had been as willing to leave London. I hope that they are well.'

'We manage with Debbie to help and the farm workers for the rough jobs,' said Edward. 'If Peter comes, he must work, too. Just because he doesn't like being beaten at school doesn't mean he can sit about doing nothing all day here,' he said sternly. He tried to sound firm but he had given in to Marian's pleadings with some relief. The plague reached out to so many towns now and Eton was close to a bad outbreak. As Marian said, what was the use of making the boy take lessons if he didn't live to use them?

'Who is Peter?' asked Sarah.

'He's my brother and we can go fishing with him,' said Alice, forgetting that she was a young lady.

Edward regarded the two pretty girls with misgivings. Sir Vincent had come to see him a few days earlier and even Marian had no idea of the conversation that followed, but Edward Verney had taken a liking to the young man and trusted him. He had not, however, enjoyed the idea of putting his own daughter in danger.

'Can you give me your word, Sir, that he will not follow her here?'

'I can only say that every way will be found to keep him from knowing where Sarah is staying,' said Vincent Clavell.

'Devil take him. Why can't he stay in London or follow the Court to Oxford?'

'I think he's cooling His Majesty's temper by staying out of his sight,' said Vincent Clavell. 'There were two girls whom he abducted without finding out first that they were well-born and so able to bring justice to bear. He very nearly landed in the Tower for one of them and was threatened by the father of the other so that he dares not show his face at Westminster or Whitehall.'

'The Richard Rouths of this world should be strangled at birth,' growled Edward. 'Lust I can understand. It is normal and healthy and every young man should have his doxy or two, but to take girls of such tender years is a sin against God and the Church and the right thinking of any good man.'

'I wouldn't trouble you, Sir,' said Vincent Clavell, 'but I am summoned away to my ship in a few days and I couldn't rest if my sister was at home with no strong arm to protect her. Here, you have many powerful men working on the farm and your own son who can fight if necessary.'

'For your sister's honour, Sir?' Edward raised a quizzical eyebrow.

'For Alice too, if need be, Mr Verney,' said Vincent quietly. 'He talked of Alice and he has not forgotten her. He even said he would call on you at the first opportunity. I came to warn you, but when he looked at my own sister with such speculation I thought that they would be safer together, and so I ask you to take her in and treat her as your own.'

'Are there not men enough at your Manor, Sir?'

'We have horses more than we have cattle and sheep and the stablehands are a rough crowd who might even take a bribe. The farmhands that my father has there are old and only there to tend the few animals and stock that we keep for our own use when in residence. My parents live more in Scotland and on the estates in Ireland.' He smiled grimly. 'I keep this estate in good heart as it may be all the inheritance I will have apart from my Navy pay.'

Edward nodded and wished again that this man would be the one to inherit all the wealth that must go to the elder son and so leave him without land. 'We will look after her, Sir,' he said. 'I will tell Christopher and leave him to watch for strangers. Alice needn't know that we may have a caller and if he comes, there are many places where the children can play and not be seen.'

And now Sarah was with them and Alice had lost her determination to dislike the young girl as soon as she saw her.

'Did your brother teach you to fish?' asked Alice.

'He taught me to ride and hunt and I ride as a man,' said Sarah proudly.

'I have never been allowed to do that,' Alice said envi-

235

ously. 'I ride well but Father never lets me ride anything but the mildest-mannered beast.'

'Vincent left me my pony,' said Sarah. 'Come and ride her.'

'Not away from the farm,' said Edward. 'If you ride, I want you to promise not to go beyond the home park and the Manor grounds.'

'We shall be safe, Father,' said Alice impatiently. It wasn't right for him to show her up as a baby in front of her new friend.

'You promise or you stay here,' said Edward, and Marian wondered at his stern voice.

'I promise,' said Alice, jutting out her chin sulkily.

'And never forget it,' said Edward. 'I want you back in time to help Kate decorate the waggon for the supper.'

Alice clapped her hands. 'I'd forgotten that it is tonight. Come, Sarah, we'll have a short ride today and then pick fruit in the orchard and make chains of leaves to go on the cart.' They went to fetch the ponies, leaving Edward with his family.

'She seems a pretty little girl,' he ventured, 'and her brother is a sober, responsible man. I hope we see more of him when he returns from sea.'

'Why the sea?' said Kate softly. 'The sea takes all the best.'

'You would not consider marrying a naval man, my dear?'

'After Robert? No, Father.' She looked at him and seemed amused. 'You haven't thought of Vincent Clavell for me, have you?'

'He is likeable and even if he isn't the eldest son, he has riches enough,' said Edward.

'He is barely as old as me,' said Kate.

'Kate needs an older man,' said Anna, who was listening and saying little. 'And Sir Vincent needs someone much younger whom he can cherish as he does his little sister.'

236

'He'll need a woman, not a child,' said Edward testily. 'He cares about his sister and with cause, but he'll look to a woman for marriage, not a girl as young as . . . Alice.' He stopped, surprised at the sudden thought. Alice was a child and not ready for marriage. No, he wasn't interested in her. Anna smiled, knowingly. 'You're quite wrong if you think he comes here for Alice,' said Edward. 'I thought perhaps Kate.' The two girls shook their heads.

Edward had a sudden and sharp vision of Alice as a small child, naked in his arms. He recalled the soft skin and the vulnerability of the tiny body, the small fingernails and the sexless shape that promised beauty. Sorrow mixed with jealousy stabbed his senses. It was years since he had dared to touch his own daughter except to kiss her and to hold her close if she fell down. Another man would do that and more – and she would smile up at him as she never smiled at any other human being. She would marry, one day soon.

'Not Alice?' he asked, hoping for a laughing denial.

'In time,' said Anna. She picked a dead leaf from the bunch of autumn flowers she was making. 'I don't think he knows it yet,' she said, and Kate laughed softly as women do when they know more than their menfolk.

'You are being foolish,' said Edward and walked out. Sarah was a new responsibility and now he had to realise that his younger daughter might be as open to threat as Clavell's sister. 'If that rogue was to lay one finger on Alice, I'd horsewhip him and then kill him,' he muttered, and watched the girls ride off, their laughter hanging on the cool breeze and the sound of hooves dying away over the hill.

Kate wrapped two cheeses in fresh butter muslin and placed them in a wide shallow basket. She put more muslin over them and added a second layer, with fresh herbs in tiny bunches round them. She hesitated and thought, If I don't take them to the vicarage and the Manor, Mother will wonder why. The vicarage was halfway to the Manor

237

where Sir John and Lady Dunstan lived and only a short walk away from the cottage that was a part of the estate. I have to pass the door if I am to see Aunt Mattie, she thought, and knew that this would take courage.

It was easy for Marian to tell her to look in at the vicarage and give the cheeses to George Silke, the young man who had been given the living only six months ago. It should have been a simple task just to walk up the uneven driveway with its avenue of yew trees and to knock on the door, and then to meet him without losing her power to speak, and to smile as she would at any of her family friends.

She pulled on her bonnet and took off her apron. I shall say that I have to go to Aunt Mattie, she decided. 'I can't stay and take tea with you, Mr Silke, nor can I stay to see the needlepoint that the ladies of the parish have done for the altar,' she pictured herself saying.

Partly satisfied, she walked slowly towards the church-yard wall and into the acre of land dotted with graves. Here, there was death with dignity; the dead were buried according to the rites of the Church and with the tears of the mourners to water the sod. Those that died in London seemed far away, extinguished rather than dying, bereft of loved ones and lacking any show of compassion. Tales had filtered through of the sickness growing worse and the city dying, but here it was difficult to imagine what that was like. Kate wandered on to the house where George Silke lived and tried to recall the face of Robert, the man she had loved and who had been swallowed by the sea. The man I still love, she corrected herself. The man I shall love for ever.

Mrs Jason opened the door and Kate smiled. He might be out, visiting parishioners or doing his duty in the church. 'I won't stay if the Reverend Silke is not at home,' she began.

'I hope that you can stay for five minutes, Miss Verney,' said a voice behind her, and George Silke strode up the path from the church. Mrs Jason sniffed and retired to the dim hallway of the vicarage and George Silke led Kate back to the church.

'I am sure that you have many calls on your time, Sir,' said Kate. 'I wanted only to leave these cheeses for you to try.' She blushed. 'At least, my mother asked me to do so and as I am going to the Manor, it is on my way.'

'Then may I walk there with you after I've taken the cheese into the larder?'

'The top ones are for you and the others for Aunt Mattie,' said Kate, giving up her basket. 'But I can't trouble you to waste time on me.'

He took the basket and went swiftly into the house. Some men look like clergymen from the day they go to school, thought Kate, but the Reverend George Silke looked more like a man who rode hard and lived well and voiced none of the mealy-mouthed platitudes that she had had to endure when Robert was killed. He was very well-shod, something she noticed in men, and his hair hung clean and thick over his dark habit. He came out again and smiled, showing white teeth in a gentle smile.

'I took a piece to try although I know I shall eat well tonight,' he said. 'Excellent. I have seldom tasted cheese that gave me more pleasure.' He held the basket and Kate had no choice but to follow him. 'You will be at the supper, Miss Kate?' he asked.

'Yes, we shall all be there.' Until now, it hadn't occurred to her that he would be there, too, but of course Uncle John would want him to ask a blessing on the food and on the harvest and to speak of the fruitfulness of the earth.

'I shall look forward to seeing you all,' he said gravely.

'It will be our pleasure, Sir,' said Kate. They walked in silence for a while and then he talked of church affairs, to fill the gap and to make her relax. Fallen leaves lay soft underfoot but many trees were still in full leaf under the amber sun. Birds hung on high branches, free of families and mating and eager for the freedom of flight when they gathered for migration.

'Nature brings life and takes it away when the time is ripe,' he said.

'Nature is cruel,' said Kate softly. 'God is cruel.'

'God brings His sickle to harvest and the cutting is hard, but after comes the new growth and perhaps a better crop?'

'No,' said Kate, but hated herself for almost believing him.

'I have to go,' he said abruptly, at the gates of the Manor, 'I hope to see you all tonight, but now I have a sorry man to visit who needs my prayers. He is sick and I think will not see the spring, nor even the leaves fall from that oak.'

Kate was left with the basket and she went up to the huge wooden door that stood half-open. Here, there was no need for locks and chains to keep out robbers. She smiled, sadly. Locks did nothing to protect the human heart. Was it right to feel something for another man? Not that he thought of her as anything more than a lamb in his flock and the daughter of a man he admired. Robert was still safe in her memory, she decided.

Aunt Mattie exclaimed over the cheeses as if they were gold dust, and Kate laughed at her praise.

'If they had been bad, you would not have been able to say so, as you taught me, Aunt Mattie,' she chuckled.

'I shall put them on vine leaves in the middle of the table,' said Mattie. 'Come and see what has been prepared.'

Kate went into the great hall and a serving maid hurried out with an empty log basket. The grates in the three deep fireplaces were ready for lighting and four huge oak tables were laden with pewter dishes and mugs, knives and wooden platters and loaves of wheaten bread. Pies with patterns of leaves on the pastry glistened with egg-glaze and smelled of all kinds of savoury fillings, from hare and game to salmon and crayfish from the streams. Venison in thick jelly, turned out from decorative moulds, and cold

240

meats with salamagundy in large bowls tempted Kate enough to make her steal a piece of cold fowl and Mattie watched her indulgently.

'It will be a real family party,' she said, and Kate was pleased at her genuine happiness in having them so near. The first feelings of strangeness had vanished almost overnight after their flight from the capital. Living away from the Manor but a part of the life there made it all easy and Marian had taken to the cottage immediately. Kate knew that her father had breathed sighs of relief as his main dread had been having to live under the feet of his wife's relatives, but now he worked as hard as any on the farm, took ale with Sir John and played chess with him, but could go back to his own nest when he needed to be alone with his family.

'It's good to see smoke from your chimney, Kate,' said Mattie. 'You have brought new life to the whole Manor. I wish that you could all stay for ever.'

'That will not be possible, Aunt Mattie,' said Kate.

'You sound sad,' said the older woman. 'That pleases me more than I can say.' She put the cheeses on a bed of leaves and made room for them on a wicker tray on the table. 'John and I are getting old,' she said. 'We have no children and sooner or later will have to pass this house and all it means on to someone ready to care for it as we have done all our married lives.'

Kate examined a pie intently. Life on the farm was far better than anything she had thought possible now that her future with a naval officer for a husband had been shattered.

'We love you all,' went on Mattie. 'We have talked about it a lot and if any of you would stay and make a life here, we would make sure that your future was assured.'

'I could not stay alone,' said Kate. 'I love the farm and the life here, but you must turn to Christopher for real help.' She smiled at the woman who had come to mean so

241

much to her. 'Find him a good wife and then see,' she said. 'Isn't it strange? Before we came here, he wanted to stay in London and look after the house there and he said he must be back again within two months. He made it sound as if he would die of boredom, and now the days are too short for all he wants to do.'

'He's a good worker and the men like him,' said Mattie. 'If he doesn't find a wife, but wanted to stay, you could tend the house for him.' Kate turned away and Mattie felt for the girl who had to face the future alone or bring herself to know that sorrow passes, albeit not without pain. 'It takes courage to make a new life, my dear,' said Mattie softly, and Kate knew that Christopher wasn't the one who needed courage; sooner or later, she must look to her own future.

'I'll take the basket back,' said Kate now. 'I haven't time to pick berries but I'll ask Alice and her new friend to come along the lane tomorrow to gather them.'

She walked back in a thoughtful mood. Life was changing for all of them and there was no telling what the future held. News from the city was worse again after a recent fall in the number of deaths. Families had returned prematurely to houses that had held infection and were now judged, wrongly, to be clean. Weary bodies slept in beds that had not been aired or cleaned, and clothes abandoned by those fleeing the plague were worn again and took a second toll from the returning crowds. The Brokers of Death sold contagion in the fabrics now put out in the market places and the figures for the end of October made grim reading.

Earlier storms had given way to mild weather and a late autumn, and the harvest had been left until the wet grain was dried. Kate couldn't think of the house they had left. There was so much to do here, and she dreaded the day when Edward would say, 'Time to go back where we belong.'

The cottage was buzzing with activity as Alice and Sarah made garlands of leaves for the great hall at the Manor and Christopher brought in logs for the fires they now lit in the cooler evenings. He piled more logs onto a cart for the Manor and instructed a labourer to take them straight away as they might be needed. Marian packed cakes that Debbie had been baking all day and Anna put jars of pickle and peach preserve into the carriage.

Even Kate became excited. There would be music and dancing after supper and visitors from neighbouring farms and manor houses.

'You will wear your blue silk, Anna?' asked Alice.

'This is the country, not London and not the theatre, Alice,' laughed Anna. 'I haven't worn anything but cotton since we came here, but soon the evenings will be chill and I must see what I have that is warmer.'

'Silk *is* warm,' said Alice.

'What are you about, Minx?' challenged Anna.

'If you wear your blue silk, then I can wear the red dress I wore to the theatre. Sarah has no dress like it and I want her to see it.'

'Is that fair? Sarah has never been far from home and so does not need elaborate gowns. She may feel ill at ease with you dressed up in silks.'

'If you don't wear the blue, then what will you wear?' asked Alice. 'Aunt Mattie said we must put on our very best as all the County will be there. Some of them go to London, you know. They can't all be clodhoppers!'

'Very well.' Anna smiled indulgently. Alice usually had her own way and what was the harm in dressing up for once? It might impress upon the neighbours that the Verneys were people of importance and not poor relations.

Once she had decided, Anna took pleasure in making herself pretty. Her hair was brushed a hundred times and the long silky darkness glowed with raven blue-blackness. I do look darker, she thought, and the blue does nothing

243

to hide it. She shrugged. Who would notice or care? She put amethysts in her earlobes and a necklace of matching stones at her throat, and when Marian came to inspect her toilette before they took the coach to the Manor, she gasped.

'You look beautiful, Anna,' she said, but hoped that Edward would not examine his ward too closely. Somewhere in the Huguenot background must have been a stronger Latin strain that emanated dignity and passion and pride as Anna greeted Sir John and his wife and they stood by the wide fireplace in the great hall. The heavy silk sighed as she walked and made Anna instinctively elegant. She turned to speak to another guest with whom all the girls had ridden on the Downs, and behind her heard the metal tread of riding boots.

'Your servant, Madam,' said Captain Bennet, addressing the lady in the group to whom Anna was talking. He bent over to kiss her hand and saw the woman in the glinting blue dress.

'Have you met Miss Anna Ruyter?'

'Yes.' He bowed slightly but made no effort to touch her hand and Anna wished that she had worn a simple dress of pale lemon or lavender. He was staring and her discomfort increased.

'I see that you have been riding, Sir,' said Anna, and felt foolish. Anyone could see it.

'I came from Oxford at the invitation of Sir John,' he said.

'Then you came from the Court?' Anna regained her composure and the Captain stopped staring at her. She smiled, and the other ladies clustered round him asking questions about the King.

'Are they still at Oxford? Does the Court move back to London soon? What of Lady Castlemaine? Has she borne another son?'

'What are the ladies wearing?' asked Alice who had wriggled closer.

'They are as elegant as Miss Ruyter, if that were possible. I took you for a lady-in-waiting, Madam,' he said, and Alice giggled. Her red dress and fair hair made the perfect foil for the darker tones and the sulky fire of the blue stones.

'Is she not beautiful, Sir?' asked Alice archly.

'As beautiful as a flower,' he said politely, with a stiff bow.

'What flower?' pressed Alice, enjoying Anna's discomfort.

'A flower I found in Switzerland when I inspected the guard there,' he said. 'Miss Anna would know which one. I think you have books on Botany.' His smile seemed forced against his will. The group drifted away. Botany was not what they wanted to hear, and Alice sensed that she was becoming unwelcome.

'I've heard of gentian,' said Anna, thinking of the deep blue colour.

'No, this was edelweiss,' he corrected her.

'That is a white flower that grows in rocky places,' said Anna. Her eyes challenged him. 'I am not snowy white and I hate the cold. Gentian is better.'

'I disagree. Gentians grow in the valley and can be picked easily, but to cull the edelweiss one has to climb and conquer and face danger.' His eyes were expressionless. 'They call it "Lad's Death" because many die picking it for their sweethearts in dangerous places.'

'I am not . . . dangerous,' said Anna. She moved away, hiding her trembling hands in the folds of the full skirt.

'Any man who sought you would face rocks and his own conscience, Madam, but I owe you an apology.'

Anna turned to face him. 'I think not, Sir.'

'I apologise for thinking you were related to the sworn enemy of England,' he said.

245

'There is no need, Sir,' she replied coldly. 'I am proud of my name and should I be judged by my true friends, I think they would look further, beyond the name and beyond my face.'

'As I look deep into the petals to find the honey,' he murmured.

'I see that you have learned pretty speeches at Court, Sir. Tell me more about Oxford.' Mattie was calling them in to eat and as if by appointment and not of necessity, Anna and Daniel Bennet drifted in with the rest.

'Oxford?' He took a wooden platter and loaded it with food. 'I found good books in many libraries there.' He began to eat as if he was starving, and Anna saw how tired he was under the determination to appear normal. She picked up a piece of bread and some game on another dish and pointed to the wide rim of the fireplace. He gave her a smile that was more natural. 'Thank you, Miss Anna. I have been in the saddle since dawn and I confess to being tired.'

He looked round the crowded room. 'Are you expecting to see friends?' she asked.

'Not friends,' he said. He ate more and drank from the fine glass that Anna filled with red wine. 'I heard that Rollo was back in the land of the living.'

'Sir Rollo?' Anna fingered the necklace and then sipped her wine. 'Then he has been ill?' She looked agitated and very concerned. 'Is he really better?' Her mind worked rapidly. Was it forty days since he had been taken ill? If he had the plague, he had recovered well and surely it was a miracle.

'You are concerned, Madam?' The tiredness triumphed and Captain Bennet's eyes were dull with fatigue and some-thing more like disappointment. 'He sent his greetings, Madam. He is fortunate indeed to have your concern.'

'I, that is, we all wondered what had become of him as

246

we heard that he was sick. He didn't come to take leave of us or offer his protection as escort as he had once promised.'

'I am also at fault, Madam. I was summoned to Salisbury and had not time to say goodbye to any but Lord Chalwood, and my kinswoman.'

'My father wished that you were with us, Captain Bennet. He mentioned you several times.'

'And you, Miss Anna? Did you wish my company?'

'I was anxious to return your books, Sir,' said Anna, with a composure that grew as his faded. She took his empty platter. 'Please stay there, Sir, and I will bring some more pie.' She smiled as she moved away, her silk gown flowing after her like a blue wake and her dark hair glistening. All men are vain, she thought. He doesn't care for me as I remind him of his enemies but he resents me caring for the health of Sir Rollo. She brought him more food and filled his glass, but refused more wine herself.

'I have to go back to Oxford in three days' time,' he said. 'My brother has been ill after falling from a horse and I begged leave from the Court to see to my father's estates.'

'Have you no other brothers who are not in the Army?' Captain Bennet drained his glass. 'I thought that there were two or three older brothers,' said Anna.

'There are, but only Michael is able to run the estates as a business.'

'And you?' He nodded. 'But you are away and cannot help your father?'

'I have no claim on him as there are so many above me in age. The Army is my career and one I love,' he said, almost defiantly. 'I may never be wealthy but I know of no other life I would rather live.'

'There are other things of value,' Anna agreed, and felt closer to him than she had thought possible. 'I was grateful for your books and have read them from one cover to the end.'

'I have more in my saddlebags and there are many more

247

in my father's library. May I call on you tomorrow with a selection?'

'What of your father's business?' asked Anna. 'It is a long ride and you will be busy, Sir.'

'I am staying here tonight,' he said, and looked away. 'I can spare half an hour to leave the books and if you are too busy to receive me then we can each go about our business.' The formal manner shut out any warmth and Anna was reminded that he enjoyed her interest in science as he would appreciate it in a man, but he had no time for sunburned girls who were half-Dutch.

Chapter 16

'Roger Carter is no writer even if he is my senior clerk,' said Edward Verney.

'He has written many pages more than I would have done,' said Marian calmly.

'He tells of the Bills of Mortality and of businesses that have failed through lack of trade, mostly those I have no knowledge of and who have never dealt with us, so they are not important; he tells of the way the river smells, but says he never ventures out if he can avoid it, so how does he know? He leaves out all that I want to hear. I know nothing of the ships in the offing which carry my goods. No, the plague is on the docks and Master Carter doesn't go there and doesn't encourage callers who could be of use!'

'I think he's wise, Edward. If he was taken sick, you'd have no news and nobody to look after your interests in London.'

'But when he does write, he could at least tell me what news I want to hear.'

'Does he mention Lottie and Sam?' Marian put down her sewing.

'Yes. He says here that he gave Sam enough money for a month so that he needn't come to the office again for a while. Don't you see, Marian, I want to know about Sam

249

and this is our only way of keeping in touch! When I send letters, I have to send through Roger, as Sam cannot read. I depend on Carter to keep me informed and to tell Sam anything I want done.'

'Lottie can read,' said Marian. 'I'll write to her and she can send a letter back. She finds it difficult but I'm sure that she will manage somehow. She used to read the books that Mary Creed kept, but her writing is bad.'

'One thing that Roger wrote puzzled me. He heard that Sir Rollo FitzMedwin had the plague and that his servants had fled the house, but last night Captain Bennet told me that Sir Rollo is down at his family home, Mersley Manor.'

'I thought the Captain looked very tired,' mused Marian. 'I hoped that Anna would cheer him but he wouldn't stay for the dancing and went to bed early.' She sighed. 'I feel that Anna's name is a great barrier to any social contact with eligible men.'

'And the sun has made her dark enough to put off any man who hates foreigners,' said Edward. 'If we had peace tomorrow with the Dutch, everyone would welcome her gladly because of her name, instead of looking at her sideways. She needs to be off our hands, much as I love her.'

'Don't send Anna away,' said Alice from the doorway.

'Nobody sends Anna away,' said Edward sharply. 'She has a home here for life if she wants it, so please, Miss, stop listening to half a conversation before you jump to conclusions.'

'Last night I made Captain Bennet pay her a compliment,' said Alice smugly. 'He didn't want to say it but I made him agree that Anna looked beautiful.'

'You deserve a box on the ears,' said Edward. 'If I was paying court to a lady and that happened, I'd have done it myself and not left it to her father.' He made a threatening gesture towards her and Alice fled, laughing.

'That girl is becoming a hoyden,' said Marian. 'She

should have a strict governess and pay more attention to her books.'

'I have it in mind,' said Edward. 'When Peter comes here, I shall ask the Reverend Silke to give him tutoring and Alice can join them. The books that Anna reads are too deep for a lively girl and of no importance later when she manages a household.'

'Alice is learning many crafts here, Edward. She can make bread even though she hates doing it and she dresses a hare for table very well.' Marian defended her daughter and couldn't imagine her sitting in the gloomy house near the church, studying Euclid. 'Soon, we may go back to our own home and she can have a companion and chaperone.'

Edward tugged at his hair, which had grown longer in the country as he never now wore wigs unless very important visitors were expected. 'We must keep a good eye on Alice,' he muttered.

'What is worrying you, Edward?' Marian asked. 'I've noticed that you often look very serious, ever since Sir Vincent Clavell left Sarah with us. She is a good child and I have no doubts about her influence over Alice. They love each other dearly.'

'I think she is safe here,' said Edward.

'Safe? Of course she is. How could she come to harm in a peaceful and law-abiding village where everyone looks after the people from the Manor?'

'You're right, Marian. If strangers came, they would be noticed and they could do no harm.'

'They look at anyone who doesn't live here,' said Marian. 'Nobody from London carrying sickness would go by unnoticed.'

'And we can see their side of it now,' said Edward. 'Sometimes I have to remind myself how we felt when we were driven away from the inn and no villagers would offer us hospitality, but what can we do if we think that our own children might suffer?' His natural sense of justice

251

made him uncomfortable at times. News from the city did little to ease his conscience when he was safe and well-fed and had no family worries. Perhaps the unstable markets and rocky businesses made up for it as there was plenty to annoy and cause him anxiety there.

'I'll just walk up to the Manor and tell Sir John the bits of news that Roger did manage to include,' he said. He enjoyed many activities that once would have made him tired or would have been beneath his attention, but now it was pleasant to walk, and to be greeted by Sir John's servants with a respect tinged with friendliness that had none of the cringing servility of their opposite numbers in the city. He stopped to consider the quality of the hay in the barn by the church and wondered if the portion of a man of the cloth would support a wife or whether the Reverend Silke had private means. At the supper the night before, George Silke had made it obvious that he was interested in Kate and she seemed to find his attentions welcome. Wise man not to rush into avowals of love, thought Edward. Kate was still bruised and would need more time, but it would be a suitable match.

He picked a cobnut from the hedge and wished that his teeth were as strong as they had been in days when he could crack nuts and eat them without having to pound them with a stone.

Sir John Dunstan met him by the stables and led him in to see his latest buy. 'Fifteen and a half hands and well-muscled,' he said, slapping the mare on the rump. 'I don't ride often enough, Edward. I became lazy before your arrival here, but now we really must hunt this autumn and the young ones can race.'

'Who is there to race?' asked Edward.

'There are many from neighbouring estates and many more who visit them and stay for a week or so for hare and birds, and we need to keep the foxes down. One of the tenants is complaining that his henhouse is in a sorry state

252

after Reynard took his toll last week.' He laughed and placed an affectionate hand on Edward's sleeve. 'We have enough room to house an army and it will be like old times. Having you here has made such a difference to Mattie and myself. If it wasn't a sin to say it, I'd hope the plague lasted for ever!'

'You've been very kind, Sir. Coming here was a wrench that took some consideration but now I almost agree with you. I've never seen my family so well and so occupied.'

'All but Alice, and she is too young to live in the country,' said John shrewdly. 'She'd get into mischief anywhere but she needs life and colour and fancy gowns.' He smiled. 'Marry her off and be rid of the care of her. There are young men staying at Mersley who are ripe for marriage if they could be pinned down so early.'

'Mersley?' Edward stared at him. 'Who is staying there?'

'A crowd from the Court who while away the time until the King returns to London. Oxford has no room for them, it seems, and they hanker after sport they cannot have there.'

'What sport?' asked Edward. 'And who are these bucks?'

'Why, Edward, you look like thunder!'

'Who is there, Sir John?'

'The family and some from Lord Carnegie. House guests like Richard Routh.' He laughed. 'A cunning youngster he was, I recall. He used to visit us at one time, but he made all the girls cry. I haven't seen him for what must be five years.'

'He makes them cry even now,' said Edward grimly, and told John what he had heard about the young nobleman. 'He is taking no short congé from Court but fled from the wrath of the King and two families who seek his blood.'

'I thought that Captain Bennet was hard on the boy but I didn't know this.' Sir John pulled at Edward's coat. 'Come into the house and talk to Mattie. We must make sure that the girls are safe.'

253

Edward regarded him anxiously. 'What has happened?' he asked when they arrived breathless in the great hall. The fireplaces had been swept and cleaned and fresh logs awaited a touch of flame; the huge tables were cleared of the food that had covered them the night before. Rushes on the floor, damped to lay the dust, were being swept up by two men with wide brooms. The autumn sun warmed the tapestries on the pale walls and showed the prowess of long-dead members of the family. The garlands made by the girls lay shrivelling in one corner and the house was returning to normal, with an air of haste that was more in preparation for a feast then the leisurely clearing up after a harvest supper.

Mattie looked flustered. 'Captain Bennet has left to see you, Edward. Did you not pass him on the bridle-path?'

'I walked along the lane,' said Edward. 'Is something amiss?'

'I hope not,' said Mattie with a look of reproach towards her husband. 'You told me that they would be men of breeding and charm, John, but I am beginning to think we are mistaken in your choice of guests! Captain Bennet was angry and left me in grave doubt about these men.'

'You told him that Richard Routh was coming here?'

'He asked, as he hoped to see Vincent Clavell again, but we hear that he is still on his ship. I showed him the note from Lord Chalwood who is entertaining Lord Carnegie's friends for racing and he said something that I can only suppose he learned from common soldiers! What are we coming to, John?'

'Richard Routh is coming here?' said Edward. She nodded.

'I wish that you had told me sooner that Clavell's sister had been threatened by that man,' said John impatiently. 'In the city such things are kept within the family for safety but here it is the opposite. If everyone knows a danger, then we have eyes and ears all over the village. Loyal folk

254

who care about us and ours and who guard their own daughters, to keep them safe for men who live and work here.' He shrugged. 'We do have bastards, but mostly from loose women and the men are jealous as there are not enough brides to go round.'

He went to the window and shouted for his groom. 'Tell the men to look out for strangers who say they are our guests. Treat them with respect but be watchful as there are some I don't trust with the girls of the village or with any who wear skirts be they nine or ninety!'

'That was direct,' said Edward with reluctant admiration.

'They are used to blunt-speaking and respect me for it. They know that their families are safe here.' He laughed and winked at Mattie. 'Even the "Droit du Seigneur" has lapsed here for several generations but who knows, a lusty new Lord of the Manor might want to take it up again, as his right.'

'This is 1665, Edward, not the Dark Ages. That custom went out of usage years ago.'

'There are still resemblances to my forbears among the villagers,' said Edward. 'Faces that came to life after the Lord took his rights on the night before the girl's marriage. There are some who still say it was good, as better blood was mingled with the common.'

Mattie knew that he was teasing her but she bridled. 'I shall keep you in sight on the eve of the Hobsons' wedding,' she said.

'I have smelled the girl at close quarters, Mattie, and I couldn't stomach her,' he replied. 'Come, Edward, we must go back to the farm and make sure that Christopher knows that the men he was eager to meet might not be as welcome as he thought.' Sir John mounted the new mare and Edward climbed up behind him, thankful that he had lost weight and that Sir John was thin and wiry.

'Is he as bad as they say, I wonder?' questioned Edward.

'It's one thing to seduce a girl from the kitchen and another to brave a house in daylight and steal away a girl from good family.' He bit his lip. 'But it seems that he has done that twice at least, and if twice, then how many more times has he struck and not been found? They say that once the liking for children is there, it's like a dog which tastes blood on the first sheep he worries.'

Later, 'Where is Alice?' was his first question as he strode into the cottage. 'Where are Sarah and Alice, Madam?'

'Picking berries and finding mushrooms,' said Anna, who was seated by the window as though looking for someone to come in through the stable yard.

'And Captain Bennet? Has he been here?'

'He came,' said Anna shortly. 'He came as he had promised, sparing me a few minutes of his time to leave this book.' She pointed to a thick volume on the table. 'He rushed in and barely said a greeting, then hurried away again.'

'Did he say where he would go?'

'He asked where Alice was,' said Anna. She felt humiliated. Her new gown of russet wool with the fine lace falling softly across the bosom had been wasted. In fact, she knew that Debbie had smiled, knowing that she dressed to make the Captain look at her twice.

'And where *is* Alice?' demanded Edward with mounting apprehension.

'I think she is safe, Edward,' said John quietly. 'The visitors are not due until dinner-time, and you can keep her indoors until tomorrow when they might be gone. I'll make excuses that we have other guests coming and they might leave us for Mersley Manor.'

'You said that you have room for an army and they will be used to hard beds or straw when they hunt or race and have to sleep in barns.' Edward was growing more and more uneasy. It was usually Marian who had premonitions

256

of evil, but now he was sure that something evil existed close to them.

'Is Christopher in the yard?' asked John.

'He went with Captain Bennet,' said Anna. She stood up suddenly. 'What is wrong? Have they seen someone with the plague?' She thought of Rollo FitzMedwin and the sickness. If he was staying at Mersley Manor, he could have brought infection with him and perhaps one of his servants now had it. Many were infected like that, after all signs had disappeared from the person who first caught the contagion in the household.

'The sickness, Anna? This sickness is of the mind and soul and needs destroying.' The two men went to look out of the window and peered in all directions. 'Which way?' asked Edward helplessly. Two middle-aged men with one horse, unless they asked for another to be saddled and so wasted time, seemed rather pointless as neither of them knew where to go and for whom they were looking.

'We'd best wait, Edward,' said John. 'I don't know if we should seek out Christopher or the girls or Captain Bennet, who also appears to have some interest in this.'

Edward looked up at the sky. 'It's nearly noon and if you expected guests for dinner, they will be here soon.' He forced a smile. 'Alice has a healthy appetite and is usually sitting at the board before the food is ready, so she may return before they come down that road.'

But of late, when she and Sarah found a baby animal abandoned by its mother, or stopped to eat nuts and berries, they forgot the time and rushed in, covered with grass seeds and dust and had to be cleaned up before they could eat. Marian had given in to the inevitable and now dressed the girls in simple gowns, easily washed, and apart from the quality of the cloth, resembling the clothes worn by the daughters of the better-shod farmers.

'When did the children go out?' asked Sir John.

'Soon after they finished shaking the beds and taking the

257

dirty linen to Debbie to wash,' said Anna. 'They have been away for over two hours and said they would bring back bundles of sorrel and some nuts.' She began to look anxious and her frozen expression vanished. 'They are safe, aren't they? What could hurt them here?'

'They are safe,' said Sir John soothingly. 'Edward is fussing like a mother hen and Captain Bennet was no better.' He laughed but couldn't hide his own anxiety. 'This is my land and my people live here. No harm could come to them even if they were lost in the woods and slept in the open.'

'Then why are you so anxious?' asked Anna. 'First Captain Bennet rushed in and out again as if the Dutch Army was after him, and Christopher was as white as a sheet and went with him, and now you are here, trying to tell us that nothing is wrong.'

'It may be nothing,' said Edward. He felt slightly ridiculous. What Sir John said made sense. How could men riding through a village and country lanes threaten his pretty Alice? They wouldn't have the time and the girls would not stay to put themselves at risk. Still any father would feel as he did, having heard about Routh's evil reputation. Edward unbuttoned his jacket and sat heavily on a settle. No man would leap out on a girl as if he was a beast. He moved restlessly and walked back to the window.

Anna went to the door. 'I thought I heard them,' she said, and went to her room to change her dress into something more serviceable, then came down to the kitchen to Debbie. 'There may be extra guests,' she said. 'Is there enough rabbit stew for two more?'

'Plenty, Miss, but if they eat hearty, they'll need more bread and I still have it in the oven.' She laughed. 'Miss Alice left it to prove but the yeast was sulky as she used water that wasn't warm enough and it took twice as long to rise.'

258

'I'll make herb dumplings,' said Anna. She fetched a big earthenware bowl from the dark shelf under the larder and Debbie brought coarsely-ground flour, and dripping from the ducks they had eaten a few days ago. The servant-girl rubbed dried herbs between her fingers until they were fine and the stems could be thrown away, while Anna mixed the fat into the flour and added a pinch of salt and soda.

Steadily adding a thin stream of water and a spoonful of sour milk, Anna mixed the dumplings and shaped them into balls. She dipped each one in more flour and as Debbie held back the copper lid of the huge pot on the fire, she waited until the gravy round the rabbit joints was bubbling and then dropped each dumpling in separately. Even as she watched, the floury balls began to swell in the boiling liquid and she reached over for the last four dumplings.

Captain Bennet lingered in the doorway to watch and Debbie giggled. Anna turned swiftly to see what the girl found so amusing and dropped a dumpling on to the fire instead of into the pot.

'I prefer mine boiled,' said Daniel Bennet solemnly. He no longer looked tired but his face showed signs of tension.

'Have you been invited to dinner, Sir? If not, then you will not be troubled by my bad cooking.'

'I have been invited,' he said, with a mocking bow.

'Did you find Alice?' she asked, and nodded to Debbie to place the lid back and told her to keep the fire hot until the dumplings were done.

'Yes, we found her and Sarah,' he said. He came into the kitchen and put a finger into the cream pail, licked it and looked into the pots on the fire.

'Well, where were they and what is all the fuss about?' said Anna, impatiently. She was acutely aware of the man watching her and angry now to be wearing a gown that made her look like a serving maid.

'Richard Routh is on his way to stay with Sir John and Lady Matilda,' he said. He came closer and Anna knew

259

that her hair was coming loose but she dared not touch it with floury hands. She raised a hand halfway to her hair and then stopped.

'Richard Routh? Isn't he the young man who was at the theatre when we saw *Solyman the Magnificent?*' she asked, and frowned. 'Is everything we hear about him true?'

'Everything bad, Ma'am,' said Captain Bennet.

'You don't like him?' She faced the man who was now nibbling at the edges of one of the hot biscuits that Debbie took from the lower half of the bread oven. Anna thought back to the night when everything was bright, the dresses of the ladies glittered and the gentlemen looked handsome, bold and tantalisingly wicked. Captain Bennet had not been as parrot-bright as Richard Routh and the attractive face had the advantage of showing no signs of conflict other than those of an amorous nature. Anna glanced at the Captain. He could be jealous of the man who had wealth and influence and until lately had been a favourite at Court.

'I do not approve of him,' said Daniel Bennet, simply.

Anna tossed back the hair that was now escaping fast. 'You are full of prejudice, Sir. Surely he is only as other young men, enjoying life as much as any can in these sad times?'

'There are ways of disporting that are innocent and some that have landed better men than Routh in the Tower,' said Bennet sternly.

'The Tower? I can't believe that Sir Richard Routh is guilty of treason.' The dark eyes that made her want to back away, and yet excited her as no man's had done even over her fan in the theatre, flashed fire.

'And if Alice was deflowered by such as he, would you say pretty things about him and beg he be spared?'

Anna brushed back her hair with her hand. 'He hasn't harmed her?'

'No, we found her and Sarah in the garden of the wood-cutter playing with baby chicks and sent them home by

260

the back lane.' He took another biscuit and frowned. 'We arrived there and the girls were leaving when Routh and two more came into the lane. Alice was running and Sarah looked back to see who was coming, and Routh saw them for a second.'

'They said nothing?'

'Routh laughed and said that the woodcutter was more of a man than he could credit him if he had daughters like that. We didn't correct him,' said Captain Bennet. 'Christopher told them the quickest way to the Manor and we followed the girls to make sure that they went home and that Routh didn't turn back.'

'So nothing happened,' said Anna. She was cross with herself for looking as she did, and now she knew that her hair was touched with white flour. Alice seemed to make this man more concerned than if she was his own sister, and Anna wondered bitterly if his concern was any more pure than Richard Routh's.

'Nothing,' he agreed. 'Is that food ready yet? Have pity on a starving man, Debbie.' She bobbed and took the hint that she should do more than stare at her betters while they talked, taking in every word they spoke, and went to lay more platters on the oak table.

Anna lifted the lid of the pot and saw that the dumplings were done. She sniffed. There would be bread enough if they ate it hot from the oven. She turned to call Debbie but Daniel Bennet stopped her. 'I'll take the bread out,' he said. 'It wouldn't be the first time.' He looked into the big pot and sighed. 'How sad that you work so hard that your hair is grey, Madam.'

Anna put a hand to her hair again but he closed his hand over her wrist. 'You make it worse,' he said, and Anna stood quite still while he carefully wiped her hair with a cloth. This is the first time you've touched me, willingly, she thought and the shock of his touch was more than she anticipated. He turned her hands palm upwards and wiped

261

away the drying flour. 'You have strong hands, Madam,' he said. He ran a finger along a line on the palm of her right hand. 'A strong hand showing a long life.' He smiled. 'I like to know that my friends will not die young.'

'That is gypsy talk,' said Anna, snatching away her hand.

'I have known gypsies who were good folk,' he said. Anna stirred the pot and refused to look at him. She knew that he had no great wealth of his own, but did it mean he was so poor that he had to pull his own loaves from the oven?

Out of the corner of her eye she watched him take the long wooden shovel and lift the baked loaves on to the cool slab by the window. The smell of fresh bread filled the kitchen and he was smiling. Anna brought pats of butter from the larder, shaped by wooden boards ridged to give a pattern, and put them on a tray. She added three loaves and carried them to the dinner table. Marian hurried out to tell the others that food was ready and when Anna went into the kitchen, Debbie was being helped by the youngest serving lad to carry the pot to table.

'Thank you,' said Anna, and walked to the slate sink to rid her fingers of the rest of the dough stuck round her nails. Her hands looked very pale under the cool water and she shook the droplets off and dried them on a cloth. The Captain did the same and as she handed him the cloth, he took her hand and kissed it. Anna hoped that she was not trembling. Many men had kissed her hand in greeting and farewell and sometimes to flirt with her, and she had never resented it. He looked up at her face as he bent over her hands and there was no flirtation in his eyes. She dragged her hands away and laughed, weakly. 'You have no need to thank me for the biscuits you stole or for the good meal you will now eat if you go in there and sit down.'

'I have another favour to ask, Miss Anna.'

'You have, Sir?'

262

'If you can spare the time, will you discuss with me the content of the book I brought?'

'I thought that you were bound for your father and his estates?' she said, walking to the kitchen door. 'You were intent on going earlier.'

'I shall stay here,' he said. 'Sir John lent me a man to take messages and to bring me news, and I have sent him with the papers that my father needed from the city.'

'And the King? What if he hears that you are not using your leave as he ordered?'

'I shall not go back to Oxford, Miss Anna. I have other orders.'

'Are you going away?' Anna felt a twinge of regret and wondered if he wanted to leave England again so soon.

'Only for a while. The East India Company have need of more men to guard their properties in Africa and I am going to organise them and find suitable officers to oversee the arrangements in case the Dutch attack again.'

'You will be missed, Sir.'

He took her hand. 'May I depend on that, Miss Anna? Do you say that you will miss me?'

'To whom shall I turn for books?' she replied demurely. 'Your father will have to manage his affairs with only your brothers to help him and Alice will have to be guarded by other strong arms.'

'Read my book and I shall require a catechism of it when I return.'

'You are hungry and I hear my uncle talking to Lady Marian,' said Anna, and reluctantly he released her hand.

Alice and Sarah were in the throes of a fit of giggles at the table. This infuriated Edward, now that they were safe. They looked so young and innocent that he wanted to shut them away from harm. Routh was too close to the cottage for his liking, and even if, as he promised, Sir John would ride back now for dinner in his own house and tell the visitors nothing about the Verneys, care would be needed to protect the girls until the party left the district.

Anna felt that the Captain was looking at her more than at his platter and for a man dying of hunger, he ate no more than she did. Her heart beat faster but there was an underlying sadness in her response to his attention. He was poor. Mrs Blackwell had said it clearly and he needed a wife with money and property to keep him as a gentleman officer. She forced herself to think of his first reactions to her; the cold aloof presence in the carriage on the way to Tothill Gardens when he first heard her name was Ruyter, and the way he had avoided touching her on each occasion of meeting.

A distant relative with a vast estate had been courted by far more handsome men than the Captain and their studied charm and extravagant compliments had been the laughing stock of the house, as Margaret was plain to the point of ugliness and no man who wasn't blind could have failed to notice it. Money is a great beautifier, thought Anna, and her great dark eyes under the madonna-like hair grew sadder. If only he would woo her for herself alone and not for her money. Was he trying to woo her now? It was impossible to say as he was talking animatedly with Kate and gave Anna not a glance.

I am dreaming like a silly girl, she told herself. Just because the Captain shares my delight in books and science doesn't mean he could ever love me, and with my name he would never want to have any more intimate contact with me, but she watched his face and his hands as he ate and talked. He used his hands like a Frenchman when he wanted to illustrate what he was saying, and Anna smiled, wondering how long ago it was that one of his family had mingled his blood with a continental. It made her feel easier. She smiled with a wicked glint in her eyes. What if he had Dutch ancestry as well? But no, that gesture was

264

more Gallic or Italian than the phlegmatic Dutch. I have both Dutch and Italian blood, she thought.

Daniel Bennet saw the smile in the dreaming eyes and wondered who it was for. Not me, that's for sure. She will never forgive me for hating her name and I could never ask her to marry me. A name and wealth were too great a barrier and she had far too much to offer any man with twice her fortune, but he saw her blush as he looked at her, and knew that the blush at least was for him.

Chapter 17

'Mr Verney is of the opinion that he hears no news of you, Sam,' said Roger Carter, seriously. He closed the ledger on the desk before him and regarded Sam with an air of reproach.

'That's not my fault, Mr Carter. You told me to stay away from here and you never come to the house, so how can he know about us?' Sam felt bolder than usual, talking to the man who had authority over his living now that the family was in Surrey.

'That's beside the point, Sam. They have forgotten the dangers here in London, with them safe in the country and no thought for the sick here.'

'That isn't true, Mr Carter. They care about us and they didn't want to go away but for Miss Alice and the other young ladies.' He approached the desk.

'Stay back, Sam. I don't know where you passed by this morning and I want no infection in here.'

'Is there news of them coming back?' asked Sam eagerly. 'When that boy came with the message that you wanted to see me, I thought that something was amiss.'

'They are well and they will stay until the pestilence is over,' said Roger. 'Meanwhile, you will see me once a month and take your wages and money for the house expenses, but each week you can see my junior out in the open and tell him the news. He has to go out to buy what I require, but it is not necessary for me to expose myself to risk as I have too many responsibilities here.'

Sam grinned. 'It's bad but not as bad as it was, with six hundred less dead this week and the weather turning chill. It might be the end of it soon, Mr Carter, and then you can come out for All Saints' Day.'

'It isn't only the sickness, Sam. There are desperate men about, sailors who have been turned off their ships when they were laid up for repairs and who now starve or steal. They lie in wait for clerks from the Navy Office and beg for money but until they are strong, the Navy doesn't want them back on board.'

'But if they starve, how can they be strong?' asked Sam.

'Exactly,' said Roger Carter. 'That's another reason for you to stay away from the city and the docks. The pressmen are out again looking for healthy men to man the boats now being victualled for another fight with the Dutch. They say that De Ruyter is out of Texel at the head of ninety ships and he intends invading us.' He looked at Sam's clean but sober working clothes and sturdy limbs. 'You'd be safer in livery but there are few carriages in London now; and those are owned by the very high and by those on His Majesty's business.'

'I'll be careful,' said Sam. 'I have too much at stake to be other than careful, Mr Carter. Lottie is nearly due, or will be in four weeks and I have to find a clean woman to look after her.'

'From the country?' Roger was alarmed. 'What nurses are left are no better than sluts and most carry the pestilence. You'd do better to send her away, Sam, while she is well.'

'Lottie won't go away and she wants our child to be born here,' said Sam. He was inclined to agree with Roger Carter but he knew that Lottie had made up her mind. He hesitated, and decided not to tell Roger that Lottie's mother wanted to come to her when she was confined. Even though the plague ebbed and flowed over the City and out-parishes, Cripplegate was still highly contagious. 'We'll have to see,' said Sam. 'If the worst comes, then I'll call in Dr Verney or turn my hand to being midwife. It can't be too difficult. I've delivered colts and lambed before now.'

Roger Carter blenched at the idea. 'I hope all goes well,' he coughed. 'Just make sure that no contagion comes to the house. My master will want to step back as if nothing has changed.' He frowned. 'Many of his private documents are missing, so I suppose they went on to Oxford with the wills and some other papers that he sent there. I hope Mr Verney does not have all his money with him, either. Who knows what robbers may attack a simple country village?'

Sam kept quiet. If Mr Verney had wanted his head clerk to be aware of the deep pit under the stables that now contained a fortune in legal papers and stocks and money, he would have told him; Sam felt again the pride it gave him to know that only he and Mr Verney knew where they were hidden.

'Do you want me to look among the books in the library, Sir? I wouldn't know what to look for but you could tell me.'

'No, leave well alone and when things are better, I'll come and look for myself before the family returns. Meanwhile, here is your money and a letter from Lady Marian for Lottie. Can she read?'

'Yes, Lottie can make out words,' said Sam proudly. 'She isn't good at writing but she can read enough.'

'So you can tell your news to Price and he can write it down for Mr Verney,' said Roger. He shuffled papers in a way that told Sam it was time to leave. 'Take care in the side roads. If you are robbed of your wages, you will get no more here.'

Sam divided the money and hid it in various purses among his clothing, then took up the cudgel he now carried

268

in a strap on the horse's saddle. The horse stood in the inner courtyard away from prying eyes but still watched over by a gaunt-faced boy as Sam hadn't the heart to refuse him the penny or so he earned by being there. He also gave him a piece of salt bacon that Lottie had spared and a bit of bread. 'Not a word to anyone, and it didn't come from here,' said Sam, knowing that Roger Carter would have no time for beggars.

'God bless you, Sir,' said the boy and stuffed the bacon under his belt, hidden by the ragged shirt. He chewed on the bread and sat by a pillar until he had eaten it, while Sam rode out into the deserted street.

The air was crisp and the smell of the city was dulled now that there was less refuse in the streets. The grisly heaps of the dead that had accumulated during the worst of the plague had now been carried away and tossed into pits. Some pits had been closed and covered with a thin layer of earth through which the corruption found an easy path and filled the surrounding air with foulness, but in the main streets, where there were no pits, everything looked more normal, if the red crosses on the doors could be ignored. The cobbled roads were dirty and weeds grew in every crevice, untended gardens and hedges grew wild and there were signs of neglect on all sides, but with the crisper weather new hope came and more people ventured forth to breathe the air.

The cry of the driver of the plague cart was a reminder that there was still pestilence about and Sam drew rein to avoid meeting the cart. He watched the small procession and recognised the Searcher. His blood seemed to freeze. Mary Creed in her long white gown and wide black hat looked like a witch carrying a white wand. She had never looked kind or sweet but now her eyes burned with power and zeal and she looked up at the man on horseback as she passed by. A smile that was as evil as a snake's vemon lit her face but she gave no other sign that she knew him.

'If I was a Catholic I'd cross myself,' Sam murmured. 'The Good Lord keep me from evil and never let Lottie look on that face again.'

So that's where they had gone. He glanced at the driver of the cart and at the Bearer of the Dead with his red staff, but neither of them was Joseph and Sam couldn't believe that the man would have the courage to take on such work. They weren't starving now they had left the Verneys' employ and if Mary earned the good wages of a Searcher, he might not need to find work. He would not tell Lottie what he had seen, he decided. Sights like that could turn milk sour or make a woman lose her baby.

He rode back as fast as he could, trying to use roads open to the sky and free of red crosses but this was a vain hope. Many streets were silent and each house had its mark of hopelessness. No guards watched as the houses were empty of life, and Sam was glad to leave them and find the well-kept house where he now lived.

'Is something wrong in Surrey?' asked Lottie. She was heavy and her legs were swollen but she looked pretty and had lost none of her sweetness.

'No. Mr Verney hadn't heard from us so he sent word to Mr Carter to find out if we were well. He also gave me a list of things he wanted done here, most of which I've done without being told.' He gave Lottie the letter from Lady Marian, written carefully in big letters to make sure that the girl understood and could read it. Lottie blushed. 'The dear lady,' she said and began to read, slowly and with difficulty, but at last she had the messages firmly in her mind.

'What does she say?' asked Sam.

'They are all well and they will stay there for another two months. Master Christopher is racing and hunting and wants to become a farmer.' They laughed, knowing how reluctant he had been to go away. 'There must be a sweetheart for him there,' said Lottie. 'The others send love and

Lady Marian says that I may take what I want from the chest in her room.'

'She knows how a body changes and needs garments to fit,' said Sam.

'She put away all the clothes that she wore when she had babies,' said Lottie. Her bodice was very tight under the arms and her skirt had tapes on the waist to make it meet and tie. 'I shall find something now,' she said happily. 'She is so good, my lady. God bless her and all of them.'

'And keep you safe, Lottie.'

'Why, Sam? You look as if I was in danger.' Lottie kissed him, with her awkward body turned sideways so that she could reach his face, and then pattered off to Lady Marian's chamber.

Unfolding the sheet that lay on the top of the clothes within the chest, Lottie took out a warm dress of blue wool that was tent-shaped and one that she knew Lady Marian had worn when she was due for delivery. There were shifts and bodices and some breast-binders for after the birth if the milk came in fast and made the breasts swollen. Lottie discarded her old clothes and dressed in the new warm ones. It was getting colder each day now and she was glad of the extra layers and the thick material of the dress.

'My baby will be dressed like a prince,' she said, examining yet again the good clothes that the family had made for her. Gently, she pushed the crib on its rockers and sent it swaying. Her bare feet were cold and she found a pair of worn leather slippers that had been discarded by Edward Verney and had not fitted either Sam or her, until her feet were swollen as they were now.

Autumn leaves strewed the gravel paths and the formal hedges of yew needed expert attention far beyond Sam's ability. Lottie sighed. I'm heavy and sad, she thought. The fall of the leaf is never the best time of the year. She shuddered, thinking of her mother in Cripplegate. They

271

said that death came easily at the fall of the leaf. Would her parents survive? Would any of them survive?

'Sweetheart!' said Sam. His gentle rough hands held her close. 'Crying, when you have such nice things to wear?'

'I miss them all and I almost wish we'd gone too,' she cried. 'All the friends I had are gone away or are dead and I can't even see my own mother.'

'You know you never get on two days running,' he said, in an attempt to see her smile. 'I took food and they have no need to go far and risk catching anything.'

'Does Mr Carter know you go there?'

'No, not a word. He's scared out of his wits that he might be infected, ever since he heard that a friend who carried the same nostrums against plague died, and so he has no more faith in haresfeet and brimstone.'

'The herbs are the best protection,' said Lottie. 'That and the silver cross that my lady gave me.' She laughed and seemed more like her normal bright self. 'In these clothes, I am a lady, Sam. I'm warm and eat well and we shall have a fine child to show them when they return. Miss Kate told me before she left that she will stand Godmother at the naming.'

'They'd better come back soon, then,' said Sam, tapping her swollen abdomen with pride. 'He's going to be a fine big lad.'

'And what if it's a girl?' Lottie smiled and he wished it was all over and she was free of the worry of birth.

'She'll look like you and be a help as she grows,' said Sam. 'We can call her Lottie, but the gentry give more than one name. Would Miss Kate mind if we used her name, if she's to speak for her?'

'I thought you said a son, Sam!' Lottie turned away. 'Look at me, and say that I am like my lady.'

'In that dress you are, for sure.'

'She said I could use it all as she is past childbearing now, and I think that when the young ladies have babies,

fashions will have changed and they will have new clothes.'
She sighed. 'Is there anyone as lucky as me, Sam? But I
am restless and think that the baby will be born soon.'

'You haven't started?'

'No, there'll be time enough when the pains come and
I'll tell you what to do when I'm ready.' Lottie longed for
a woman of her own age who had borne children, or a
comfortable, clean older woman who would let her have
her first good cry on her shoulder, but she dared not permit
anyone from the City into the house. 'Perhaps my lady will
send a woman from the country,' she said, but she knew
that this was impossible. No woman would come to London
now.

'I'll manage,' said Sam awkwardly, hiding his own very
real fears. 'It will come out somehow. They do, Lottie.'

All day, Lottie paced the house and garden, picking
herbs and filling every space on sills and on tables until the
house smelled bitter-sweet and Sam told her to rest.

'If the frost comes, they will die and I want to dry as
many as I can,' Lottie said.

By nightfall when the owls in the stable drifted out like
ghosts and the moon rose, Lottie put extra covers on the
bed and wished that she could sleep in the big four-posters
of the family and draw the curtains close against the
draughts, but Sam was warm and big and cradled her in
his arms, and she fell asleep.

'What was that?' Sam sat up, letting in the cold air and
Lottie tried to cover herself again. 'Someone's out there,' he
said, and reached for his breeches. Lottie shook the sleep
from her eyes and shrugged into the thick woollen gown
she had worn that day. She could hear the tapping now,
insistent and louder as if whoever was there needed help.

'Be careful, Sam,' she said. 'It might be robbers.' He
picked up the cudgel that never left his side now and
walked to the window of the room overlooking the front
door.

'Who is there?' he called. Lottie lit a lantern and he held it over the sill. Shadows from the high porch made the two figures difficult to see but the lantern gradually threw them into relief as Sam's eyes became accustomed to the dark.

'It's us,' said Dora Moor in a harsh voice as if she had little breath left and had been running.

'You can't come here,' began Sam.

'We have no other place and it's your duty to look after us,' said the whining voice that Sam detested.

'The Good Lord bless you, Sam,' said Lottie's father, more cautiously than his wife spoke. 'Would you see Lottie's kin without a roof or food?'

'No roof?' Lottie stood on a stool to peer out. 'They couldn't turn you out.' She had no desire to let them in but had a sinking feeling that they meant to stay.

'And why come now, so late that only the plague carts and the sick are out?' Sam said. 'Stay here, Lottie. I'll see to them.'

'Let us in.' The woman beat on the door and her voice rose to hysteria. 'Let us in, my girl, or you're no daughter of mine!'

As if there was anyone to hear, Sam hurried down and unbolted the heavy front door. 'No!' he said as Dora tried to push past him. 'Not in the house. Mr Verney made me promise not to have anyone here but me and Lottie.' Instinctively he knew that once inside, he would never be rid of them. 'You can stay above the stables where we live when the family are here.' In the lamplight, Dora saw his scowl and knew that for tonight at least, she must bide her time. She shrugged and shivered. The night air was colder than it had been for months.

'Bless you, Sam,' said Mr Moor. 'We haven't come to cause trouble.'

'Why have you come?' asked Sam as they climbed the stairs to the loft. Dora looked about her and smiled. It would do well and was far more comfortable than she had

274

imagined. 'We left it ready for us when the family come back,' said Sam. 'Mr Verney wanted us to live in the house until he gives the word, but this is ours and I suppose you can use it, but why here tonight?' he repeated.

'The plague,' said Mr Moor, and his wife gave him a violent shove.

'Not us,' she said hastily. 'We are clean, I swear it! The people below us have it and the Searcher said she would seal the whole house even though we have nothing to do with that family. There are five whole families and only one sick but she put the red cross on the door and sent for the Watch to guard and chain the doors and windows.'

'You should have gone to the magistrate, not to us,' said Sam. 'If they find you, they will kill you.'

'Who will find us here?' Dora smiled and lit another candle from the lantern flame. The shadows faded and she picked up a pot from the shelf, sniffing at it to make sure it held no mould.

'There's water in the yard and meal left in that bowl,' said Sam. 'That must do until morning. Stay here. If you come to the house, even once, I'll turn you out, Lottie's folk or not,' he added grimly. 'How do I know you are free of contagion? You mustn't touch Lottie. She is near her time.'

'But a mother's place is with her daughter and she'll need help,' smirked Dora.

'If you touch her, I'll kill you,' said Sam, and Dora backed away from his controlled fury. 'I'll do everything she needs. We want a healthy child and Lottie needs peace of mind. Stay here and you'll be . . . welcome, but come to the house and you are out on the streets.'

Dora flushed but her husband put a restraining hand on her arm. 'We all need sleep,' he said. 'Take care of our Lottie for us, Sam.'

'As I have done since we married.' Sam gritted his teeth. He strode to the stairs and the light of his lantern jerked

275

angrily over the walls and down the path through the stable yard. Horses, disturbed by the voices and light, whinnied and stamped but the night settled when the light vanished and the cats slunk away to hunt among the straw.

'Are they all right?' asked Lottie.

'Now you're not to worry about them,' said Sam, trying to keep the panic from his voice. 'They are well and have food and a place to sleep for tonight.'

'But what will they think of me, Sam? You didn't even let me see them properly!' Lottie rubbed the arm that Sam had gripped roughly to thrust her behind him as soon as he saw who was at the door. She walked awkwardly over to the milk heating by the fire and poured it into clean earthenware mugs before adding brandy. Her movements showed her resentment and he went behind her and touched her hair gently.

'You have to rest, sweetheart,' he ventured but she shrugged away from him and handed him his mug of comfort as if that was all the comfort she would give him.

'She is my mother and she wouldn't be here unless she was afraid.' Lottie hid her tears and scrambled back under the warm bedclothes. 'I know you don't like them and I have little time for them now, but I know my duty. I should be there making sure that they are comfortable and lack for nothing.'

'They came to get all they can out of me,' said Sam harshly. 'They know you are soft and can be wheedled into giving them food and so they hang on to us like leeches.'

'They never have before now, Sam,' she told him. 'Tell me what has happened back there in Cripplegate.' Her eyes were wide and dark in the firelight and she made room for her husband at her side. He glanced down at her and his heart was filled with love and protective care. She was back in bed with the clothes up to her chin, like a child in trouble.

'As I said, they are well,' began Sam. He hesitated,

knowing that Lottie needed some explanation for their being in the stable loft. 'There is plague in the house but not close to their rooms, or so they say, but the whole house is to be sealed and the families with no infection have fled. I suppose they had to come here,' he added reluctantly, 'but you *must* stay away from them until we are sure they bring nothing to harm you.' He saw her troubled face. 'The baby must come first, sweetheart. Whatever happens, the baby must be our concern.' Lottie nodded. 'Even if one of them is ill, you must stay away. Do you hear?'

'I will, Sam.' The baby moved and she wanted to run away to the country where the air was free of the vile pestilence and where her baby could be born among friends. 'The baby comes before any one of us,' she said. 'If I should die, remember that, Sam. The baby comes first.'

He buried his face in her soft breasts and she felt them stir as if for a child, the nipples tense and ready for suckling. 'You will not die,' he murmured. 'I shall be here and we will bring this child to life.' He tried not to think of the number of deaths in childbirth he had read in the Bills of Mortality over the last year. Lottie was hale and strong and his seed would give her a strong baby. The only girls he had taken had been clean and he had not slept with another woman since knowing Lottie.

Lottie slept but Sam lay inert and full of vague anxieties. He could control Dora when he was there but what if she sneaked up to the house when he went for supples? What if they did carry the contagion? What if the Searcher knew them by name and found them here? What if Lottie lost her baby? Or died? He turned over and cuddled up to his wife. He heard the owls and the distant bark of a dog and the lonely sound of cartwheels that seemed closer tonight. He slept fitfully and heard someone drawing water from

277

the pump in the yard and hoped that Lottie's parents weren't always such early risers.

Dawn came with a sneaking wind that rustled the dry leaves and made the chimney echo. The loft might be cold, he admitted when he heard the sound of an axe on wood and knew that there would be a fire soon in the iron grate in the room where he and Lottie had lain so often making love. He kissed her gently and softly rose to put on his clothes. The newcomers would need food and he wanted to give her parents no excuse for coming to the house. Sam found six eggs in a bowl and some bread and salt pork. Lottie had made apple turnovers with spices in them and he took two of those with the rest of the food in a wicker basket. A flagon of ale completed his load and he walked slowly across the yard and went up the stairs.

'Who is it?' The voice was low and terrified.

'Sam! Who did you think? The Devil himself?'

'Dora is asleep.' The man stood in the doorway and all Sam could see was a mound on the palliasse in the corner. He handed over the food, not sorry to miss an early encounter with his mother-in-law.

'Leave the basket by the end stall when you need more,' said Sam. He turned to go and the door closed after him abruptly. He washed under the pump and drew water for the animals and for the kitchen. The huge earthenware jug was heavy with ale from the dairy and the bucket of water balanced him as he went back to the main kitchen. Lottie was still asleep so he brought in enough wood for two days and cheese from the dairy, aware that Dora might go there to see what she could discover. The kitchen was now well-stocked and he made a dish of tea for Lottie, knowing how she liked this luxury. He called her name and heard a sound that made the hair on the back of his neck rise.

'Lottie? What is it?'

'Nothing, my dear,' she said and smiled. 'It's just the baby. I had a pain but it wasn't bad.' She touched his tense

278

face with one finger. 'Did I cry out? Take no heed if I do. They say it is better for a woman to do so and to bite on a cloth, but I have no need of that as yet.'

'You ought to stay in bed,' he said.

'I know, but I can't think it right. Animals get relief moving about and so do I. I shall lie down when the pains come but it's easier doing simple tasks and keeping occupied.'

'Are you sure?'

'Please, Sam, if you are to help, you must be calm or I'll have to send for Mother.' Her face reddened and she put a hand over her next contraction. 'It's over,' she said. 'I wonder if she ought to be here.' Sam looked agonised. 'No, you are right, Sam. The baby must be free of risk and so must I if I am to feed it.'

'Just tell me what to do,' he said, and for the next few hours he remained calm and rubbed her aching back and brought in the baby clothes for the tenth time, patiently and without demur, for her to look at and treasure.

The fire burned brightly and he fed her thin gruel which he recalled was what women in labour needed but which Lottie hated. She demanded one of her own apple turnovers and they sat together munching them and talking of what they would do when the family returned.

Lottie clutched at his hand as the pains grew worse and her calm beauty changed to anxious heat and damp hair as she laboured. At last, she let him put her to bed and Lottie lay on a thick pad of rags when the waters broke and she pushed down, gasping at the sudden agony and the sensuous joy of release. Again and again the surge of pain swept over her, leaving her wet and spent and yet eager for more effort.

Sam forgot that he was a man and so not the right person for this work. He saw only his wife, gripping his hand until she fetched blood under her fingernails, giving him a pain that he relished, and wanted in some way to take away the

279

terrible wonderful tremors that engulfed them both. He shared every change and each new effort and watched the thin line of hair emerge at each contraction, the ebbing and flowing of the birth force and the emergence of a tiny head covered with waxy cream and blood.

Lottie took a deep breath as if she had tired of the effort and wanted to have it finished, and her face was suffused as she pushed hard and Sam felt the new life slip into his hands. Lottie was breathless. 'Tie the cord tight, Sam,' she said as the baby cried. 'Tie it twice and cut between and give me the baby while you wait for the afterbirth.'

He did as she told him and removed the caul from over the baby's head. 'She'll never drown at sea,' he said, repeating the tradition that anyone with a caul was safe from a watery grave.

Lottie pushed again, expelling the afterbirth, and lay exhausted while Sam, with strangely gentle hands, wrapped the child in a binder and warm gown and swaddled it in a shawl. 'A girl,' he said gently. 'We have to wait for our son, Lottie.'

'Do you mind?' she asked, and smiled as she drifted into a deep sleep.

'I shall love her as I love you,' he murmured and touched a tiny hand that escaped from the shawl. 'Little Lottie Katharine,' he said, and began to cry.

Lottie woke and asked for the baby. 'Heat some water and I'll wash now and see to the baby,' she said. With Sam's help, all was clean and sweet and the signs of birth were removed. 'Keep the caul safe, Sam,' said Lottie. 'Keep it about you to protect you. It is a powerful nostrum.'

'I'm not a sailor,' he said, joking, but pleased that she was miraculously well and able to order him about. He folded the dried membrane into a piece of linen and put it in his pocket. 'I'd best tell your parents that they have a granddaughter,' he said.

'Don't let them come here,' said Lottie immediately, and

Sam saw a new light in her eyes. He had seen it in the eyes of a vixen with cubs, an expression primitive and protective. He recalled the sudden curl of the lips and the hiss of warning as he approached the lair that his dog had found, and his own reluctant admiration for the female fox that was ready to die for her young.

'I'll keep them out but they can see the baby from the window,' he said. 'I promise they shall not come in here.'

'Make me some gruel, Sam. I fancy it now,' she said. Her breasts were filling and she put the baby to suck even though there was nothing but the colostrum there, and the sucking brought back tiny labour pains to seal off the last of the seeping blood vessels. 'My ankles are down and my heart doesn't beat so heavily,' said Lottie. 'I shall get up tomorrow.'

'Women stay in bed,' said Sam, not knowing for how long they were confined but remembering that his sister had done so.

'I'm not sick and I have a lot to do,' said Lottie. 'I shall sit while I make bread and rest when I am tired,' she said as she saw Sam's chin become stubborn. 'You must get more food for all of us and I shall be well in a day or so.'

'I'll tell them about the baby now,' said Sam. He looked out of the window. Someone was walking on the gravel with iron-soled pattens. He started back in horror. Mary Creed was looking up at the windows and listening for signs of life. Sam went down quickly and stood in the doorway. Mary eyed him with speculation.

'Living in my rooms, I see,' she said.

'Mr Verney told us to move over here,' said Sam.

'And how is Lottie?' Mary came closer.

'That's nothing to concern you,' said Sam. 'Go away, you witch! You bring the plague on your clothes. I've seen you with the white staff.'

'I left my white staff behind,' said Mary, 'but I look for

contagion even when I'm not working.' She scanned each window and listened, then looked disappointed.

'You'll find none here,' said Sam. 'If you aren't gone I'll set the dogs on you.'

'They know me,' said Mary. 'They'd never bite the hand that fed them. I'll go, but I may be back. The two Moors have escaped a sealed house and if they come here to Lottie, then you'd best be gone from here.' Her smile filled him with cold dread and as he watched her go, fury and fear mingled and made him lean for support on the wall.

Sam braced himself. 'I'll tell them of the baby but they'll have to go,' he muttered. 'I'll give them what money we can spare but they must go.' He crept back to the house and found money and more dried fish and smoked meat for the couple in the loft and walked across to the door.

The door was opened a crack. 'Has she gone?' asked Lottie's father.

'You saw her and recognised her?'

'She is the Searcher who came to the house, and when she asked who lived there, someone mentioned our name. I didn't know that she was the Mary Creed who worked here. We wouldn't have come if we'd known,' he lied.

'You must go. She said she'd come back,' said Sam. 'I've brought you money and more food but you must go. Make for the fields and at night get down past the out-parishes and into the country. The plague is dying out and they say the King will be back soon.' He tried to convince himself that with the return of the crown to London, all would be well.

A movement from the room made Sam crane his neck to see what Dora was doing. She pushed her husband aside and stood before the horrified young man. 'You're too late, Sam,' she said. 'I have to stay.' She tore the shift away from her meagre breasts and he saw the roseate circle of the plague round a soft white bubo on her neck.

282

Chapter 18

'Soon, we may go back,' said Marian. 'Sam and Lottie are well and the baby is expected in only a little while. The sickness is less each week and Mr Carter says that some ships have come in laden and ready for trade.'

'Humph!' snorted Edward. 'He says so little again and I wonder if he really does know anything of importance. The King is still at Oxford and the *Intelligencer* talks of the Court staying until after Christmas.' He scowled. 'I wish that the King, the Court and all the rag-tag that goes with it would go back and leave us in peace.'

'You can't be worried about Alice now, Edward? She plays with Sarah and seldom leaves the garden or the village.'

'That cub is at the Manor and shows no sign of leaving. Mattie dislikes him and he upsets the servants. The other gentlemen are better but take their cue from him and hunt over sown fields and fight when they are drunk.'

'Perhaps Sir Rollo FitzMedwin will have a better influence, Edward,' said Marian. 'Mattie said that he is expected soon and he was very attentive and courteous the last time we met in London.'

Edward grinned. 'He had a narrow escape by all accounts. It was weeks before even his friends believed that he was free of the plague and welcomed him back into society. He's looking for a wife and Mattie asked if he could call on the girls.'

'He has a bad reputation, Edward!' Marian was alarmed. It was one thing for him to flirt a little and make himself amusing to the young ladies, but marriage was different.

'Wild oats, Madam. He is ready to settle down and make something of his estates, and we can't keep Anna with us for ever. Kate will wait for a while and Alice is too young, but Anna is ripe for marriage and can match his wealth with her own dowry.' He saw the sadness in his wife's eyes. 'You can't keep every fledgling, my dear. Christopher will marry at the turn of the year if I'm any judge and Kate might take the parson in time.'

'I know. It's selfish of me to want them here and if we were back in our own home, it would all seem right to match-make for our family, but here I need their company. I miss young children about the house, not that I would want to bear more myself. I wonder what Lottie will have. Pray God she lives through childbirth.'

'She can stay when we go back,' said Edward indulgently. 'You can make much of the child until Kate and Anna have babies and then you will find no time for anything.'

'Captain Bennet stays longer than he intended,' said Marian thoughtfully. 'I'm glad, as he is teaching Peter to ride and to shoot when Christopher is busy on the farm.' She smiled. 'He's good with him and makes him go for his lessons to the vicarage. Even Alice does as he tells her and goes with Peter, so Mr Silke has three pupils now that Sarah is here. It leaves Anna free to ride as she no longer teaches Alice.'

'And Captain Bennet kindly rides with her in spite of her name,' said Edward.

'I sometimes think he finds her beautiful,' said Marian. 'They keep my mind at rest as they go to meet the children from lessons and bring them home safely. Alice is restless

284

and likes to explore but she is contented enough once she is home with Peter and Sarah.' She looked up as Captain Bennet walked into the room without even pausing to tap on the door.

'Is Alice here?' he demanded. Edward jumped up. 'Miss Anna caught her sleeve on a branch so we were delayed, and the girls had left the parson before we arrived to fetch them. Peter went fishing in the brook and Sarah came home with him, but Alice stayed to pick medlars in the garden of the empty cottage by the woodyard. I rode there but she hadn't arrived.' He looked anxious and Anna came in, her tension showing.

'She has a taste for chestnuts,' said Edward. 'She'll be in the wood behind the yard.' Daniel Bennet turned away and ran to his horse.

'Do you think she's safe?' asked Marian. 'What could happen to her so close to home?'

'Richard Routh came by the church with his man,' said Anna. 'He called to us and asked where the woodman kept his pretty daughters, and he had been drinking.' She twisted her hands in her skirt and couldn't hide her agitation.

Why did we linger? she thought, passionately. Her mind was a confusion of guilt and sweetness and a heavy sense of foreboding. The sharp tug of the rough branch that brought her almost off the back of her mount had started it. She cried out and the Captain rode back to her and brought his horse close in beside her, carefully untangling the twigs from her cloak and freeing her. But it had not made her free. He had dismounted and held out his arms to help her down and give her time to recover, and his lips brushed her hair. Anna hung her head and wondered if he had touched her by accident, but he held her close and made no attempt to let her go.

'You are hurting me, Sir,' she whispered.

'Not as much as you hurt me each time you look at me,

each time you pass near and I wonder if you have any feelings at all for me.'

Anna looked up, startled, and saw pain and a kind of anger in his eyes, a resentment mixed with passion as if he willed himself to refuse his own instincts and yet was powerless to ignore them.

'You have been kind to me, Sir,' she faltered. 'I hope we are friends. Our mutual interests have given me much pleasure and I hoped that you enjoyed my company.'

His hair against the dimming afternoon light was dark and his eyes burned. Anna gave a long shuddering sigh and closed her eyes as his mouth came down on hers in a long kiss of hopeless desire. All thoughts of mutual scientific interests, the pleasures of riding and sport and the exchange of witty trivia faded in an emotion that she had never suspected except in fantasies. He kissed her hair and closed her eyes again with his lips, murmuring, 'My love, my damned darkling love.'

Anna tried to escape. His kisses were almost savage and she knew that he embraced her against his will and better judgement. She tore away and stood with her eyes wild and her breast showing the agitation of her heart.

'You don't love me!' she cried. 'You have no respect for me. You hate my name and avoid mentioning my background and yet you try to take me as you would a scullerymaid!'

His hands clenched and then dropped limp at his sides. He shook his head to free his mind of the thoughts that obsessed him and made no further attempt to touch her. 'My apologies, Madam. Blame yourself, and keep away from low branches in future.'

Anna put a hand to her bruised lips and tasted salt on her tongue, from blood or tears she couldn't tell. He took a step towards her but she backed away to her horse and swung into the saddle with all the grace of a dancer. He watched her, then stiffened. 'Alice! I forgot!'

Anna urged her horse on along the glade and heard him behind her. They had delayed far longer than it was possible for one embrace to last, surely? But it was growing dark under a cloudy sky. Daniel Bennet caught up and passed her and then reined in his horse. Richard Routh stood in his path, with one of his bullies.

'Still here, Bennet?' he asked. He swayed and leered at Anna. 'Not much sport left. Killed all the hares and never a pretty ankle to see or a sweet child to touch.' He eyed Anna with speculation. 'None that aren't locked up day and night or taken,' he added.

Anna rode on, trying to hide her confusion and knowing that her dishevelled hair would mean only one thing to the man so practised in seduction. Daniel Bennet followed quickly and when they saw the parson walking towards the church, they knew that Alice had left for home.

'I hope her medlar jelly is better than the plum jam she brought me,' said the man with a smile. 'It was so hard set it took a knife to get it out of the pot.'

'Medlars?' queried Anna.

'The others went on but she wanted to pick some for jelly.'

'This way,' said Anna, and rode fast, her cloak streaming behind her and her face concerned although she knew that Alice wouldn't stay out after sunset. But Alice was gone and the heap of rotten fruit, sorted from the good, was the only sign that she had been there.

'I'll go, too,' said Anna now, when Daniel Bennet had left Edward and Marian.

'I know where to look.' She went to the door. 'I'll go on foot and take the short cut where a horse cannot go under the low beech trees.' She ran, unsure of what she sought or what she would find. She even smiled a little at the thought of Captain Bennet being torn from his horse by low branches as had nearly happened to her. Dry leaves underfoot were soft and silent and she drew her cloak closer to keep free of the grasping wood. In the copse, the light was muted.

She stopped to draw breath and listened. Small sounds from the undergrowth and the cry of a yaffle bird made the silence deeper. She went on and trod on ripe chestnuts in the grove. She bent to pick one up and it lay smooth and cold and the colour of a man's hair.

From the lane, she heard hooves cracking the dry twigs and a shout. She leaned over a bank where elder tangled with bramble and barred her way, and saw Richard Routh and his man holding a struggling girl. Anna gasped as Captain Bennet rushed into the clearing, shouting to the men.

Alice turned like a cat and sank her teeth into the hand of the man gripping her arm. He cursed and loosened his grip and Alice twisted free. She ran into the copse and didn't look back and Anna followed her. She saw the girl gain the safety of the lane by the cottage and then stopped again. Daniel Bennet hadn't followed her. The back of her throat was harsh with running and fear for the man who filled her mind with thoughts that frightened her. She went back to the clearing and saw the men fighting. Daniel Bennet used his fists well and the hired bully had a hand to his jaw as he stumbled away from further damage, but Richard Routh brought a short stabbing knife from his belt and walked unsteadily towards the unarmed man.

'You Puritan, Bennet,' he slurred. 'You take what you want but you deny me an innocent diversion. You're like all the rest at Court.'

'Put it down, Routh,' ordered the Captain.

'I'm not one of your soldiers. What will you do if I disobey, Captain? Clap me in the Tower as they wanted to do with me last month? Keep me confined just because I tasted the sweetness of two worthless little virgins?' He came closer and Daniel Bennet saw the bloodshot eyes and smelled the sour breath of depravity.

288

'You go too far, Routh. That was the kinswoman of Sir John, your host. That was Alice Verney.'

'S'death! I thought I'd seen her somewhere! As sweet a kernel as a milky cob.' But he stopped and seemed to check his thoughts. 'Older than I thought but sweet for all that.' He grinned. 'And with spirit enough to make our play exciting. Tell me, is she spoken for? Maybe I should marry and be in favour with the King again.'

'You could never have her,' said Daniel scornfully. 'They would never give her up to your corruption. Get out of this wood and out of this county before I send word to the Court about today.'

'But you may dally in the woods with that foreign witch and be applauded for deflowering such as she.' The insolence was back and Routh waved the knife in the air.

'You will swallow those words, Sir!' cried Daniel. Disregarding the knife, he came at Richard Routh with clenched fists, his eyes blazing with madness. From the barrier of brambles, Anna saw the men come together and the knife-blade glint as Routh held it high.

She screamed as the hard fist of the man she tried to hate smashed into the laughing face and the knife pierced the leather jerkin of the Captain. Routh stepped back, horrified at what he had done and turned to his man. 'Run, man! Run and never say what you saw today. If he dies, I am finished.'

'I heard a scream, Sir!'

'A rabbit in a snare,' said Routh. 'There's no time, man!' They disappeared into the trees and Anna struggled past the thick hedge of thorns, gasping and crying as she tore her hands and clothes and at one time seemed imprisoned. She called for Christopher and Edward and anyone who could help and as she sank to the ground by Daniel Bennet's side, Christopher came into the clearing.

'Who did this?' he demanded.

'Richard Routh. No, Christopher, you must stay and get

the Captain to safety! Dear Lord, may we stop the bleeding!' She pulled up her skirt and tugged at the linen petticoat, ripping it at the hem. Daniel lay senseless and the patch of blood on his side spread slowly and his face became pale and pinched. Christopher took out his knife and cut away the clothes over the wound, and Anna folded the linen into a hard pad and held it to the slashed skin.

'I'll get a hurdle and some men,' promised Christopher. He ran back to the cottage and in a minute, Peter and Kate and Edward followed him back with a wattle hurdle and the boy from the stable. Anna held the pad tight and willed him to live as they lifted Daniel and carried him to the couch hastily prepared in the main room.

'Stop that noise, Alice,' said Edward testily. 'You aren't hurt and we can't be bothered with the vapours now.' Alice looked between her fingers and dried her eyes. It wasn't fair! She was the heroine of the day and now Captain Bennet was stealing all her glory. Sarah stared at the wounded man and forgot that her friend had been attacked, and everyone was far too busy rushing about with hot water and linen cloths and healing salves to bother with one hysterical girl.

'We need a surgeon,' said Edward. 'Christopher, ride to the Manor and tell them how it is here, then take the curricle into Reigate and bring back a doctor.'

Marian took charge in a way that astounded the others. Her life in London made her seem warm-hearted, a good wife and mother but lacking in anything that needed courage, but now she brushed aside Edward's clucking and cleaned the wound again now that the bleeding was less. She looked into the gaping hole in his side and said, 'The blade scraped his ribs and didn't go into the lung or he would have frothy pink blood here. His breathing is shallow but even and he has lost far too much blood to need bleeding. Bring me linen thread and a stout needle, Kate, and we must sew this up.'

290

Edward tried to dissuade her but she shook her head at him. 'I think you should wait until he is better, my dear,' he said.

'It's best now when he cannot feel anything. I have sewn cuts on animals before and his skin is softer.'

Anna held the bowl of warm water for Marian to use to clean the skin, and smothered the wound with juice from the house leek growing on the tiles, to stop further bleeding. A tight binder of linen kept the pad in position and when the surgeon came four hours later, Daniel Bennet lay clean and pale but conscious before the fire.

'I see that I am not needed, Madam!' said Mr Barnes. 'You have done it all and I shall leave it as it is until tomorrow.' He sat drinking some of the fine Madeira from Sir John's cellar and made himself comfortable in Edward's favourite chair. Anna and Kate flitted about quietly while the doctor talked and the rest of the family listened.

'Is he staying?' asked Kate in a whisper. 'Do we take in food yet or wait until Father asks for it? Shouldn't we give the Captain something to drink or eat?'

Marian looked from the doctor's red face to the pale one on the pillow. 'I think that the Captain needs rest,' she said at last, seeing the growing discomfort of the man, as the bruised and cut nerves now ached and throbbed.

'To be sure,' the doctor said. 'Give him a draught, Madam. You have laudanum?' She nodded and Kate prepared a warm drink of oatmeal and milk with the opium mixture in it. Daniel drank thirstily and Anna mopped the cold sweat from his brow. He gazed up at her with pleading eyes and she knew that he recalled that they had parted with bad feelings. She lowered her gaze as she saw the doctor watching her with interest, and took the empty cup back to the kitchen.

The doctor sniffed. 'It grows late, Ma'am, and we all need our suppers.'

'Will you stay?' asked Edward. The savoury smells from

291

the fire couldn't be ignored any longer. 'It will make it late riding back but the lanes are clear and the weather calm.'

For the first time, the doctor showed signs of caring for his patient. 'I feel I should stay, Ma'am, and relieve you of all worry.'

'But what of your other charges, Sir?' Marian forced a smile but had taken a dislike to this overweight and dictatorial man, who had done nothing to help since his arrival.

'I am on leave from the Army and have time to spare. My brother is the doctor you sought but he is out dealing with many sick and I find little to do. I can sleep here quite well,' he said, looking at the deep cushions by the fire. 'A little supper and perhaps a game of something to while away the hours and tomorrow a look at the wound after dinner, and then I really must go back.' He looked round for grateful approval and Kate stifled her laughter.

'Supper and dinner tomorrow and he'll charge for his time,' she said as Anna helped her at the table. 'I wish we'd never bothered him. Mother is good with wounds and so are you, Anna. I hate the sight of blood but you seemed as if you had tended the wounded all your life.'

'I had to do it,' said Anna. She looked at Kate's untroubled face, so calm now after her time on the farm. My troubles are just beginning, thought Anna. I had to help him and let no other but Lady Marian do what was needed. He is my charge as we are equally guilty over Alice and I love him. The admission made her sad. What a hopeless love it would be, and yet the savage kisses had stirred her into an answering passion that now lingered in tenderness.

Supper was over and Edward and Christopher tried to pretend they enjoyed playing at cards. Daniel Bennet lay in shadow by the fire and from time to time, Anna gave him water or bathed his face and made him more comfortable. The doctor saw her devotion and his sharp eyes missed nothing. Alice was consoled, once the anxiety over Captain

Bennet receded and word came from the Manor that Richard Routh had returned from his ride in a fine old state, packed his bags and gone with no explanation.

'I think he's gone to Lord Carnegie but he could be anywhere,' said Sir John, during a brief visit to the cottage.

'If he has gone for good, then we can rest better,' said Edward. He told Sir John what had happened and the old man was furious.

'I'd have whipped him myself if I'd known,' he thundered. 'I shall send word to the King that he has done this and I shall write to his patrons and demand an apology for violating our hospitality.' He stayed to drink a glass of wine and to look down on the sleeping man. 'You are fortunate in your champion, Edward.' Kate went with him to his carriage. 'By the way, my dear, Sir Rollo has come and will call to see you all tomorrow. He is most anxious to renew acquaintance.' He glanced at her unselfconscious smile and knew that the young rogue would get no encouragement there. Perhaps Anna, he thought as he buttoned up his coat against the cold air. She looked pale tonight but it was natural to be concerned over Alice. 'Poor child! A sorry business but no harm done. . . .' No harm done to any but the good man lying there wounded. He sighed, wishing that he and Mattie had been blessed with a strong son to take over when they left the farm and the Manor.

Kate went back into the warm and approached the sick man. He smiled slightly through his pain and asked for a drink. Kate turned to get it but Anna was there before her, with freshly-made barley water and brandy. She touched his brow and it was hot, and his eyes seemed as deep as the inner petals of tiger-lilies, with black pupils dilated by laudanum.

He clutched at Anna's hand. 'Stay near me,' he whispered. 'Stay with me and say that you forgive me.'

'I think you do little to cool him, Madam,' said the doctor who had come to see his patient before retiring for

293

the night. Anna drew away and said nothing. 'He is flushed now and the poison will out. I have seen many such on the field of battle. Men who have lost limbs and some poor devils with little left to lose. He may recover,' he added, but pursed his lips. 'It is impossible to tell, and all my skill can't save him if it is the will of God that he should be taken.'

'Your skill, Sir? What now? We are here to do what you think is necessary,' said Kate.

'Let him sleep if he will and give him drinks and cool cloths and if the fever is worse, poultice the wound and we may have to put on leeches.'

'All this is commonly know,' said Kate when the doctor had gone to the room that Christopher normally used, having decided that cushions were not enough for his large body. 'He has done nothing and told us nothing we didn't know! Mother has learned much from Uncle William Verney and I wish this one had not come. I'm sure his voice is enough to make the poor man much worse.'

'I'll sit with him until he sleeps,' said Anna quietly.

'Call me if you want help,' urged Kate. She hesitated. 'If he is worse, I will go for Mr Silke.' She blushed. 'He would be of great comfort.'

The big room grew quiet as the family went to bed, leaving Anna by the low bed in the firelight. She put more logs on the fire and made a tisane for herself and another cool lemon drink for the wounded man.

'Miss Anna?' His voice made her start.

'I thought you were asleep,' she said. 'Are you in pain?'

'All the time but it is bearable if you are here.'

She held his hand and felt the heat of his body. The sweat might chill him, so she gently took away the bedcover and sponged his chest and arms, drying the hard chest carefully and longing to hold him close and say that she loved him. His eyes brightened and his lips moved as she put on fresh warm covers but his words made no sense.

He sipped the drinks she offered and when he moaned, she gave him more laudanum until he slept and she sank into a fitful doze by the fire, waking suddenly from time to time to look at him.

'Anna?' She started up, thinking that something was amiss. 'It's dawn,' said Kate sleepily. 'Stay there and I'll bring you a drink.' She kicked at the half-burned log and sent sparks up the chimney before putting on more fuel and walking to the kitchen, where the kitchenmaid lay on the truckle bed by the fire. 'Wake up,' said Kate. 'There is work to be done, Deborah.'

Anna washed her face and hands and brushed her hair before drinking the hot ale that Kate brought to her. Daniel Bennet lay still and she dreaded touching him in case he slept the last sleep and she had lost him, but his skin was still hot and as he turned, she saw that he had been in a deep and healing slumber.

'A drink, please?' he asked, and when she held it for him, he rested his head on her shoulder weakly, taking deep draughts of the warm ale. He turned his face and buried it in her breast and Anna shuddered, sensing her response to what was not lust but weakness. Even so, she moved his head away and propped him up on pillows.

'A good night, I trust?' The booming voice was back. 'Just a jug of ale and some bread and perhaps a bit of that ham I had last night,' he ordered.

Kate watched Mr Barnes sit at the table and told Debbie to serve him. He had done no more than glance at his patient and she began to wonder if he was a doctor at all. His bag lay unopened and he had not given any instructions, and when Marian insisted in opening the dressings and showing him the wound, he was unenthusiastic.

'I'm sure you've done your best, Ma'am, and no blame can come to you if he dies.'

'I have every intention of seeing him better,' she said,

with obvious annoyance. 'Kate, bring warm water and Anna the fresh dressings.'

The doctor watched and talked all the time to the patient about military matters. 'Safer in the Army than in the City of Westminster, my boy,' he said. 'Better still out here in the country, safe from infection, eh, Sir?' He chuckled. 'I'd stay here for a while with all these pretty ladies to look after you.'

Anna left with the soiled dressings and Marian touched the edges of the wound gently. There was inflammation and tenderness and she looked at the doctor for advice. He prodded the wound with a finger that was none too clean and made Daniel wince. 'I've seen worse,' he said.

'Shall I poultice it?' asked Marian.

'If you think it might help,' he replied. 'Good nursing wins more than loses and I can do no more.'

'I think it will help,' said Marian, trying to keep her temper. 'And if nursing will save him we have plenty of willing hands here. Miss Anna stayed up with him all night.' And you, she thought angrily, snored so much in Christopher's room that nobody slept a great deal.

'A goodlooking wench,' said the doctor, glancing at the door to make sure that Anna had gone. 'Just right to tend to the sick but she's foreign, isn't she?'

'Her mother was English and of noble family,' said Marian, flushing slightly as she sensed his disapproval. 'Her family is good, Sir, and she has a fortune of her own and a lineage that many would envy.'

'And her father?' he asked. His eyes were hard and the twist of his mouth cruel. 'Foreign and unacceptable to the Church?'

'No, Sir! Anna is our ward now and has no father and she is a good churchwoman.'

'But her name, Ma'am?' he asked, and his smile was cold silk and iron.

296

'Ruyter,' Marian admitted. 'But not *De Ruyter* of the Dutch navy.'

'Your husband told me, Ma'am, but I couldn't believe my ears.' He raised his voice and his glance flickered to the Captain and again towards the shadow by the door. 'Quite a catch for anyone who has no feelings one way or another about our enemies, but no wife for an officer in the King's service, eh, my boy?' He laughed. 'Good sport, no doubt, but you'd lose your commission if you dabbled deep there. Ruyter! You have my sympathy, Ma'am, if you have the care of her. If I was ten years younger, I'd set her up in Whitehall myself. A fine-looking woman.'

Anna stood in the doorway and didn't drop the tray she carried, but pretended that this was just one more overheard insult of the kind that had once followed her occasionally in St Paul's. This time, however, she knew she must either rid herself of her name or leave the kind family who loved her and seek refuge in France, away from all she held dear and away from the man who could never marry her.

Chapter 19

'The Bills of Mortality are up again, Sam,' said Mr Price, Roger Carter's assistant. He sat with Sam in the inn close to the office and they drank ale and exchanged news. 'My master is worried and grows more and more into himself. If he had friends or wife and child he wouldn't receive them now, but sends me to do his messages and asks where every crumb was made.'

'Tell him that Lottie was delivered of a girl last week,' said Sam. 'They are well and Miss Kate would want to know. I might try to take them down to the farm.' He tried to speak unhurriedly but longed to rush back to his wife and to know she was safe.

'Would Lottie want that? She has parents in Cripplegate, hasn't she?' Mr Price eyed him with suspicion.

'She never sees them,' said Sam hurriedly. 'Mr Verney forbade it. Give the family our blessing for Christmas.'

'You look pale, Sam. Not ill, are you?' Sam shook his head. 'I'll not say as much to Mr Carter or he'll think you've been to Cripplegate and got the plague.'

'You don't look healthy, either,' said Sam quickly. 'And you've never delivered a baby, I'll wager!'

'Thank the Lord!' said Mr Price. 'I think my wife would be very upset if she produced an infant after all these married years.' He grinned. 'As for Mr Carter, he wouldn't know one end from another as he's never been wed and has no close relatives with children.'

Sam drank up his ale as if he was ready to go, but his companion sat back, enjoying the unexpected conversation. 'It's icy on the roads,' said Sam. 'The river is freezing or so they say and my horse doesn't like it.'

'You should put a blanket over him,' said Price comfortably. 'Take more ale or perhaps some Sack to keep away the Devil.'

Why don't you give me my wages and let me go? thought Sam. 'Any more news from the country?' he asked out loud, to hurry things on.

'That young rascal Sir Richard Routh has been arrested for trying to rape Miss Alice, and Mr Verney says that he hopes to come up to London soon if the cold kills off the plague after Christmas, but there is a new outbreak by the docks and along the waterfront. Some of the sailors caught it and brought it back and now they are begging and stealing and some even stoned the windows of the Navy office while Mr Pepys, the Navy Secretary, was at work there.'

'They should pay them,' said Sam.

'Not everyone cares for their own as Mr Verney does,' said Price. 'You have more than most, with the house and garden and fowls and horses and food, away from us at risk here.'

Sam tried not to think of the low moaning he had heard that morning as he passed the door to the loft on his way to water the horses. Lottie was feeding the infant and never asked after her parents. It was as though she had no thoughts for anyone but the baby and, in a secondary way, for Sam. She was well and had enough milk to feed two and Sam dreaded the time when he would be forced to tell her that her mother was probably dying of the plague.

'Well, you'd best take your dues,' said Price at last. He handed over the package of money and letters and Sam put his cross to show that he had received it.

'I'll see you next week,' said Sam, and left the rest of his ale as he hurried away. Price looked after him and then reached over for the mug. He lifted it to his lips then put it down again. It was tempting to drink the good ale but Sam hadn't looked well and there must be something wrong if he left his drink.

There had been rumours of houses in Cripplegate where Lottie's parents lived being shut up and the inmates condemned to stay for the statutory forty days. He'd keep his ears open but not say anything to Mr Carter yet. Maybe Sam didn't know, but if he did then was he in contact with the Moors?

Sam dug his heels into the horse's sides and made all speed to the house. Silence greeted him and then the wail of the baby ready for more food. He smiled and relaxed. They were safe and once Dora was recovered or dead, he could take Lottie away to the country, late one night, and leave Mr Moor to sort out his own troubles. He stabled the horse and made sure the hay was within reach, then turned to get water.

'I thought I told you to stay away from the pump,' he shouted. 'I'll get all the water you need!'

'I didn't know when you'd be back,' said Mr Moor sullenly. 'Why can't I take the cart and put her in the pest-house? If they find her here, we're all lost.'

'How is she?'

'Better today, worse last night, with the buboes fading.'

'You think she may recover?' Sam hesitated. He looked up at the blank windows of the house. Dr Verney might help, but if he came then the infection would be public knowledge and not even Dr Verney would be able to save them. 'I brought some new remedies,' said Sam. 'And give all her drinks warm or the fever will fight it and she'll die.'

'Are the carts out?' asked his father-in-law.

'Not here,' said Sam quickly. 'And the Searchers have to keep to their own districts. With more cases, they are

300

busy enough without coming out to the big houses here.' He glanced back, half-expecting to see Mary Creed. Perhaps the evil woman had at last succumbed to the disease and wouldn't trouble him again, but it was with a sigh of relief that he sent Mr Moor indoors and went to find Lottie. He took in the fowls and flour and the big bag of meal that had cost him far more than it had done three months ago. With extra mouths to feed, even the good allowance he had from Mr Verney would be stretched to feed them all, and Lottie needed good cheese and flesh and milk.

'She smiled,' said Lottie. Her body was back to normal except for the tense breasts, and she looked desirable. Sam fought guiltily against his lust. It was unchristian to lie with a woman delivered under six weeks, and Lottie didn't look at him in that way. He kissed her and bent to kiss his daughter. 'You see, she smiled at you, too.' Lottie went to the window, carrying the child. 'My mother hasn't seen her yet, even from here. Perhaps tomorrow,' she added, as if she didn't really want to see her but thought that it was her duty.

'Yes, perhaps tomorrow,' said Sam hastily. 'I hope that they go soon. We have enough to do feeding ourselves without them taking anything.'

'It's so cold, Sam. We can't turn them out until the weather changes.' She stood at the window with the child swathed warmly against the chill.

'Come to the fire,' he said, but she stayed looking out at the dark wintry scene.

'No bells this Christmas, Sam. No hot ale and apples to make merry, and no dancing.' There were tears in her eyes.

'Come into the warm, sweetheart. There will be other times and better ones,' he said. 'Miss Kate and Miss Alice will be married one day and then we'll see a dance or two.' He tried to speak lightly but he wondered how long it would be before Lottie had to know. There had been a smell of corruption from the stable loft when he had passed by and he had avoided the midden where the night-pail was emptied. 'The family are well and Mr Verney sent kind messages for us. We can go there whenever we like and he will be coming to London soon when the Court and the Exchange are back.'

Lottie smiled and gave the child to him to hold while she prepared their food. She seemed so happy that Sam wanted to weep. Outside, the sky was black and the wind howled, and there was a distant crash as an elm went down and then the sound of breaking tiles, but Lottie smiled, knowing that the storm couldn't touch her baby. She served the stew and Sam dipped his bread in it and ate, wondering if his depression was due to lack of food or something worse.

That night, he examined his body for marks but his skin was whole, and he had been very careful not to touch anything dirty. He let the water run freely from the pump when he drew fresh and tried to forget that Mr Moor must have touched it when he found him there, and the days slotted one inside another as the winter cold sealed off the land.

Sam tapped on the door of the loft each day and was told that Dora was still alive. Her husband seemed apathetic and had a kind of hopeless fatalism that let him care for her and not think of the future. He accepted food and drink and made no effort to come to the house and Sam began to think that Dora would recover and that nobody need know that the loft had been tainted. The baby was fat and very good and Lottie was happy, but growing restless. She wept sometimes when she thought of her good friends who would have shared her joy over little Katharine, and longed to show her off to Lady Marian. 'When will it be over, Sam?' she asked, time and again. 'When can I take her out and let Miss Kate see her?'

'She'll see her, Lottie. Be patient,' he said, and told her

302

severely that the yard was no place for her as the mud was thick and foul.

'I could draw the water sometimes,' she said. 'It flows badly in the cold and you have enough to do.'

'Stay in and keep warm for another week or so,' he insisted, and prayed that whatever was to happen in the loft would be over by then. The Bills of Mortality were less and yet there were new outbreaks as if it had died in one out-parish only to flare up in another. As the plague changed direction, so the Searchers were given new areas to work in, and he was afraid when he heard of cases closer to home.

Each morning, he listened for the death cart's rumble and heard it come closer. He went to see Mr Carter and told him that the baby was well and that they were warm and in good health, and bought expensive nostrums against the sickness on his way home. Once, he saw Mary Creed and she shook her white staff at him with a curse and a threat, and he wondered again if Joseph had died of plague.

'You don't need those,' said Lottie when she saw the elixir, and the salve to be rubbed into the throat day and night. 'I place my faith in natural herbs and my cross.' She looked pensive. 'I haven't seen either of my parents since the night they arrived,' she said. 'It's warmer today. I'll take the baby out into the yard and they can see her.'

'No!' She stepped back as he shouted. 'No, Lottie,' he said, more quietly. 'They've gone away. They didn't like it here and Dora wanted to see some friends.'

'Just like them,' said Lottie angrily. 'They've gone and not bothered to say goodbye. Well, they can come begging to see Katharine and I'll not let them take a peep at her! You'd think they'd have had a little care for their own grandchild.' She put the baby back into its crib almost roughly. 'I'll go and give that place a good clean. My mother never cleans properly and I don't think she'll have left it wholesome.'

303

'Leave it until the weather is warmer and we can open the doors and the window to air it. We don't need it yet and we'll have to do some spring cleaning here in case Mr Verney comes back,' said Sam desperately. 'That will take all your strength, Lottie.'

'I'll leave it,' she agreed, but she wandered about the house, not really working but unable to leave well alone. 'I wish I could come when you see Mr Carter,' she said more than once. 'I hate being shut in here for so long.'

'I have to go tomorrow,' said Sam, 'and he may tell me good news. In any case, I think we should get a few things together and go to find the family as soon as you are strong and the roads are drier.'

'I'm strong now,' said Lottie eagerly. 'Tell Mr Carter that we are going and ask his advice about the way we should take.'

Early the next day, Sam tapped at the door to the loft. The face that showed through the crack of open door was thin and sad. 'She's asleep,' he said.

'You said that yesterday and the day before that and all last week!' The smell from the room was overpowering. 'She's dead, isn't she?'

'Yes, she's asleep. She fell asleep nine days ago and now I just have to wait.'

Sam backed away. 'You are sick, too?' He swallowed hard. 'How long?'

'I have a hard token in my thigh,' said Lottie's father. 'They say that with that, I have no chance. Go away, Sam, and take Lottie with you. You can do nothing here.' He smiled. 'I saw such a token but not as big as mine on the man in the room below us.'

'You went into that room? You swore that you had not been tainted.' Sam was angry and at his wits' end. 'You brought it on yourself!' He stepped back 'What now? I ought to tell the magistrate.' He put the food he had brought on the step. 'Keep inside and use this.' He left the elixir on the step with the food and walked away as soon as the door closed. The food had gone but the bottle of physic was left behind.

'One of the horses has a cough,' lied Sam when Lottie remarked that he looked upset. 'I'll not be long, and we can begin to plan for our journey. Stay indoors and open to nobody.' He took the younger of the horses and cudgel and rode to Lincoln's Inn, and Lottie watched him go.

A bright sunbeam made her push the crib away from the window in case the sleeping child was disturbed. It was warmer and Lottie felt energetic. Sam fusses, she thought and smiled. He's been so good and so patient with me and the baby when she cries. The yard was dry, with less mud after the rain, and she collected a pail and scrubbing brush and soap and put on a coarse sacking apron. The sun would sweeten the loft after she had scrubbed it and then she could think of finishing the mending. The baby was fast asleep and wouldn't awaken for at least four hours, so Lottie crept out into the yard.

From the stables, which she couldn't see for the angle of the house, she heard voices. So they hadn't gone! What had Sam meant? She drew back as someone screamed. Robbers or beggars desperate for food? She ventured further round the corner and saw a man disappear into the loft stairway and heard more commotion. She called. 'Mother? Father? Who is there?'

The man came down the stairs, followed by Mary Creed. 'That one,' said Mary, pointing with her staff. She chuckled. 'One in, one out.'

'She looks clean,' said the man. 'Perhaps she doesn't live here. Where are you from, Miss?'

'Don't listen to her. I know her,' said Mary Creed. 'She's their daughter.' A bumping on the stairs of a heavy body slumping from wooden step to wooden step filled Lottie with dread. Another man dragged the body of Dora Moor into the light and flung her naked on the waiting cart.

305

'No!' whispered Lottie. 'Oh, Mother, I didn't know.'

'Take no notice but do what you must,' said Mary Creed. 'She has a baby.'

'I had a baby but it died,' said Lottie, reading the inexorable hatred in the woman's face. She felt the hand on her arm and tried to get away, but the two men forced her into the loft and slammed the door. All colour left her cheeks and she vomited as the stench of death reached her. Her father lay on the soiled bed but he didn't know her. She went to the small window and looked down. The man with the red staff went away, ringing his bell to warn of his approach with contagion and Mary Creed watched the red cross being painted on the door, her face ecstatic as she pictured the pretty girl up in that foul room with her dying father.

Mary Creed looked gloatingly at the main house. That could wait until she brought her own cart and took what she wanted, alone. When Sam returned, he would be caught and put in with his wife but first, she must find a strong man to set on watch. The door was chained and the lower window barred so there was no chance of her prisoner escaping and the upper window was not big enough for a child to pass through. Even without the guard, Sam could not reach his wife, nor could he save her. 'The Lord is good,' Mary Creed said and hummed a hymn as she went to find a guard.

Lottie shook the door but the bar was firm. She climbed up to the small window and put it wide but when she tried to wriggle through, she couldn't get more than head and shoulders out. She looked fearfully at the man on the bed and the scattered filth in the room, and knew that she would never see her baby again. The light changed and noon passed. Sam would be back for dinner and he would rescue her. She wept bitterly. Sam must not touch her. She was tainted with the plague as surely as if she had the tokens already. She was a pariah who must stay until she died or was clear after forty days. 'The baby must come first,' she said again and again as she walked round the room and avoided the man on the bed in the corner. She was thirsty and drank from the ewer of water that Sam had left earlier and then wondered if the contagion was in the air.

Hoof-beats came clearly as Sam rode back to the stables. Lottie pushed as much of her body as she could through the small window and shouted, praying that the guard had not arrived.

'Lottie!' Sam jumped from the horse and let it run on its own into the yard. 'Lottie!' His cry of agony made her weep but she controlled her voice.

'Sam. Listen! Mary Creed did this but she doesn't know I have a live baby. The baby comes first! You said it and so did I and we have a sacred duty to her.'

'Wait! I'll fetch a crowbar and let you out.'

'Not now. There isn't time. You must take the baby to Mr Carter and tell him to see her to the farm.'

'I must get you out first.'

'No, Sam. The guard will come soon and then you will be taken, too. Take the baby,' she insisted. 'For the love of God, take her to safety and then do as you will!' He hesitated. 'There's no time, Sam! Take the baby and go away with her if you will, for I am gone. I am tainted now or soon will be with my father dying here and my mother taken to the pits. Give me money that you can spare to buy food through the Watch, but go now, and God save you, my sweetheart. The baby must come first!'

Sam threw a purse in at the window and ran to the house. He snatched up the baby, then thought more clearly. He put her down on the cot and filled a basket with her clothes and bedding and then wrapped her in a thick shawl and placed her in the basket, too. The horse was cropping rank grass by the gate and Sam led her to the mounting stone and put the baby in the basket in front as he sat on the horse. Steadily he rode back to Lincoln's Inn and fortunately baby Katharine didn't wake up. Mr Carter would help. He would *have* to help. Hadn't he admitted that Mr Verney gave instructions for him to give Sam and Lottie and the child every assistance? The streets were deserted but for beggars and Sam ignored the outstretched arms and thought that they were better off than he.

I shall leave the baby and get straight back to Lottie. I'll kill the guard if I have to, he thought grimly, but I'll get her out before harm touches her . . .

The office was dark but for one candle in an upper window and when he knocked boldly on the door, it flickered and brightened as another candle was lit. Footsteps came warily down the stairs and a voice called, 'Who is there? State your business and speak clear.'

'It's Sam. I have to see you, Sir.'

'Has something happened to the property? Have you let robbers break in?' The bolts were drawn back and the door opened. Mr Carter stood in his long woollen gown over his nightshirt and stared at the basket that Sam held out to him.

'Lottie has been set on and can no longer care for the baby. You must send her to Lady Verney and keep her safe while I go back and see to Lottie.'

'She has the plague!'

'No, Mr Carter. Lottie and the baby haven't stirred from the house since the birth and the baby hasn't been touched by any but Lottie and me. Take her, and God bless you. She will need a wetnurse but not from here, so she must go soon!' He thrust the basket into the bemused man's hands. Roger Carter blinked up at the sky as if surprised that it was still afternoon, even though a dreary dark one, and Sam stepped back, in a suddenly desperate rush of longing to pick up the child again and run with her back to Lottie. He clenched his hands and knew that he must thrust away all feeling, all love, for the sake of the future.

'You can't leave me with this!' Roger bleated.

'Please, Sir . . . as you value Mr Verney's goodwill and the blessings of Heaven, take her by coach and find a wetnurse out of the city. Ask the local doctor. He will find one, but hurry, and take care of my little daughter.' His voice broke.

'You mean I go too?' Sam nodded. 'I can't do it. Coaches for hire are not clean and I might catch the plague myself.'

'No man has caught plague from a carriage since long gone, Mr Carter. Take her, and God bless you, for she's all we have in the world. It's her only chance!' he said and could bear the agony no longer, but ran into the street and walked his horse slowly into the main road. At the corner, he paused. What if the man didn't cooperate? He left the horse with a boy and sat in the alehouse at the corner to watch, and half an hour later, when he was almost giving up hope, he saw Carter emerge, dressed for travelling and carrying the basket with care. Sam watched him hurry down to the Post House and the coach to Kensington and then sat with his head in his hands, weeping for a few minutes. He must get back to Lottie, he decided at last. She'd be anxious and if they were to get away, they had little time left. They needed to escape, then to prove that she wasn't tainted and to go on to the farm and retrieve little Lottie Katharine. He walked out into the dusk and saw that the horse had gone. He cursed himself for carelessly leaving it in the care of one small boy. Many had lost horses like this if they were in view of the road. He walked along the cobbles and tried to avoid the worst of the ordure, then heard the sound of running feet. Two men ran breathlessly past him, pushing him aside, and before he could recover and make out what they were shouting, four men came up behind him and seized his arms and legs, making him helpless. Sam struggled with all his might, and desperation added to his strength but the men were practised and

309

well-built and at last he lay exhausted, face downwards in the mud.

'A good strong one,' said one of his captors. 'Better than three when they tame him.'

'I have to get back. My wife is sick,' said Sam.

'So is mine.' The kick in his ribs was agonising.

'I have the sickness, too,' said Sam.

'A great healthy brute like you?' They laughed. 'What if you have? If it doesn't show, then you are healthy and we get paid for every healthy man pressed. Come on.'

Sam was heaved roughly to his feet and led manacled to the docks. He looked back helplessly to the lights glowing in the City and prayed that Katharine and Lottie would be saved. The masts of a tall ship latticed the skyline and the twenty-oared whaler took him out over the choppy water to the dark side of the ship. Tarred ropes and oakum-caulked timbers smelled like the nostrum he had left on the steps of the stable loft and Sam wept as he was thrust into a dark hold until he was needed.

Above, he heard the sound of laughter. Not the coarse laughter of the seamen but the light laughter of men at leisure, officers who were in power over the ship by right of ownership or birth, often regardless of their skill at sea. Activity was everywhere and the windlass turned and creaked, pushed by men singing to forget aching muscles and the fact that they might not see London again for months. The anchor moved and dragged into the locker with a rattle of chains so close to Sam's head that it seemed in the same dark space. A movement that was foreign to him and made him queasy told him that they were underway and that the wind and tide carried them down to the open sea.

'Lottie!' he cried into the darkness and as he stirred, his foot touched another man, also chained.

'It's no use shouting,' said a muffled voice. 'We're pressed for the Navy and you'd better get used to the idea.'

'What do you know of it?' asked Sam.

'I deserted once but they don't know it. I was a fool to be caught twice but I was starving and so didn't try to escape. Do as they say and it's easier. Resist and you are flogged, but you'll eat and drink and if you have any love for England then you serve the King,' he added with an ironic laugh. 'That should make up for losing all you hold dear!'

'For how long?' said Sam.

'Depends. You might like it and rise in the ranks. You may get sick and be thrown overboard. You may serve three years and be discharged honourably or you might catch the eye of one of the officers and be let off, to go into service with him. That's what I'd like to do. Livery and a full belly and when the plague goes, a life in London.'

'I wear livery,' said Sam.

'You should have worn it today, my lad. That's the only thing that would have saved you if the crest was high enough at Court.'

Sam felt his chains but they were firm and merciless. Even if he freed himself of them, the hold was barred and there must be a guard. He sank back in misery and eventually slept among the moans and snores of the other men who lay with him on the hard wooden floor.

Above him, the officers supped and then spread charts over the table. 'De Ruyter has ships here and here,' said the Captain. 'We go there by the Texel and catch any booty we may and bring back to the supply boats. With newly-pressed men below, we can't put ashore until they settle and we want none of the mutiny of last month.'

The sailors among them talked of tactics and the way that other battles had been lost or won, and the sons of noble houses, sailing for prestige and diversion, talked of the Court, of women and of the wealth they might have through the sacking of De Ruyter's fleet.

'First catch your ships, Sir,' said the second-in-

311

command. 'He's a wily devil and a good sailor who has cut our tails often enough.'

'We had old ships then,' said one, the amount of wine he had drunk showing in his agressive manner.

'We still need more and better ones,' said Vincent Clavell. His neatly-braided hair and fine woollen uniform made him a man worth watching and his assured and work-manlike ways made his Commander nod in agreement. 'We need better-fed men below and those who want to serve his Majesty, so that they take pride in what they do and create no more mutinies, but with so many disbanded and left to rot while we furbish new ships is it any wonder that we have few volunteers? We need the men and yet the ones with any skill on board lack the strength and health to work hard, and some carry the plague even yet.'

'If we had the right ships we could root that devil out of the seas,' said his Captain. 'The *Defyance*, just built, has too much freeboard and was built bigger than the plans and no man wants to command her.' He smiled. 'A chance for you, Clavell, for your first real command?'

Vincent Clavell shook his head. 'I still have much to learn, Sir, and wish for no better ship than yours now we are on our way from the Thames and bound over the Channel.'

'Does it not bother you to leave England now? Most of the young gentlemen are already pining for female company and their families.'

'I am anxious to end this strife and I am happy to go now as my family are well and my young sister is being cared for by people I trust. The only threat to her was Routh who followed her to the country but he is in the Tower having tried to assault Sarah's friend. Now, they are both safe and can play and ride and grow into pretty young women.' Clavell smiled. 'They are alike and both comely.'

'And marriageable?'

Clavell frowned. 'That is something I wish to forget until my return. Let them be children until the Court removes to London, and may heaven protect them both.'

'With the King back in his palace in London and the Exchange full of all who left in haste to escape the plague, trade will increase and we have great times ahead, Clavell.' The Captain eyed him with concern. 'But forgive me. I forget your troubles. Your eldest brother died of the sickness in Westminster.'

'Another reason for me being glad to leave, Sir, until the family are out of mourning. We were not close, but I do grieve for him and his childless bride.'

'And your other brother who serves in the army?' the Captain asked.

'He is in East Africa with his men and couldn't be here to comfort my father.' Vincent Clavell sighed. 'So I had to take the place of the heir in all but inheritance.'

Chapter 20

'One of us must go back,' said Edward firmly. 'I get no sense from Carter and who knows what is happening to our house?'

'Please may we have Lottie's baby here, Father?' pleaded Kate. 'I lay awake last night thinking of the poor little soul with a strange nurse and nobody who really cares about her future.'

'I can't say!' said Edward, with a sudden burst of temper. 'Where is Sam? He is the father and my servant and not a sight nor sound has there been of him since Carter took the child to his cousin in Kensington and then to the wetnurse who is looking after it! Price went to the house and swears that a red cross is on the stableyard door, but not on the house. If the baby is sick then we must not have her near us and if she isn't, then she is still safe where she is and I will pay the nurse.'

'Can we all go?' asked Alice, her eyes shining at the prospect of returning to London.

'Not you, Miss. You stay with Sarah and Peter until he returns to Eton after Easter. By that time, we may all go back,' he added, with none of the eagerness of his young daughter.

'They say that the nobility are back with their carriages and that the King may give permission for the theatres to re-open soon,' said Alice. 'I read the new *London Gazette* and it gives details of the Court entertainments and the engagements of the Royal Family.' She sighed longingly. 'It must be wonderful to live at Court and to see and hear everything amusing and fashionable. Sarah and I could ride to Vauxhall and watch the carriages.'

'It's only the banking and merchantmen's offices that are busy as yet,' said Christopher. 'Covent Garden and Vauxhall are still quiet and there is no entertainment apart from a few inns opening their doors, one by one.'

'But people are going back to live,' said Alice stubbornly. 'There were some passing the village with carts loaded up and they said it was now safe to go back.'

'With a red cross on any of my doors, be it only a hoax, there'll be no going back for you, Miss!' said Edward.

'What if Lottie is there, sealed up?' said Marian. The idea had haunted her ever since they had received the letter from Roger Carter written at the inn near Kensington while he waited for the wetnurse to come and take care of the baby.

'That is not so,' said Edward, annoyed again. 'Carter states that Sam said Lottie was set on and hurt and that the baby had never been touched by any but her and Sam. My brother will find out how it is with them and I expect to hear today. Until then, I shall stay in readiness to go, unless Christopher will do this for me.'

'I'll go,' said Christopher. 'There's little to do in the fields now apart from mending harness and carts and sorting root vegetables, and Peter can help you there. I'll ride alone and hire as I go so that I can reach the house in three days, stopping at inns.' He grinned. 'I hope to have a better reception on my way back than we had on our way here.'

'Those rascals will make a fortune when more and more go back and they can charge what they like for rooms.'

315

Edward reddened at the memory of his humiliation. 'They should be pilloried, and the women ducked.'

'I would like to go, too,' said Anna. 'I could arrange for servants to clean the house and if you could spare Deborah we could stay until you return, Lady Marian. Someone must do that before you arrive,' she added when Marian looked shocked.

'You have enough to do looking after Captain Bennet. If it wasn't for your devotion, he might have died,' said Edward.

'The Captain is better now,' Anna said firmly. 'He is walking and eating more and his wound has healed at last.'

'In spite of that doctor!' said Christopher. 'Did you know his wig was full of lice and I had to spend a day getting rid of them from my room?' He looked concerned. 'Has Captain Bennet said or done anything to upset you, Anna? I'm sure he is very grateful for all your nursing.'

'I have no need to nurse him now, and like Alice, I long for London again, or even France.' Her face was pale. 'I think it might be better if I left you for a new life on the continent where I might be well-received.'

'Leave us, dear Anna?' Alice flung herself against the slim girl and hugged her. 'I won't let you go.'

'That isn't the answer,' said Marian. She smiled gently. 'We must talk, Anna.' Day by day, Marian had seen the girl grow paler and thinner and sensed that what was once a labour of love was now an embarrassment to both Anna and the Captain. At times, they seemed happy in each other's company, arguing over books and listening to Alice and Sarah playing on the viola and harpsichord. She had seen the Captain take Anna's hand to his lips and her answering blushes, and knew that wherever Anna went in the room, his gaze followed her hungrily.

'You can't go to France,' said Peter. 'Mr Silke told me about the French now being at war with us as well as the Dutch.' He bit into a shrivelled russet apple, the last of

316

the stored fruit. 'He said that we might end the war with De Ruyter but be in bigger trouble with France. The Danes are not our real friends and the Swedes may help but they also are not our real friends.' He looked round with the air of one who knows everything. 'Mr Silke says,' he went on, but Edward waved him away, having heard what Mr Silke said a dozen times, and now tired of having his young son under his feet all day.

'Mr Silke studied the situation and he knows,' said Kate, wishing that Edward was more tolerant of the serious and scholarly man who spent so much time at the farm with them all.

'I notice that *you* don't offer to go back,' said Edward.

'I would like to stay here for ever,' said Kate simply.

'And be a wife to the parson?' Edward laughed. 'Don't look so worried, Kate. He asked me and I was pleasantly surprised that he has means other than his living in the church.'

'He offered for me?' Her delight was obvious. 'Oh, Father, I shall be so happy.'

Edward turned to Anna. 'You can't leave us yet, child. Kate will need you as bridesmaid and even in London, marriages are being conducted again in church.'

'Come, Anna,' said Marian, laying a soft hand on the girl's sleeve. 'I need you to help me sort silken underskirts and if Christopher is going to London, then he will need fresh linen.'

'I must go away,' said Anna in a voice low but full of passion.

'And do you think you can forget him if you do, my dear?' Anna looked startled. 'I know how you feel about him but it will pass, Anna. Just because he was helpless and you had so much to do with his care, it was easy to think you loved him, but consider. He is a man without a fortune and only his commission to keep him.'

'I know all that,' said Anna. 'If I go away now, and can't

317

see him, I shall be happier, but if I stay . . .' She bit her lip.

Marian was alarmed. This was more serious than she'd imagined. The Captain was gaining strength and with it the virility of a young man of passion and Anna was capable of a passion to match his own. She moved restlessly about the room and neither of them started the task they had set themselves. It was impossible, of course. Marian glanced at the lovely face and proud carriage of the young woman who had brought such happiness to the family, and inwardly grieved, but Captain Bennet needed Royal permission to marry a foreigner and one with such a name! If he did marry her, he could be labelled an adventurer, and lose his self-respect.

'Sir Rollo is coming today,' continued Marian, watching the girl's face. 'He is being a perfect guest at the Manor and Sir John is pleased with him.'

Anna remained stony-faced. 'I'm sure you will welcome him, Madam,' she said and began to fold the linen and to look out what Christopher would need.

Marian sighed. 'He asked after you, Anna, with great respect, and hoped that you would receive him.'

'If it is your will, Lady Marian, then I will bring in refreshments,' said Anna coldly.

'I wish it,' said Marian. 'You could find your escape and salvation in such a match, Anna. The young man is handsome and wealthy, and in the eye of the King now that he has sobered beyond all expectation.' She smiled. 'They say it is because of a woman and I think we haven't far to look to find her. When he was ill it was after he had followed you by barge in the hot sun and now he has come here from friends to see you, and I hope you will receive him well.'

'He comes to see you all,' said Anna. 'Relatives of his host must be treated with courtesy. I shall meet him in the same spirit and enjoy news of the Court.'

318

She bent to her work and Marian knew that it was no use asking more of her. When dinner was on the board, Anna sat as far from the Captain as she could and talked only to Peter and Sarah, ignoring the glances from the other side of the table. It was a situation that couldn't continue. The previous afternoon, when the birds sang after rain and the new leaves grew soft over the beechwood, the Captain had asked for her arm and to be led down to the stream.

Anna looked about her but they were alone. Sarah and Alice wanted to see if the foal was back in the stable and Peter had gone into the wood to shoot rooks, while Kate took yet another basket of invalid food to the cottage next to the church.

'There is only you, Miss Anna,' he'd said, and smiled in such a way that she was reassured as to his intentions. They talked of the book just arrived from St Paul's and of the news that many plague carts were now employed for removing the dirt and débris from the streets instead of for their original grim purpose.

'We can go back soon,' said Anna. 'It seems like a dream that we can live in London again and listen to the sounds of the City.'

'You would never live in the country by choice?' He eyed her with curiosity.

'Never. I love the people here, and if I have to be in the country then this is better than any place I know, but I long for the street cries and the gossip and the theatre.'

'You have to go back and I have to go away,' he said flatly. 'What are we to do, Anna?' He sat on a log and watched the sheen of willow pollen on the water. 'What do I do without you?'

'You are nearly well, Sir.' Anna tried to free her hand but he drew her down beside him with surprising strength. 'You have no need of nursing now.'

'I have need of you, Anna. I need you more than ever,

after knowing your soft hands on my body when I was half-delirious.' She blushed. How much had he noticed when she sponged the burning limbs and he seemed unconscious, four days after his wounding? How much had he known of her gentle kisses on his brow before she made him groan with the heat of the poultices she laid on the inflamed wound? And now, how could she hide her love from his intent eyes?

'I want you, Anna. I have never wanted a woman as I want you and I burn whenever you pass my chair or touch me.'

'They say that gratitude may be mistaken for love, Captain Bennet. I was the one you saw and the one who tended you when you were sick, so you came to depend on me.'

'I love you, Anna. I love you with all my soul and I think that you are not indifferent to me.' He kissed her hand. 'Such strong gentle hands, with love in every finger's touch. No! You can't stop me now. You deny that you love me and you lie! I can think of nothing but you, and long for the sound of your voice each time you leave me.'

'You have no right to speak like this,' she whispered. 'It is hard for me to listen, knowing that your love can never be enough.'

'Enough to take you in my arms and make you mine,' he cried, and his arms were as strong as they had ever been. She felt his hand on her chin and was forced to look at him. 'Come to me, Anna. We could be happy, and later, when my commission ends, we could marry.'

'I said that your love would never be enough, Sir.' Anna turned her face away from his eager kisses and trembled. 'I am no strumpet or a slut to follow the regiment.'

'It wouldn't be like that!' He tried to embrace her again but she sat stiffly and his arms slid from her waist. 'I want you for ever, but without my commission, what am I? If we married and lived on your fortune, I would never regain the respect of those who now call me fellow officer and friend.'

'But I can live with strumpet written large wherever people meet, and be scorned by many less than I?' Her head tossed proudly. 'That is not love, Captain Bennet. If you loved me, you would never notice my name or my lineage, though both I suspect are prouder than your own.'

'Change your name, Anna, and I will ask the King for permission to marry you. Mr Verney will take you into the family as his daughter and nobody could object to our marriage.'

'I have been insulted many times because of my name and because people think I am a foreign witch but I have borne it all, thinking that some day I would find a man who loved me enough to marry me without thinking of these things.' She gave a sad smile. 'I hoped he would love me not even knowing of my fortune, but that is being as childish as Alice and as cloudy-minded. All men look at what they can have along with a pretty face and a healthy body, but is it too much to think a man could love me and my fortune and make me happy?'

'I love you and would love you if you had nothing, Anna. If you had less, it might be easier.'

'If I was plain Anne Verney with no fortune,' she said bitterly.

'Be Anne Verney and to hell with the world, my love,' he said passionately.

'And then you would marry me?'

'Tomorrow!'

'And then you'd go away and fight for the King and forget that I languish at home?'

He forced a laugh. 'That is the way of life, Madam. Men fight for King and Country and for all they hold dear, and women have children and look to the estates.' He pulled her to her feet and held her close. 'But we would have so much. We love art and science and all the things that

321

matter. We would have time together when the battles were won.'

'Or lost and you came home wounded like this.' She pressed on the healed scar and he winced. 'It hurts still, Sir, and yet you talk of reporting back to the King at Whitehall.'

'Mr Verney told you?' She nodded. 'I have to go soon or the King will think I shirk my duty. I may have to go to Africa but he will instruct me.' He touched his coat over the wound. 'I shall ask his permission to marry but I know he will not grant it until my return from duty.'

'So even Anne Verney would have to wait,' said Anna with a slight smile. 'You would use me and leave me deflowered until you come back.'

'Devil take it, Madam! What more can we do?'

'We can do less,' said Anna, and walked on, leaving him to follow. 'Until I marry, I leave my body and fortune intact, Sir.' He couldn't see her face, twisted with the effort not to weep nor know the heavy sorrow that made her want to run to him and let him do whatever he wished, and whatever she wanted with all her heart.

And, as Lady Marian now said, Captain Bennet had received a dispatch from Whitehall summoning him for examination by an army surgeon to see if he was fit for duty. 'If we can get his clothes ready, he can leave with Christopher to care for him on the way, tomorrow. I have mended his leather jerkin and his coat where the blade slashed it and it is as good as new,' said Lady Marian with satisfaction. She glanced at Anna. 'It is better that he goes now, my dear. You need time to consider everything and to make up your mind about taking our name.'

'He told you?'

'Edward talked to him and he does seem sincere, Anna, but there are others more worthy of you whom I hope you will consider.'

'And for Rollo FitzMedwin you bring out crystal and the best silver, Lady Marian?'

'Wear your russet dress Anna, and I'd be obliged if you'd oversee Debbie when she makes syllabub this evening.' Anna inclined her head. At least Rollo FitzMedwin was no threat to her as he was not the marrying kind whatever his friends might hope for him. She changed her dress and smelled of sweet pot-pourri from the muslin bags she kept among her shifts. She brushed her hair until it shone and made the table shine too before laying out silver dishes and fine knives and new salts, until the room once used by humble yeoman farmers gleamed with all the trimmings of London society.

Young leaves and spring flowers stood in bowls on sills and the floor was scrubbed and newly-laid with rushes. Anna put pewter mugs and silver goblets for ale and wine and when Captain Bennet came down from the stables where he had been with Christopher, discussing the journey, he opened his eyes wide.

'A special supper before you go, my dear,' said Marian, her face pink with exertion and slight embarrassment.

'You expect more guests?' he asked.

'Mr Silke and Sir John and Lady Mattie and their guest,' she added, as if they were of no consequence, and laid linen napkins by each setting.

'I wish I could do you justice,' said Daniel Bennet. 'I brought little enough with me and now what I have is packed ready for an early start.' His blue suit of chambray made him seem darker and the hollows of his cheeks seemed tonight to show that he was not yet ready for active service. Anna busied herself with the arrangements and when Sir John and his party came in, she was in the kitchen beating cream and hoping that it wouldn't turn buttery before it reached its peak.

'Anna, come quickly,' whispered Alice. 'Sir Rollo has arrived and I nearly swooned when I saw him.' She rolled

323

her eyes with great dramatic effect and clutched at her dress over the spot where she fondly believed her heart was situated. 'Oh, Anna, he is so handsome and you must see his clothes! I had forgotten that men were so beautiful and well-dressed. I remember him at the theatre but he has changed. Perhaps his fright over the plague has made him more serious, but he has a wonderful smile and told me that I was the most beautiful lady he's seen today, and he wants to hear me play after supper.'

'Take a deep breath!' said Anna, laughing. 'You'll choke if you don't stop for a minute. I shall come when I have finished this cream. Lady Marian wants everything of the best tonight.'

'I know. Isn't it exciting? Christopher and Captain Bennet leaving for London and Sir Rollo visiting us and now Kate and Mr Silke will announce their betrothal tonight. Sarah and I will soon be old enough to be married, too, Anna. I shall look for someone very rich and handsome.'

Anna looked down at the shining eyes and pretty hair. 'And you'll find them making a line to court you in turn,' she said affectionately.

'Will you be my bridesmaid, Anna?'

'Probably,' said Anna. 'I doubt if I shall be married first.' Books and good works and the children of my friends will fill my life, she thought as she carried in the tray of glasses and the wine to put in the cooler.

Sir Rollo FitzMedwin rose from the stool on which he perched elegantly, his calves showing to the best advantage. The flared coat of peacock silk fitted over a waistcoat of embroidered yellow velvet and his stockings were pale green and without a wrinkle. His natural hair shone with gold lights and as he came to greet Anna, his eyes glinted with triumph, knowing that she must receive him as a guest of the house, and an honourable suitor.

Anna inclined her head slightly and murmured the

conventional words of greeting while he took her hand and held it tightly before kissing it with panache and evident enjoyment. 'Your servant, Ma'am. More lovely than ever, Miss Anna, though a little thinner. I hope that means you pined for me,' he said.

She was aware of Captain Bennet's pale face watching every moment and she smiled into the eyes of the man who had escaped the plague. Somewhere behind the smile, she sensed the same ruthlessness and the same predatory urges, but it was exciting. Let Mr Bennet know that other men desired her and didn't scorn her name. She drew her hand away, not because it felt strange in his clasp but suddenly she was aware that country life had made her hands rougher and she needed unguents to smooth the skin.

Did Rollo smile because he found them all too rustic? Did he laugh at Edward's jokes to make him feel at ease in his own house, or was he genuine in his delight at meeting her again? Anna blushed and looked down and Rollo was entranced.

They ate and drank and left the table to be cleared before they played cards, and tonight even Edward enjoyed a hand or so and plied his guests with more wine and sweetmeats. George Silke and Kate sat apart and said little, but were in a world of their own, and Captain Bennet retired early to the tiny room made over to him as soon as he could be moved from the fireside. He pleaded weariness and the early journey the next day and indeed he looked drawn and solemn and not in the mood for play.

Anna glanced at the closed door at the end of the main room and Marian beckoned to Debbie. 'Go to the Captain and ask if he has all he needs,' she said. She smiled at Anna in a warning manner. 'There is no need for us to disturb ourselves. Captain Bennet is no longer an invalid and he has his own responsibilities to take on tomorrow.'

Rollo looked across at Christopher. 'You will go to Lincon's Inn after you go home?' he said. Christopher

325

nodded. 'Would you call at my house and see that it is still locked up? I left it locked securely but in a hurry, and I hope that the good souls living in my loft are taking care of it.' He handed over a bag with coins in it. 'If they have done well and kept thieves away, give them this.' He laughed. 'I go to London only with the Court until the infection has gone completely. Who knows who might see me and think I return from the dead if I show my face?' He sounded flippant but his eyes were hard, recalling that someone might have seen him or suspected him when he killed the watchman guarding his house.

'I'll go,' said Christopher. He put the bag in his pocket and soon went to bed, leaving the party to break up after prolonged leave-taking.

From his bed, Captain Bennet heard Rollo calling that he would come at ten to take Miss Anna riding, and he turned to the wall, finding that his wound ached as if his heart was stitched with it. What did a name mean? What had that to do with a loving heart and a beautiful body and a fortune? He had been clumsy, goaded by the remarks made by the Army doctor. The man had no skills and might be an even greater fool in this. 'I'll ask permission,' he said in the darkness. 'If I'm not too late to find her again.'

'Don't disturb him now, Anna,' said Marian as she saw the girl put a hand on the door of the Captain's room, later on that evening. 'He has all he needs and must sleep. Come, my dear, you are tired too. We are all tired after the excitement. Go to bed. Alice is still awake and so is Sarah and will not settle until you go up.'

Anna went up to the room under the eaves that she shared with the girls and listened to their chuckling and whisperings long after the rest of the house was asleep. She drifted off to sleep and when she woke, she heard voices and the sound of horses. She rubbed her eyes and went to the window. Christopher was mounting and settling

326

between the full paniers on his horse and Captain Bennet had already left the yard and was slowly riding along the lane. Christopher looked back and waved to Edward Verney and Peter, who still wore nightgowns and shirts, but Captain Bennet looked ahead and kept a straight and lonely back.

Anna stuffed the bedclothes to her mouth to prevent her sobs from wakening the girls. He had gone and it might be for ever. Last night he had looked ill again but that might be the contrast between him and Rollo FitzMedwin. She rubbed lanoline into her hands and then wiped them clean. They were still rough, so she put more on and stayed in bed with cotton gloves until Alice woke and asked for a drink of water.

On the kitchen table she found a note addressed to her. *'Keep a place for me in your heart, my dear Anna. I will return and make you my own.'*

As wife or doxy? Sharp tears of grief and anger made her fold the note small and put it in her ribbon-box. No hint of when she might see him again, and no hint of anything but his need of her.

'You saved his life and now he is gone,' said Marian when she saw Anna looking out at the lane. 'He will go back to a man's life, but Sir Rollo can give a woman what she wants and deserves.' Her kind face had a shrewd expression. 'He's changed for the better, Anna, I know it, and whatever he's done is in the past. Don't be hard on him because he once was foolish and didn't know you well. He respects you and anyone can see that he wants you. Be wise. To him, your name and fortune mean nothing and it's time you married well.'

If it rains, I shall take it as an omen that I must not ride with him or encourage him in any way, thought Anna, but by half-past nine the house was clear and her horse saddled ready for the ride. She dressed in a habit of bright green wool and pinned a cap of green velvet to her hair. She put

327

fine French leather gloves of dark red on her hands, the leather as smooth as a chestnut and smoother than her hands, and the sun shone with real warmth, making the spinney soft with mist as the vapour rose above the ground.

'Miss Anna.' Today, Rollo was dressed soberly in grey and purple with polished leather leggings over grey stockings and boots. He came into the house to take a draught of wine before the ride and Alice watched with envy as the riders set off towards the Downs. Carelessly, Rollo hung his feathered hat on his saddle and spurred his horse to a gallop. Anna rode with him and they reached the top of the Downs breathless and exhilarated. The whole of the County lay before them, pure and bright under a light blue sky and they saw carts with household goods down in the distant lanes, all going towards London.

'It's over, or nearly,' said Rollo. He looked at the lovely face by his side and kept his own lust under control. This time, he must woo her gently but swiftly if he was to steal her from that sober-sided Captain who had a head start on him. Not that she had given anything. The man's eyes followed her too much for that. Wasn't there a saying that a man looked after a woman wherever she went until he had his way with her, and then she was the one to watch everything he did while he glanced away?

'Yes, I begin to think it may be over,' said Anna. So much was over, the plague, the sorrow; and yet the hope was gone, too. Captain Bennet and Christopher would be stopping for the night somewhere beyond that hill and soon would be in London, forgetting her and everything here.

She smiled. 'I haven't been to that ruin yet. It's been too wet and cold and I had no companion.'

'I'm at your service in every way, Madam. I am your slave!'

'With a name like mine?' Anna looked up at him with suddenly sad eyes.

'You can change names, Miss Anna. If it bothers you,

then change it for mine.' He kicked his horse's flanks and rode away, leaving her to follow. So the name worried the not-so-gallant Captain! Rollo laughed aloud. It would be easier than he had dreamed. A name? He had wealth enough to buy off disapproval and no place in the Army or Navy that needed sanctions to any match he might want to make. The King would be glad to have him tamed by anyone and the Verneys were important in their own right.

Anna rode back slowly after the ride. Rollo kissed her hand but refused to stay to dinner and left her in a glow of fresh air, flattery and the idea that her name didn't displease everyone.

Chapter 21

'You are silent, Daniel,' said Christopher after the first five miles of their journey together. The roads were good over the grassy tracks and the horses took their own time.

'And you have little to say,' said Daniel Bennet. He smiled. 'It's good to breathe the air and to look away at distance.' The land undulated over the gentle green hills and far away they saw the young bracken and dew ponds of the Heath. Late primroses and bluebells dying in the grass gave off scents that reminded them of childhood and Christopher couldn't drag his mind away from the farm.

'I hate the thought of London,' he said aloud. 'Much as I wished to stay when we left, now I could be happy never to see the place again.' He pictured Abigail at the side of the road, up early to wave him goodbye and crying softly. They had passed through her father's estates and Christopher felt a rush of pride at the thought that one day, he would own many acres of that land and take Abigail for his wife. How could any man wish for cities when there was heaven in the country?

'I shall miss the comforts of your home,' said Daniel. He eased his back and felt the ache of his wound again.

'Let us stop soon,' suggested Christopher. 'The horses can drink at the stream and we can go to the inn for news and ale. Neither of us has broken fast and soon the sun will be high.'

Daniel looked at him sharply, not wishing for any favours, but Christopher showed no sign of the concern he felt for the man at his side. In the house, everyone had become used to the gradual loss of weight and gaunt features and Anna had been the one to see him more than any of the rest of the family, but here, out in the sun, riding as a normal healthy man, he looked all wrong and Christopher doubted if he'd have the energy to reach their first night's stop.

As they sat by the fire in the inn parlour, Daniel sighed. 'I'm not used to the saddle,' he admitted, but attacked his bread and meat with a good appetite.

'We'll take longer than I thought,' said Christopher, pretending chagrin. 'I don't fancy the nags they have for hire here and we have no need to change if we rest ours well. If we push on until late afternoon and stay for the night, they will be well-fed and rested.' He knew now why Anna had whispered, 'Take good care of him. He isn't well.' Last night at supper, he thought that Daniel was sullen because Rollo FitzMedwin was there, making an elegant leg to show the ladies while Daniel sat in his sombre suit that looked two sizes too big for him, but now he saw how the man had suffered.

'We owe you a great debt,' said Christopher impulsively. 'I have been wrapped up in my own concerns and never said so, but you nearly gave your life for Alice.'

Daniel flushed slightly. 'Any gentleman would have done the same and I, too, owe much to your family. Without their care, I would have died when the poison set in.'

'That was Anna and my mother, but mostly Anna,' said Christopher. He smiled as if he saw the lovely young woman. 'She is a wonderful girl and worthy of the best in the land. I love her as a dear sister and so does my family. One day, she will marry and be as happy as Abigail and I

331

will be, but before that I hope she does find happiness in the country. She loves to ride but hates sport where blood is spilled, which made us all amazed that she could tend you so well when your wound needed dressing four times a day.'

Daniel bent over his platter. Each word twisted in his heart and showed how selfish he had been. 'She is dear to me, too,' he said awkwardly. 'She is indeed good, with no thought for her own comfort when there is work to be done.'

'She sat up with you for four nights when you were out of your mind with fever and let nobody take her place until dawn, when you slept.' Christopher rhapsodised over Anna until Daniel wanted to shut his ears and cry, 'Enough, I know it all and I have been a fool!' How could he have suggested to her that she become his mistress? Now, he felt the miles between them and more than that, he felt a distancing that was nothing to do with time or place. She would try to forget the rough army Captain who insulted her, and take comfort in the scented arms of that facile idiot, Rollo FitzMedwin.

Captain Bennet stood up. 'I am fit enough to go on,' he said firmly. The sooner he joined his unit the better he would be – and to Hell with women and love and kindness, and soft hands that were tender even when roughened with soda. Even in his note he had been incapable of saying all he felt for her. Two lines of nothing, when Rollo could say more with his eyes. He tugged angrily at the reins and made the horse slide away towards the ditch, then recovered his balance, mentally and physically. There was more colour in his cheeks when they stopped for the night and he took satisfaction in the knowledge that he had ridden as well as his companion.

'I go to the house and the office and you to Whitehall and the palace,' said Christopher, over supper. The inn was full of people going back to the City and the inn-keeper looked red in the face with pleasure at the extra business. No turning away of travellers now, thought Christopher. Everyone was coming from healthy districts and none from the plague. The man stopped at their table, however, and frowned. He knew that they came from the country, but the Captain looked as if he had been ill and it brought back some of the fear.

'You go home to the City, Sir?' he asked.

'I report for duty,' said Daniel shortly.

'The Captain was wounded and is now recovered,' said Christopher, seeing that some explanation would help to ensure service.

The man's face cleared. 'A gentleman soldier! We have need of you, Sir. They say the beggars in the City are looting and getting bold, entering sealed houses and so spreading the last of the plague along the docks. It isn't safe on the streets, or so they say, and you'd best look to your baggage in inns closer to the town.'

'I am not the Watch or a Constable,' snapped Daniel. He was tired and aching and needed sleep. Christopher took their saddlebags and paniers to the room they shared with three other travellers and wondered how he had ever liked such places, with the noise and laughter and cursing in the rooms beneath them.

Before dawn, Daniel woke and went out to the yard. He cupped his hands at the pump and drank the clear cold water before sluicing his face and hands. He couldn't forget the expression on the man's face when he thought that Daniel might carry the plague. In uniform, he was respected and even feared by the general public, although he had never indulged in the excesses of his fellow officers. There had never been a time when he felt threatened by any but the enemies of the King and he had absorbed the belief that officers of the King were above censure.

True, he had little in the way of wealth, but neither had many of his friends and it was a game to see who could find a wife rich enough to supply the needs of a man wishing to rise to high rank. There was no disgrace, and no shame attached to being poor. He shook the drops of water from his hands and dried his face on his kerchief, a spotless square of muslin folded by Debbie only last night.

He walked back to the parlour and called for the first draught of the day. That look was one that followed Anna Maria Ruyter wherever she went among the ignorant mass in London. She suffered indignity whenever the name of Ruyter was mentioned and whenever her dark beauty aroused comment. And yet . . . she kept her pride and was the more beautiful for her impassive dignity under stress. He wanted to ride back and kneel at her feet and beg her pardon. He wanted to ask her, with tears, to marry him and he would give up his commission, but the road back was already filled with carts and horses and even two carriages, and he knew that the King expected him.

'We'll make a start and rest later when the sun is higher and the horses need a drink,' said Christopher. He saw that the man with him was as pale as yesterday but stronger and his eyes had lost their dullness.

As they approached the villages outside London, they saw rough shelters in fields away from the streets, where families had taken refuge and now had no other place to live until they could go back to their homes. Beggars were more in evidence and children ran barefooted, thin as stripped twigs and empty-bellied. Some chewed at raw young carrots stolen from fields and some fought over bread thrown out of the inn kitchens.

'We'll go further and eat our own food,' said Christopher. 'Bless Anna! She insisted that I pack enough food for a few days in case we found difficulty in the City. She said it might not be safe to buy from shops newly-opened until I see Roger Carter and can tell which are safe.' He laughed. 'Her ancestors had to travel and take what came when they faced persecution and it's in her blood. She could make all the victualling for an army on the move if she had to, and travel with them.'

'A good wife for a soldier,' said Daniel.

'My mother has other ideas for her,' said Christopher. 'The man who has Anna for a wife will have to satisfy all of us, from my father down to Peter, who loves her dearly.' Christopher laughed again. 'Alice will find what she wants and take no notice of us, but Anna has made her life with us and takes heed of what we say. I would break the man who caused her pain. She's worth a king's ransom.'

They rode through rutted roads, now dry after the rain, and some better roads covered with gravel or broken stones and slabs of hewn stone. Signs of more gentle living showed in the glimpses of tall chimneys behind trees and wide driveways and flowerbeds. By night on the second day, they reached the Oxford Road and rested before venturing past Tyburn gibbet with its grisly burden swaying in the wind, and the road into the City.

At St-Giles-in-the-Fields, Christopher paused. Everything was shabby and in need of paint and care. Weeds grew among the cobbles and many houses had the fading red cross on their doors. Some were open and white crosses showed that the period of forty days had passed and the rooms were free of the plague. It was all so familiar and yet the two men stared as if they had never been there before this moment.

'We'll ride together to the Strand and I'll look in at Sir Rollo's house and then take the two horses while you go by water to Whitehall. After that, I can be free to seek out Roger Carter and then go to our house. If you need me, come to the office and Roger will tell you where to find me, as I shall sleep away from the house until I know what has happened there.'

'Thank you, Christopher. I shall report and then if I am not needed, I shall stay with my aunt who is back at her country house at Deptford. I can't say how indebted I am to you.' He clasped the other man's hand and for a moment they paused as if this was a turning point in their journey and they half-dreaded what lay beyond.

By the Strand, Daniel dismounted and took his bundle from the saddle. 'Give my humble regards to your family, Christopher,' he said. 'Don't forget me, and please, if you love her, have a care for Miss Anna and give her my best love.' He turned to the lane leading to the boats at Whitefriars Stairs and Christopher led the horses along to Dorset House and beyond to the town house of Sir Rollo FitzMedwin.

Here, there were no crowds and no beggars. The big houses he passed had all been free of the cross except for one, and Rollo's house, which he now approached, had a white cross on it. Christopher grinned. It must have been placed there when it was known that Rollo was not infected by the plague. He looked again. The doors were chained on the outside as if sealed, and even when the key he had been given turned freely, he saw that he would need crowbars and cutters to take off the chains before he could enter.

Christopher wondered if he need bother, as at least the house was doubly secure, then curiosity made him wander down to the stables to seek an axe or something to remove the chains. The road outside was obviously not used by heavy carriages but the wheels of a small cart had rutted the land leading to the stables. He followed the path and smelled horse manure. Rollo had mentioned the couple caring for his stables and Christopher recalled the purse he was bound to give them if they had done what they promised, but he couldn't make out when Rollo had seen them, if he had escaped the guard.

The horses smelled water in the trough in the lane and Christopher led them to it while he went further to enquire. An old cart sat in the middle of the lane with a nag hitched to it ready to leave. On the seat was a woman who started when she saw him and then tried to smile in an ingratiating way.

'Mary Creed!' exclaimed Christopher. He recognised the cart he had given to her and Joseph when they were turned away from the house in disgrace. 'So it was you that Sir Rollo FitzMedwin trusted to look to his house?'

'We had to take his loft as we had no other roof,' the woman whined. 'The Watch let us stay and when nobody came after Sir Rollo died of the sickness, we lived here to look after his house until someone claimed it.' She looked at him slyly. 'We did it out of charity in return for a roof.'

'You are lying,' said Christopher scornfully. 'Where is Joseph? Perhaps he will give me the truth.'

'He is dead,' said Mary.

'Of the plague?' Christopher backed away.

'Not that, although I have seen many who did,' she said with a dry chuckle. 'He was careless and was crushed by one of the massy posts, under carriage wheels. Not the plague, but he went the same way to the pit, and in his good livery, too.' She eyed him craftily. 'Have you come home, Master Christopher?' His saddlebags and dusty clothes told her that he was still travelling and might not have seen the house.

'I am due at the office in Lincoln's Inn and then I shall go home. We have had word of strange happenings and my father needs to know that all is safe.'

'I know nothing,' she said, and wondered if there was anyone who might endanger her with the Verneys. 'I have work to do that takes me far from Holborn and Gray's Inn, but I did hear that Sam was taken.'

'Taken of the plague?' Christopher was shocked.

'No, they told me at the alehouse by Lincoln's Inn that the pressmen had a good haul one day there, taking three men and one of them Sam.' She laughed. 'So that pretty wife lost him and her baby. The Lord is good and defends the Righteous, Master Christopher.'

'So that's why we didn't hear! And Lottie, what of her?'

Mary Creed shrugged. 'I know nothing of her but I know the baby died.' She licked her lips, remembering the cries of the girl shut up in the loft and imagined that some of her grief was for the dead child as well as for Sam. Her face at the window when Mary had shouted up the news that Sam was pressed for the navy had held a mixture of grief and hopelessness but also a kind of relief which puzzled Mary and took away some of the pleasure. In one way, he was safe and had escaped her, but she had consoled herself that he had nothing left, with his baby dead and his wife about to die.

'The baby? The baby is safe with a wetnurse! Mary Creed, you know more about them than you say! And what do you do for a living? You look well-fed and the nag is looked after.'

'I collect old clothes,' she said. 'And goods that people have no use for after they die.'

'Plague goods?'

'No bedcurtains or clothes from bodies, and I stay here in the hope that someone from the FitzMedwins may pay me for my trouble.'

'He will come soon, but he told me to give you this and I must, although I hate to give you anything.' He tossed the purse over to her and her eyes widened. 'Sir Rollo will be back – so make sure you keep faith with him,' he said.

'He is alive?' she whispered. 'That is impossible.'

'He escaped and went to the country. He had sunstroke, not the sickness, and is free to mingle with society.' Christopher edged away. 'Roger Carter is expecting me and I have much to do before I find an inn.'

The woman seemed to be mad. She now mumbled to herself and had forgotten that he was there. Christopher led the animals back to the Strand and Mary Creed sat for quite five minutes planning what she must do. If Sir Rollo had escaped, then the body by the door was not his and she had seen nothing of the guard since that morning; but the white cross had been put there too soon for the house to be clear. Her smile of admiration changed to cupidity. Good luck to him if he had killed the guard. It wouldn't be the first time it had happened during the past year or so, but Sir Rollo might turn her over to the authorities if he saw the rich harvest of silver and pewter and glassware she had in his stables. The good, clean clothes she had selected from the house where she had once cooked would take some explaining away and so would the crested dishes of Lady Marian's which he would recognise as they bore a crest similar to his own.

She whipped up the horse. There might just be time to act. First, Lottie must be silenced and then justice must be done against Rollo FitzMedwin. Master Christopher was tired and would stop for refreshment with Roger Carter. She went by back streets and arrived at the house at two in the afternoon. The guard stood by the door and the cart with the Bearer of the Dead waited. To her relief, Mary saw that the man was one of her cronies; he had no taste for silver but an insatiable appetite for young and pretty women.

'Is she dead?' she asked urgently.

'No. The man is dead but the girl has not touched him and might be clean.'

'I'll see.' Mary took her white smock from a bag and her wide hat of office and undid the white staff from under the cart. Now, she could go in officially. The guard hung back and the man and woman mounted the steps and stood aside on the bay by the grain-shaft to let the body of Lottie's father be dragged down on hooks to the cart; then went inside to the terrified woman who cowered on a bed of fresh straw in the second small room which she had scrubbed and which showed none of the filth of the room in which her parents had died.

'As neat and clean as on your wedding night,' said Mary

Creed, eyeing the clean straw that Lottie had begged from the guard and breathing the fresh smell of the herbs burning in a dish in the middle of the floor. The elixir that Sam had left for the Moors was half-gone and Lottie had the small window propped open.

'I am not infected,' cried Lottie. 'Let me out. If the Verneys knew they would have you whipped!'

'That's what we've come to find out,' said Mary. All the way to the house, she had turned over in her mind what she could do. Her revenge was incomplete. What price was big enough for this woman to pay for taking what was Mary Creed's by right, the comfortable rooms and good food and the life of a valued servant? She recalled the way that Joseph had looked at Lottie and couldn't believe that he had not taken his fill of the soft and comely body.

Sam was alive and could come back to claim his child. 'You told me your child was dead,' said Mary. 'I hear that it lives.' She intended a rebuke to make the girl cower the more, but Lottie smiled and her face was again beautiful.

'Safe, thank God,' she said. 'And Sam is safe, if not free. You taunted me with it, but even pressed he will live.'

'Where is the child?' Mary advanced and her shadow bent across the wall.

'Safe!' cried Lottie. 'The family know and have taken care of her.' She stepped back from the straw, her arms wide. 'Sam will find her when his time is done and you can't touch her. We vowed that she must come first and the Good Lord listened to us. She is safe and I am not infected. Time is passing, Mary Creed, and when forty days are up, I shall walk out of here!'

'Time is passing,' said Mary. 'I must see if you have a token. I can do so by law as I have my staff with me.'

With a swift gesture, she put aside the staff and pulled at the bodice that Lottie wore. The thin cotton ripped and exposed the tight binder over the tense breasts. Since the baby went, Lottie had slept little, the pain of unrelieved

340

milk nearly driving her mad, so she had bound her breasts as she had heard they did for women whose babies died, to stop the flow of milk, but each time she thought of the pink fingers and soft skin of Lottie Katharine, her milk had flowed again, stimulated by the image, and making her cry with pain and desperation.

The Bearer stared and his mouth dribbed saliva. 'A milky doe,' he said harshly. 'You never told me she'd be as sweet, Mary.'

'No!' Lottie tried to get away, sliding along the wall and staring at the debased hands that moved towards her.

Mary chuckled as the man brought out a small sharp knife and held it to Lottie's face. 'It's no use shouting. No one will hear and if they do, they will think the sickness is taking its toll.' He slit the breast-binder with the knife and it fell away, revealing the heavy white glands threaded with blue veins. Milk dripped from the engorged nipples and he caressed them roughly. Lottie tried to take the knife but he had no need of it now and forced her down on to the straw. It dropped from his fingers as he tugged at her clothes, like a wolf eager for entrails. Mary looked on, mumbling lines from the writings of the prophets of doom who foretold death to the Sinners.

Lottie struggled but was too weak to escape. She smelled the breath of corruption and felt the hard body merciless inside her and then found the knife, in her twitching hand.

'Sam,' she whispered. 'I am unclean. Katharine, my love, be good and happy.' She seemed to have forgotten the man panting above her as she plunged the knife into her side. Blood poured over the straw and Mary Creed gasped.

'You fool! You used the knife! It could be noticed on the way to the pit, and she has no tokens.'

'She did it, the bitch,' he said, and kicked the unconscious body, but he hastily put back his clothes and wiped the blood from his hands.

341

'We can't take her unwrapped and they remove all the clothes to let the quicklime work faster. They will say we murdered her.' Mary felt a sense of injustice but there was no time to dwell on her lost triumph.

Christopher Verney would come soon and know that she had been there if she didn't remove the cart from the lane. If he came now, and saw the body on the death cart, he would have no mercy. Mary caught up her staff and pushed the man towards the door. 'Go quickly,' she said. 'Go with the other one and say she isn't dead yet. Say they can come for her tomorrow.'

She took the smouldering heap of herbs and blew on them to make them dance into flame, then tossed them on to the dry straw. As she ran down the steps, she left the door open and the draught from it was drawn up and out of the open window. Flames erupted and licked at the lathe and plaster walls and Mary watched the death cart disappear round the corner before taking her own away from the house and hiding it behind some trees. She paused for breath and felt something pricking her hand. In her haste, she had gripped the reins and noticed no pain but now, her hand was sore. She opened the palm and there, on the broken links of the chains that Mary Creed had torn from her neck, was Lottie's silver cross. Mary cried out as if it was the touch of the Devil and threw it far away, into the hedgerow, where it sank among the lacy periwinkles and buttercups, and she could try to forget the girl burning in the blazing stable loft.

In the distance, she heard shouts as the smoke was seen above the trees and someone decided that this was not just another fire at a street corner to purify the air against plague. Two men came along the lane past the place where Mary Creed was hidden, but they just looked at the blaze and tried the pump handle before shrugging and moving away. The stable block was away from any other building and already, the roof was caving in. A whinny from the

342

terrified horse made Mary take up her reins and quiet him, and when the men had gone, she ventured out and saw no other soul on the road back to the City and to the magistrate.

Mary Creed stood before the magistrate, wearing her hat and staff, and smirked when he sat back as far from her as he could. When the plague ended, she would no longer stimulate such fear but her wealth would win her respect enough. She told a tale of a man sealed up who killed his guard and got away to friends in the country, saying that only now had she found that the man was alive and not dead of the plague. She swore on the Holy Bible that Sir Rollo FitzMedwin was a murderer and added that now the plague was almost over, she would like to hand over her staff and recover from months of hard work and anxiety.

'You have performed your duties with commendable zeal, Madam,' the official said. 'If the rogue is free then we must find him.'

'He has friends at Court,' said Mary quickly. 'It is only the word of a poor widow against his, Sir, and I only told you out of duty.'

'I see.' The magistrate paced the floor and then realised how close he was to Mary and went back to his desk.

'He could be accused but not charged if he agreed to stay out of London . . . for a time,' she added hastily.

'He must be examined, and then we shall see if his friends come to his aid. Leave this to me, Madam. Whatever we may or may not do, we will put no blame on you.'

Mary looked down as if embarrassed. 'If he finds out that I reported this, he will turn me out of the stable room where I have been living and caring for his interests, Sir.'

'Have no fear. I shall make an order that you are not disturbed, come what may, until such a time as the property is sold, if that is his will.'

And the law takes its time, and longer in these troubled times, Mary thought complacently as she dressed in her neat grey gown and went to find the best tavern where she could treat herself to a good dinner. The Good Lord had filled the stables and there was no more room, so she had no need of the treasure from other houses. Her next task and a pleasant pastime, would be to sell off the silver, piece by piece, and find some good investment for her money.

From one of the houses, she had taken firearms and powder. Mary slept with one primed by her bed, regretting that such measures were necessary in this city of beggars and thieves, but conscious only of the chest of money and the heaps of treasure that she must guard.

What a shock for Master Christopher, she thought, amused to imagine his horror and the letter he must now send to his parents. Buckingham, the Bearer of the Dead, would feel deprived of his sport, but he could never tell tales about Mary even if he was denied the pleasure of Lottie's dead warm body.

I will give him something to keep my memory sweet, she decided cautiously.

Chapter 22

'Why must we talk here, Christopher?' asked Edward Verney. He walked away from the midden where flies hovered and the air was foul. They went along the lane by the stables and Edward sat firmly on a log as if this was as far from the house as he was prepared to go.

'I wanted you to hear this in private, Father.'

'You've hardly said a word since you came home late last night.' Edward gave his son a shrewd look. 'I suppose you stopped on the way to see Abigail and forgot all about the report I was waiting to hear.'

'No, I rode hard from Kensington and rested the horse for short periods only. I don't think I winded her but I'll have to keep an eye open for distress when next I ride her.' He picked at the grass. 'I left the other nag in stables.'

'Yes, yes! But what of London and Roger Carter and my house? You came in and ate as if you were starving, hardly spoke to Sir Rollo who was supping with us and retired without saying goodnight.'

'I have things to say that are for family ears only, Father.' Christopher looked stubborn and Edward saw that he was still suffering from some kind of exhaustion or strain.

'Well, you're home now, my boy, and we are all alone,' he said more gently. 'What is amiss?'

Christopher took a deep breath. 'I found much that was

345

amiss, Father. There has been a fire and the stables have been gutted.'

'All? What of our valuables? And the house?' His father looked deeply shocked.

'Not the valuables, nor the house,' said Christopher quickly. 'Thank heaven that the stables were well away from the main buildings.'

'And thank heaven that there was no living thing, either horse or dog or man in there,' said Edward. 'Well, son?' He put a hand on Christopher's arm. 'There's more?'

'No horses, but someone died in the fire. I found the place smouldering and a guard from the magistrate standing by, wondering what to do as he had been sent to guard the stables which had been sealed against the plague.'

Edward groaned. 'Not Sam?'

'Not Sam, Father, but I don't know how we can tell the ladies. Lottie was in that fire and perished.' He passed a hand over his eyes as if to shut out the memory of the smoking ruins. 'It was a confused tale I heard when I went to the magistrate to find out who was sealed up there. It was the two Moors who were infected and not Sam or Lottie. They lived in the house and were not touched by it and the baby was safe. That at least is true and we need have no fears for the baby, or Sam when and if we ever see him again.'

'He wasn't with Lottie? I don't understand. He disappeared after thrusting the baby on to Roger Carter for safekeeping.'

'Sam had been pressed for the Navy and couldn't return.'

'How did you come to know this!'

'I went to Sir Rollo FitzMedwin's house after I left Captain Bennet and found Mary Creed there, living in his stables. She thought that Sir Rollo had died of the plague after being shut away and swore that she had been given leave to live in the stables by the guard watching the house. She must have said she was still employed by us but was staying in London while we were away, and was looking after the premises for any family of FitzMedwin who might come to claim his estate. The magistrate was surprised when I said that she and Joseph had been dismissed.' Christopher laughed bitterly. 'We had no idea what a wicked woman we nurtured, Father. She is now a Searcher and as such reported that there was plague in our stable loft and a young woman who had to be sealed up – tainted, so the Bearer had to obey.'

Edward paced the room as he did when puzzled. 'Mary Creed thought Sir Rollo dead, you say? Then she could not have spoken to him and he must have escaped by some means before she could see him.'

'One of the watchers disappeared but so many collapse at home or in the streets with the sickness that nobody thought twice about him.' Christopher frowned. 'A body from that house porch was taken by the Bearer, wrapped up in a sheet. It could have been Rollo or the watcher, and maybe Rollo killed the guard before his day partner arrived. A body was there and accounted for and yet Rollo is alive.'

Christopher avoided his father's eye. 'How deeply involved is Anna with FitzMedwin? I know that you and Mother have encouraged his suit and that he is setting his cap at Anna, but she should be saved from him.'

'Why? He escaped and we have no proof of what happened. He may have been a rascal in his youth, but a murderer? *No!*' But Edward looked uncomfortable. Marian had talked of little else but Anna's future if they could arrange this marriage and the man was certainly making all female hearts flutter with his smooth talk and fulsome admiration of all they did.

'He had no contagion and so was right to escape and we have no proof of how he managed it,' Edward went on. 'I would try to escape and so would you, my boy, and I have no doubt that the man who died was dying even as he watched the house. May God have mercy on all who died thus,' he added piously.

'But Mary Creed knows the truth, or so she swore before the magistrate. After she saw me, to make her own case secure I've no doubt,' said Christopher with an ironic sneer, 'she went to the law and accused Sir Rollo of murder.'

'Did you say he was here with Sir John and Lady Mattie?'

'No.' Christopher looked down. 'It is better to leave them to find him if they must. Sir John is not young and this is not an upset I would wish on his doorstep.'

'And Mary Creed may well be lying,' said Edward firmly.

'I thought of that and in a way I sympathise with Rollo if he needed to escape. Many would have done the same and with the security of the King's patronage, I have a doubt that any charge will be made.'

'You are right. It will all blow over and be as lasting as the ripples in a pond after a pebble is cast.' Edward eyed his son with anxiety. 'You have told me everything?'

'I saw the baby, Father. She is fat and well and so like her mother that it was a shock. Sam will be suffering with no word of her and she needs a home until he returns.'

Edward pulled on his sleeve as if the rough fustian that he wore in the daytime on work days was irritating his wrists. 'I am paying for the wetnurse,' he said.

'And after? Lottie and Sam have no remaining relatives who could care for her. Their parishes have enough to do to give succour to the many homeless who have wandered away from the plague and are being pushed from one place to another to lessen the Poor Rate. Would you have Lottie's child suffer, Father?'

'She can stay where she is for a while and then after she is weaned, we'll see,' said Edward, and Christopher smiled. Just let Mother see the child once, and nothing that Father could say would make her give the baby to the parish.

'And Anna? As you say, Father, nothing has been proved

348

against Rollo, but he did try to seduce her once and he had a very bad reputation with women before this happened.'

'Should we believe Mary Creed? Remember, Christopher, that Mary hated Anna for her foreign looks and her name and might want to ruin her chances with Sir Rollo.'

'She did know that he wanted Anna,' said Christopher slowly. He laughed. 'She might even recall the night she was embraced by him in mistake for Anna! And she is vicious enough to want Anna to suffer.'

'So we say nothing to her for the moment?'

'Nothing for a while, Father, but we must make sure that his suit is honourable and never give him a chance to take advantage of her.'

'More easily said than done, as they ride each morning alone and today she has gone to the Manor for the day to watch racing.' He saw the remnants of anxiety. 'Anna is a dignified and moral lady, Christopher. I am sure that she will have no truck with philanderers. Sir Rollo will rejoin the Court soon and who knows, we may all be back in London before the month is out.'

'Not this month, Father,' said Christopher quickly. 'You forget my wedding and then we have the hay to bring in, and the first fruits.'

'Soon,' said Edward. He mopped his hot brow. 'That is if the weather doesn't bring back the plague to the city. It's as hot as last year and even with the King back and the houses of commerce working, there is more infection that could flare again than I care to face for my family.'

'Kate and I will never return, Father, but I shall come to help you move back.'

'What did you see in the stables?' asked Edward.

'All is undisturbed, Father. I left the ashes to cover the floor and told the men I employed to clear the site for new buildings to take only the charred wood and leave the rest until we send word. Nobody will suspect that there is anything left of value and we can makeshift for the horses

349

in outhouses on the other side of the main building, once we return.'

They walked back to the house talking of more peaceful matters, and Christopher shook off his depression and made for the stables to work until he could ride over to meet Abigail.

Edward sighed and braced himself for the tears that were now inevitable when he told the ladies of Lottie's death. If fate had decreed otherwise Christopher would have fallen in love with Anna and kept her fortune in the family. However, the land owned by Abigail's family would serve well in the long run, together with the Manor Farm that Sir John had decided to leave to Christopher.

'What is it, Father?' Kate came down the path to meet him. 'Where is Christopher?'

'He's working and he's told me about his visit to London. Come in, my dear. I have something to say to you all.'

Kate found Marian and Alice and they gathered in Edward's favourite window where they could see the orchard, and as the sun made shadows and the gentle breeze moved the leaves, Kate found everything blurred as her tears fell. Alice wept noisily and Marian sat white and tense, picking at her skirt and swallowing hard at intervals until at last the tears came to her and Edward crept away to leave them to recover.

'The baby must come to us,' said Alice. She brushed away her tears. 'Sarah and I can look after it and make pretty clothes for it.'

'This is a baby, not a doll,' said Kate huskily. 'She is a little girl baby and I offered to give my name at the christening, so it is right that I look after her.'

'You will have babies of your own, Kate,' said Alice jealously.

'Lottie was my maid and was more than a servant,' said Marian. 'I miss the sound of children's laughter in the house and it's my duty to look after her for a time.'

'Only for a time, Mother?' Kate looked anxious. Many children were put out to service very young and had many hardships. 'I know that George loves children and we shall have room in the vicarage.'

'You all forget Sam,' said Marian. 'One day, God willing, he will come back from sea and expect to claim his own flesh and blood. We can look after her in trust for Sam but never think of her as ours. She is all he has left and he will make her a good father. He can work here and Debbie can help us look after her.'

'May we see her soon, Mother?' asked Alice eagerly.

'Not until we go back to London,' said Marian. 'Debbie can go to make sure the woman is clean and that the baby lacks nothing, and when we all return, we will take her into our home to wait for Sam.' She held up a hand to stop Alice protesting. 'While she needs milk, we can give her nothing and babies are better with only a few faces round them. Roger Carter can pay the woman and send someone to check often.' She laughed shakily. 'What a shock the poor man must have had when he was left with a baby! Many men would have balked at it but he takes his duties and loyalty very seriously and the baby is safe, thanks to him.'

'May I tell Anna?' asked Alice, jumping up when she heard Anna's voice outside, handing her horse over to Christopher.

'Back so soon?' said Marian, glancing out of the window. Sir Rollo FitzMedwin followed Anna into the house, looking sullen.

'Back too soon, Ma'am,' he said. 'We had many more races to watch but Miss Anna wouldn't stay.'

'You could have stayed, Sir,' said Anna. 'I have no need of protection in these woods.'

'I am to ride after dinner,' he said. 'I came in only to pay my respects and to hope for an invitation to supper.' His smile was marred by the irritation he felt. There was

351

more ground to cover before he could claim Anna as his own. 'It seems that Miss Anna wants news of her servants more than the company of her most humble servant.' He kissed the hand that Lady Marian held out to him and she smiled as she invited him to supper, as she had done each day for the past week. Edward watched from the doorway and was glad he had not aroused suspicion in any of the other minds. Best to let matters ride, he thought. It's enough that they mourn for Lottie.

'What happened in London?' asked Anna. 'Alice, you have been crying.' She looked from one to the other. 'You've all shed tears,' she said.

'Is something wrong?' asked Rollo.

'One of our servants has died,' said Marian.

'There are many to step into his shoes,' he said lightly. 'I will ride back if I may and see you later.'

'How can he speak like that?' said Alice. 'He didn't even ask who it was.' She had lost her first admiration for the handsome man who now ignored her most of the time and spent his evenings flattering Lady Marian and Anna.

Marian broke the news of Lottie's death to Anna and held her close as she wept and grieved for the girl who had never bothered with names or race and had been a warm and loving companion as well as a servant. 'I had a feeling that something was wrong,' she sobbed. 'I wanted to come back sooner but Sir Rollo became quite annoyed and so I stayed until there was a pause in the races.'

'He looked very cross,' said Alice with satisfaction.

'Yes.' Anna brushed her hair back from her eyes. Today, she had seen a man whom she found it hard to recognise. He had put money on horses that ran badly and cursed openly when they lost. His temper was short with grooms, even when they were not of his entourage, and once he had caught a stable lad across the ear with his whip and made the blood flow. The laughter of his friends had become loud and ribald and they were drinking early in the day.

Rollo had remained quite sober but Anna had sensed that he was making an effort for her sake and without her presence might have been as bad as the rest.

'Are you going back to the Manor, my dear?' asked Marian when dinner was over.

'I have a headache,' said Anna. 'The sun is hot and I have no heart for watching races today.'

'Sir Rollo will be disappointed,' said Marian with a hint of reproach.

'He will be here this evening,' said Anna, and the thought gave her less pleasure than it would have done a few days ago.

'Captain Bennet will be sorry to hear of Lottie's death,' said Kate. 'He said once that a true friend among servants was above price, and he knows how we valued her and Sam by what we said about them.'

'Yes, he would care,' said Anna. She went to her room but there was no privacy there as Alice was playing with two kittens on her bed, so she wandered in the spinney among the shade and sweet summer smells. Captain Bennet could care about servants, but he thought of her as less than that. How could any man plead real love if he wanted only physical satisfaction and no dignity of marriage?

She thought of the gaunt face and thin body that had been in her care and the passion in his eyes when he looked at her and took her into his arms. She shuddered, recalling her own response, and wondered why she felt no answering passion to Rollo's advances. His kisses were teasing and light as if he played a game, but once he had let slip the mask of dalliance and rained hard kisses on her face and neck, pawing her breasts and body until she broke away and fled up to the house.

'I'm sorry, Anna. Please believe me that I was overcome by your beauty and nearness, and you are so cold to me.' He had been profuse in his apologies and had taken her hand gently, his manner formal and his eyes full of remorse.

353

'I shall try to forget it, Sir,' said Anna. The force of his passion had made her uneasy and yet exhilarated as her slumbering passion was stirred, not as it had been with Daniel Bennet but in a more primitive way. She tried to forget that evening. Are we not above animal heat? she wondered. Kate was so lucky. She could marry a man who loved her and had never taken a woman before marriage. They would live in harmony and raise children in this peaceful place and die like the leaves of autumn, gently and without drama.

'That's not what I want!' Anna whispered up through the kaleidoscope of leaves and sunshine. 'Life must have more than that.' She pictured the dust and heat of Africa and the men who suffered under alien suns, and longed to share it with a man she could honour and follow wherever he led her. But not as a kind of camp-follower, she told herself severely, to rid her mind of Daniel Bennet. At least Rollo offered marriage and a background of wealth and influence. He loved her and his lapse from convention only showed his youthful impulsiveness and need for her.

She was heavy and her head ached as it did each month. That's what makes me cross, she thought and resolved to be kind to Rollo when he came to supper.

'The parcel of silks has arrived from London,' said Alice when Anna returned. 'Kate says that she has found a good dressmaker and there is a shop in Reigate that sells thread and ribbons enough for all of them.' She danced ahead to show Anna what had arrived. 'The silk for Mother is very fine, and yet Kate says she wants to be married in a simple gown of dimity.' Alice made a face. 'We have so little opportunity to dress well and I mean to have the yellow silk. What will you have, Anna?'

In spite of herself, Anna began to be interested. 'The bird's eye silk is beautiful,' she said, fingering the finely-patterned fabric of blue with the overall pattern in light amber. 'It needs a simple style and I can sew it for myself

354

as there isn't enough time for one dressmaker to make them all.'

'A summer wedding is good,' said Marian happily, and Edward was pleased to see them have an interest that took away some of the sorrow that hung over the house.

'Lottie would have helped,' said Kate softly, then turned her attention to the materials. 'Has Abigail decided what to wear?'

'I said that I'd give her the material for her wedding dress,' said Marian. 'The cream taffeta is for her, and her mother will sew it. This evening, Christopher can take it over and soon they must set a date for their wedding.'

'Why can't you have a double wedding?' asked Alice. She clapped her hands. 'Do get married at the same time, Kate!' She glanced at Anna roguishly. 'Is it possible for three couples to wed at the same time?'

'Not unless you have a husband ready for yourself, Miss,' said Anna, with composure.

'Sir Rollo would look magnificent,' Alice went on, teasing.

'He'd look fine anywhere but I doubt if he'll be here for Christopher's wedding,' said Anna, pretending not to understand. She felt the soft silk again and imagined herself wearing it in a great church in London, floating down the aisle on the arm of a man in the uniform of a Captain of His Majesty's Guard, and a tear fell on the edge of the bird's eye silk. She caught up the length of cloth and spread it ready for cutting on the long table. The work it entailed would keep her busy and give her an excuse to stay at home for a day or so.

'A double wedding?' said Edward later. 'A good idea. They all need to get settled before the autumn and we might be going back before long.' He sighed. 'I would like Captain Bennet to be here as he became one of the family but I hear that troops are busy fighting in the Dutch lands in Africa and he may not be home for months.'

'Is there more news?' asked Christopher. 'May I take the *Gazette* to Abigail's father this evening?' He glanced at the list of names of officers killed in battle. 'None here I know,' he said with relief, then read again one line. 'No, for a minute I was afraid that Sarah's brother was wounded.' He glanced up to make sure that she was not in the room. 'One brother died of the plague, didn't he?' He looked uneasy. 'Vincent Clavell is in the Navy?'

'Oh, Christopher, his name isn't there, I hope,' said Marian.

'Not Vincent, but Justin Clavell,' said Christopher. 'Would that be the same family? An officer in the Army?'

Edward took the paper from him and held it away from his face. 'The print gets smaller every year,' he grumbled. 'It was a better paper when it was the old *Intelligencer* and I could read it.' He handed it back to his son.

'Justin Clavell died of wounds on the way back to England from the fighting in Africa,' said Christopher.

'Poor Sarah!' said Anna.

'I doubt if she knew him any better then she did the other brother who died. They were both much older than Sarah and quite senior to Vincent.' Edward looked pensive. 'Quite a catch for some young lady,' he said. 'Vincent is now the heir to a great estate, unless this one had a son?'

'He wasn't married,' said Christopher. 'Now there's a man for you, Anna,' he laughed, but he exchanged glances with his father. 'More wealth than Rollo FitzMedwin will ever see and a better man to boot.'

'He's very young,' said Marian.

'He and I are the same age,' said Anna demurely. She smiled. Surely they wouldn't try to make her marry him? First Sir Rollo and now every mind seemed to be assessing Vincent as a possible partner for her. Two likely men and one who she might never see again. 'We couldn't marry,' she said, and bit off a piece of thread. 'If he is an officer in the Navy, he must ask permission to marry, and as the good doctor said when he was here, that would never be allowed with my name and lineage.' She held her head high but looked pale and Edward cursed the coarse man who had upset his household when Captain Bennet was at death's door.

'The war can't last for ever,' he said awkwardly. 'If you would take our name, Anna, any family would welcome you and the King would be pleased to link any noble house with Lady Marion's escutcheon.'

'I shall wait,' said Anna. 'I have my books and riding when I am here and once we are back in London, I shall study science and literature.'

'Yes, wait a while,' said Edward eagerly. 'There is no rush to get you married. You are young and must take time to make up your mind.'

Marian looked at him in amazement. He had been so eager to get Anna married and now he was pleading with her to stay. Sir Rollo wouldn't be pleased and nor was she. 'If Anna wishes to marry soon, that's her affair, Edward, and we must never stand in her way.' Besides, she thought, a woman needs a man older than herself. She watched her younger daughter flit about the room like an angel in pale pink and smiled briefly, then stood up and smoothed down her dress before going to tell Sarah that her brother was dead.

'Two deaths,' said Kate. 'Who is the third?'

'That's easy,' said Christopher and told them that Joseph had been killed by carriage wheels. 'If Mary Creed is to be believed,' he added, then refused to say more about London and rode off to see his sweetheart, his heart filled with eagerness and love. From the lane he saw Rollo Fitz-Medwin riding slowly and cautiously as a man might if his horse was lame or he was incapable of riding.

'Christopher!' Rollo waved his whip and clutched at the saddle.

'Steady, man!' Christopher dismounted and held the

head of Rollo's horse. He grinned. 'It was a good day, was it?'

'No, it was bad. I lost money and came off my mount at the fence.'

'You can still sit a horse.'

'Only just,' said Rollo and swayed until he slid from the saddle and sat on the ground.

'I think you are in no state to meet the ladies,' said Christopher. 'Another glass of wine and you'd be asleep.' Or worse, he thought, seeing the bloodshot eyes and the mean curl of his mouth.

'The others have gone wenching but I came a-courting,' said Rollo. 'I have to act the gentleman until she is mine,' he mumbled, forgetting that Christopher was foster-brother to the woman he desired. 'But I miss the old days and the company of real men, real women. Anna is a drug and a tease and I must have her.' He began to look maudlin. 'She inflames me, damn her! She blows hot and cold and never lets me touch her and yet I want her more then any woman I've met.' He tried to stand but his legs gave way under him. 'I've had a glass too many,' he announced with surprise, and belched.

'A few too many,' said Christopher. He heaved the man up and made him hold the saddle then pushed him up to lie across the horse's back. 'I'll take you back to the Manor,' he said and walked, leading both horses by the slack reins, imagining Lady Marian's concern if she saw her favourite popinjay drunk and incapable. Not to speak of Anna, thought Christopher and his mouth tightened. How could she marry him even if she loved him? All the things he had heard about the man came to mind and he no longer doubted the tale that Mary Creed had told him. Anna was precious and must not be wasted on a murderer.

After leaving his sad bundle at the Manor, where Rollo was put to bed by his servant, Christopher rode on to see Abigail. 'I have to go back,' he told his fianceé, and

358

explained that Rollo had been invited and could not take supper with Lady Marian. 'Come too and have supper with us.' Abigail perched behind him on the horse and they rode back slowly, slipping off the horse halfway to embrace and exchange sweet words that meant nothing to the birds, and when they reached the house, Lady Marian was watching for Rollo and looking anxious.

'Did he have an accident? Have you seen him?' she asked.

'He did come off his horse but suffered no harm,' said Christopher. 'I met him in the lane but he was not fit for company, so I took him back to Sir John and his tolerant hospitality.' Edward saw the set of his son's jaw and hoped that there had been no hard words or worse between the young men.

'He *was* hurt!' cried Marian. 'Anna – you must go over and look after him!'

'No, Madam,' said Edward firmly. 'I think not.'

'But if he is sick . . .'

'I think he may be, Mother, but not from a fall. He was helplessly drunk when I found him in the lane and might well have been thrown before long,' said Christopher.

Anna flushed. 'You did well to save us that,' she said, and wondered why he looked so angry. Men did often drink more than was good for them but she was sure that there was more to this.

'He may be here to apologise tomorrow, Mother, for not keeping his supper appointment, but I think that I saw the real man tonight.'

'You said he was drunk, Christopher. That doesn't mean he is wicked,' said Abigail gently.

He squeezed her hand. 'Fine feathers, my dear. Fine indeed but not for my family.' He looked at Anna. 'The sooner he goes back to Court the better. He doesn't belong here.'

'Of course he doesn't,' said Alice, laughing. 'He is far

359

too sophisticated for this small spot. That's why he is out of place. When we go back to the City, we shall meet men like him with manners and spirit and Sarah and I will find rich husbands.'

'Not like FitzMedwin,' muttered Christopher. 'And you are far too young for that sort of talk,' he scolded his sister.

Chapter 23

Marian stepped back to admire her handiwork. The fresh damask table cover was spotless and made the big oak board appear even bigger and more imposing with the swags of leaves and late roses across the front. Piles of fresh fruit with dark purple grapes from the orangery of the Manor and rich red plums from the orchard shared a bloom with the peaches on the silver plates.

Outside, under the huge cedar tree was another table made up of many small boards but covered as the main one with a cloth that hid the joins. Here, huge jugs of ale and metheglin waited for the servants of both the Manor and the Home Farm Cottage to come after church and drink the health of the newly-married couples. On the whole, Lady Marian Verney was satisfied but it was a pity that all the celebrations couldn't be in one place.

'I think you did well to have dinner here and supper at the home of Abigail's parents,' said Edward. 'Poor Sir John couldn't stand too much of the guests who have been included by obligation, and they will be more drunk at night than here for dinner,' he added shrewdly.

'Most of the men have gone back to Lord Carnegie, now that their sport is over, and only Sir Rollo and two of his friends remain,' said Marian. 'What has happened between Rollo and Anna, Edward? She seems to avoid him whenever possible and never goes riding with him alone any more.' She laughed. 'Perhaps she is shy with him and finally falling in love. Many girls become distant when they are most taken with a man. You know, my dear, I would like to see her happy before we go back to London, and he is very attractive.'

'He has an axe to grind,' muttered Edward. 'He might even feel he needs friends who are above reproach and can speak for him.'

'He has money enough and a family of distinction,' said Marian in puzzlement. 'They were connected with my own family a few generations ago, and he has no disgrace from the bar sinister on his armorial bearing. Half the Court have bastardy in their families and the King has at least ten or twelve ennobled bastards from Lady Castlemaine and his other mistresses, and who knows how many by whores?'

She spoke hotly and Edward regarded her with surprise. She seldom mentioned the gossip from the Court and he knew that she had become attached to the handsome and eloquent young man. 'Well, he's here for the wedding with enough powder on his hair to lime a bird on a branch! As for his pantaloons, they would fit the stage better than a small country house.' He grinned. 'Take your fill of the sight, Madam. If Anna refuses him again, he will be off, mark my words. His patient manner is wearing thin and Sir John has asked him to leave. The Court are settled back in London and he must have matters to which only he can attend.'

'Perhaps today,' said Marian hopefully. 'Alice thinks he looks wonderfully handsome today and what girl could resist such a beau when everyone is talking of marriage?' She straightened a silver knife. 'We must walk over to the chapel,' she said. 'I hear wheels and voices and we must be in our places before the brides.'

They walked across the buttercup-spattered grass

through the churchyard, the way taken by generations of the Lords of the Manor, and a man pulled on his forelock as he opened the gate for them. Many servants in clean sober clothes stood in groups waiting to be allowed into the back seats of the chapel, and the carriage bringing Abigail's parents arrived as Marian and Edward reached the porch.

Candles burned on windowsills among bunches of wild flowers and herbs but none on the altar as this was a simple church with no hint of the forbidden religious decorations that could have them accused of Popery. Anna sat with Alice and the sun picked out the light and dark of their hair and the brightness of their gowns. Marian was escorted to the family pew of Sir John and Lady Matilda, which fortunately was large enough to take the leading members of all the participating families. The cold and slightly disapproving cast of an ancestor and his lady, somewhat marred by the remains of bat droppings, watched yet another generation joined in Holy Matrimony and the two Canons of the Church invited from Westminster made the eyes of the simple villagers widen with respect and awe, almost as if they practised black magic and not the rites of the established Church of England.

Marian closed her eyes and thought back to her own marriage, arranged by her family who needed an infusion of money and property and had only their daughter to offer in exchange, with her own title. Edward had been good-looking in a solid way and his manner had never been that of a courtier, but it was a good marriage and one that had stood firm in joy and sorrow. They had fine children and she had never lacked anything, but what if a man like Sir Rollo had crossed her path twenty years ago?

She glanced at Anna, and wondered guiltily if she was trying to relive her own life with a slightly more romantic element included, taking vicarious joy in another's adventures. Sir Rollo sat by a pillar and looked bored. His face in repose lacked the strength of Christopher who stood with his bride before the altar, his shoulders set and pride in every fibre of his body. George Silke looked well turned-out and his sensitive face was full of love and the promise that Kate would never know infidelity in her choice of husband.

How many women had Rollo taken? Marian wondered, and as the words of the service impressed her yet again with their solemnity and holy vows, she also wondered if Rollo would be capable of keeping any he made before God or man. Anna looked up at the stained glass window and the rays of the sun fell in colours over her hair. It was not right to think of such things but she looked like the Virgin in an old Catholic painting, and more beautiful.

Tears pricked at the back of Anna's eyes as she followed the service and heard two young women vow to honour and obey and love until death. Captain Bennet was far away, unaware of any marriage here today, and he might even be dead or dying of fever. For several days she had been so occupied that there was no time to day-dream, but now, in this grey old building, steeped in the family happenings of centuries, she could think only of the man who wanted her but dared not take her with honourable marriage. The scent from the silk coat of the man behind her wafted over like a frivolous incense and she knew that he was watching her.

Soon, today or tomorrow, I must make up my mind, thought Anna. Rollo was exciting and she yearned for the sophistication and colour of the city after all the months of spartan rustic life, however enjoyable. It was interesting to make butter and to feed hens and the riding was superb along the short-turfed paths and over the Downs, but on bad days she would gladly exchange the mud of the country for the mud of the London streets and the cries of the vixen for the street cries of pedlars.

But were the pedlars back? Was anything the same? Or

was she holding fast to a dream that had never been as she recalled and could never again be as good? A sensation of panic filled her. So many had died from the plague and even now, Edward was cautious about returning to the City as more cases had appeared on the docks and a wave of contagion swept Cambridge and Colchester, destroying over four thousand lives and leaving the city of Colchester a skeleton that could never again be well-fleshed.

She looked at the simple dress worn by Kate and the hardly more elaborate one of Abigail. They were meant for this life of rustic simplicity but did any other manner of living exist after the plague? Anna looked back at the man by the pillar to convince herself that beauty and adventure and gaiety were still possible. She saw the rich silks and powdered hair and the bright blue eyes of the man who swore he loved her and would give her his name. Daniel Bennet was a gaunt wraith who might never come back.

Rollo saw her misty smile and rejoiced. It hadn't been a waste of time coming today! The atmosphere at weddings made women cry and melted all but the stoniest of hearts. One wedding led to another and he must make sure of her tonight. His smile was sweet and his eyes seemed to hold caresses as Anna dropped her gaze and looked at the altar, but his hands twisted the fine silks of his skirted coat as he felt his body harden. Soon, he told himself grimly. A man couldn't deny himself for ever or his virility would die and his mind would go. If she refused him now, then he would take her as he would a whore. His mouth grew tight and his eyes hard. She had teased him long enough.

He moved uneasily on the hard wooden seat and picked up the cushion that his fidgeting had pushed to the floor. I want to marry her, he thought, and was angry at his own reluctant response to the vows exchanged. With Anna even fidelity was attractive and she would vow to honour and obey him. Obey! That would be the summit of his triumph. He saw the slender neck and the tilt of her proud head.

There would be sport there enough to make any man happy.

The service ended and the candles on the sills were snuffed, leaving a smell of burned tallow. By Marian's elbow, one of the candles had fallen into the bunch of flowers and herbs and a man rushed out with the smouldering bunch to make it safe. The burning herbs came as a remembered breeze across a stricken city. Lottie had such faith in herbs, thought Marian. Such utter faith and yet she died. The tears that she now shed were not those which mothers weep at weddings when they see their sons and daughters leave home to make their own nests, but nobody but Marian knew it. She prayed for Lottie's soul and for the safety of Sam and the child, and when she opened her eyes, was amazed to find that everyone else was laughing with joy.

'Anna!' Kate clung to her and smiled with joy. 'You look wonderful and I wish that you could have such happiness.' Anna smiled and hugged the girl who was a sister to her and then embraced Abigail. 'Now we have another sister,' said Kate, 'and I shall need Abigail if you insist on returning to London to live.'

'London and the Court need Anna,' said Rollo Fitz-Medwin. He eyed the simple gowns of the two brides with mild amusement. Such rustic charm was not for him. He led Anna away to find food and drink. 'You are as a peacock among sparrows, or one of those outlandish handsome birds they call Birds of Paradise, that sailors bring back from far lands.'

'Outlandish I am,' said Anna.

'That was a slip of the tongue, but what man wants the ordinary when he can have such beauty, such variety?' he said quickly, seeing the sadness that crept into Anna's face whenever she was reminded of her background.

'You are kind, Sir,' she said, and accepted the dish that Debbie held out to her, thus preventing Rollo from taking her hand. Debbie smiled mischievously. Everyone at the Manor knew Sir Rollo and his tantrums and his liking for a hand up a skirt or into a bodice and she hoped that Miss Anna wasn't taken in by his scent and manners. Rollo saw the smile and took it to mean that Debbie was not averse to a kiss or so or even more, but there were more important affairs to settle before he could lay another servant girl.

The great hall was filled with colour that set the old grey stones and flags glinting with unaccustomed tones. Tapestries that looked lustrous when the room was empty now hung in faded dignity and the open doors let in bright sunlight. Even the two church dignitaries laughed and enjoyed the good food and drink provided and Rollo was at his best, careful to see that he didn't overstep the mark of good manners but flattering, courting and plying the ladies with Sack or Madeira until their eyes sparkled.

Alice and Sarah sat by the window and watched the others, remarking on dresses and hose and the figures cut by the younger men. They giggled and ate and stole more than their share of the syllabub. Today, they were dressed as they might be at the theatre and tossed back fair hair bound with pearls and ribbons, conscious that they were grown-up and attracting attention from the men with Rollo FitzMedwin.

'Vincent!' cried Sarah suddenly, and ran outside, forgetting that she was now a lady grown. She hitched up her skirts and ran after the horseman riding slowly along to the stables. 'Vincent! Stop, Vincent, it's me!'

Vincent Clavell slid from his horse and tossed the reins to the lad who came out of the kitchen wiping his mouth free of ale. 'Sarah!' He hugged his sister and kissed her cheek. 'They told me at the farm that there was a wedding here today,' he said. His face was drawn and tired and he was obviously making an effort to smile. 'By the look of that gown, it could well be you, my dear.' He regarded her earnestly. She was older by far more than the few months since he had last seen her. She tugged at his hand and dragged him back towards the Manor.

'You must be hungry,' she said. 'Kate and Abigail were both married today and we are still feasting.'

'Not to each other, I hope,' said Vincent, and sent his sister into peals of laughter.

'I must tell Alice,' she said, and giggled again.

'You have made a good friend of her?' He saw the eager eyes and soft mouth, and a flood of gratitude for the family who had taken Sarah into their care almost overwhelmed him, after the hard life at sea.

'She is my sister,' said Sarah firmly. 'Even if she doesn't let me ride her new pony as often as I wish.'

'That sounds like a sister,' he said, and his smile was more relaxed. 'I'll wash away some of the dust and change my clothes before I am seen by the guests. I'll go in through the back way and ask for warm water and a place to put my clothes. Tell Sir John that I am here and Mr Verney, too.'

Sarah danced away and told Sir John that her brother had arrived and a buzz of speculation ran round the room. Was the war over? Was he here because he had lost his ship? Had De Ruyter once again forced the Blue Squadron back to the safety of British waters?

Lady Matilda ordered wine to be taken to the room that Vincent was using and forbade anyone to bother him until he came down to them in his own good time. 'He will be weary,' she said firmly, and the party turned back to the lighter discussion of weddings and dowries. Rollo looked ill-at-ease but smiled and made the ladies laugh again, although Anna refused to be alone with him. She longed to see Vincent and to ask about the war and what news there might be from Africa, and Rollo saw how her eyes turned to the narrow door beyond which the man rested, and wondered if she had been waiting for Vincent Clavell. Another officer? He laughed, softly. These stiff-backed

368

soldiers and sailors gave far too much loyalty to the Crown and left the way free to more liberated minds. If she thought she had a chance with Vincent Clavell, who had no real fortune, she could be disappointed and have to turn to other arms.

'Isn't it sad?' said Kate. 'Vincent has lost another brother.'

'Of the plague, Madam?' asked Rollo. She must mean the eldest son of the family, who died months ago.

'No, Sir, this is the other one, who died of wounds returning from Africa. Haven't you heard? Vincent may have to leave the Navy to care for the estates as his father is in very poor health and never leaves the family home in Ireland.'

'He is the heir?' Rollo looked annoyed. They were of the same age as far as he knew and it was possible that Clavell had come back to claim a bride. 'Anna?' Rollo said softly. 'I must speak to you. I have to go back to the Court and I am in agony.' She glanced at him sharply and wondered at his sudden seriousness. 'You must give me an answer today and it must be yes!' They stood looking out of the window and although he made no attempt to touch her, Anna was acutely aware of him. 'I love you, Ma'am,' he said softly. 'I mean to marry you but first I must go to London and bring more money and clothes with me.'

'So suddenly?' she asked.

'The King wishes to see me and I have debts to pay and business to attend.' He sounded evasive and glanced back into the room to assure himself that Vincent Clavell was not there. 'In church today, I was ready to make all those vows before God and I saw your face, my darling. You are ready for marriage and with me above all men,' he said fervently. 'I can give you everything you desire and we shall make ours a passion to end all passion.'

Anna stared out at the wistaria drooping over the rough walls and smelled the moss roses in their shaggy green

369

calyces. Wine and the words she had heard in church rang in her head and the voice beside her throbbed with everything she had wanted to hear from Daniel Bennet. 'I must have more time to think and to consult my family,' she said weakly.

'You don't say *no!* Then I am halfway to *yes!*' He touched her hand briefly. 'Tonight, when we go to Abigail's home, you shall say yes, my darling. There is no other way for us, Anna. There is no other man for you.'

He left her abruptly before she could say more and went to Lady Marian to fill her glass and to talk and flatter, telling her that she was more lovely than any young bride.

Anna tried to appear happy but she wanted to rush away to her bed and cry. I have to give an answer and there is no reason for refusing him, she thought. He loves me and perhaps if he marries, I can change him and make him settle down. She looked at the throng of brightly gowned women and smartly-dressed men and then at the face of Abigail raised to listen to what her new husband was saying. The thread of belonging, that shone less bright than heady passion, made her envious. There was love in their faces but also something that Rollo could never give any woman. She tried to tell herself that Daniel Bennet was far worse and could give her neither passion nor caring, if he ever came back, but she knew that she lied to herself and did him injustice.

'Sad on a wedding day, Miss Anna?' Vincent Clavell had slipped into the room unseen and now raised her hand to his lips.

'These are sad times and I forget to smile,' said Anna, and then smiled delightfully. 'But I'm so pleased to see you again. Thank you for lending us your sister. She is so like Alice and together they are good for each other.'

'It does my heart good to hear that,' he said and smiled tenderly. 'My parents are both ill and I have had more to do with Sarah than anyone. My brothers were older and left us together while they hunted and attended to business.' He sighed. 'And now we are the only two left. I think the news of my brother's death will kill my parents, too.'

'You have many friends who care about you,' said Anna. Her lovely face was gentle. 'Sarah will grow into a perfect lady who will do you credit and you will marry and make your own family.'

'I dislike the ladies at Court,' he said. 'I like life in London and much of what is offered there but I shall have to look further for someone less spoiled and used than the ladies I see there.' He laughed. 'Isn't it a pity that we can't love each other, Anna?' She looked startled. 'You see, it had never occurred to you as possible, and it isn't! Besides, I think you have lost your heart to someone far more worthy than me.'

'You are mistaken,' said Anna abruptly. Was it common gossip that she might take Rollo FitzMedwin? She saw the indulgent smile that was not for any liaison with Rollo. 'Who do you mean?' she asked hesitantly.

'Daniel Bennet. He told me of his love for you and begged me if I saw you to give you his love.' He laughed. 'That was long ago, I'm afraid, as I have been at sea and he is busy in Africa.'

'Captain Bennet and I can never marry,' she said.

'Why not?' Debbie came with food and placed it on a small table away from the main party, and Vincent tore at a chicken wing and devoured it hungrily.

'You know my name,' said Anna. 'Officers must have the Royal Consent before marrying foreigners who stem from the enemy.'

'Sometimes, but now we have several Dutch deserters pledging allegiance to our Crown after being ill-used by De Ruyter, and the climate is good for more to come over. Only a few weeks ago, Lord Arlington married a Dutch woman, Isabella van Beverweerd, and you are half-English.'

371

'It doesn't follow,' said Anna. 'Captain Bennet doesn't wish to marry me and I have had another offer.'

'You haven't accepted?' Vincent paused for a second from eating.

'Not yet,' said Anna.

'Then do nothing!' Vincent wagged a lamb-bone under her nose, severely. 'You saw him when he was weak and helpless and know nothing of the real man.'

'He recovered enough to make his position perfectly clear,' said Anna. 'He rode to London and rejoined his unit, so he was better.'

'In body and mind? Please promise me to wait until he returns.'

'I have no promises from him and nothing to expect,' she said softly. 'Many have heard from officers in Africa and yet I have had not a word since his farewell note.' She raised a sad face to him. 'I know nothing of his heart, Vincent, and I must think of my own. He may not come back to us again.'

'He must. He must make his home with me if he wishes. I owe him a debt and so do you, unless you think nothing of Alice as a sister. He saved her and probably saved my own dear little sister, too. How can anyone forget that, Anna?'

'I don't forget. I nursed him when he was very ill,' she said. 'I think he loved me a little because I tended his wound but now that he is better, he has forgotten.'

'They say that some troops will return this month, and the Navy has orders to convoy them safely. I shall not be there, but I think you should wait, Anna.'

'Coming back?' Her eyes shone and she knew that it was no use hiding her feelings from Vincent. 'Have you heard? Is he well? He isn't coming back because of more wounds?'

'I have heard from him recently.' Vincent's eyes twinkled. 'He says he is well and asked that he may come to visit the Verney family to pay his respects.'

'Of course. Lady Marian will be delighted,' she said. He must come back to tell them that their care had been of use and after that he would be free to go away again and live a man's life in barracks and battlefields. 'I see Mr Verney looking this way,' said Anna. 'If you have finished refreshing yourself, he will want to see you, over there with Sir John.'

Vincent laughed. 'I have so much to tell them and I'm sure they are curious to know what is happening, as I am curious about affairs here.' He walked away and then swung back to face her. 'A curious coincidence! Sam was pressed into the Navy and was on my vessel until last week. I saw him wretched, the day after we put to sea and the pressed men were allowed on deck, and I recognised him!'

'Is he well?'

'He was pressed without pay which is against the rules but has made the best of it, only worrying about his family. He's strong and works well and I hope to get his release as soon as I can because he was taken so badly and no pay was sent to his family. The Navy Office has no money and so the poor men leave their wives to starve unless they have kind masters such as Mr Verney.'

'Vincent, my dear boy!' Edward Verney shook his hand and introduced him to the new members of the family. Anna sank back and thought of Sam and wondered if he knew that Lottie was dead. The plague was erupting in some other houses in the city and one rich family had died, leaving only one member free of the disease. If it struck again there was no knowing where it might go and who would die. Life was short and if Daniel Bennet had nothing to offer her but the status of mistress she could die an old maid, having never tasted the sweetness of conjugal bliss.

'Isn't he handsome?' whispered Alice who had come beside her.

'Who? Sir Rollo?' asked Anna, having heard nothing but his praises since dawn.

'No, of course not!' Alice looked shocked as if she had never found Rollo in the least bit attractive. 'No, I mean Sarah's brother.'

'Handsome?' Anna smiled. Vincent was a fine-looking young man with strong features, unlike his sister who was small-boned and fairer with a delicate chin and pink cheeks. 'He has a good face,' she said, with truth. 'He's kind and good company.'

'And very, very rich!' said Alice. 'Sarah wants me to go to stay with her and Vincent. Do you think Mother will let me go?'

'I'm sure she will,' said Anna.

'We're going riding tomorrow morning,' said Alice. 'He *is* funny. He asked if I wore such clothes as the ladies at Court favour, and was cross when I said I would like to have a long coat like a man and a periwig as they do now for riding. He said it was wicked to ape men and if I wore anything like that he would never ride with me.'

Anna glanced across at the young man who was talking earnestly with the two older men. How long will it be, she wondered, before Vincent knows that he must fall in love with Alice? Riches made any man handsome in Alice's mind and her heart would soon follow her thoughts.

Rollo FitzMedwin had gone to change and brush the powder from his hair. His clothes suddenly seemed unsuitable for wooing Anna and if he was to take her out into the evening alone, silks of light colours would not be practical. He dressed with care, soberly but with style, and knew that he looked better than any man in the house. His friends, wearied of parochial cheer, had gone back to London, leaving Rollo with his own carriage and one manservant to follow them to London at his leisure.

Rollo toyed with the idea of abducting Anna if she proved shy or unwilling, but had confidence in his own charm to take her tonight, with the firm promise of marriage as soon as possible. He sipped the strong Sack that flowed so freely

374

today at the Manor and when it was time to move on to the big rambling house by the river where Abigail had spent her childhood, he went out to the stables and asked for his carriage to be ready.

We shall ride and talk and then, if I can be patient, she will be mine, he exulted as he checked that the velvet cushions were clean and scented and that there was strong liquor in the box. His man eyed him with speculation. Who was His Lordship after this time? It was an exercise repeated often in the past but never since they had come to the country, after the master had sent for him from the other family house in Hertfordshire. Tales spread even in times of bad communication, and he also wondered if Sir Rollo had done something really bad this time. They had kept away from the City even after the Court had returned but now they had to see the King and do duty in the Royal entourage.

He gave the harness an extra polish and hoped they might get to London soon, as apart from cock-fighting and wenching, there was nothing left to do in this simple place.

With reluctance, Sir Rollo FitzMedwin went back to the party, ready to offer the use of his coach to any who lacked the means of getting to the other house except on foot. It would give him the excuse he needed for having the carriage there. The great hall was almost empty and the remains of the dinner were being taken back to the kitchen by Debbie and the other servants from both the Manor and the farm.

'Has everyone left?' he asked.

'No, Sir.' The young maid bobbed politely. 'They are changing and getting gifts to take.'

Almost absentmindedly, Rollo bent to kiss her and placed an arm round her waist. She had soft lips but smelled of onions. Anna would fill every need, he thought hungrily. How had he ever bedded girls such as this one? Anna had spoiled him for any but her and she must come to him.

He heard a sound from the door. 'FitzMedwin? What are you doing here?'

Rollo swung round. 'I am a guest of Sir John's. I have been here for some time.' He saw the amazement in the eyes of Vincent Clavell and laughed. 'I have not died of the plague, Sir, if that's what you were told, and what of you? I thought you were fighting the King's enemies on the main and had little time for country life.'

'I came to visit my young sister,' said Vincent. He seemed ill-at-ease and inclined his head in a stiff bow before leaving Rollo staring after him. He looked about him and the empty room, denuded of its food-laden platters and the bright flowers that now wilted on the sills, seemed dark and almost forbidding. He shivered. Outside, it was still day but the sun had gone in and the little servant brought candles ready for lighting.

One by one, the guests gathered to fill the curricle and the two carriages that were ready to take all who found the short walk difficult and the ladies who dreaded what might happen to their satin shoes on the rough paths. Rollo hung back, hoping to catch Anna alone again, but saw her swept away with Alice and Sarah and Lady Marian as they had to be with Abigail's parents to greet the guests at the second reception. He cursed softly then made himself useful, taking a full carriage of aged relatives and coming back for more.

There was no sign of Edward Verney or of Vincent Clavell. Too busy putting the Navy and the Court to rights, thought Rollo, but wondered what they were discussing behind the heavy closed doors of Edward's library.

Rollo looked into the great hall of the Manor and went to the side table to help himself to more Sack. Tonight would resolve all his plans and make the future clear. He watched the candles being lit and was glad to be alone for a few minutes. The carriage was ready and in it he had put some clothes in a box as he was not averse to the idea of running off with his prize once he had captured her heart. His hands trembled with excitement. It was the eagerness he felt before hunting wild boar in the New Forest or watching a good dog bait a bear in the Bear Garden by Southwark. So, a few more hours of talk and smiling flattery, and then he would take Anna aside out into the cool sweet night.

He heard a horse shake the gravel as it swung to a halt. If it's unshod, it will have the Devil to pay for hooves, he thought angrily. A moment later, a man strode into the hall and gripped him by the hand.

'Rollo! Thank God you are here!'

'Alan? I didn't know you were invited to the weddings. Not your kind of sport but I might find a pretty maid for you before the evening is over.'

'No time for wenching, Rollo. I wonder you haven't heard, but you couldn't have done or you'd be miles away.'

'What's amiss, Alan?' Rollo stared at the dusty face of the man who used to carouse with him in London, a squire from his father's estates and a lifelong friend and fellow lecher.

'The King ordered your return to Court,' said Alan Denzil accusingly.

'I was summoned,' said Rollo lazily. 'I have been summoned before and each time I rode fast to obey, he had forgotten or moved on to hunt or visit or was too busy with his women to remember why he had commanded my presence.' He shrugged. 'I am on my way, but I have a little unfinished business of my own to consider first. Next week I shall stand before our dear monarch and dance to his bidding.'

'Next week, if you don't ride fast, you may well dance on the end of a gibbet!'

'My dear fellow,' began Rollo.

'No time! I see your carriage ready for a journey. I thought you must have heard and were even now leaving.

Come on, Rollo. There's no time to lose. A warrant is out to find you for the murder of a watchman at your house near the Strand. They want you to appear before a different court this time, not the one at St James's.'

'But where shall I go?' Rollo FitzMedwin sank onto a stool and forgot everything but the fact that he must escape. 'I must get away until it blows over,' he said.

'You must make for Dover and France. You have property in Belgium and money can be got to you there.'

'I can't leave England!' Rollo shook his head as if to shake off a bad dream. 'You don't know what you are saying. Calm down, man, and tell me that this is a foul slander and a joke. Who accuses me and of what? I killed a watchman?' He laughed. 'How many have died and not been missed, dropping dead at the door of the house they guarded and most like plundered? Where was this and who saw it?' His confidence returned. 'Who saw it happen, Alan? And what would the Court have to say apart from finding it amusing?' He poured out ale for the traveller but Alan Denzil waved it aside.

'There's no time for that, Rollo. Are you mad? You must leave this house at once and be out of the country by morning or you will end up in the Tower.'

'I'll stay and face my accusers,' said FitzMedwin in a haughty voice. 'My name and position will brush away all these lies.'

'Go! It's all you can do to save yourself,' said Alan bluntly. 'Even if this is not proved, it will give courage to the many who think you have slighted them or taken their wives or daughters. Once a finger points, then every coward becomes brave and will accuse you of everything simmering in the past. The accusation comes from a Searcher and they have power. Some say thay have charmed lives and some say they are the instruments of prophecy. Whatever it is, they do have the ear of the magistrates. The City is muttering mutiny against the rich as many starve, and if

378

they think that there is one justice for them and another for the mighty, there will be trouble.'

'The plague is over, or nearly, and people forget,' said Rollo desperately.

Alan gave a bitter laugh. 'Memories can be longer that you think and the King has a long memory. He recalls that a king's head fell not so long ago and is afraid of insurrection. They would throw you to the wolves if it gave them the approval of the masses.'

'There is a lady,' began Rollo. 'Tonight, I go to her and take her away as my bride.' He smiled. 'Give me a few more hours and I can take her with me. She is half-foreign and might welcome a different country.' He laughed with anticipation. 'That's what is best, Alan, and I may bless the day you came here to push me on!'

'God's Death! Have you not heard me, Rollo? You don't have a few hours. They are at your heels and will be in this house early tomorrow morning. A lady? When hasn't there been a lady? There will be ladies wherever you go. They say the wenches in the Netherlands walk slowly and are easy to catch! Come now, get your cloak and what you need and take these papers and gold. I have them from your family and they will give you safe passage in any country you choose.'

The sight of the documents did more to convince Rollo of his position than anything his friend could say and he ran to get riding surcoat and another bag of belongings and valuables. 'Ride to Dover and then take the barge I describe here,' Alan instructed him. 'The Captain is an old friend and will take you and the carriage. Make for France but don't stop until you reach Belgium. Even the Court of France isn't safe as we have our differences with them even now.'

'Miss Anna . . .' said Rollo, but Alan shook his head. He bundled Rollo into the coach. 'I could call at the house and fetch her?'

'Not if you value life and liberty. Leave your servant. It's best to travel alone and have no tongues loosened in alehouses. Trust no one until you are free of the country and God Speed.' Alan touched the lead horse with his whip and watched the carriage lurch away through the darkness of the lane. He waited until he heard the wheels turn to the road leading to Dover and breathed deeply. The fool had the sense not to go to the house for his wench.

Silence filtered back and there was no more movement in the lane. Nobody had seen him arrive except for a girl who took him to be one of the guests, and Alan Denzil slipped away through the woods, leading his horse, and soon it was as if he had never been at the Manor. He slept in a barn a few miles from the village and rode back to London in stages, wondering if Rollo had found the barge and what his future held.

Alan chuckled. Rollo might go to the Dutch asking for refuge against injustice or he might go further, but whatever he decided, he would be free. Rollo FitzMedwin would survive.

Chapter 24

'Who was that man with you this morning?' asked Marian as Edward walked into the yard and back to the house. 'There were others in that black coach by the church. Had they anything to do with your visitor?'

Edward sighed. 'I might have known that he would be noticed, even after leaving his men away from the house.'

'Who was he?' Marian became impatient. 'What is wrong? Has something more happened in London? Has Sam been drowned? Have your ships foundered? Why don't you confide in me, Edward?'

'Come into the dairy where we can talk alone,' he said. 'The men came for Sir Rollo but I was able to tell them that he didn't stay here with us but was a house guest of your kinsman.'

'You sound as if you wanted nothing to do with the poor young man, and that after all the efforts you made to marry Anna to him!'

'He's a poor man indeed, Marian, but one who will never again be welcome in this house. The magistrate sent men to take him back to London on a charge of murder.'

Marian gasped. 'It isn't true! Who has been spreading such lies?'

'Lies they may be, Madam, but he has to stand and answer for them if he is to clear his name.' Edward shrugged. 'Young fool! He's bolted. Must have had word and taken the bit between his teeth and fled. I saw no one yesterday among the guests who could have warned him. None came from his family and most of his friends had left Sir John's house before the weddings.'

'He had the carriage ready but I thought it was for the use of the wedding parties.' Marian regarded her husband with curiosity. 'Did you suspect he might have done wrong? Your attitude suddenly changed towards him and you no longer seemed to want him to marry Anna.'

'I heard rumours but believed them to be just that, stupid and malicious rumours spread about a young man with charm and position.' He thought uncomfortably of Christopher's dislike of the man and his son's reservations about his integrity. 'Anna will be upset,' he added. 'Do you think she wanted him?'

'I can never tell with Anna. At one time she seemed flattered with all the attention he paid her, and that must have been like a breath of fresh air after the sombreness of Captain Bennet, but of late she has avoided him until the wedding, when I thought she softened towards him.'

'Is she still asleep?' Edward was suddenly very agitated. 'Go to her room Madam, and make sure that she is there!'

'I have seen her this morning, making cheese with Debbie and then loading up the dogcart with linen for the Manor, as they used so much yesterday that Mattie swears she hasn't a napkin to her name. Anna knows nothing and I shall not say anything until we hear more of this sorry tale. I cannot believe that Rollo is bad, and soon he will ride back to us and amuse us all.'

'I hope they do not worry Sir John,' said Edward. 'I'll ride over and make sure that all is well there, but the Constable wanted to know what Sir Rollo had done since he was here and a great deal about his family. Sir John, I know, would object strongly to saying anything against a guest or his family.'

Edward asked for his horse and rode slowly through the lanes to the Manor. He passed the cottage where Christopher and Abigail had begun their married life and the dull grey vicarage that Kate had entered with such joy late last evening. He couldn't bring himself to disturb either of the men and both houses had a shuttered look as if the world was not the concern of the occupants. He smiled. Two good matches and one day even Alice might be off his hands.

'This is a fine to-do,' said Sir John when Edward entered the study. 'I had those fellows here for over an hour. I believe they think I know more than I do but I could tell them nothing save the fact that Rollo was here and left to go back to Court. I thought it insolent to take my hospitality and leave without a word of thanks or goodbye, but the young are rash and shoot off when the fancy takes them.' He sighed. 'I enjoy having young blood about the house, but I confess that I'm not sorry to see that crowd go. I treat my servants with respect and justice but they annoyed the grooms and seduced at least two of my maids. Mattie will be cross if we have to turn them out. As yet we don't know if they have fallen, but time will tell.'

'You think he went back to Court, Sir John? I wondered if he had been warned that he was being sought and had fled the country.'

'If he has done that, then he dare not come back,' said Sir John grimly. 'It is an admission of guilt to run away and that is the truth of it, Edward. The young man must be guilty if he's taken off, and I want to hear no more of him.'

Sir John helped himself to ale and bread and cheese and Edward joined him, hungry after no breakfast and now easier in his mind. The man was gone and it was for the best. Anna would find another suitor and life would return to normal as soon as he could get his family back to London.

'Christopher will go back to London next week to see what needs to be done. Some work has been in hand, repairing broken locks on chests and some windows where thieves went in to take what they could carry, and now we must set up curtains again and have the house cleaned. I shall go up to my offices and talk with Roger Carter, and visit my brother who is miraculously still alive – even after prolonged contact with plague carriers.' Edward talked and Sir John listened. 'I have to send to Oxford for papers but they can wait for a while,' he continued, 'and I shall have money enough to pay the workmen once I have seen Roger.'

'Christopher will be a blessing to us, Edward. I can forgive whoever sent the plague for that alone. He would never have come to us and married Abigail if you hadn't left London.' Sir John smiled. 'And dear Kate. It's as if we have children of our own at last and soon we may have grandchildren to run over the fields.'

'We have been happy here, Sir John, and I know that Marian will miss the farmhouse, but business is getting better and I must go back. It seems only a few weeks ago that we came here and yet it also feels as if we have lived here for years. Now, with this coming September, it will be time to plough and plant for next year, whether it is in the fields or in the City. Alice will go to Sarah's family, an aunt and uncle, as Vincent's parents are sick and could not entertain them, and she will stay there until the house is to rights again.'

'She will be a lady by then, Edward. Mattie has some fripperies that she will like, some pearls and a few emeralds that belong to the family and which Kate would never wear even if offered them.' He smiled. 'Young Alice's wedding will be far too grand for us, I fear.'

'She is a child,' protested Edward.

'She has already chosen her husband,' said Sir John. 'At least that's what Mattie tells me, and my wife is never wrong in such matters.' He chuckled. 'I hope the poor man knows or it may be a shock to him. I was interested in what he said about the fleet last night.'

'Vincent Clavell?' Edward's face was full of surprise. Then he smiled. Why not? Why not indeed?

'He said the Dutch ships burned in August were brought to our notice by a renegade Dutchman, ill-used by De Ruyter. We burned a hundred odd ships and landed at Terschelling to plunder a small town there and caused much havoc.'

'Who commanded?'

'Sir Philip Howard, and Vincent regretted that he was not of that party but came ashore dismasted from the earlier battles. The bells rang from Bow that day and long after, and even the poor were given some relief, as bounty for the victory.'

'But still they give nothing to the pressed men,' Edward complained. 'My servant Sam is among them but healthy still, thank heavens, and Vincent will bring him out soon. His ship will return with the convoy protecting soldiers from Africa. They are due back this month and if we are reinstated in London, we shall have much to rejoice us.' Edward coughed slightly. 'Much indeed, now that you have made Christopher your heir to these lands, and added to Kate's dowry. All this after your kindness in taking us in.'

'Life will never be as good again, Edward, but much better than we expected in our old age.' Sir John stood up. 'You have many things on your mind and I must help Mattie to pay for the extra help we had for the weddings and be here as whipping boy when things go wrong! Mattie swears that I employed two rascals who stole some of the pewter last night, and I must set the law after them.'

Edward went back to the farm and for the next few days worked hard preparing his books and accounts for Roger Carter to take over. He had documents sent down for his signing and found that he had neglected some. 'I shall work better when we are back in the peace and quiet of the City,' he told himself. Who could call the country anything but noisy? Birds shrilled and cattle moaned and horses' hooves clattered in the stableyards, and more people than ever came to visit and gossip and drink his good ale. An office would be a haven of quiet and a place sacred to his work and inner thoughts.

Tomorrow, he mused, Christopher would see Roger Carter and the house and they could go back on September the tenth to see the servants into their quarters and hire more help. By then, the house would be clean and Debbie could oversee the females. If only Sam was there to see to the men, all would go smoothly indeed. Edward walked to the cottage where Christopher lived and they talked far into the night about their plans.

'Another month begins in four days, on Saturday, and God willing, September will be free of plague and unrest and everything that has troubled this land,' said Edward. 'Get everything in hand, my boy, and your mother and I will be eternally grateful.' He put a hand on his son's shoulder. 'I am sorry to drag you away from your bride so soon, but you will be rid of us in the near future.'

The magistrate's men had left the village and the two houses in a state of worried conjecture. Marian still vowed that Rollo could never have committed such a crime but the servants gossiped and agreed that he must be guilty, adding their own tales to make his character even darker. Anna was pale and quiet and Marian was concerned.

'Are you unwell, my dear?' she asked.

'No, Lady Marian.' Anna went about her duties and took long walks through the woods and said nothing about the man who had given her such pleasure in his company and humour. He has gone without a word, she thought. First Daniel Bennet forgot her and then Rollo took off into the night before saying goodbye. She blushed with humiliation, knowing how close she had once been to accepting his proposal and worse, how close she had been to allowing him to make love to her.

'I could go to London with Christopher tomorrow, Lady Marian,' she said. 'Debbie will feel strange and has no knowledge of hiring servants. I need to go,' she added in a low voice.

'Then go, Anna,' said Marian impulsively. 'I hate to think of you alone in that great house but locks have been made and most of the repairs have been done and Debbie and Christopher will be with you. The stage-coach is fast again and you can travel in that while Christopher takes the curricle earlier, and changes horses.'

'Debbie can stay with me a night on the way, with the stable lad who is going to work at the house, and we can arrive home early to visit any shops we need. It will be an easier journey than the one we made coming here,' said Anna. Her cheeks were less pale and she hurried to pack her box as if she needed the exertion, and Debbie talked about places they both knew and had loved in the City.

'You are lucky,' said Alice enviously.

'You are packing too to stay with Sarah,' reminded Anna.

Alice pouted. 'I thought it would be fun but Vincent won't be there until next week. He says he has to be on duty, talking to a lot of stiff Admirals and Navy Office people and has no time to pay calls on us.' She folded her dresses with care, however, and Anna smiled. Only the prettiest gowns disappeared into the box that Alice was packing and all the trinkets she had collected in her short life.

Sir John sent a light carriage for the boxes and other baggage to be transferred to the stage at the nearest post-house, and Anna and Debbie left in a flurry of goodbyes and tears.

'You will take care and not go out alone?' insisted Marian. 'I hear that London is a dangerous place now and no woman is safe.' She worried now that Anna was dressed for travelling and wished that she could go too, but knew she had far too much to clear up at the farm to think of it seriously.

'I wonder what we'll find,' said Anna, when they stretched weary legs at the inn that night.

'Oysters!' said Debbie. 'I haven't had a good oyster since we left London.'

'And lobster and fresh fish from the barges,' said Anna. 'I hope to forget that there are such things as cabbages and turnips and wild rabbit.' They ate supper and shared a small room, while the stable lad slept in the loft with other men and Anna wondered if Christopher had managed to reach Tyburn and the out-parishes.

The country receded, like another world. All that had happened there was now a dream and from it they could wake to reality and their life where they belonged, firm and stable, imperishable through the storms of the terrible sickness. London would be home once more and in it, Anna might find comfort and learning. Cocks crowed and the horses champed at their bits and the travellers on the coach were still in the country, but the air was different to Anna and the eager servant girl with her. As the sailor smells the salt and the promise of the sea, they sensed the great city, and in spite of her depression Anna felt her pulse quicken and her eyes strained to read signs and milestones and began to find familiar landmarks.

The last leg of the journey took them through fields that were bereft of grass. Small huddles of makeshift tents and lines of washing showed that the many who had left the capital were still waiting for the red crosses to go from doors before returning to make what they could of property left a few months back.

Further in, they saw red crosses and doors torn from their hinges. Piles of rubbish lay in alleys, and signs of robbery and pillage were everywhere. Grass grew up between cobbles and under windows of houses left unattended, and hedges that needed cutting waved shaggy privet over unkempt gardens.

'Miss Anna, I'm frightened!' said Debbie. 'What if the plague is still here? Look over at that man in the doorway. He has healed sores on his neck and is begging from the coachman.'

'We are safe,' said Anna with more outward confidence than she really felt and she wished they had brought bunches of herbs with them, but as they came through St Giles-in-the-Fields, the rubbish was less and carts were collecting refuse to take away to laystalls where house-holders could be free of flies and stench. The streets were used more here and the grass grew only by the side of empty houses as carriages kept the cobbles clear.

'I saw a shop open,' said Debbie, and craned sideways to watch a pedlar with his vast tray of goods hung round his neck. 'I feel better now. Those rascals were the first to leave and the first to sense that it is safe to come back.'

Anna closed her eyes as the coach jolted into the yard of the post-house. The cry of the pedlar did more to comfort her than she liked to admit, and she was going home. Soon, she could wander in the shops and stalls in St Paul's churchyard and Covent Garden, picking up books and papers to fill her days and mind. The smell of kitchen fires and fresh bread from the inn persuaded the two young women to stay there for dinner before hiring a hackney to take their baggage to the house near Holborn, and soon they saw the big chimney and the driveway they knew so well.

Christopher heard the wheels and was at the door. He smiled a welcome and helped the boy bring in all the boxes and parcels. 'There's a lot to accomplish but we can make do until we have what we need.'

Anna wandered through the empty rooms, noticing the lack of bedcurtains and the broken locks of chests now newly-mended. She made lists of necessities and asked

Christopher to take her to their old seamstress and to shop for fabrics for curtains. She looked with distaste at the heap of curtains brought in by a woman who had cleaned the floors, and asked the boy to take them to the stables.

'There are no stables, Madam,' he said.

'A shed or an outhouse then,' she said impatiently. 'Lady Marian would be angry if she knew that these had been brought in here. How do I know if they came from a clean place? Everything must be new. Take them away and sell them if you can but never bring them back here.' She examined the bills for items bought and pursed her lips. 'It's high time I was here to see to things,' she said. 'Debbie, go to the shops for food and ask if anyone can sew. There's work for half a dozen for a week here.'

Christopher saddled horses and they inspected the local shop and the stall selling fish and oysters. Everything was clean and they stocked up with provisions enough for a week and ordered fresh fish to be sent each day. The house where the seamstress had lived was empty with a fading red cross on the door, and as they went closer to the City more crosses and more gaping windows met their gaze until Anna could hardly stop her tears, but when they returned Debbie was in high spirits, with tales of gardens open again for strolling, alehouses having a lick of paint and eating-houses taking in great stacks of wood to fuel fires that would cook venison pasties and roast meats.

'And I have found two clean women from the country who came here only last week and need work. They sew and bake and one is full of milk as her baby died of convulsions.' Debbie eyed her mistress with caution. 'She thought to wetnurse a child but would rather live in with a great family, Miss Anna.'

'We must send for Lottie's baby,' said Anna. 'Tell her not to bind tight until I see her and if she still has milk by next week she shall take over the baby, but you must care for the child, Debbie, until Sam comes back and takes a wife.'

The stableyard was clear now of burnt wood and Anna hated to glance that way, imagining Lottie in the flames. If the girl had the plague then the end was merciful, but if not . . . Anna gulped and turned back to the house and made up her mind that Lottie's child must thrive if they could make it possible. If I have a child, she thought . . . then tried to think of bed-linen and curtains and food and to forget the two men who might have given her love and a family.

On the sill in the drawing room was a pamphlet that Debbie recognised. She tried to make out the words but her reading was as bad as her writing and she was poring over it when Christopher found her. He took it to read and threw it down with a curse. 'Mary Creed!' he said. He bent to pick it up again and read it slowly, his brow creased with annoyance, tinged with fear.

'What does it say, Sir?' asked Debbie.

'It's one of Mary Creed's papers written by madmen who think they see into the future. This is Mother Shipton and her prognostications. She foretold a pestilence, but the country has seldom been free of some sickness over the centuries.'

'She was right about the plague,' said Debbie.

'She made a good guess,' said Christopher. He screwed up the paper, forcing a laugh. 'But I doubt if she is right about the next.'

'There is more, after the plague?' Debbie's eyes widened. 'I did hear something about destruction, but many preach hellfire and the fall of the monarchy and nobody listens.'

'She says that London will perish in a great fire, the like of which has never been known.'

'No wonder the law forbids stacks of firewood against wattle walls and makes bakers have iron chimneyplaces instead of timber,' said Debbie.

'Not because of these mad people. That law makes sense in a crowded place with bakers and pudding-makers and cake ovens like the City. There have been fires, but with the long rakes supplied to bring down thatch and rafters, and the new pumps on London Bridge and in the parishes, any fire can be killed in half an hour.'

Christopher threw the paper ball at Debbie. 'That's one fire you *can* start, my girl, and then bring some food. I'm starving.' He walked away, slowly. With the paper, he sensed the evil woman again and wondered if she was still alive. The locks on the doors and windows had not been broken like the ones on the inner chests and rooms, which made him think that someone had had a key. Joseph Creed had owned one when he was employed as coachman and lived in the house. If he had kept it and given it to Mary, his wife, she would have been free to enter and steal what she wanted. What had she said? 'I take things that people have no use for, and clean things. Not bedcurtains and linen from infected houses.'

He looked about him. She had taken everything movable except furniture, for he felt sure that the thief was Mary Creed. What treasures did she have stored in Sir Rollo's stables? Grimly, he decided to visit her soon to find if anything she had was stolen from this house. It would have to wait for a week or so, though. He hurried back to see if the stores were unpacked and saw Debbie and Anna making up beds with linen they had brought from the country.

The horses were bedded down in a dry outhouse and the curricle safely stowed away in another and servants and their betters all sat together to eat and drink and talk about the future. Candles were lit and would have to do until lamps were bought, and a fire in the huge hearth glowed red in the chilly evening. Sparks flew up, and in the crimson depths each one saw his own pictures and let weariness overtake the day.

Debbie snuggled deep into the truckle bed in the room where Anna lay on the uncurtained four-poster. The night was dark and they could hear hooters from ships in the offing away beyond Greenwich, often heard on higher ground better than closer in the valley of the river.

Was Daniel Bennet out there, making his way home on a troopship from Africa? thought Anna.

Was Sam sailing home, bringing the soldiers back? wondered Debbie. She longed to hold Lottie's baby and to show her to Sam, pink and white and bubbling with mirth. 'As if she was mine,' murmured the girl, and slept.

Anna woke early and saw the dawn light streaming in through the exposed windows. Today, there would be so much to do that she couldn't stay in bed a moment longer. She washed in water from a clean bucket as the china from the washstand had gone and brushed her hair vigorously. Debbie stirred and sleepily dressed and went to prepare food and pour ale for the first draught of the day.

Christopher was up and ready to leave, but tore off a piece of bread and drank some ale. 'I may be away all day,' he said. 'It's wonderful to have you here, Anna. It would be out of my power to see to all the domestic matters that you manage so easily. I have to see Roger Carter and some of Father's banker friends and then I have to go to the docks to track down some tallies.'

'You will see what ships are in,' said Anna.

'I have the name of the ship on which Sam may be sailing and Vincent gave me letters to present to get him released.' He looked at the girl who shared his home and was as a sister. 'And Daniel Bennet? If he is there, shall I wish him well from you?'

'I am sure you will give him good wishes from us all,' she said. 'I am here and if you bring him, I shall make him as welcome as our present means allow.' She looked down and hoped that Christopher couldn't hear the catch in her voice.

'I wonder if Rollo got away,' said Christopher. Anna looked up, startled. 'You do know that he might be a murderer, Anna, and fled the country? Word came that he took the tide to Calais and escaped. You had a very lucky star over you, Anna. I hope he didn't hurt you.'

'No, he did nothing to hurt me. I found him entertaining. I shall miss his company but that is all.' Anna looked up into the kind eyes of her dear friend and near brother, and he held her close for a second, making her want to sob at his understanding, but she found that Rollo had vanished from her thoughts as quickly as the sights and sounds of the country. Here, she had work to do and a future in a city where her mind need not go to seed. Some day, she thought wistfully, I shall marry and forget the two men who left me without a goodbye.

'There are carriages belonging to the King!' cried Debbie. She ran into the house, breathless. 'I saw them when I was with William, the stable boy. We went to fetch bread and found a shop down near the Oxford Road and two carriages were going empty towards Whitehall.' She sank on to a stool. 'Miss Anna, they gleamed and the seats were covered in watered silk of gold and crimson and the livery was fresh and bright and the footmen were so handsome.'

'Soon, we shall go to Vauxhall to take the air and watch the Royal parties as we did before the plague,' said Anna. Would everything they did now be marked by it being before or after the plague? 'We must get everything ready here first and when Lady Marian comes back we shall have a feast.'

'I saw good fabrics and everything we need for curtains, and the whole lot came from the north where no plague has been. Some came over in ships to Yarmouth from the Netherlands and they are free of the plague.'

'We'll take the curricle and fetch everything today. With so many families returning, some goods will be in short supply.' Anna pulled on her shawl and the stable boy drove them on their errands until they had all they needed for a long time. 'Now we can work and waste no more time looking for Royal coaches,' said Anna, with mock severity. 'There are rooms to prepare and the boy can cut back all the rank grass by the ruins. Work begins there as soon as Father returns, and there is far too much growing where they need to put wood for cutting and shaping.'

She showed the boy what to do and gazed for the first time without flinching at the ruins. Christopher had told her that Mary Creed had been here and she couldn't get Lottie out of her mind.

'Master Christopher found Mother Shipton's curse, Miss Anna,' said Debbie who had come to hang out clothes. 'Mary Creed left it here, but I don't know when as I cleared away all her tracts on Lady Marian's orders when we sent them packing.'

'She came here,' said Anna. 'Christopher believes that she stole from the house.' Debbie gasped. 'She is an evil woman and full of hate, Debbie. She killed Lottie as sure as if she put a knife in her, and we shall never know exactly how she died, or if she knew we loved her.'

'We have her baby,' said Debbie. She bent to pick up something bright from the cut grass. Debbie rubbed it dry on her dress and held out her hand to Anna. 'It's her cross, Miss Anna. She never left it off even in bed and swore that it would protect her from the plague.'

Anna took the slightly tarnished silver cross and the broken chain and tears filled her eyes. 'This was taken from her by force. The chain was quite strong but has been broken. Lottie would never have thrown it away here.'

'May I have it, Miss Anna? I will have the chain mended and put it away for little Lottie Katharine as a keepsake from her mother.'

'Yes, keep it safe,' said Anna. 'Have it cleaned and a new chain fitted and I will pay.'

Chapter 25

'I wish you would worry less, Roger,' said Christopher Verney. The man looked as pale as a green plant kept in a dark room and about as healthy. 'You have done so much to look after my father's affairs that I know he will have nothing but praise for you when I report back to him.'

'But the house has been robbed Master Christopher, and I should have prevented the fire there.'

'Nobody could have done that,' said Christopher firmly. 'Mary Creed had a key and the fire was an accident that could happen to any place in dry weather. Come now, keep the books as well as you have and try to get out into the air. The plague has gone and we are safe now.'

Christopher looked at the row of bottles on the side table and the pile of herbs that sent a bitter pungency into the air, enough to make him catch his breath. The whole office reeked of remedies against the contagion and with it was mingled fear in the man who had stayed loyally in the City to look after his master's property.

'I did go out yesterday,' ventured Roger Carter, 'but not for long as the pressmen were out again and I have no wish to go to sea.'

Christopher suppressed a grin. Roger looked so thin and pale that no man would try to take him for service. They exchanged news and Roger Carter gave up the keys to the strong-box so that Christopher could take what documents he needed for the banks and the ships in port. 'The river is the safest way if you have to go to the Tower or Greenwich,' suggested Roger, glad that he was not asked to go there too.

'I'll complete as much as I can today,' said Christopher. 'Tomorrow, I must go to the house where Sir Rollo Fitz-Medwin lived and look for Mary Creed. If I find one silver spoon with our crest on it, or one curtain from my mother's room in that stable, she will go before the magistrate.' He picked up the leather cover containing the papers and walked briskly to the door. 'That woman is evil and deserves to be hanged.'

He went to the landing stage at Milford Stairs and took a boat to Whitehall after seeing various bankers in the City and arranging for men to undertake more repairs at the house. It was hot and dry, and the ale and oysters in a newly-opened inn were welcome for dinner. News of Dutch battles and the devious behaviour of the French passed round the place and Christopher wondered if any of the idle men from the Court knew any more than he did, fresh from the country.

Christopher gulped the last of his ale. The sooner he finished with London the better, but there was a lot more to do. He went by boat again to the docks by the Tower and as he passed the place where Rollo FitzMedwin had his London house, he wished that he had time that day to look for Mary Creed, but the letters from Vincent Clavell almost burned his pocket and he made for the Navy Office.

The ship on which Sam had served was being victualled and watered for another sortie against the Dutch and the sailors had been given shore leave, except for the pressed men who had not been paid and might escape legally. The clerk scrutinised the papers and sighed. The rich could save a man even if he had no dependants, and this man had been in livery for a great house. Also, he had not been given a penny for his wife and child, so the papers were signed and Christopher went to find Sam and bring him back from Woolwich.

The tide was against the boat and the oars made little impact on the Thames. Sails drooped wearily against the masts and most of the passengers alighted and continued their journeys by land, risking the bad roads and many beggars that lurked in every alleyway. Christopher looked up at the sky. The sun still shone brightly but it was getting late. He landed and took a carriage down to the ship, dozing a little on the long ride and yet eager to reach the dock.

'Christopher!' A man strode forward before Christopher could reach the door to the office. He was tall and his shoulders had a width and firmness that had never been apparent when Daniel Bennet lay half-dead on the bed in the farmhouse. His face was bronzed by weeks in the African sun and his cheeks had filled out into firmness. The well-cut uniform of an Army Captain fitted his hard lithe body and he bore no sign of his old injury.

'I didn't know you!' Christopher embraced the man who had made his home with the Verneys after saving Alice. 'I came to see you and to bring my servant Sam back to civilian life. He was pressed for Navy service but I have here his discharge.'

'Not tonight,' said Daniel firmly. 'It's too late and too hot and you look tired. Come and tell me what you have been doing and I'll send word to the bosun to let Sam go ashore to lodgings until you take him tomorrow.' He slapped Christopher on the back and laughed. 'I'll be but a minute and then you must come to my lodging and have supper and a bed before going back. I want to know all your news and everything about your family.'

'I'll see Sam first,' Christopher insisted, and went through all the wearisome formalities necessary to achieve freedom for the man. The last pieces of the puzzle of

398

Lottie's death sadly came into place as Sam described what had happened that day, before he had thrust the baby into Roger Carter's terrified arms for safe-keeping.

'And my child? My little Lottie Katharine?' Sam looked bemused. Last week he had been wracked with such terrible seasickness that he had thought never to see his baby daughter again, and now here was his young master with a magic paper that set him free.

'Well and growing fast, I hear,' said Christopher. 'Tomorrow, you shall go to Kensington with Debbie and another wetnurse we have found and bring her back with you.'

'And then I shall seek out Mary Creed and kill her,' said Sam softly.

'You must think of the baby. The baby comes first, Sam.'

'That's what Lottie said.' Tears formed and he brushed them away angrily. 'We'll see, Master Christopher. We'll see.' He picked up his bag and went to the lodging at the inn, and was ordered to report once more to the office before leaving with Christopher the next day.

'Now we can eat,' said Daniel Bennet at last. He ordered venison and they ate fresh lobster while it was cooking and drank wine that had been taken from one of the captured Dutch ships; a wine that went softly over the palate as if it was as innocent as mother's milk but which made both men sentimental and slightly garrulous.

'I married the sweetest little girl you ever saw,' said Christopher. He described the wedding and the cottage and told of his new inheritance until Daniel broke in to ask about the rest of the family.

'What of Mr Verney, and Lady Marian?' asked Daniel.

'They are well and anxious to return to London.' Christopher chewed a piece of bread and filled his mouth with wine.

'And the others?' Daniel tried to hide his eagerness.

399

'The others?' Christopher shrugged. What news of them? He found it difficult to think clearly. 'Kate married her vicar and Alice has gone to the Clavell estate with Vincent's sister Sarah until we are settled back at the house.' The venison was well-prepared and savoury and he ate hungrily, leaving no space to talk, and Daniel watched him impatiently. At last Christopher pushed away his platter and took more wine. 'I was famished,' he said.

'You have had a long day,' said Daniel. 'You told me about Alice and Kate. What of Miss Anna?' He threw a crust into the fireplace and drank more wine.

'Anna?' Christopher's eyes had a glazed expression 'Anna came back with me to see to the servants. Sad about Anna. Sad about Rollo, too, but he is a rascal.' His head sank on to his arms and he fell sound asleep.

'Christopher! What of Anna? *Anna?* Come on, man, tell me! What of her and Rollo FitzMedwin?' Daniel's eyes glinted with impatient anger and he shook the limp shoulders to no avail. He cursed under his breath and called roughly to the servants to carry his guest to bed. Daniel sat at the table until long after the house was quiet and everyone slept. 'Anna,' he muttered from time to time. 'Anna?' as if to conjure her face before him. With the clearness of thought released by wine before oblivion, he looked back and despised his own behaviour. On British soil again, he was closer to old problems and old desires, and with his new-found health and strength, he knew he should have written to her and told of his undying love.

What had happened in the country after he left? He was tormented by the vision of Anna in the lecherous arms of Rollo FitzMedwin, forgetting the gaunt and shabby figure of the man who had asked for her body and left her unsure of his love. He stood up, unsteadily. Tomorrow, the *Gazette* would show his promotion to Colonel and he would ask permission to marry a woman half-Dutch. If it wasn't too late! He slept deeply, thankful for the wine and forgetfulness, and woke with a headache enough to burst his brow.

Christopher eyed him through bleary lids and grinned. A draught of ale helped and the two men planned their day. 'First, I must take Sam and set him up with clothes,' said Christopher. 'He can't collect his child in those rags.'

'I have work to finish here and then I must report to Whitehall. May I call on you later?'

'Come to stay if you have a mind to see Anna, but we are not straight yet.'

'I have leave and can help. I am used to discomfort and even that will be better than the open desert,' Daniel said, as casually as he could, but his heart beat faster at the thought of seeing her again. Had she forgotten him? Had Rollo forced her to think of no other man than the dressed-up buck and his wealth?

Sam was anxious to leave, partly in case the Navy changed its mind about him and partly because he longed to see the last link he had with Lottie. 'Has she the same smile as Lottie, Master Christopher?' he asked when he was dressed in a new suit of sober grey that would do for work later when he had full livery again.

'So Debbie said when she saw her.' Christopher glanced at the man beside him in the boat as the wind took them up towards the Tower. Sam would never look as carefree again. The marks of pain and fear were etched deeply beside his mouth. Sam gazed across the water, torn between his longing to see his child and the desire to leap ashore at Blackfriars Stairs and seek out Mary Creed.

'Sir Rollo's house is further along,' said Christopher, reading his thoughts. 'Time enough for that later, Sam. I'll come with you as I have a score to settle there, too.' He saw the stubborn chin harden. 'We'll do it the right way, Sam. No killing, but the law may well do that for us.'

'If you say so, Sir,' said Sam with the false submission

401

he had learned the hard way, over swimming decks under the lashes of cat and tongue as the ship wallowed.

The sky looked red as if the dawn was late, over to the west. Passengers crowded to one side of the boat to see a fire that came from somewhere west of the Tower of London, until the lighterman shouted to them to trim the boat or end up in the river. Flames could be seen high above the narrow streets round Pudding Lane and Fish Hill Street, and several men got off the boat hurriedly at London Bridge, saying that their houses were close to the fire. Two children cried as their visit to relatives in Old Palace Yard was abandoned and more shouts of wonder turned to anguish.

'There have been fires aplenty in these crowded streets,' said Sam. 'But there should be water enough from the new culverts and the pumps on wheeled cisterns to quell fires ten times that size.' Yet the sound of cracking wood came clearly over the water and as the wind freshened, the flames shot high and enveloped a church tower, then subsided as the wind dropped.

Boats with hand-pumps were busy at landing stages, filling buckets and sending thin jets onto houses not as yet affected, and wells, low on water after the hot weather and the sudden return of hundreds of families to the capital, were dipped dry in an effort to stem the tide of flame.

'It's more than a house fire and more than can be put out with buckets,' said Christopher. 'I have business in Dowgate by the steelyard. We can do the business and then eat at the Old Swan near London Bridge.' He stared. 'The Bridge is on fire! And look, Sam, it's spreading to the steelyard. We can't stop there. We must get home and warn everyone that the fire is getting worse.' He had no need to tell the boatman to hurry and soon they were put ashore at Milford Stairs, off the Strand.

'I'll warn Mr Carter,' said Sam. 'The fire won't touch Lincoln's Inn but you know how it is with him. He worries.' Sam reddened. 'I want to thank him for looking after the baby, so if I can be spared, I can see him and do that.'

Christopher nodded. 'I'll go back and tell the servants to buy more food. If the fire reaches the warehouses on the riverside, stocks will be low and we may have many mouths to feed if houses are burned and the people flee to our parish. Go to Roger and bring him to the house if he is afraid, and make sure he has food there. He looks half-starved.'

'I'll come home as soon as I can. At least the people running away bring no plague this time,' said Sam bitterly, remembering his mother and father-in-law. He thought of the people he knew in Cripplegate and wondered if any lived. The fire was a long way off and would be out before evening. Tomorrow, it would all be over and he could search for Mary Creed, but now he must do what he could to help his benefactors and his own kind.

Sam hired a hackney after much trouble. 'I'm not going into the City however much they pay,' said the driver. 'They load up with goods so that the poor beast can't take it all and then blame the driver for having weak nags. Most of them want to save their goods and who can blame them, but I'm not going far in this heat with a horse that's been out for hours.'

They made slow progress through Wich Street and past the Duke's house in Lincoln's Inn Fields, avoiding the carts laden with everything snatched from the advancing jaws of the fire. Horses and donkeys loaded with bedding and small pieces of furniture crowded the narrow roads, and carts of every kind, hired from men out to make an extortionate profit, lurched over the cobbles. Some families still wore night-clothes and their dazed expressions showed a deep degree of shock.

Shouts and the noise of falling timbers died away as Sam reached the offices and found Roger Carter staring out of a top window at the haze of red and black smoke over the City. 'Is it coming close?' he asked anxiously. 'I've made a pile of everything valuable here and if you think it should go, take it to the house.'

'I think it's safe as there is a lot of open ground between this place and the fire, and already the militia is destroying buildings in the path of the flames to make more breaks, but maybe we should take anything that is valuable and I think you should come too, Mr Carter.'

'No, I'll stay. I'm not afraid of something I can see and I've a pair of legs to carry me away if the fire comes here, but the papers are important. Take them, Sam, and keep them for Mr Verney.' Only then did he realise that Sam was free. 'It's good to see you again,' he said, less frigidly than usual. 'How is that baby of yours?'

'I came to thank you, Mr Carter. She is safe and well and will be coming back to the house soon.'

'Poor motherless child,' said Roger gloomily. 'You'd best find a wife again and quickly, Sam.'

He helped to load the hackney with the documents, after Sam had told the driver that they wanted to take papers and not heavy goods and that there would be a good meal for him at the end of the ride, then he sat among the packages thinking deeply until they came to the house.

'A solid place,' said the driver. 'Above ten hearths, I reckon. It would take a big fire to knock this one down and it would never leap over the grounds.' Sam led him to the kitchen and asked the new maid to give them some food. She looked concerned, wondering who they were, until Debbie flew down the stairs and hugged Sam. She pushed them into seats and brought strong broth made from fowls and vegetables, and sat watching while the men dunked dark bread into the juices.

'I'm coming with you to fetch the baby,' said Debbie. 'We found another wetnurse who wants to work here after the baby is weaned and I shall look after little Lottie

404

Katharine until . . .' She blushed. 'The Master says you'll have to marry again, Sam, or the child will have no real mother.'

The driver left and Sam looked about him at the familiar room and the table marked with spilled ale that Lottie had tried so hard to clean. He drank more ale and felt comforted by Debbie's light voice and laughter. She told him about the weddings in the country and how Miss Anna had nearly been taken by Sir Rollo FitzMedwin. 'But I know that she didn't love him. He was fancy enough with his hand kissing and smooth tongue, but she needs a real man like Captain Bennet. I think she misses him still but not a word has he sent her. You'd think if he cared about her, he'd have written letters or sent messages.'

'He's back and will be here soon to stay the night and to eat with us,' said Sam, and gave her all the instructions that Christopher had sent.

'There's food enough and more as Miss Anna made the girls buy what they could in the market this morning. We can feed many mouths if we have to take in those who lost homes in the fire, and two of the stable hands are still out buying food. Miss Anna is upstairs this minute. I'll tell her that you've come back, and Sam, I'm so happy.'

Sam bent to kiss the upturned face and felt deeply sad. No woman could take the place of Lottie, but as night follows day, he would marry the girl who would look after his child. He kissed her again with more warmth and found her mouth willing and her body soft under his hands. Later, he thought. First he had work to do down in the City to help the sailors and militia to fight the fire, and then there was Mary Creed.

He changed into old clothes and carefully put his discharge papers in an inner pocket in case of being accused of desertion or if anyone tried to press him again, but as he rode back towards the fire, he knew that today there

405

would be no pressmen, not a single Constable and no person of any rank to bother with the likes of him.

No rank at all! he thought later as he watched the Duke of York, richly-dressed but covered with black smuts and ash, riding among the workers with the King himself, as badly dirtied but seeming to be one with the masses as they raked down walls and urged the pump workers to even greater efforts. Carts jolted in every direction and mobs of frightened people fled their homes to find the green spaces of Moorfields and the land round Bishopsgate, anywhere outside the London Wall that might save the rest of London. Sam seized a rake and joined a band of sailors sent from ships by the Tower. They were told to rake off the roofs of houses as yet not affected, but they found resistance among those who prayed that the Good Lord would not let their houses be burned.

'It's the command of the King,' shouted the warrant officer of the militia. 'We must make breaks.' He swore. 'They've been cutting open pipes to get water and none flows down to the lower street, and the culverts are empty. This is the only way when there isn't enough water.'

They hacked and pulled and poured what water they could pump on to the next row to damp down the sparks already flying over the leads of the City onto the tinder-dry lathe and plaster of the narrow stews. Time and again the fire was quelled only to flare up as balls of flaming material came down as scouring rain. A distant sound as of thunder told them that another warehouse on the side of the river had exploded, sending more fireballs of burning oil and tar and molten lead over the heads of the workers and even onto the boats trying to take goods away by water.

Sam wiped the grit from his eyes and wished he had a yard of ale to settle the dust, but the work was neverending and the spirits of the men flagged as their arms ached and their throats grew dry. They retreated, group by group, to rest and look for an inn that still had food to serve, but as the day wore on, no supplies came through by land or water and even the great had to eat what they could and use nothing but grimy fingers as spoons.

At dusk, Sam went back to the house, taking his horse from the deserted mews where he had left her hidden. It's as bad as the plague, he thought. Every cart taken and people fighting at each of the City gates to get through with far too much to carry. Back at the house, he dismounted wearily and went into the kitchen, where Debbie and three girls were making more soup under the eye of Anna. Debbie sat him down and fussed over him and he began to enjoy the touch of her hands and her ready smile.

Anna talked to him while he ate and at last asked what was on her mind. 'Have you seen Captain Bennet?' she ventured.

'This morning, Ma'am, but not since, not that he isn't near and coming tonight,' he added. 'He had work to do and then I heard that his men were working with the King's party by the Exchange. They are using gunpowder to blow up houses now, and for that they use the military.'

'Is it dangerous?' she asked. She looked out of the window at the empty drive. 'It's still light,' Anna said in a voice full of awe. 'It's lighter than it was at noon and now it's nearly midnight.' But the glow was red and more menacing than noon in summer and the hot air was full of ash and fragments from afar, now blackened and harmless but frightening. She put a hand to her throat. To die of the plague was terrible, but what if there were souls trapped in that furnace?

Debbie called out, 'Master Christopher is coming, Miss Anna, and he has a man with him. Shall I serve ale or some supper for them?'

'Bring warm water and cloths first, Debbie and then put food ready.'

Christopher held out blackened hands for the maid to wash as if he had no will left, then sank into his seat and began to eat without saying a word. Anna thrust away her disappointment. The other man was a neighbour who had worked with Christopher all day and had shared a carriage with him to bring him home. He too was weary and ate before going home, unable to think of doing more even if the whole of London burned. Anna served food and made sure that the two men had everything they needed, then went on to the leads on the roof to look down over the City.

Fires raged everywhere and the wind was up from the east. Far away she saw flames round the outer perimeters of St Paul's. She caught her breath. Surely that would never burn? There were priceless books and works of art in the shops and libraries in St Pauls's Churchyard where she had spent such happy hours. Daniel Bennet would feel as she did, she decided. That at least they had in common. If he should die now, she could never again believe in God.

This was to have been a fresh start, free of the plague and free of everything that broke her heart, and now London was in flames, threatening safety and everything to which she had looked forward, and Daniel Bennet was back in the country with never a word for her. 'I hope he stays away,' she said and wondered if he had changed. 'He is a man without a heart,' she told herself and wondered if his mouth was still soft with passion when he kissed.

Explosions followed shouts of warning deep in the City and more wine and oil in the warehouses added fuel to the fire now sweeping along Thames Street and by the Strand, licking inwards to Cheapside and out along Bayards Castle. Anna turned away and felt her way down the steep steps from the leads. Voices from below told her that there were more visitors and she hurried down to welcome them.

Three weary Army officers sat sprawled by the open windows with mugs of ale in their hands. Debbie fussed about, serving slices of venison pasty made earlier in the day in case of need and the men seemed oblivious to everything but food and drink and rest. One man fell asleep with the half-eaten pasty in his hand and another yawned and stretched out on the floor as if it was as comfortable as a featherbed. The third raised himself on one elbow and stared at Anna through blackened lids.

'Forgive me if I don't rise, Ma'am,' he said. 'We are all plaguey weary and have to go back in an hour.'

'You can't! You need sleep and more food,' said Anna. This meeting lacked the tension she had expected and once again, she was the one to tend this man and so could act naturally. 'Your hand is burned,' she said, and hurried out to get warm water and oil and linen. Gently, she washed the red area and applied the oil and when she looked up she saw him looking at her ringless hands.

'Not married, Miss Anna?' he asked.

'There are other things in life, Sir,' she said coldly and took away the tray of dressings. From time to time, she glanced at him asleep on the floor and wanted to place pillows under his head and to kiss the hard lines from his face. Christopher and Sam were up again after only three hours' sleep and roused the officers. They grumbled and staggered up stiffly, and Anna peeped in at them when she heard them talking, having slept fitfully and aware of the mounting menace of the fire. She dashed water over her face and hands and brought bread and ale into the main hall.

'Thank you, Ma'am,' said one of the men. 'Heaven alone knows when we shall eat again. Yesterday even the King had to take what was offered from a stall not yet empty, and ate with his fingers like any common soldier.'

'Today it will be worse,' said Daniel Bennet. 'Many of the houses on the other side of the Wall are full of people fleeing the fire, and there is nothing left now that the warehouses are aflame. I think you may expect more here, Miss Anna. Houses on this side will surely escape but I know of many that will go.' He peered out at the darkened

409

garden. 'There is a carriage now filled with goods coming here.'

'It's William Verney and his family,' said Anna. 'Hurry and bring them in, Debbie.' The girl went slowly to the door, yawning, and the whole household was now awake and half-dressed.

'You must have food,' said Anna. 'Where are you going?'

'To Moorfields after we blow up houses down by the stairs at Whitefriars,' said Captain Bennet, and showed her a chart of the City and the road the fire had taken the previous day. 'With the wind still coming from the east, it will follow this path, so the Duke of York has ordered more gunpowder from the arsenal at Greenwich, with more men from the ships. It should be ready now and we must go.' He hesitated. 'Later, the King will be at Moorfields to talk to the people camped there. If you could send food later, we shall be glad of it.' He smiled for the first time. 'Even the King would be in your debt.'

'Why is he going there?' she asked. 'How do you know?'

Daniel Bennet turned away to buckle on his sword, and Anna asked one of the other officers the same question.

'Many think the fire was started by the Papists, Ma'am. Foreigners are not safe on the streets, and yesterday a Frenchman was torn limb from limb when the mob thought he carried fireballs.' He laughed. 'They were tennis balls, Ma'am, but it shows how the mood went. Can't say I blame them as more fires sprang up far from the City docks that must have been started deliberately, and with the Dutch making a nuisance again, opinion is hard against any who are not English.'

'If you are going down by Whitefriars, we shall come with you,' said Christopher, and Sam stood a pace behind, grimfaced. 'I know this is not the time for private quarrels, and we can help with the work, but I must see if Mary Creed is alive.' He drew Daniel aside. 'I'll keep an eye on

410

Sam. He has murder in his heart and isn't safe to let loose if he sees that woman.'

'Be careful!' cried Debbie as they left the house. 'Oh, Miss Anna, they are so brave. I wish I was as brave but fire frightens me and I could never go near it.'

'There's no need. You'll have work enough to do here. Bake more pies and bread and see that Dr Verney has a comfortable room and water for washing. His family will need to sleep.'

'You need sleep too, Miss Anna.'

'Not now, there are many matters that come first.' While he is out there in danger, I shall not rest, she vowed.

Chapter 26

The air was full of dense smoke, hanging over the river like a pall of fog and carrying sparks and blazing fragments of wood and molten glass and lead. Soldiers pushed back the people who still hoped to save more from the houses already condemned to fall to gunpowder and not to the fire, and the cries of those whose houses were now destroyed were as doleful as a Greek tragedy. Captain Bennet gave the order and the air was once more clouded with smoke and fumes, and ratings and men employed to rake the wood away rushed forward to clear the area.

'Bring it over here,' shouted an officer. 'Shacks built of wood and an empty house that must go. Looks like stables belonging to the big house and the row of small ones on that side.'

'That's Rollo's house!' exclaimed Christopher. 'And that lane must lead to his stables. Stay your hand!' he called. 'There may be someone living above the stables. We'll go in and see.'

'You have five minutes,' warned the officer. 'If you aren't out by then, it goes up and if you are in there, it's your own fault. We can't stop now or sparks will set this alight and the wind is still fresh.'

Sam ran down the lane and stopped. The old cart that they had given to Joseph when he was dismissed was in the middle of the lane, piled high with goods. The cries of the nag, frightened by the smell of fire and enraged by the furious whipping that made his flanks raw, increased as Mary Creed hit him about the head and hocks like a woman demented. She tried to pull the cart but one wheel was stuck in the rutted path and was in too deep to get free unless the cart was unloaded.

As the men watched, the cart lurched and tipped over, spilling goods and sacks of pewter and silver over the path. Mary Creed shrieked at the horse and dragged two huge sacks away from the cart. Her hair was dishevelled and her eyes blazed with fury. 'My gold and silver! My treasures!' she groaned.

'You must leave them,' called Christopher. 'Come away, Mary Creed. You will be killed if you stay here.'

'My treasures! I have more in there. Get a cart and help me!'

'No! You have no time. Come now and face the magistrate, Mary Creed. You have much to answer for,' said Christopher sternly.

She started as if she had only now recognised the men. Her slow smile was wicked and venomous. 'It's Sam the groom, back from the sea, but there was no pretty wife to greet you and warm your bed, was there?'

'Come away, Mary!' Christopher backed and grasped Sam by the arm. 'She's mad and there's nothing we can do. Leave her to whatever God she thinks exists in that shrivelled mind. We can do no more.' Sam clenched his fists but was dragged away. A shout went up from the officer and as Christopher and Sam ran out of the lane, a small river of flame left the tinder and hungrily followed the fuse to the stables. A moment later, the explosion hurled the dead horse higher than the walls along the lane and the leather traces snapped as the cart hurtled into the stableyard, sending a rain of silver and pewter, gold coins and bright jewellery glinting through the smoke. A fire

413

started as the scorching took rich velvets and brocade and men rushed forward to quell the blaze before it did damage to the next building.

'Rake the rubble away and lay more powder,' ordered the officer in charge. 'There's more that must go if we are to save Essex House and Arundel.'

Six men were ordered to go among the ruins and secure the valuables until such a time when their owners could be found, if they were still recognisable, and one man tried to walk in but stumbled back with the leather of his boots smouldering. The warrant officer grinned. That heat would keep the goods safe until an armed guard could be put on the carriage sent to collect them. Sam glanced along the ruined lane and then worked as hard as the rest until the cobbles cooled. Fragments of ashes and flying glass made him bend his head as he finally went back, cautiously walking on the remaining yellow grass to avoid the heat.

Devastation of the stables made him pause. Surely nothing of Mary Creed could be left now . . . He went on and found a broken cartwheel and another bursting sack, and saw a figure carved of charcoal, curved round a bag that had burned through, leaving Mary Creed embracing a crumbling mass of fine porcelain and silver. Naked, as her clothes caught fire, she had still clung desperately to the last of her treasures as the world about her disintegrated, and Sam gave a great sigh. 'Go the Devil, Mary,' he said. 'If he'll take you.'

A sparse amount of water was rushed to the ruins to stop an outbreak of fire and when the sweating men looked up, the space was enough and the anger of the fire licked hungrily at a break that had no substance and could not feed it. A faint cheer went up and Christopher called to Sam, 'There's nothing more for us here, Sam. Come to Moorfields and let us see what we can do for the homeless. Debbie and the boys from the yard may be there and need help if they are not to be robbed before they can give out food fairly.'

By back ways, they rode to the fields where hundreds were gathered among as many of their possessions as they had managed to take with them. Faces blackened with smoke and some grey with pain and shock eyed any bundle brought by those who came to help, but most were too weary to demand anything. Two horses stood apart from the crowds, each laden with heavy baskets. Christopher stared, then cursed. 'It's Anna. Is she mad? Doesn't she know the mood of the crowd? They are seeking out foreigners and she looks darker than ever after the summer sun.'

He spurred his horse and joined her. 'Oh, Christopher, I'm so glad to see you,' she said. 'I thought they would want help but they murmur against me and say I carry fireballs in my packs and want nothing from me.'

'Stay close by me, Anna,' he said. 'Sam, ride on her other side, and you,' he said to the stable lads, 'take the first bag and give it out to the women and children. Let no man have anything until the children are fed, and leave the rest here until Captain Bennet comes. His men have worked until ready to drop. They shall be fed.'

Anna smiled, but her mouth trembled. She sat straight on her saddle as if there was nothing to worry her, but her hands clenched the reins and she spoke little.

'Stay here but dismount,' said Christopher. 'Sam, remain with her until I come back. I'll try to find Daniel.'

Anna slid from the horse and felt less secure now that she was on a level with the crowds. Sam placed his sturdy body between her and two men who eyed her with more interest than he liked, and Anna saw a woman with two tiny children sitting under the shelter of a bush. The children were crying softly as if they had no strength for wild grief and the woman sat pale and still and hopeless.

'Give me some bread and a bottle of ale, Sam,' said Anna. 'They are starving.' She knelt beside the woman and

415

offered the children bread and butter in small pieces. The woman drank some ale and shuddered as the warm, bitter brew hit her parched throat then drank more, greedily. One of the men came forward, ignoring Sam, and tried to take the bottle from the woman.

'She needs it,' said Anna firmly. 'There is a flaggon of water over there and the cistern on wheels brought from fighting the fire. You look less worn than most so give it out in small amounts to make it last.'

'I'll have no foreign spy telling me what to do in my own country,' the man said. His face was contorted with hate and Sam seized his arms to restrain him. 'Papist!' spat the man. 'Foreign spies for De Ruyter! Who knows what they bring? Poisoned water?' He struggled to get free but Sam held him.

By now other men had gathered, murmuring against the Dutch and one called out to Anna, 'Fine clothes while we lose everything? What is she? A foreign whore in the pay of the Dutch?'

Sam looked about wildly as the mood grew savage. Blackened faces seemed to loom up out of nowhere and a dirty hand tried to grab Anna's skirt. Sam lashed out with his fists and the men drew back like hyenas ready to wait for their kill. Anna stood tall, her face showing nothing of her fear, and as Daniel Bennet rode quickly towards the disturbance, he saw her, calm and proud and beautiful.

The uniform of the Royal Guard made a way through to the silent woman and the men cringed back before the bright blade that the Captain held ready to strike. 'Back!' he said. 'Get back. Don't you recognise a lady when you see one?' They muttered 'Spies' again and he laughed. His voice was clear and could be heard even by the King's party that followed him. 'This lady is well-born and saved my life. She is no spy unless you dare to accuse me of spying, too? I am to marry the lady as soon as this pesky fire is out, and I have the King's permission to do so.'

Anna was aware of only one face, one voice. The others faded into the blur of grass and tired bodies and green leaves covered with dust. Daniel Bennet bowed solemnly and turned his horse sharply, making it rear and send a shower of hot dung over the men who had threatened Anna. Sam began to hand out food to the soldiers who lined up wearily, their once-smart uniforms soiled and dusty and their throats parched with smoke. Over on a ridge, the King spoke to the people of London, reassuring them that the fire was no Papist plot or a part of enemy invasion which had been rumoured. He told them calmly and compassionately that this was an act of God that nobody could prevent, caused by a spark and the dry weather.

The people listened and noted his lined face and tired red-rimmed eyes, the dirty shoes and silk pantaloons, and forgot that this was the man who lived so extravagantly, emptying the nation's coffers quicker than they could be filled and siring a score of bastards but no rightful heir.

His Majesty promised a new London, built of brick and stone and with less thatch and wattle even among the poor. He held their attention and growing affection and many pressed forward to touch him as they had done when he received many with the King's Evil, before the plague.

Christopher took food to his retinue and at last even the King was pleased to eat some of Debbie's venison pasty and the soldiers brought more food from houses saved by the gap made by gunpowder, taking all that they had for the homeless. London Wall held and the wind changed, but it was too late to save St Paul's, packed with books and fabrics taken there for safety at the beginning of the fire.

'The Exchange has gone but the Guildhall is safe,' said Sam. 'All the warehouses along Thames Street have burned and the markets in Cornhill, but the flames have stopped by Smithfield and Pye Corner and will die out in a day or so.'

417

'What of the Tower?' said Anna. 'Not that as well as St Paul's?'

'They say the wind changed at the end of Seething Lane where the Navy Secretary lives, charring only the face of the clock at the end of the road. The Tower is safe.'

Christopher touched Anna's arm. 'Come home. We have done what we can and the Duke of York is organising relief and food from the country. Come, Anna.' He pressed her hand, smiled and helped her to mount her horse. 'There is still much to do and many to feed. Daniel will want a bed and some of his men can sleep in the library and the other rooms on the floor.'

'Did you hear what he said?' she whispered.

Christopher rode beside her and looked anxious. 'I heard him, Anna. What does it mean? Has he declared himself? Is he the man you want to marry or have you still a feeling for Rollo? If you want him, then tell him when he asks. He is a plain man with no time for flirting.'

'He has said nothing,' said Anna. 'He spoke as he did to keep the crowd from me, but by now he may have a wife in Africa! He never sent me word that he was well or that he missed me.'

'Don't be proud, Anna. I know he loves you and I know the Duke holds him in high regard. Besides, a wife half-Dutch will be of use when the war is over. The King will want ambassadors, and who better than you and Daniel? We shall hear more later, but the King is indebted to Daniel over gains he made when away, and he apparently knew your family when he was in exile.' He smiled. 'We have only a few days before the rest of the family comes back. Marry soon, Anna, and follow him where he is sent.'

'You talked of me?' she said, with wonder. 'We parted on bad terms.'

'We talked of you and he asked me to be his envoy. He may fight the Dutch and have no fear, Anna, but you

418

frighten him out of his wits and speech until he knows that you prefer him to Rollo!'

'Rollo has gone for ever,' said Anna.

'I wonder. His accuser is dead and what other proof is there? He can come back and regain the favour of the Court after a spell abroad unless he has sworn allegiance to the Dutch or French.'

The house was grey with spent ash and everywhere that Anna could see was covered with the fine tilth that would remain until the rain washed it away. News came that ash had blown as far as Oxford and over the fields and herds far out in the country. A grey world, thought Anna, inspecting a finger that she pressed along a ledge. Dust lay on the kitchen dishes and everything had to be washed before eating as well as after a meal, and still the greyness settled and thickened and the heat from the City smote like a furnace as the breeze caught it up and tried to spread it again.

Anna shook out her dress and stood in her shift. Warm water in a hip bath had made her clean and she could now forget the smell of smoke as she smoothed scented unguents into her skin. She buttoned up the night-robe of red silk and made the cuffs fit tightly as she did up the rows of many tiny buttons that matched the front fastening. The colour cheered her and she went down to oversee the meal being prepared. None of the men were in the house and it was well past midnight, but Anna could not sleep until they were fed and rested. 'I shall sleep in the small linen room,' she told Debbie. 'Captain Bennet shall have my room, so put fresh water by the bath when you empty mine.'

'It doesn't seem right that a man should sleep in your pretty bed the first time the new curtains are up, Miss Anna.' She giggled. 'Not alone, Miss Anna.' Anna boxed the girl's ears lightly and laughed. 'The Captain will be too tired to notice if he has a bedfellow or not, tonight. Be

419

quiet and get on with that bread. It may be midnight, but they will need food whatever time they come in.'

She carried candles to the many rooms that would hold weary men that night and lit the lamps in her room. Listening every few minutes, she heard nothing but distant shouts from the City, and then, when she had almost given up expecting them, a door banged and the house was full of people. Debbie rushed to put bread on the table, hot from the oven, and Anna served bowls of thick broth and told the new maids what was expected of them. Dimly, Anna saw Daniel Bennet at the head of the table, eating and drinking and wiping the darkening sweat from his eyes. Some men slept on the floor where they had eaten and some staggered as far as the library, but Debbie took Daniel up to the airy room where the new velvet curtains surrounded the big fourposter bed and the creamy feather pillows lay ready and inviting.

Anna followed slowly, carrying fresh linen begged from Christopher, and put it on the table. Daniel pulled off the tight tunic and looked at the bed and then at the warm water. At the door, Anna saw him begin to remove his other clothes and she turned away. It was easy for a girl like Debbie with no feelings in the matter to stay and help him into the bath, and to scrub his back if he needed it, but she blushed, glimpsing the white flesh where the sun had not reached, remembering that in the past she had done more than scrub his back when he lay helpless at the farm.

A surge of deep emotion made her feel faint. I'm tired, she thought. He's tired too, and today he may have said more than he intended. She opened the door to the small linen room and pushed the bed against the wall to make more space. In neat piles were shifts and napkins and towels, rows of spotless items that the dust had not sullied . . . she suddenly remembered that she had left no fresh towels for the Captain. Anna picked up two towels

420

and walked along to her room. Debbie had gone and the man in the bath looked as if he might be stuck. 'Help me out. I'm so bone weary that I shall tip it over, Debbie,' he said, without looking up.

Anna draped a towel over his shoulders and rubbed them dry, then put a hand under each arm and he rose from the murky water, rubbing his wet hair with the other towel she gave him. Anna hesitated. 'Have you everything you need, Sir?' she asked softly.

He swung round, the dark hair flicked back from his face. 'Anna?' He almost stumbled towards her and she tried to smile as if it was every day that a naked wet man seized her hand and kissed it with such passion that he forgot he was exhausted.

Tentatively, she touched his bowed head and he gave a great sigh. 'You need sleep,' she said.

'I need sleep, I need peace of mind and I need you, Anna. Can you forgive me? Can you ever forgive me for treating you badly after everything you mean to me?' He kissed her cheek, half-afraid of being rejected. 'You are not married,' he said. 'I heard that Rollo FitzMedwin asked you.'

'He did. He offered an honourable marriage and his name, with no thought of mine or of my lineage,' she said softly, with a hint of reproach that was fast fading as she felt his hands round her waist straining her close to his body.

'And I offered nothing.' He sensed her submission. 'I offer myself now, in the humble hope that you will take me as husband, Anna. I have the Royal Assent and land given me in thanks for my time in Africa, and I need you by my side wherever I go.' He searched her eyes for his answer and found her lips sweet and eager, but she pushed him away at last.

'You need sleep, Daniel. We both need rest.'

421

'Stay with me,' he begged, and led her to the bed. 'Stay with me now, and we will marry soon.'

'I'll come back later,' she said, and handed the clean nightshirt to him.

The lamp gave gentle light and a peace that filled Anna with joy. She left him alone while she cleared the bath and took his soiled clothes to the kitchen for cleaning. Soon, the Verneys would come back and plan her marriage, if there was a church left standing. The Great Fire would be dead and the City cleansed of the plague, please God for ever. Soon, and she opened the shutters to look over the deserted, smouldering City, out of the dust, she could find her future and her love.

She smiled when she peeped in later. He was sound asleep and she crept back to the tiny room and the bed among the clean linen.